THE ELEPHANT
WITHIN US

THE ELEPHANT
WITHIN US

Peter Peeters

Book Guild Publishing
Sussex, England

First published in Great Britain in 2011 by
The Book Guild Ltd
Pavilion View
19 New Road
Brighton, BN1 1UF

Typesetting in Baskerville by
Keyboard Services, Luton, Bedfordshire

Printed and bound in Great Britain by
CPI Antony Rowe

A catalogue record for this book is available from
The British Library

ISBN 978 1 84624 638 8

*To Catherine Meakins
for unfailing support*

Prologue

How the hell did I get myself into this? thought John.

He tried to move but the straps on his arms and legs prevented him. From the corner of his eye he just managed to see Klaus' back.

'Stop fiddling!' grumbled Klaus. 'Look what you've done now! Everything has gone out of tune. I have to start fine-tuning all over again just because you are unable to control yourself. This will not do! It just won't! How many times have I told you that any movement, even the slightest, creates electrical interferences? So don't move! You are just about allowed to breathe – but very quietly and regularly.'

'All right. All right! I'll try.'

'You still want me to carry on, do you? You still agree?'

No, thought John. 'Yes,' he said.

Coward, you coward, he thought. *If you think no, then why not say no? Why pretend to be braver than you are, you stupid fool? You're scared and you don't dare show it. Is this the result of years of obeying social conventions, of having your behaviour determined by what's expected of you?*

He'd always had the knack of getting himself into sticky situations, but never in his whole life had he managed as brilliantly as this time: he was lying on his back, tied to a sort of operating table, and with God knows how many probes fastened onto his scalp.

This can't be true, he thought. If anyone had told him a month or two ago, back in Chicago, that this would happen to him in eight weeks' time, he would have laughed and shrugged his shoulders. Yet here he was, ready to be sent to another era – not in Chicago, not even in the USA, but in Naboru, capital of one of those unstable East African countries.

But maybe it isn't real..., John mused. *Maybe nothing is going to happen. I'm getting all worked up for nothing, that's it! If I had really believed deep down that Klaus would be able to whisk*

1

my brain away to another era, I certainly wouldn't be lying on this table.

Or maybe ... maybe he really did want to get away from it all, from life's misery and unhappiness. He was getting fed up with the bad luck fate had been sending his way. If what he had been through so far was life, he had seen enough of it; it simply wasn't worth waiting for more. All that could happen to him from now on was more of the same. Or worse: getting slowly older; less successful; less attractive, and lonelier. Wasn't it better to quit now at thirty-nine rather than wait for decay to set in? What the heck!

Then a frightening thought struck him: what if his brain were to suffer irreparable damage and he had to spend the rest of his life locked up in a mental institution?

'Can't you keep still?' came Klaus' irritated voice. 'I just cannot work if you keep sending huge brainwaves my way. I told you not to think! Or if you absolutely need to, think about something nice. Something very quiet.'

'OK, OK, so sorry,' replied John. 'I'll try. Is it still a long way off?'

'Not if you collaborate. Just relax. Think of something that makes you feel good ... or of a place where you feel secure. Think that you are ... let's see ... well ... in your mother's womb or something like that.'

My mother's womb? thought John. *How did it feel in there? I really haven't the faintest idea.*

He now tried to imagine a situation of total relaxation. Maybe the moment after having made love was like that? Suddenly he wondered how it would have been with Veronica. Yes, with her it would have been total relaxation, he was sure of that. He saw himself lying in her arms... It would all have been so wonderful... If only he hadn't been such an idiot ... Veronica!

'What's this?' he heard Klaus remark. 'What are you thinking about now? I told you to relax, not to get excited!'

'Sorry, sorry, I'll try to think of something else.'

He began to imagine scenes from his youth back in America: kettle on the fire in the winter, cat purring on his lap, contentedness ... or else: green meadows, soft summer breeze, the rustling of the wind in the leaves...

'Wonderful, wonderful!' exclaimed Klaus. 'I've got it all set up. We can start now...'

Suddenly John panicked: *No! No! I can't go through with this. I must tell Klaus...*

PART
ONE

1

By the time he landed in Naboru where he had gone to join an elephant project, John had spent more than twenty-four hours on planes and in airports and felt utterly exhausted. He followed the other passengers to the baggage claim area like an automaton, collected his bag and went through customs. *At last*, he reflected, *I've got here. My troubles are over.*

Night had already fallen and as he passed through sliding doors and emerged into the dimly lit arrival hall, the heat and humidity hit him in the face. A strong smell of acrid sweat rose from the crowd gathered there: hundreds of Africans were milling about, some holding names written on cardboard above their heads, others just shouting them. It was total chaos.

I suppose this is where the government official will be waiting for me, thought John, and he began looking at the names on the boards in the hope of finding his own.

The first man he approached had the name Davenport on his board, and as John read it, the man pressed forward shouting: 'You Mr Davenport? Follow me.' He nearly wrested John's bag from his hands, shouting: 'Give me your case!'

At the same time another man accosted him, screaming: 'Taxi!' He grabbed John by his jacket, but John pushed him away, shouting back: 'I don't want a taxi! Leave me alone!' And struggling to keep possession of his bag he yelled: 'I'm not Mr Davenport!' to the other man, and managed to move on.

After shaking off in turn the African carrying the board with the next name, and a number of others who seemed unwilling to believe that he was not called Mr Mercier, Mr Branding, Mrs Bottlefinch and several other names, and having pushed the taxi driver away maybe ten times, he finally came to the end of the row of men carrying boards without having encountered his own name.

He now tried to listen in case someone was shouting his name, but he couldn't distinguish anything among the noisy cacophony. After half an hour or so most of the passengers who had arrived with him had gone. The crowd had visibly thinned out and John suddenly had a sickly feeling that he was being abandoned to his fate in a country where he didn't know anyone. In the plane he thought that his spirits were at a low ebb, but now he realized that they had sunk lower still.

Suddenly the cab driver popped up again with a big smile. 'Taxi, Sah!'

John finally surrendered. He had arrived at the state where he would have given anything to get out of the airport. 'OK,' he said.

'Your bag, Sah?'

'What about my bag?' said John defensively. 'There's nothing wrong with it, is there?'

'No. No. I carry it for you, Sah.'

'No need for that,' replied John. 'I can carry it myself.'

When they got to the cab and John was seated inside, the driver turned towards him. 'Where you want to go?'

'I don't really know,' replied John.

'But you got to give me address,' protested the driver. 'Not possible just sit here!'

'Well ... I just can't think any more. The truth is that I'm at the end of my tether.'

'At the end of what?'

'My tether.'

'Maitetha ... Maitetha ... let me see.' The cab driver pondered for a while. 'I don't know that address,' he finally admitted. 'Never heard of it.'

'Oh God!' groaned John. 'Just take me anywhere. Wait! Isn't there a nice cheap white guesthouse in town?'

'That difficult, Sah. Many guesthouses are white in daytime. But at night they are dark, Sah.'

'I mean a guesthouse with white people inside. People like me.'

'Now I get it,' said the driver and he turned to John, showing a set of flashing white teeth in the dark. 'You European. You mean guesthouse with Europeans inside?'

'Yes, yes, that's it. But actually I'm an American.'

'Right! I know some place. Many Americans stay there. I take you.'

8

The cab was a ramshackle affair. It didn't have air-conditioning and it was stifling inside. Once it had left the airport behind, the car proceeded slowly over a potholed road through the dark African night until they arrived near the shantytowns: shacks upon shacks sprawled along the road; their scattered dim lights made the darkness appear less deep but still, coming from America, this seemed altogether a different planet.

The cab driver seemed to have been pondering over something while they were moving along, and suddenly he asked: 'Why you not want taxi in first place, Sah?'

John who had almost dozed off, woke up with a start, saying: 'Hey, what?'

'I wondered why you push me away at beginning and wait so long to decide, Sah?'

'Oh, that! I was expecting to meet a government official.'

'A government official, Sah? At this time of night, Sah?'

'Well, yes. It was arranged that I should be picked up.'

'How much you pay, Sah? If I may ask, Sah?'

'I don't understand.'

'How much you pay the government official for that service?'

'I didn't pay anything! I'm going to work here and the government is going to pay me, if you really want to know,' retorted John, slightly offended.

'The government pay you, man? Haha! That's a good one, hahaha … Oh man, oh man…' The driver was howling with laughter, tears rolled down his cheeks, he started banging the steering wheel, the cab swerved dangerously and nearly collided with a bus coming from the opposite direction.

'Hey, watch out!' shouted John. He didn't want to get mangled the very first hour he was in Africa.

After a while the driver quietened down somewhat. 'I see you never been in this country, Sah. Let me tell you that in Africa governments don't pay. They take. You want service. You want anything. You pay. No problem for you, Sah. You are American. You rich. But why you want government to pay in worthless shillings when you have so many dollars, I do not understand.'

'But I'm not rich,' protested John. 'I'm poor.'

'Haha, Sah. If you permit me to say so, Sah, you joking. We walk to our villages – you drive in cars. We take bus to travel

– you take airplane. I seen your movies, Sah. You don't fool me. Everyone is rich in America. Women are covered in gold and diamonds. You got big cars. Big houses. Big money. We Africans all want to get out of here and go to America. And you say you come to this country to work here for miserable shillings! I cannot believe that, Sah.'

'But I assure you...'

'Come now, Sah,' said the driver as if he were talking to a deceitful child, 'don't try to hide truth from me.' Now that he had a genuine American in his cab he was keen to verify some of the wilder rumours he had heard. 'Tell me, is it true that when babies are born in America, the government gives them lots of dollars? Don't laugh, Sah. They say so over here ... and also that people have so much money, they lose many dollars every day without noticing. I heard that, if you keep your eyes open, sometimes you can pick up a fortune in the street.'

They were now in the city, and John was utterly tired and fed up. 'Well, if you say so...' he replied vaguely, hoping to put an end to the enquiries.

It didn't stop the driver, who carried on eagerly: 'Are black people in America also rich?'

John thought of the inner city of Chicago, of the squalor of the black quarter. 'No,' he replied. 'They are poor.'

The cab driver suddenly flared up. 'There you have it!' he exclaimed. 'Racism! Always the same! Keeping the black man poor.' He grumbled for a while in a local language, and then drove on in tense silence. At long last he stopped in front of a large low building. 'Here you are,' he said gruffly. 'White guesthouse for white Americans. That'll be fifty dollars.'

'Hey!' exclaimed John, now fully awake. 'That's a lot!'

'It's not,' contested the cab driver. 'This was long drive at night. And you're a rich American, and I'm a poor African.'

'I think thirty dollars is plenty,' said John, rummaging in his wallet.

'It's not!'

'Look here, I'll make it forty, but not a cent more.'

The driver grabbed the banknotes and John just had time to get out with his bag before the cab raced off.

There was a light above the entrance door and John rang the bell. An elderly white woman in a sort of uniform opened and John presented himself: 'I'm Mr Garfinger from America...' he said.

He was just about to ask if they had a free room and how much it would be for the night, when she said: 'Oh yes, of course. Do come in; there's a room ready for you. Follow me, please.' And she led the way through several corridors to a modestly furnished room. 'You have time to freshen up,' she informed him, 'but don't take too long, please. Dinner will be ready in ten minutes. Just follow this corridor to the end, turn left, cross the open space and you'll find the dining room.'

How strange, thought John. *I've never been to a guesthouse like this one where they don't even ask for your credentials.*

He got ready as quickly as possible, all the while thinking: *That woman didn't even tell me the price! I should have asked about the price. You never know.*

When he entered the dining room everybody else seemed to be already present. He found an empty chair at one of the tables, and just as he sank down they all stood up and began to sing. It was a hymn of praise to the Lord for the food they were about to receive. When it was over they all sat down again while supper was served by a few stout African women. He looked around: it seemed to be a mixed company, men and women, mostly white, some quite old, some younger. They ate in silence, as if eating was a very serious business. It suited John perfectly; he had reached the point where he was too tired for any type of conversation and just wanted to be left in peace. When supper was over they said a short prayer of thanks, and as everyone got up John quickly retired.

What a strange place, he thought when he was lying in bed. *I wonder where I am? Must be a religious sort of guesthouse. Anyway, I'm beyond caring. I've got a bed to lie in and that's all I need.*

And he fell asleep within seconds.

2

Immediately after breakfast next morning he was called into the office of a man he presumed to be the director of the place. A thin ascetic man of maybe sixty was seated at a desk facing the door and, as John entered, the man looked up and studied him attentively. He didn't speak for several seconds, but eyed John in what seemed a very unwelcoming way; it made him feel uncomfortable. At last the man asked: 'Are you a reformed sinner?'

John looked aghast. 'Wha ... what?' he mumbled.

'I was certain of it!' The man almost growled, as if he was going to bite John any minute now. 'I studied you this morning at breakfast. You did not appear to know any of the hymns. Just pretended you were singing, but that didn't fool me.' Then he said with scorn in his voice: 'You are most certainly a sinner. One look at you is sufficient to see that. And you have not repented! You continue to sin!' screeched the man, wagging his finger at John.

John recoiled under the unexpected attack. *My life has not been exemplary*, he thought, *far from it. But that doesn't give this fellow the right to call me a sinner.*

'What's the matter?' he stammered. 'I don't understand any of this. Where am I?' The thin man didn't answer. Instead he asked: 'How did you get in here?' as if accusing a criminal.

'A cab driver dumped me here last night coming from the airport. He led me to believe that this was a guesthouse where many Americans stayed. I gave my name and was shown to a room. That's all.'

'What's your name?'

'John Garfinger.'

'So that's how it happened!' exclaimed the man. 'We are expecting a Mr Gorfinder, a member of the American branch of our Congregation. I was away last night and Sister Anna who opened the door must have mistaken you for him. So that explains the mistake.'

'Did you think I wormed my way into this place under false pretences and full of bad intentions?' asked John who was getting really upset now. 'I'm here through no fault of my own. The mistake is yours! And even if I'm a sinner – which, by the way, is what you call me without any proof whatsoever – that's no justification for you to give me a most unchristian reception!'

He turned and was about to leave the office when the director called him back: 'One moment, please.'

John turned around. 'Yes?'

The director looked slightly embarrassed. 'I have judged you rather hastily and, I realize now, unfairly. I feel that it's my Christian duty to make up for a mistake which, I understand, occurred through no fault of yours. As you are occupying the room reserved for Mr Gorfinder, I'd like to ask you to be our guest until he arrives. Mind you, he is due any day and you may have to leave tomorrow for all I know.'

John reflected for a second or two. He was still rather upset, but was calming down. *I mustn't let my emotions run away with me*, he thought. His financial position was far from brilliant and in the situation in which he found himself it would have been foolish to refuse a free offer. So he said with as much grace as he could muster: 'Thank you. That's most generous of you. I assure you that I won't be a bother to anyone.' And he added: 'I may even be able to learn a hymn or two,' with a glint in his eyes, which the director fortunately failed to notice.

'I would if I were you,' nodded the director, who began to see the possibility of saving another soul. 'Hymns are very uplifting.'

'I do find them beautiful,' agreed John.

'May I ask you what you came to Naboru for?' inquired the director, who seemed to have become interested in John's case.

'I am going to help with a project.'

The director appeared keen to find out more. 'Something in our line? Saving sinners? Or maybe helping the weak and unprotected?'

'Nothing to do with humans, I'm afraid. It has to do with the protection of animals.'

'Well, they are God's creatures too,' conceded the director with a touch of disappointment in his voice. 'So why did you come to us instead of going to the project?' he added after some reflection.

'A government official was supposed to pick me up on arrival at the airport, but if he was there I certainly didn't notice him. A cab driver finally caught me and as I don't know anyone in this country and was at the end of my tether...' John chuckled quietly at this point as if savouring a private joke, making the man behind the desk stare at him, somewhat puzzled, '... I let him take me to what he claimed was a guesthouse for Americans. But I've explained that already.'

'Fine, fine,' mumbled the director. 'What are you going to do now? What are your plans?'

'I shall have to find the people responsible for the project,' replied John. 'I have the name of the Minister of Wildlife who signed the contract. A Minister Kimbabe.' John looked the man opposite him straight in the eyes. 'How do you think I should go about contacting him?'

'Well, hmm ... I suppose...' the director shifted somewhat uneasily in his chair. 'You know what? A member of our Congregation has to drive into town this morning. Why don't you accompany him? He can drop you in the centre of the town where the ministries are, and you can find your way from there.' He rang a bell and a servant appeared a few seconds later. 'Take Mr Garfinger to Howard and tell him to drop our guest downtown,' he commanded. And as he waved John out, he added: 'Good luck.'

3

At about the same time two men were having breakfast a few miles further in town.

'How's the machine getting on?' inquired Sam Goldstein. 'Any progress?'

'All right so far, I think,' answered Klaus in a distracted way. He was a tall, wiry fellow with a slight limp, a brainy-looking forehead and a pointed chin.

Sam waited a few seconds for more to come, but that was all Klaus seemed willing to convey and he began to feel slightly irritated. *He really looks like an owl with those round gold-rimmed spectacles sliding onto the tip of his nose when he bends his head forward*, thought Sam as he stared at Klaus. 'Is there no progress then?' he insisted. 'How far have you got?'

'Oh! How far? Well, I'm still working on the electronics.'

'How much longer do you reckon you need before putting the machine into practice?'

'How much longer?' Klaus rubbed his chin and bent his head slightly to the right, with the look of a surprised owl on his face. 'Let me see now ... that depends.'

'On what?'

'Well, you see ... it would help greatly if I had a real brain...'

'I sometimes wonder what's going on behind that bulging dome of yours, but I never doubted that there was a real brain inside,' commented Sam acidly.

'No, no, my friend. You misunderstand me. I'm referring to a *Versuchskaninchen* ... how do you say that in English? ... Ah, yes, a pig from Guinea, isn't that it?'

'What do you want a pig from Guinea for? I don't think we can get them easily in this country. What about any other animal? I mean one available over here?'

'No, no. Not an animal pig. I'm referring to a *human* pig. One with a human brain.'

'Ah, I see now what you mean. I think it's possible to get

15

you a human brain if you really need one. With the road accidents that happen all the time around here and the violence in town, it shouldn't be too difficult to find you a relatively fresh brain. But we'll have to keep it quiet. Anyway, what do you want a human brain for?'

'*Mein Freund, mein Freund...*' Klaus shook his head. 'I sometimes wonder whether you are really dim or whether you are playing the game? But no, you are a reputed scientist and so you must be playing the game. To fine-tune the machine I need a human with a live brain inside. I thought you knew that all along.'

'Do you mean to tell me that the wiring and programming are nearly finished and that you're ready to try the machine on a human? But that's wonderful!' Sam jumped up and began to pace back and forth. 'That's really great!' he exclaimed. 'I'd no idea you'd got this far already.'

'Now, now! Let's not get too excited. Yes, the wiring and programming are nearly finished, but as the proverb says: Don't run before you can walk. A lot of practical settings are still missing and it would help if I could start working on a real brain soon. I need to scan brainwaves and a lot of other things besides.'

'That's no problem. I'll pick up someone tomorrow.'

Klaus was moving his head from left to right, as if weighing the case carefully before pronouncing a verdict. His spectacles were on the tip of his nose and his round eyes were bulging like small globes above the shiny spectacles. 'That would take me some way, yes, some way ... but I don't think that's the ideal solution.'

'Why ever not? What's the problem? A brain's a brain as far as I can see. I get you someone to lie on your lab table, you scan his brainwaves and fine-tune that time machine of yours, and hey presto, we're ready for the great day.'

'You do not understand, my friend. One brain is not like another. Ideally the fine-tuning should be done on the person who is going to be zoomed back a few million years to the epoch of the hominids. Otherwise I shall have to start everything all over again when we find the right candidate. And that would take at least a week or two.'

'I see. So it's no good working on the first passer-by. We have to start looking for someone more specific. How would you define the ideal candidate?'

'Well ... if you ask me...' Klaus' face took on an expression of intense concentration. 'The ideal candidate would have to have a well-developed brain. By this I do not just mean that he or she must have a high IQ.' He held up a thin index finger, wagging it. 'Remember that the candidate is going to be sent back in time for a very specific purpose. If our collaborator is to fulfil the high hopes you place in him or her we have to be very strict in our selection criteria. The minimum is someone with a degree in science and some experience.'

'You don't say,' replied Sam, taken aback. 'I'll see what I can do. I'm sure we'll get someone.' But his voice had lost some of its cocksureness.

4

How different a city looks by daylight, thought John as Howard drove him towards the town centre. Some of the avenues were quite wide and lined with smart buildings, and the sidewalks were enlivened by bright billboards. John read a few as they drove along. One showed a gleaming battery out of which sparks shot. The text read: 'Ever Ready – the battery that never lets you down.'

'Hey, look! They've got good batteries here!' commented John.

Howard sneered: 'Yeah. Don't try them. The locals call them: "Never Ready".'

'What about this then?' asked John, pointing at another billboard, which carried the inscription: 'The *Daily Star*. The paper that tells you all you want to know. Everyone reads the *Daily Star*!'

This time Howard's reaction was contemptuous. 'They should have put: "The paper that tells you what the government wants you to know. Everyone reads the *Daily Star* because it's promoted by Minister Mamab..." No, I mustn't drop names!'

What a negative attitude, thought John, who refrained from making any more comments. He was in a fairly optimistic mood after a good night's sleep, found Naboru attractive, and felt sure he was going to sort out all his problems that same morning. Just then they passed a large building with marble steps leading up to big front doors. It carried the proud inscription 'MINISTRY of AGRICULTURE' on its facade in big copper letters. 'Hey, drop me here!' exclaimed John. 'This will probably do. They'll be able to put me on to the right place.'

He ran up with springy steps and opened the big double doors, ready for action, but he stopped in his tracks when he discovered that he was not the only one to have gone to the Ministry of Agriculture that morning. Thirty or forty Africans were pressing against a counter behind which three employees were sitting, visibly unconcerned about the commotion that was

18

going on at the public side of the counter. Two had retreated somewhat into the background and were busily reading the *Daily Star*, whilst the third one was gazing in front of himself looking bored, pretending not to see the visitors who were shouting and gesticulating, and trying to attract the attention of the government officials. It was total chaos.

No need to queue up, thought John. *There is no queue.* For a minute or two he was at a loss as to what to do. *Hell*, he thought finally, *if I wait my turn I'll wait forever.* Then he decided upon a line of attack. He was the only white man in the room and, racial equality or not, he realized that this was the one thing that distinguished him from the others. It was his only trump card and he was going to play it for what it was worth. He pressed forward with all his weight, shouting: 'I've come from America! I'm an American!' pushing the others out of his way. It seemed to work. The Africans stopped shouting, surprised by his odd conduct, and let him pass through.

By the time he got to the counter even the government officials looked up, astonished at having an American in their midst. 'What you want?' asked one of them.

'I want to contact the Ministry of Wildlife!' barked John, as if he were an important person used to ordering others about.

'Wild life? You come for the *wild* life?'

'Yes, yes!' shouted John impatiently. The crowd was beginning to press in upon him and he felt that his advantage wouldn't last long. 'I've come to study it.'

When they heard this, the three government officials left their desks to face John across the counter. 'You come all the way from America for the wild life in Naboru?' asked the first official as if he wanted confirmation.

'Yes, yes,' nodded John.

The man now turned to the other two employees and, although they had heard everything, he repeated, pointing his thumb at John: 'This here American feller has come for the wild life in town! To study it he say!' And they all began to laugh.

'No, no!' shouted John who thought he was misunderstood. 'It is not in the town. It's in a park!'

When the officials heard about the park they roared so much with laughter that they had to sit down while the Africans, who had closed in around John by now, began to shake with mirth.

19

John was getting more and more upset. *This must stop*, he thought. *I've been told not to waste my time with lower officials in African countries. People who know told me to go straight to the highest official level, and they were right.*

'I want to see the Minister of the Parks,' he said with as much authority in his voice as he could muster.

This seemed to set off an even louder roar, which continued for some time. Finally one of the officials made a movement, which John interpreted as 'I'll tell him', and between hiccups of laughter he explained: 'Ministers don't go to no park for the wild life, man ... Haha ... The wild life ... hahaha ... it comes to the Minister ... hahaha ... to his office...' He was almost unable to finish his sentence and burst into loud howls after the last word.

Just then a door opened at the back and a woman, well provided for by nature and heavily made up, appeared. 'There goes the Minister's wild life...' shrieked one of the officials. 'But you ... haha ... you no Minister ... You better go to the park to study the wild life...'

And everyone exploded again with laughter. Some people shook so much that they could no longer stand and had to sit on the floor, holding their sides, and one government official was so convulsed with laughter that he fell off his chair. He rocked to and fro and rolled about helplessly while tears streamed from his eyes.

By now John had begun to understand their insinuations. The disgusting pigs! If they thought they could treat him like that they were mistaken. They needed to be put in their place! 'I want to see the Minister!' he shouted. 'I insist!'

'You want to see Minister?' asked one of the officials. He shook his head. 'Not possible. Minister very busy right now...'

'Yeah, he studying the wild life!' cut in another official, laughing heartily.

The first official carried on, trying to steady his voice: 'You better write letter. Or come back tomorrow...'

'I want to speak to him right now!' yelled John, banging his fist on the counter.

Suddenly the official in front of him became serious. 'Man,' he said, wagging a disapproving finger at John, 'you not important. Important people, they not come here. They go to Minister's residence.' Then he added, shaking his head: 'You American fellers! You always in hurry. Never have time. This no good, man. I give you advice. You go back to your country and tell them folks over there to take time to live. And when they understand, then, maybe, they will be happy. Maybe even have time to laugh, maybe...'

When they heard this, all the Africans nodded while staring at John with eyes full of compassion. It was obvious that they were willing to help this unhappy being, but it was equally obvious that they thought it a near impossible task because there was so much the poor man didn't understand.

John wasn't going to wait for more. He pushed his way through the crowd and left the building, fuming. Had such a thing happened in the States, he would have filed a complaint for unethical behaviour, put a lawyer onto the case, and those revolting employees would have been kicked out in no time! As he turned around to cast one last glance at the Ministry of Agriculture, his heart was filled with black thoughts.

What kind of a joint is this? he thought. *This is really beyond the pale. I should have gone straight to the American Embassy. There at least you're sure of honest personnel and decent service. With the American authorities at least you know what to expect.*

5

He hadn't taken ten steps when an African walked up to him, approached his ear and whispered: 'Psst ... change.'

John stopped in his tracks, surprised, but as the man seemed unwilling to explain, he shrugged his shoulders, gave him a stern look, and went on. At the next crossing the same thing happened: as he began to cross the street, another fellow caught up with him and he heard again in his ear: 'Psst ... change.'

What the hell! thought John. *What's wrong with me? Why do they want me to change?*

Finally one African said: 'Change dollars, man?' and John got it. It brought home to him that he didn't have any local currency and needed to change some of his dollars. He walked on but the man glued himself to John, insisting: 'Good rate, man. One hundred shillings to the dollar.'

John hissed: 'Leave me alone,' accelerated his steps, and finally managed to shake off his tormentor.

What kind of a country is this? he thought. *Government employees who don't do their duty and laugh in your face. Ministers who occupy themselves during office hours with private affairs that defy all norms of decent behaviour. And they do it on the premises! People who accost you in the street to change money illegally. It's unbelievable! This whole country is rotten to the core. Such attitudes are the death of all values, of all decent behaviour. I am a law-abiding American citizen and I refuse to go along with this kind of overt corruption.*

Just then he passed in front of a bank. *Ah,* he thought, *that's where they change money in a normal country. Right! I will show these shady street dealers how a decent citizen behaves.* And he went to the swing doors and resolutely stepped inside.

A man in uniform came up to him as he entered. 'What is your business, Sir?' he inquired.

John looked surprised. The inside of the bank was not what he had expected. The public area was separated from the rest by a huge counter. There were armed guards at each end of it, and

22

behind this counter maybe half a dozen employees were sitting in front of their desks, shifting papers and looking generally bored. The strange thing was that he seemed to be the only customer.

The doorman repeated his question. 'Eh?' replied John, somewhat bewildered. 'Oh. Yes. I want to change money.'

'Follow me, Sir.'

The uniformed man stepped to the middle of the counter, motioned to one of the employees and then returned to his position next to the entrance.

The employee now came forward, bent over the counter and asked John in a subdued voice: 'Will you please state the nature of your business, Sir?'

'I want to change money.'

The employee seemed to hesitate.

'You don't change money?' uttered John, taken aback.

'It depends, Sir. May I ask you to be more precise?'

'I want to change American dollars into local currency.'

'Ah,' said the employee, looking relieved. 'That is possible.'

John was beginning to feel annoyed. 'And may I ask you why you hesitated? I would have thought that one of the things a bank is there for is to change money.'

The employee seemed embarrassed. 'Did you arrive recently?' he asked in a very low voice.

'Last night.'

'Ah. So you are not aware of the situation. You see, it is, umm … let us say, extremely rare that someone comes here to change dollars, so I feared that you wanted to exchange shillings into dollars.'

'And what's wrong with that?'

'Well, ahem … I am afraid that such a policy is … let us say, not promoted by the government.'

The man now withdrew and began to talk to someone at another desk. Some sort of quiet consultation seemed to be going on, and at last the other employee disappeared into one of the back doors. After what seemed to be an interminable time an important-looking man appeared, accompanied by a young woman who was carrying a set of papers.

When they stopped in front of John the man leaned forward. 'You really want to change money, Sir? Here in the bank, Sir? I have not misunderstood?'

23

'Well, of course!' exclaimed John who was getting very impatient by now.

'In that case, would you please fill out these documents? I'm sorry to have to ask you to do it in triplicate, Sir. We have run out of carbon paper.'

The young woman presently spread the documents on the counter, turning them around so that John could read them.

When John looked at the papers, his mind refused to believe what his eyes saw. It was not just his name and surname, nationality and passport number they wanted to know, but how he had entered the country, the flight number if by airplane, how long he was going to stay, what his business was in the country, his father's and mother's name, the company he worked for, and more apparently irrelevant questions. It was mind-boggling. And in triplicate. *Well*, he thought, *I started it all and I'm going to finish it!*

For maybe ten minutes the only sound in the building was that of his pen scratching the paper, filling out the forms while the woman stood in front of him, looking on encouragingly. When he had given all the requested details he came to the main object of the exercise: quantity to be changed. After some reflection he decided on two hundred dollars.

When he had finished and signed everything, he handed the completed documents and the money to the woman. 'Your passport, please,' she said, holding out her hand.

'I beg your pardon?'

'We also need your passport, Sir.'

Good heavens, thought John. *What next?* But he gave her his passport.

The woman smiled approvingly and withdrew into the back office. The important-looking man now appeared again and made a sign to one of the employees who came to the counter. 'Could you await your turn on that chair over there, please, while your request is processed?' said the employee. 'Here is your number.'

'What do I need a number for?' John asked surprised. 'I'm the only customer here.'

'You need a number, Sir, so that you can come forward when your number is called, indicating that it is your turn,' replied the employee coldly but politely. 'That is the correct procedure, Sir.'

As he sat down John stared at the big copper plaque he had been given. It carried a number 2 in its centre. *I'm the second one who has been caught in this administrative spider's web today,* he reflected. *Or is it this week?*

After what seemed ages the important man reappeared. He went to a safe in the back, accompanied by two employees. They fiddled for a while with a key and the knobs on the door, opened the safe and then set about counting money. Finally one of the employees called: 'Number two! Your turn now. Number two!'

John came forward and handed over the metal plaque. The important man in turn put John's passport on the counter together with a wad of used, dirty banknotes of small denomination.

'Here you are, Sir,' he said. 'Five thousand shillings.'

'Is that all?' John stammered. 'Where is the rest?'

'The rest, Sir? There is no rest, Sir. This is correct, Sir. Twenty-five shillings to the dollar; two hundred dollars, that makes five thousand, Sir. We checked it several times on the pocket calculator. There is no mistake, Sir.'

'Hey, but a dollar buys a hundred shillings, not twenty-five!'

'Sir, you are in an official bank here, and twenty-five shillings to the dollar is the official exchange rate,' stated the important man in a voice that tolerated no contradiction.

'But that's scandalous!' exclaimed John. 'That is outrageous!'

'Sir,' said the important man, 'I explicitly asked you whether you were absolutely certain that you wanted to change here in the bank. As far as I recall, you contested affirmatively. We have now concluded our transaction and I consider this meeting terminated.' And picking up a paper lying on the counter, he added: 'And don't forget your proof of official exchange.'

John swore as he left the bank. *This is broad daylight robbery! With my own ears I heard a hundred shillings to the dollar, and here they give you a miserable twenty-five. The thieves! The scoundrels! This is immoral! No wonder people give the government a wide berth. Who wants to abide by the law when it is as rotten as that? And look at the waste of time. They kept me in there for a whole hour just to relieve me of the little cash I possess. But I have a paper proving that I exchanged at the official rate,* he jeered. *Isn't that wonderful? Proving that I'm a dim-witted ass, yes! Lord, this is a world on its head. Nothing of what I've learned or been used to so far seems to apply here.* And mumbling and grumbling, John proceeded along the sidewalk, hissing: 'Too late!' at a fellow who sneaked up to him whispering: 'Psst ... change?'

6

At around the time John left the bank, some sixty miles further north a safari bus was drawing close to an elephant.

'Can you get any nearer?' whispered Veronica under her breath.

'It's dangerous enough as it is,' replied Ron nervously.

They had got to within fifteen yards of the bull elephant and the animal was becoming very agitated. It was staring at the safari bus, its ears stood out wide, and it had lifted up its trunk. The bull looked huge from such a short distance,

'Right,' said Veronica, all tense. 'I think I can do it.' Slowly, she raised the gun, aimed carefully and pulled the trigger.

At the sound of the shot the elephant emitted a loud trumpet call and stormed forward. Ron, who was sitting at the wheel, a bundle of nerves, just managed to get the safari bus out of the way and kept going till there was a safe distance between them and the elephant.

'My God!' he exclaimed, wiping the sweat off his brow. 'That was dangerous. Why the hell am I doing this?'

Veronica looked back at the bull elephant: he had slowed down and stood there, appearing stunned, his body swaying to and fro.

'The tranquillizer is acting!' she shouted. 'Look, he's sinking to his knees, he is rolling over! Quick! Move nearer! We've got about fifteen minutes before he comes round.'

'I don't want to go any nearer!'

'Oh come on! It's safe now.'

Ron kept on grumbling, but he did move the bus a little nearer. Veronica quickly picked up her equipment box, jumped out and ran towards the fallen elephant. As she approached, a few of the tickbirds, which look for insects in the folds of an elephant's skin, flew up. At once she set about taking samples of saliva, skin, and some dung that clung under the tail. The most difficult part was the blood. The animal's hide was so thick that she had to start again three times before she managed to push the syringe through. *Thank God that's done*, she thought when she had collected a sufficient quantity of blood. She packed everything away in her box and rose to leave. It was then that she noticed that the safari bus was no longer there.

She looked about dumbfounded till she saw the bus. It was at least three hundred yards away, and she was just about to run towards it when she heard a rumbling sound behind her. She turned around like lightning and to her horror saw that the bull elephant was coming to. He started to rock back and forth until, abruptly, he stood on his legs. *But this is much too early*, thought Veronica as waves of red-hot terror rushed through her body. *The anaesthetic should have kept him down for at least another five minutes. Maybe it wasn't strong enough for this huge bull!*

The elephant had regained consciousness by now and suddenly noticed her. He was still slightly dazed but he started flapping his ears, his trunk went up menacingly and then he began to move towards her trumpeting loudly. Veronica's thoughts ran feverishly through her brain: *If I turn and run he'll catch up and thrash me to pulp. My God! Don't panic, don't! If this is the end, be calm.*

And she calmed down and stared at the elephant, not ten yards away, looking him straight in the eyes. Then she spoke to him: 'I'm your friend,' she said softly, 'I don't mean any harm. I'm here to protect you. Be my friend too. I trust you. Please don't kill me.'

For one tense moment the elephant stood in front of her, moving nervously. Then Veronica's soothing voice, or maybe the strong waves of supplication emanating from her, seemed to quieten him: he swung around and walked away swaying heavily.

The effort to control herself, and the emotion, had been so strong that Veronica suddenly felt weak and dizzy. She crouched, hid her head in her arms and started trembling.

A loud hooting made her look up. The safari bus was rushing towards her and presently Ron jumped out. 'Hey!' he shouted. 'You shouldn't sit here. It's much too dangerous. You're lucky that bull elephant is at a safe distance or he might get wind of you and attack. Come on. Get in! You'll be safer inside with me.'

'Where have you been?' asked Veronica in a shaky voice.

'Oh where? I saw a herd of Thompson gazelles and a few giraffes further down and drove over to shoot some pictures with my telephoto lens – for my safari tours you know. Always nice to show customers some good pictures; they like it.'

'Idiot!' whispered Veronica under her breath as she got in and sat down without another word.

'No need to get huffy,' retorted Ron. 'You're not alone in the world. We all have to live and consider our own interests, you know.'

I wish I had my Land Rover back, thought Veronica. *Then I wouldn't have to count on the goodwill of this unreliable fool.*

7

An hour later, after having finished a frugal lunch in Elephant Camp, Veronica sat staring out over the horizon feeling downhearted: she was worrying about the safety of her elephants. She had been running everything on her own for two years now, with some local help: Steve Mutele who drove her jeep and had become good at elephant spotting; his wife, Faithful, who did household tasks such as cooking and cleaning; a handyman, and a few casual workers. So far she had felt up to the task, but lately there had been rumours of poachers in the area, and what could she and a handful of unarmed African helpers do against poachers?

Elephant Camp was a wooden house set in an enclosed yard in the middle of an animal reserve. It was just an outpost, miles away from the nearest village; and it took a two-hour drive through the open savannah to reach Naboru and civilized life. How could she defend herself against anyone wanting to harm her?

Veronica did not ask for much, but living conditions were primitive and she lacked some of the most basic comforts. Above all there were times when she yearned for company, for someone to talk to and share her thoughts with, especially in the evenings when she sat alone by the light of her petrol lamp and had run out of reading material. She had been trying for months now to contact the World Elephant Fund. She had been sending reports about the various problems she was experiencing with suggestions as to how to improve the situation. They were sympathetic but it seemed that money was scarce. How they expected her to monitor five hundred elephants spread over a huge area was beyond her. On a shoestring budget! Without any real help!

Still, there was good news. One of the top people from the Fund was going to visit within the next few weeks to see what could be done. Better still: they had promised her an assistant who might turn up any day now. *Everything will be so much easier with someone qualified to help me,* she thought. *I wish he were already here.*

8

When John consulted his watch he realized that it was past noon. *Probably too late for the American Embassy,* he thought. *Damned ministries and banks. Impertinent people! They laugh openly in your face and rob you in broad daylight! I've wasted my time with them. I'll now have to wait till the afternoon to go to the Embassy.*

Just then he passed a set of red plastic chairs and tables on the sidewalk and read 'Njami's Salad Bar', painted in big letters on the windowpane. *This looks attractive,* he thought as he read on: 'We offer a wide range of fresh homemade salads. From the fields straight into your mouth. Njami – the best salads in Africa!' Underneath they had hand-painted an assortment of colourful salads.

This at least is good private initiative, thought John, nodding approvingly. *Just get the government off their backs and look what Africans are capable of doing! Small-scale private enterprise, that's the future here. And the food looks healthy. So different from all the mass-produced junk we are force-fed in the West. This deserves encouragement.*

Presently an African, his round face split in half by a wide smile, came out of the bar motioning to John. 'Please be welcome, Sah. You want to try salad, Sah. Very, very good, Sah.'

As John sat down, the man advised: 'You try Njami's special, Sah.'

'What's in it?'

'All sorts, Sah. Very tasty, Sah.'

'All right.'

'And drink, Sah? I propose soft drink. Or better: milkshake? Or home-made fruit juice?'

'Sounds good to me. What have you got?'

'Pineapple...' Njami looked at the white man expectantly. 'Orange ... passion fruit...'

'Passion fruit it shall be,' affirmed John. 'Wonderful!' *Can anything be more exotic?* he thought and he sat down contentedly while Njami went inside to prepare everything.

When it was finally brought to him, the salad looked big and appetizing. It indeed seemed to contain all the coloured vegetables of the hills served on a bed of greenery, as stated in the menu which he had picked up while waiting. John was very hungry by now and he fell upon the salad and accompanying breadsticks like a starved lion, at the same time gulping down mouthfuls of passion-fruit juice. *Yum … delicious*, he thought, and ordered another big glass of juice with ice cubes.

He felt contented and sated when he had finished it all, ready to go out and face the wide world again. He paid his bill, which was hardly extravagant. *Such a lunch on a terrace in one of the main avenues of Washington would set you back at least thirty bucks*, he thought. *I'm beginning to appreciate Africa.*

Njami had explained how to get to the American Embassy, and John now began to stroll in that direction at a leisurely pace. He had covered maybe half a mile when suddenly he felt pangs of pain shoot through his stomach. Then his bowels began to contract and within minutes he was doubled up with cramps. He hailed a taxi, stumbled inside and gave the address of the Reformed Sinners' guesthouse. 'Quick, quick!' he groaned at the cab driver, fearing he would be unable to contain himself. He just sat there, his hands on his belly, praying that he would get to the guesthouse in time.

After what seemed an eternity the taxi stopped at the gate. 'That'll be twenty dollars,' said the driver, turning to his passenger who was as white as a sheet by now, sweat dripping from his forehead.

John didn't even argue at this overt extortion. He handed over a twenty-dollar note, ran to the gate almost bent double, rang the bell and, as Sister Anna opened the door, forgot to say 'Hello'. Instead he rushed straight past her to the nearest lavatory, shot in, slammed the door, managed to pull down his trousers and sank down in relief.

He sat there moaning and groaning for a long time while his bowels kept rumbling and ejecting all the coloured vegetables of the hills. After maybe half an hour the pain had somewhat subsided. *I don't think that there can be anything left inside me by now*, he thought. *Even my intestines must have come out.* He got up, opened the door, looked carefully around and then retreated hastily to his room where he washed and changed. He felt somewhat better and was just about to lie down on his bed when a renewed bout of cramps shot through his bowels and he had to run out again.

The scenario repeated itself at lengthening intervals. By six in the afternoon the worst seemed to be over, but John felt weak and slightly feverish. He decided to go and see the director, and found him in his office.

'Any success today?' the man asked.

'Not really. Nothing but bad luck. And I ate something in town that has given me terrible diarrhoea.'

'Hah!' exclaimed the director. Then he leaned forward, wagging a finger. 'I prayed for you this morning, but prayers can do only so much. Nothing can help you until you see the light. Retribution will remain your lot until you become a Reformed Sinner and join the flock.' He paused, leaving time for his words to sink in. Then he said: 'I'm sorry to have to add to your misery,' not looking in the least sorry but seeming rather pleased. 'Mr Gorfinder is going to arrive tomorrow and you'll have to vacate his room in the morning. I have done what I could – it is my duty as a Christian to assist you. But more I cannot do. Your fate is now in the hands of the Lord.'

'Oh ... ah ...,' groaned John as he felt another cramp shoot through his bowels. 'You wouldn't ... ouh ... have any medicine,' he asked imploringly.

'Go to Sister Anna. She will give you something. So, tomorrow after breakfast our ways must part,' repeated the director. 'Of course, Howard can drive you into town. We do what we can to help. But the Lord's ways are inscrutable, and only He, in His almighty wisdom, can decide when a sinner will be saved.'

9

John felt slightly better the next morning. He had received and swallowed a bitter-tasting white powder, skipped supper, and passed a reasonably quiet night. He hadn't eaten much in the morning but had drunk a lot of water, as he had been advised to do.

By half past eight Howard dropped him in front of a large double gate. 'The American Embassy,' he said, pointing his thumb.

The American Embassy! At last! For a moment John surveyed the impressive building standing proudly in the background behind the solid-steel gate, with several huge American flags hanging from poles along its facade. He felt his spirits surge as he looked upon these symbols of freedom, equality and justice. As he went through the open gate into the space behind, his bag slung over his shoulder, he breathed a sigh of relief. It was a short step, but it was loaded with symbolism. *I'm stepping out of Africa*, he thought, *and into my home country. I'm saved. No more nasty surprises. Nothing can happen to me now.*

He had advanced no more than five feet when a couple of marines pounced upon him from out of nowhere, he was thrown to the ground, his bag was pulled off his shoulder, and as he lay sprawled on the gravel face downwards, one marine had a foot on his back and held a big gun against his head shouting: 'One move and I'll blow your head off!' The other threw the bag as far away as he could and shot at it as it fell down, but missed. He seemed overexcited now, and was about to shoot again when a sergeant stormed out of the embassy yelling: 'What's happening? What you got there?'

'A terrorist!' shouted the marine who had his foot on John's back. 'He may be carrying explosives! Shall I blow his head off?'

'Don't shoot!' ordered the sergeant. 'We need him alive. We want to interrogate him first!'

'And the bag?' asked the other marine. 'Shall I blow it up?'

'What you got in that bag?' bellowed the sergeant, bending over John.

John was about to turn and answer when the marine pushed the barrel of his rifle against his head and yelled: 'Don't move or I'll shoot!' Finally John managed to say in a croaky voice, barely audible because he had his mouth in the gravel: 'My clothes.'

'Speak louder, man!' yelled the marine, kicking John in the side. 'The sergeant can't hear you!'

The vicious kick hurt John's ribs and he lay there for a while, trembling, before he was able to repeat: 'My clothes,' in a slightly stronger voice.

'What?' shouted the sergeant.

'I think he says his clothes,' said the marine.

'Your clothes?' The sergeant bent down over John, yelling: 'What you mean by that?'

'This is my travel bag,' came John's hoarse voice from below.

'Open that bag!' the sergeant barked at the other marine who during all that time had kept his rifle pointed at the bag.

'What if it's a bomb?'

'Open it!'

By that time a crowd had begun to gather outside the gate, following the goings-on with great interest and cheering when the marine threw himself on the ground and crawled forward as if he were under enemy fire, one arm covering his head. When he had made contact with the bag he began to finger it cautiously. Nothing exploded. Then he sat up, slowly opened the zip, and hesitantly felt inside. He next looked into the bag and rummaged through it. 'Nothing but clothes,' he finally said with a hint of disappointment in his voice.

The sergeant now swung into action. 'All right!' he bellowed, turning to the marine who had his foot on John's back. 'Let him sit up. But keep him covered while I interrogate him.' Then he turned to John, yelling: 'Who the hell are you? And what are you doing here?'

As John sat up, his body sore all over, a strong reaction set in. He began to shake violently and was unable to utter a word. He just sat there shaking, a truly pitiful sight.

'Speak man, speak!' ordered the marine, poking him with the barrel of his rifle. 'Answer the sergeant!'

'I'm an American citizen,' John finally managed to say. 'I came for information concerning a job.'

Suddenly the sergeant realized that what had begun as a brave act to stop a terrorist attacking the American Embassy, an act that would have got the marines a promotion, had turned into an embarrassing situation. This fake terrorist had not lived up to expectations! He had to be removed from the public eye as soon as possible before reporters arrived. The sergeant now looked at the marines with eyes like a double-barrelled gun, and shouted: 'Take him inside to security.'

John tried to stand up, but was unable to. He felt ill and weak. What with the diarrhoea of the previous day and the traumatic experience of the last ten minutes, his legs just refused to carry him.

'Get him inside!' ordered the sergeant. 'And don't forget his bag!'

Flanked by a marine on each side, his arms around their shoulders, John was dragged away, led into a side entrance and dumped on a chair facing a small room. Through the open door he noticed several screens showing all the approaches to the embassy. Two big men who had their backs turned to him were watching these intently; they seemed to John to be at least seven feet tall, and were built like heavyweight boxers. The spectators outside the gate hadn't yet dispersed, and one of the gorilla-like men was gesticulating at the screen which showed that particular entrance, shouting: 'Leave us alone, you damned assholes!'

Suddenly he became aware of John's presence in the corridor and turned around as if stung by a wasp. From the belt on his big belly protruded a huge handgun. 'What are you doing here?' he yelled while his hand moved to the gun. Then he noticed the sergeant, and pointing a thumb at John he repeated: 'What's that feller doing here? Wait! Isn't that the one you just floored?'

'Yes. We brought him in. Better to get him out of the way with all those gaping guys out there.'

'Is he dangerous?' the gorilla wanted to know, his hand still on his gun.

'I don't think so.'

'Has he been frisked?'

'No, but he's an American citizen. I think we made a mistake.'

'Shh!' warned the gorilla. 'Not a word! Nobody is asking you for your opinion. Take him to the Chief of Security.'

John was now dragged through the corridor and kept waiting outside an office while the sergeant went inside. He couldn't hear the conversation, but he did catch a few words, shouted loudly, which sounded like: '... you assholes...' and '...bad press'.

A moment later the sergeant left with burning cheeks and John was called inside and invited to sit in a chair opposite a heavy man in white shirtsleeves. The man was wearing a badge with a photo, which was an identical copy of himself but smiling. It carried the inscription 'U.S. Embassy Chief of Security' above the photograph and the man's name underneath it.

'Can I see your passport, please,' he asked.

John produced his passport and the Chief of Security studied it for a while. 'Yes,' he said, 'you are an American citizen.' He rubbed his chin, lost for words. 'Look,' he said at last, 'we do all we can to protect the lives of our citizens, abroad as at home.'

'What they did to me at the entrance didn't seem much like protection,' retorted John, whose spirits were slowly reviving.

'You should have shown them your passport,' countered the man.

'Shown ... my ... passport?' John laughed aloud, cynically. 'That's a good one! Do you think they left me time to show anything?'

'Ha! That just demonstrates how efficient our men are. Very efficient when it comes to doing their duty, which is to protect the embassy. I'm certain that you will understand and appreciate the good services our men are doing for our country.' He paused for a while, and then continued: 'You must realize that you shouldn't have walked in through that entrance.'

'Why not?'

'It's the main entrance, reserved strictly for official delegations. And as it happens, we're on maximum alert today because we're expecting an important visitor. And,' he added with something of reproach in his eyes, 'you shouldn't have carried a bag when coming to the embassy. That was a big mistake.'

'Just my luck', replied John bitterly, 'to pick the wrong entrance on the day when you're expecting a big shot.'

'So,' continued the man, 'what do you expect? They took you for a terrorist.'

'Do I look like a terrorist!' exclaimed John. 'Come on now!'

'No, no … not to me,' asserted the man, trying to soothe John. 'But with all these terrorist attacks nowadays, we can't leave anything to chance. Our men have strict instructions.'

'So anyone innocently entering the embassy hoping to get some much-needed information is going to be jumped upon, thrown on the ground, and is liable to be shot first before they ask a question?'

'Come now, don't exaggerate the gravity of the situation! But I see you're pulling my leg,' the man said, holding up a hand to stop John from interrupting him. He continued: 'Now, wasn't it comic that they took you for a terrorist, considering that you're not even an alien?'

'I fail to see the comic side of it,' replied John with a face like thunder. 'I shudder to think what they would have done if I *had* been an alien. If I had been a Cuban, let's say?'

The man visibly recoiled. 'You're not a Cuban?' He looked horrified.

'No. But supposing I had been one, I see the treatment would have been different. They would have shot a Cuban?'

'Don't quote me saying that! I didn't say it!'

'Why should I quote you?'

'You might speak to the press. I strongly advise you not to do that. Don't misunderstand me. We are a free country. The greatest democracy on earth, as you know very well. We like the press. We're all for it. But there have been a few cases where … well … where the situation was misrepresented by some people out to discredit our country. You see, most of our press understands and respects us. The press is generally trustworthy. Solid. But there are always some distorted minds who are trying to ferret out something sensational that would put our country in a bad light. Those evil people don't stop at anything to reach their aim. They make up things. Or they blow them up. They're the ones we don't like. Now, this unfortunate slight incident might easily be misused by some of the less scrupulous members of what is otherwise a highly respectable profession.'

John had sat speechless through this long monologue. Then he countered: 'Yeah. I see! Journalists blowing things up! The only ones I've met so far who were out to blow things up were your marines!'

'Tell me,' asked the Chief of Security, eager to change the subject, 'why you wanted to see us.'

'I'm a biologist,' replied John, 'and I've come to join a non-governmental project. It has to do with elephants in one of the animal parks out in the bush. I'm going to work there for two years.'

'You're going to stay two years out there in the bush. That's very good news ... I mean ... that's very brave of you.' His face relaxed at the thought that this embarrassing guy would be out of the way somewhere in the bush where he certainly wouldn't meet American journalists. And for two years!

'But there's been a snag,' continued John. 'A government official was going to meet me when I arrived at the airport two days ago, but no one showed up. And when yesterday I tried to find out what happened I couldn't get a decent answer from any of those rotten civil servants I met at the Ministry of Agriculture.'

'What the hell has the local government got to do with your job?'

'They are going to pay me while I'm staying over here. A Minister Kimbabe signed the papers.'

'My God, the local government is going to pay you? That complicates matters. Wait, I'll see what I can find out for you. Minister Kimbabe you say? Wait here,' he ordered, leaving the office.

When he returned after what seemed ages, his face was sombre.

'Well?' asked John, hoping for the best but knowing deep down that the worst was to come.

'Kimbabe is no longer Minister of Wildlife,' the Chief of Security finally replied. 'He was relieved of his functions a week ago.'

'But why? From the letter he wrote me he seemed a decent fellow.'

'We cannot tell you the reason.'

'And what happens to the project I am going to join?'

'I've been given to understand that all Kimbabe's ministerial decisions have been nullified retroactively.'

'What! And my job?'

'I'm afraid that your job has been nullified too. No job for you. No payment,' commented the man with a wooden face.

'I can't believe this! What a country! They sack you before you have even started! Everything is just one long nightmare over here. OK then. I'm returning to the States! I'm sure I'll have no trouble finding a few journalists who'll be delighted to hear what has happened to me in this country.'

'Wait. Wait!' The official held out a hand to stop him. 'Maybe there's no need to return so quickly. Just give me some time. We may be able to find you something. Let me offer you a cup of coffee while I find out what we can do for you.'

The official got a cup of weak, sugared coffee from a coffee dispenser in the corridor, handed the plastic cup to John and disappeared again. He returned after ten minutes, all smiles.

'I've got good news. Excellent news in fact! There happens to be an American research lab in town run by a Dr Sam Goldstein, and they are trying to hire someone to do advanced research. I'm sure you've got the perfect profile. You have done research before, I presume?'

'Yes. But why should they want me? Nobody seems to want me nowadays.'

'Don't be so pessimistic. Look, here's the address of the lab. Shall I call a taxi to take you there?'

'Are you proposing to pay the fare?' asked John who seemed to be getting wiser by the minute.

'Well,' said the man, taken by surprise, 'I ... I ... of course,' he concluded.

'Give me twenty dollars then, and I'll find my way,' replied John.

'Twenty bucks! That's a lot for a taxi ride!'

'All right. If you don't agree...' replied John, pretending he was put off and ready to leave. '... Bye and see you in the States.'

'Wait!' The Chief of Security began to fumble in his wallet and with a long face handed John twenty dollars while thinking: *I wonder how I'll be able to claim this back from the embassy.*

10

John was at a loss as to what to do when he left the American Embassy. After having very nearly been killed and then been told that he should forget about the project he was supposed to have joined, he felt completely dispirited. However certain the Chief of Security had been about him getting a job with this Dr Goldstein, he did not feel at all sure about it. *I'll walk for a while,* he thought. *That'll calm me and give me time to think.*

He had progressed no more than fifty yards, apprehensively looking left and right for anything that might pounce on him out of the blue, when a taxi drew up along the sidewalk and the driver shouted: 'Sah! Taxi!'

John gave him one disdainful look and then ignored him but the cab driver, who hadn't had any business come his way that morning, was not so easily put off and kept driving alongside him, every now and then calling out: 'Taxi!'

This went on for a hundred yards or so till John got fed up. He turned aggressively towards the driver, and shouted: 'I don't want a taxi! I'm going to walk!'

If he had imagined that this would put off the cab driver, he was mistaken. The moment John had spoken, the driver felt that the battle was half won and he now redoubled his efforts.

'You no walk, Sah,' he said. 'Walking no good.'

John was caught in the game. 'Why not?' he replied. 'Why shouldn't I walk?'

'Maybe dangerous, Sah? They may attack you? Maybe steal your luggage, Sah? Who knows what may happen. Better take taxi, Sah. Also speedy and comfortable.'

'Go away!' shouted John. 'I laugh at danger!' The risk of being attacked in the street seemed a child's game after what had happened to him at the American Embassy.

The taxi driver felt that he had better change tactics. 'You white man, Sah,' he now said soothingly. 'White man, he don't walk, Sah. White man, he drive. And if important, he is driven! You sure are very important white man, Sah. I drive you, Sah.'

What's all this about white man! thought John furiously as he walked on stubbornly. *I hate to be labelled: white man! As if there was only one single white man. A stereotype! Do Africans truly believe that all white men are the same? What nonsense! There are hundreds of millions of white men, all different! I don't want to be lumped in the same bag with them all. I'm an individual.*

The taxi was still keeping pace with John and the driver, unaware that he was interrupting such great philosophical musings, now called out: 'You decided, Sah?'

What a bother that man is, what a real bother! thought John. *Is there no peace anywhere?* Just then he passed a coffee bar and suddenly he had a brainwave. *That guy can't follow me in there,* he thought. He shot inside, sat down and quickly stared out. The grin had disappeared from the cab driver's face, and he looked defeated as the taxi began to gather speed and disappeared among the traffic.

John was mightily pleased with himself. *Victory,* he thought. *I've managed to do the right thing and choose a safe place. I'm beginning to react properly. At last!*

He ordered a cup of strong coffee, put his bag down and began to relax. As he did so, nature called for his attention. He had drunk a lot of water that morning and hadn't been to the restroom since leaving the Reformed Sinners' guesthouse. He quickly got up and disappeared into the back of the bar. When he returned a few minutes later, relieved at last, his bag had gone.

11

'Where's that human pig from Guinea you promised me?' complained Klaus. 'I don't want to be bothersome, but I must tell you that I won't be able to carry on much longer if you can't provide me with such a pig.'

'I've done my best,' sighed Sam. 'I phoned everywhere, but there doesn't seem to be anybody around who's as clever as you require. It's a real nightmare. Can't we make do with someone ordinary?'

'I told you that we need an educated pig!' Klaus seemed upset. 'Just think of it: I put all this work into the project! I conceive the greatest experiment ever. And then you want me to perform on someone unqualified. It will not do!'

'But surely, wouldn't any intelligent person with a good dose of common sense fulfil the requirements?'

Klaus shook his head in disbelief. 'Do I have to repeat that we need someone with an advanced scientific education – someone used to statistical methods of research? And I would like to add more: he or she should also have some years of practical fieldwork, and ideally possess a good knowledge of the morphology of different strains of hominids and of the environments they used to live in.'

A hollow laugh escaped from Sam's lips. 'Now, that's going to make it really easy, isn't it? Tell me if you know one person in Naboru, or in this country for that matter, who fulfils these requirements?'

Klaus rubbed his chin for a while; then he hit his forehead with the palm of his hand and exclaimed: 'I do!'

'Who, then, is that marvel? Come up with it. Tell me.'

Klaus pointed a thin finger at Sam. 'You!' he declared.

Sam recoiled in his chair as if someone had hit him with a wet towel. His face went white and his mouth fell half open. Finally he said hoarsely: 'You must be joking.'

'No, no, *mein Freund*.' Klaus spoke as if to a silly child. 'Think.

Who has a big brain, education and excellent training? And on top of that knows the problems of the hominids like the inside of his pocket? Nobody else but you, *mein Freund*. And who is so thirsting for knowledge that he is willing to spend his good money to find the answer? If you go back to the epoch of the hominids yourself, you will be able to see with your own eyes instead of having to rely on a second-hand eyewitness. Believe me, my friend, when I tell you that you are the ideal candidate and that we should not waste any time looking further.'

Sam now drew himself up to his full height and gave Klaus a contemptuous look. Then he spoke, throwing out each word as if it were the lash of a whip: 'Let me tell you that, if you believe even for a single moment that I'm going to lie on that table of yours and risk my life letting you fiddle with my brain, you're very mistaken!'

Klaus was visibly hurt. His hands began to tremble and suddenly he shouted: 'So you don't trust me, eh!' He stamped his foot on the floor. 'You don't believe in anything I'm doing, eh! *Donnerwetter!*'

Sam at once realized he had gone too far. If he pushed Klaus over the brink and he left, all his efforts to solve the riddle of the hominids in this very original way would be wasted!

'Come now, Klaus,' he said soothingly. 'Don't take it personally. It is because, contrary to established research institutions, I did believe in you that I wanted you to work for me and that I pay you so well. You know that my admiration for you knows no bounds. You are one of the greatest minds the world has known … maybe the greatest ever. You have made a revolutionary invention and are preparing an experiment that is unique in the history of mankind…' He spoke in measured cadences, like a politician trying to convince a suspicious public, leaving time for his words to sink in. And sink in they did. Klaus had calmed down by now and his head was bobbing up and down, nodding in agreement. 'But you will admit that there is always a risk in new experiments,' carried on Sam. 'You can never be one hundred per cent sure, isn't that so?'

'There is always a risk, obviously, however carefully I have calculated everything,' admitted Klaus reluctantly.

'See! Suppose something goes wrong, you'll have to revise the experiment and someone has to finance it. And who would do that if I disappeared? So you understand why I don't want to be the person who gets to be the guinea pig.'

'*Genau*. I see … I had not thought of that aspect. But that leaves us with a big problem. How are we going to find the right pig?'

Suddenly there was a knock on the door and the head servant entered, announcing: 'A gentleman to see you, Sahib.'

12

A moment later the door opened and John appeared. He stood there for a while, as if uncertain of the welcome he would receive. 'I'm looking for a Dr Goldstein,' he finally said in a hesitant voice.

'I am Sam Goldstein.'

'And I'm John Garfinger ... Dr Garfinger ... Hem ... is it all right for me to come in?'

Sam looked at the stranger in astonishment. Then, suddenly, it flashed upon his mind: *This may be the guy I need.*

'Well, come in, come in,' he replied, trying to sound as welcoming as possible. 'Make yourself comfortable. What can I do for you?'

John stood there, dazed. He had expected a dog to attack him, the ceiling to collapse upon him, anything, but not a welcome. He stared at Sam, then at Klaus, and seemed lost for words. Would he dare say what he had on his mind? At last he raked up his courage. He might as well speak out, be refused and thrown out. 'I'm looking for work,' he managed to say in a voice so low that it was barely audible.

When Sam heard these words he was overcome with joy, but he made a great effort to hide his feelings and replied in a calculated, businesslike tone: 'Well ... we may have something ... but naturally it depends on your qualifications. Maybe you could tell us your background, where you worked before, and so on?'

'I'm a doctor in biotechnology ... I don't know if that's any good for you? And I've done research at the Argonne Laboratory, then worked for an American biotech company and recently lectured at a Belgian university...'

'Great!' This time Sam was unable to hide his pleasure. This man really was a godsend! The answer to his prayers. 'Great,' he repeated.

Klaus coughed as if he wanted to speak. 'Yes, what is it Klaus?' asked Sam, his eyes sparkling.

47

'You know that I worked at the Argonne Lab for a while – in the physics department of course. I don't know this man personally, but I can vouch for his credentials in an indirect way. I often saw him at lunchtime in the restaurant.'

'Wonderful!' Sam felt so pleased that he wanted no further confirmation. 'But with such fantastic references, why are you here in this godforsaken corner of Africa looking for work?'

John seemed pained. 'It's rather a long story, I'm afraid. The Belgian university I worked for did not renew my contract last time round, so I went back to the States trying to find work in the private sector, but I had a nasty shock: it seems that I'm reaching the age limit for hiring people. They said that they had no use for my experience and that, furthermore, they would have to pay me too much. It seems that I'm overqualified! Imagine that! I would never have believed that it's easier to get a job if you're less qualified had I not heard it with my own ears.' John sounded vexed.

'But how did you end up in Africa?'

'I finally unearthed a non-governmental organization, the World Elephant Fund; they were offering a job to a biologist in this country. I applied and they hired me. The Fund gave me the plane ticket and some pocket money, but the local government was supposed to be paying my salary over here. And that's where the problems started. When I got to Naboru airport a couple of days ago there was no government official waiting to receive me as I'd been promised. Worse, it seems that the Minister of Wildlife who had signed the contract has been relieved of his responsibilities, and my contract's been rescinded. Would you believe such a situation possible?'

Sam just smiled. 'Yes, I would. This is your first time in Africa, I guess?'

John nodded. 'Finally I went to the American Embassy, asking for help.'

'You mean to say that you walked in just like that without an appointment?'

'Yes. And you know what happened as I walked in carrying my travel bag?'

'Why the hell did you take your travel bag with you to go to the embassy?'

'Because I'd just been chucked out of the guesthouse where

I'd spent a few nights – at least I thought it was a guesthouse. A cab driver had dropped me off there the first night, but it wasn't a real guesthouse; it was a religious kind of place, catering solely for Reformed Christian Sinners or something like that. I only got in by mistake – they took me for someone else.'

'And you didn't qualify as a Reformed Christian Sinner?' asked Sam, unable to hide an amused smile.

'No. I didn't know any of the endless hymns and prayers...' John suddenly seemed to hesitate. 'I hope I'm not offending your religious feelings by saying so?'

'That's OK. So the upshot was that you walked into the American Embassy carrying your bag.'

'Yes. And I'd hardly set a foot inside the front garden when the marines pounced on me. They mistook me for a terrorist! They had me lying on the gravel face down before I had time to say hello, holding a big gun against my head. They were wondering what to blow up first, my brains or the bag?'

'Oh my!' exclaimed Sam. 'You didn't really have a very good day then?'

'A rotten day. Nothing has worked out for me since I set foot on this continent.' John sighed deeply, as if all the troubles of the world had settled down on his shoulders. 'But today tops it all.'

'Let's look upon the bright side,' proposed Sam soothingly. 'You've escaped alive and you've come to us. Why don't you stay with us for a while? We'll show you the lab and what we're doing here and maybe, if you're interested, we can fit you in. But relax first. The manservant will lead you to a room. Where's your bag?'

'My bag ... er ... yes. After I left the embassy I went into a bar to have a strong coffee. And when I returned from the restroom I found that my bag had disappeared. Stolen!'

'So you have no change of clothes?'

'No,' affirmed John in a voice like an undertaker's. 'Not even a toothbrush. Just the clothes I'm standing up in. It's lucky I carry my papers and money on me. At least I still have a passport to prove I exist. I shudder to think what would happen if I had to go to the American Embassy again, this time as an unidentified person applying for identity papers.'

Klaus had been listening to the conversation with great interest and thought it was about time to brighten up John's somewhat sombre mood: 'This time they would be sure to shoot first before asking questions. You would be considered a UFO: an Undesired Frequent Offender!' And he began to laugh heartily at his own wittiness. 'Isn't that a good one? Hahaha ... Isn't that a good one?' he repeated, but quietened down when he saw the warning look on Sam's face.

'Don't take too much notice of our mad scientist there,' intervened Sam, trying to cheer up John who looked positively gloomy after Klaus' jest. 'And don't worry: we'll find you some gear this afternoon. But let's have something to eat first.'

13

After lunch Sam called in his head servant. 'Kibu,' he said, 'you wouldn't know of any store where we can buy clothes for the gentleman here who's going to join us?'

'He needs clothes, Sahib?'

'Yes, his bag was stolen an hour or two ago.'

'I'm sorry to hear that, Sahib. Does he want new clothes or second-hand ones?'

Sam looked inquiringly at John who replied: 'Second-hand clothes will do.'

'There are several stores that carry a wide choice,' answered Kibu. 'But may I make a suggestion, Sahib?'

'Yes, go ahead, Kibu.' And noticing that Kibu seemed to hesitate he added: 'What is it?'

'Well...' proposed the head servant, 'it might be useful to pay a visit to the large open-air market, Sahib. It is known locally as the thieves' market,' he added with an even face.

'Do you think they may have anything that will suit our friend?'

'Very likely, Sahib. And with a bit of luck he may even be able to find his own clothes and buy them back. You see, the bag has probably arrived at the thieves' market by now, and it is unlikely that the contents will already have been sold.'

'What! Buy back my own clothes!' fumed John. 'You must be joking! If I see my bag there I'll make a big stink and call the police!'

'I would advise the gentleman not to take such a course of action, Sahib,' warned Kibu, turning to Sam. 'It would be most inconvenient and possibly land the gentleman in jail.'

'Do you hear that, John?' insisted Sam. 'No rash action! If you happen to find your clothes, keep calm. Don't even hint that they may be yours; just buy them back. You'd better let Kibu do all the dealing ... Yes, Kibu?'

'May I also suggest that, for the duration of the visit, the gentleman refrains from carrying on himself any of his remaining papers and valuable possessions? It would be safer to leave such objects in his room if he is to visit the … well, the second-hand market, Sahib.'

'OK, John?' Sam looked up and saw John nod. 'Well then, here's some money, Kibu. Please take the gentleman to this, ahem … second-hand market.'

When Kibu and John got there they found a maze of passageways flanked by a jumble of stalls selling anything, from car wheels and tyres to radios, colourful plastic plates and cups, cutlery, furniture, watches, woodcarvings, tom-toms, musical instruments, clothes … anything under the African sun. So many Africans were pressing through the narrow passages between the stalls, stopping and discussing – skinny peasants and huge women dressed in bright flowery outfits – that it seemed impossible to make any headway. Everyone seemed to be talking at the same time, music was blaring out of hundreds of small radios, and the heat and smell were overpowering. Yet Kibu managed to work his way through the throng and John followed close behind.

They finally arrived at the clothes area and Kibu began to inquire in Swahili, but the stall owners just shook their heads or pointed further along as if to say: 'Ask there!' Presently they came to a stall where several battered pairs of jeans and shirts were hanging from hooks; a man with a face like a crook was peering out from between them.

I wouldn't fancy meeting that man in a dark alleyway at night, thought John.

He was about to withdraw further behind Kibu's back, when Kibu pushed him forward while asking something in Swahili and pointing at the jeans John was wearing. The crook began to poke around his wares and came up with a pair that looked as if an army platoon had driven over it. Kibu now began to speak English for John's benefit. 'The Sahib is not impressed,' he said firmly.

'No. This here jeans very second-hand,' agreed the crook.

'Anything better? Like the jeans he is wearing? Any fresh arrivals maybe?'

'Maybe,' replied the crook and he went to the back of his stall, bent down and started rummaging. A minute later he returned with a pair of jeans that looked exactly like the ones John was wearing.

'But ... but...' started John. Kibu stopped him immediately and turned to the crook. 'Let me feel these,' he said, and began to finger the jeans, pull them and hit them on the side of the stall.

'They're old and worn,' said Kibu with a long disapproving face.

'Yes, but originally good quality, very good ... *originally*.'

'How cheap are they?'

'Not very cheap. Good quality!'

'Have you more of these? Show me more.'

When the man had disappeared in the back of his stall, John whispered: 'But these are my jeans!'

'Shh...' warned Kibu, 'leave this to me, Sahib.'

The man now returned with another two pairs. 'What about these?' he said. 'Good, eh?'

'I don't know,' replied Kibu. 'It depends on what the gentleman wants.'

'Why not buy all. They fit, I can tell. Good fit. Sure!'

'Are they cheaper if we buy the lot?'

'Maybe. Want other things? I see gentleman likes this style. Wait, I got whole bag there.' He went to the back and returned a minute later with John's bag, and, as he dumped the contents on the plywood board that fulfilled the function of counter, some of the smaller items fell on the ground.

Kibu began to select some shirts and other items, and he now started haggling over the price with the crook, while John was almost unable to hide his excitement.

After some time Kibu inquired: 'How about this bag? Can we buy it to take our shopping home?'

'Yes, yes. Here you can buy everything. But this good bag. Expensive bag!'

They haggled again for a long time. Finally, Kibu said: 'Good, I'll pay your price, but only if you add all the remaining contents.'

'Man!' exclaimed the crook. 'That not possible! Look what remains: books, underwear, even good toothbrush not much used, and tube of toothpaste half full. No. Not possible!'

'OK,' said Kibu and turned around, motioning to John to go.

'But ... but...' stammered John, unwilling to go.

'See!' triumphed the crook. 'White man not want go.'

Kibu turned back and the discussion took off again. After

another five minutes they seemed to have reached an agreement satisfactory to both. As the crook dumped everything in the bag, John pointed at the few small items that had fallen and were lying in the dirt on the ground.'

'These you get free,' concluded the crook with a big smile, picking them up and handing them to John while looking with great pleasure at the banknotes Kibu was counting in front of his greedy eyes.

'Did you have to pay a lot?' John wanted to know when they were safely in the car, driving back.

'Not too much, Sahib. I think the price was more or less correct.'

'It seemed a lot of money to me. I saw you put down a pile of hundred-shilling notes. That man must have pocketed more than five thousand shillings.'

'Ten thousand shillings to be correct, Sahib. Or a hundred dollars if you prefer. But he does not pocket all of it. He will have to pay some 30 per cent to the man who brought him the bag.'

'But that's scandalous. I mean, they steal your possessions and you have to pay them for the service. A hundred dollars! It's outrageous!'

'Pray, let this not upset you, Sahib. It is all part of the grand scheme of things. Let us look upon it as a redistribution of wealth on a small scale.'

'Still, it is plain robbery!'

'Let us not judge in haste, Sahib. Anyway, it is Sahib Goldstein who is paying.'

'That doesn't make any difference. There's no reason why his money should go to those thieves.'

'With all respect, Sahib, may I make a comment?'

'Yes, fire away.'

'Sahib Goldstein inherited the money from his father, and how do you think his father made his fortune?'

'I haven't got the slightest idea.'

'It is not my intention, nor my role, to criticize, Sahib, but I am forced to note that he made his fortune by practising redistribution of wealth on a grand scale. And in his case the redistribution was unidirectional: it went systematically from many others towards himself.'

Just as he uttered these philosophical observations, they reached Sam's huge property. The double iron gate opened automatically when the car arrived, and closed after its passage. A manicured lawn stretched from the gate to the front of the big house, which was surrounded on both sides by tall trees. As they pulled up before the entrance steps, an African servant came running out to open the car door and let John out. When he noticed John's bag, he took it, motioned to John to proceed inside and followed him with the bag.

14

John was lying on the table of Klaus' time machine, probes on his head from which wires protruded, connected to an array of electronic devices. While he was fiddling with the settings, Klaus was singing at the top of his voice: '*Muss ich denn, muss ich denn zu-um Städtelein hinaus, Städtelein hinaus, aber du mein Schatz bleibst hier…*' His hips were swinging slightly to the rhythm of the song while he was keying in some data.

The sound was shrill, high-pitched and slightly irritating to John and after a while he could stand it no longer. 'Hey, hey,' he said, trying to attract Klaus' attention, 'can't you tune it down a bit?'

Klaus looked up. 'The electric pulses are too strong for you, yes? Strange. It seems all right on the screen.'

'I'm referring to your singing. It is not all right on my ears!'

'What? My song? You don't like it? I thought you Americans liked nice music. You know that this song has been interpreted by one of your most famous country singers? What was his name again? … I always forget … I don't know much about foreign singers. I mainly like romantic German music. And operettas, yes, I do like these. Ah, I've got it: Elvis Press-hay. Yes, that was his name. Mind you, he did not sing it as well as I do. His German accent was not so good.'

John sighed. Once Klaus had started upon a subject it was difficult to deviate him from his chosen path. *I must lead him on to something less painful to the ears*, thought John. *Ah, I've got a question that might interest Klaus.*

'Sam…'

'Yes, what about him?'

'Is he very rich?'

'I don't know how rich he is exactly but yes, his father was very rich and Sam inherited his fortune when he died unexpectedly.'

'Unexpectedly, you say?'

'What?' asked Klaus who had turned his attention again to his fine-tuning.

'I asked how he died?'

'Ah, that! I understand that his father died in full ... *wie sagt man das auf Englisch? Ja*, that must be it ... on the battlefield. And he left his fortune to Sam who was his son, you see.'

John looked up, somewhat puzzled. 'No need to emphasize that Sam was the son of his father, Klaus,' he said ironically. 'I believe that's the usual condition of sons.'

'*Ja, genau.* Must be my scientific attitude ... I always think that two proofs are better than one; that it never harms to overstate your thesis; and so on...'

'How did his father die such a heroic death?'

'Heroic death? I don't know about that,' replied Klaus vaguely, distracted by John's remark. 'Just a minute...' and he continued to fiddle with the knobs. After a while he carried on: 'So, as I said, he is very rich now and has decided to consecrate his life to science. Very useful to have a personal fortune in such a case; otherwise you have to go begging to the government, or universities, or other such mean institutions.'

As John nodded in agreement, Klaus shouted: 'Hey, *Ruhe*! Keep your head on the table. Don't move! Just lie there like a ... well, like a Bratwurst or something like that. But no, you must think and a Bratwurst does not do that. It just lies there. So imagine that you are a thinking Bratwurst. But think quietly, evenly.'

'I'll do my best,' replied John sarcastically, imagining himself to be a thinking sausage lying on Klaus' table.

15

'I didn't know you had such a heroic father,' said John when he saw Sam later in the day. 'Did he die in Vietnam? No, that's too far back. Probably in the Gulf War, is that it?'

'I don't understand what you're talking about.'

'About your father. Klaus said that he died on the battlefield.'

'The ass! One can never be certain that he understands anything fully or says things correctly.'

'So he didn't die on the battlefield?'

'In a way ... Well, I suppose it did represent the battlefield for him. A stroke felled him on the floor of the New York Stock Exchange during a battle with a rival for shares.'

'So he was a hero then – though not of the military but of the financial world?'

'Yes, he was an absolute master of the art of buying shares cheaply and selling them on expensively. Buying and selling was his way of life. And making a lot of money his aim.'

'Why didn't you follow in his footsteps? Your career would have been all laid out for you.'

'He wanted me to. But my interests are elsewhere. I suppose that I resemble him though. I'm not talking about financial abilities, even though I'm doing a good job at managing the fortune he left me. No! What I mean to say is that I have the same kind of mind he had. He was obsessed with making money – I with discovering the origins of mankind. Nothing else counts for me. I don't know whether you are acquainted with the dispute about these origins. It's been raging on for many years now and I want my name to go down in history as the one who settled the question once and for all. And since I found Klaus I feel that this goal has come within reach.'

He had got up while he spoke, a medium-sized, inconspicuous, brown-haired man with sloping shoulders, but as he spoke he seemed to swell and grow, and his eyes shone like two brown lasers whose burning light he now turned upon John.

58

John suddenly became wary. *Hey*, he thought, *I don't know this man at all. He looks inoffensive enough, amiable, but I've just had a glimpse of his true personality. He sees himself as a shining beacon, a giant – maybe as one of the most important men who ever lived. I must be careful not to cross him.*

16

Little by little John got used to the daily routine of working with Klaus. He had felt stressed for months worrying about his future, and settling down in this house was a relief. Sam took care of all his problems and expenses, and he was invariably in such a good mood and was such an entertaining person that John's confidence soon returned. Living on his property was like living in an oasis, shut off from the rest of the world, its ceaseless roar and unending troubles. John felt as if he were enveloped by a protective shell: it was a quiet, comfortable life, with no thought for the morrow. He just lived each day as it came and this suited him perfectly.

Yet, after a week or so, he began to feel somewhat restless. One night he suddenly remembered why he had come to Naboru: he had come to work in an elephant reserve and wondered whether the people out there in the bush knew about the government's failings. Maybe they had no knowledge of anything and were still expecting him? The least he could do was to go and tell them that it was all off; that he was sorry but that the government had broken the contract.

The next morning during breakfast he expressed his concerns to Sam.

'Well,' said Sam with a fatherly expression on his face, if it puts your mind at rest, why not? I think you have a right to a free day anyway, so why don't you take the old car and drive out there?'

'But I have no idea where it is. Is it far from here? And who directs that elephant reserve?'

'I vaguely know the person who runs the project: a Veronica de Ville. Met her once or twice. I honestly don't understand why she wants to do that kind of job. There's no money in it, the reserve is in the middle of nowhere, and she has to live without the slightest comfort or security. Rumours have it that she is obsessed with elephants; that would explain it. But she is alone in her battle to save the animals. The government doesn't care, and I hear that the Fund which employs her has taken on more than it can handle. It seems that she got the job only because no one else was interested. There's no future in the whole thing and, frankly, it's dangerous.'

'Lucky I got out of it!' exclaimed John. 'Still, I would feel better if I went to tell her that I'm out of the picture. So, how do I get there?'

Sam called his head servant. 'Kibu,' he asked when the man appeared a few seconds later, impeccably dressed in bright robes as usual, 'do you know how to get to the elephant reserve run by Miss de Ville?'

'Yes, Sahib. You take the road north until you reach the small town of Bulamonga. On the north-west side of the town there is a track leading to the elephant reserve. I have never been that way myself, but I believe that Elephant Camp, where the Memsabu lives, is quite a distance through the savannah, some thirty miles of rough track. Does the Sahib want me to drive him there? Shall I get the big car ready?'

'No, it is John who wants to drive there. You'd better get the old car ready.'

17

As he was advancing slowly through the savannah two hours later, John reflected that he would have done better to spend the day in an easy chair, reading. Driving to Elephant Camp no longer seemed such a good idea. The old car was not made for dirt roads and it was bumping and rattling along as if it were going to fall apart any minute. This was a really uncomfortable experience.

I've never driven on such a rough track in my life, thought John. *And they dare mark this as a road on their maps!*

The dirt road seemed to carry on endlessly through a landscape of scattered thorn trees and tall yellow grass. There were no clear landmarks. Far on the horizon John could make out what seemed to be a range of purple-blue mountains, but they appeared fuzzy because of the heat haze. The air visibly quivered as it got hotter and the sun bore down on the Earth. Everything seemed unreal. Sometimes he could make out the dark shapes of animals far away, maybe a herd of buffalo, but that was all. There wasn't a sound, not a sign of human life, not a vehicle around.

John definitely did not feel at ease. *What if I break down?* he thought. *This is an old car and I don't really know anything about mechanics – just where to put the petrol and a bit about checking oil and water levels. And it's full of wild animals out here. There is not even a fence to protect me from lions and other prowling creatures!*

All of a sudden he felt very lonely, vulnerable, abandoned on an inhospitable, primitive Earth. Had he got lost? He'd been driving for an hour now but the track just kept stretching towards an ever-receding horizon. What if he were on the wrong track? But there had been only one road leading north-west out of the small town of Bulamonga. He had furthermore asked a few Africans, and they all had assured him that this was the 'big road' to Elephant Camp.

The more he saw of this bush country, the less he liked it.

That was certain. How he could have thought of working here was beyond him. Of course he had never seen the African savannah before, and a few weeks ago he had jumped at the opportunity to get a job. It had all looked like a wonderful adventure back home in the States. Now he felt relieved that fate had decided otherwise.

If only I could reach this Elephant Camp, have it all over and done with, and get back safely to Naboru, he thought. *I never ever want to come here again. Never.*

18

Veronica was watering some flowers which she was trying to grow around her wooden two-storey house, when she heard the sound of a car engine. She was not expecting anyone and wondered who was putting in a surprise appearance.

A minute or two later an old green car appeared in the alleyway that led to her house, moving slowly, almost hesitantly. *I've never seen that car*, thought Veronica. *Who can it be?*

The car stopped in front of the enclosure some fifty yards away instead of proceeding through the gate, and presently a man emerged from it. Veronica eyed him with interest. He had seen her too, and as he approached her somewhat reluctantly she couldn't help thinking: *What a handsome man. Tall. Seems unsure of himself. Simply dressed too.* She mentally made an approving nod. This was exactly the type of man she liked. Not one of those muscular watch-me-here-I-come fellows. Not one of those peacocks dressed in designer clothes, expecting the girls to fall for them like flies. *I can't stand men in expensive clothes*, she mused. *Men such as Ron: impeccably dressed; big car; big noise but a windbag! This man has an old car, old clothes, but he's someone. He is most definitely someone.*

As the man approached, smiling at Veronica, he seemed somehow familiar to her. *I know him, I'm sure I know him*, she thought. When he had got to within a few yards she recognized him.

'John Garfinger!' she exclaimed. 'What brings you here?'

It seemed amazing to John that she knew him. He stood in front of her ready to shake hands, saying hesitantly, 'Veronica de Ville?' when suddenly, without knowing why, he bent forward and kissed her on the cheek, one hand on her shoulder. He then looked at her in admiration and before he had time to stop himself he blurted out: 'How pretty you are!'

Veronica was indeed a very pretty girl, used to being admired, but she blushed visibly when she heard this unexpected

64

compliment. As he saw her look of surprise, John turned bright red and mumbled: 'Oh ... I ... I'm sorry. I ... I do apologize. I don't know why I said that.'

'I don't mind,' replied Veronica with a mischievous look in her eyes. 'Don't bother. Girls like compliments. But tell me: what's the aim of this surprise visit?'

What a most awful situation, thought John. How could he tell her the bad news he was bringing? He had no idea how to set about it and just said, trying to put off the moment: 'Over in the States there was a non-governmental organization advertising for someone to help out with the technical analysis of an elephant project. Do you ... do you know about this?'

'Of course I do. That must have been the World Elephant Fund.' Veronica looked very pleased. 'I pestered the management long enough to get some assistance. And they are going to send me someone to help me. Isn't that wonderful?'

John felt truly embarrassed now. He would have to disappoint this really nice girl. 'Well...' he began hesitantly, 'I'm really sorry ... I don't know how to tell you...'

'What is it?' A worried look was spreading over Veronica's face.

'I have come to tell you that ... that no one is going to help you.'

'What!' Veronica recoiled. 'I don't believe this! How can that be? And how do you know about this?'

'You see ... I came over here for that job. The problem was that the Fund didn't have a lot of money, so they arranged for the local government to pay me. And would you believe it: the minister who signed the contract has been fired, all his contracts have been nullified, and the government is not going to pay anything. So here we are, you without an assistant, and I stranded in Africa.'

'But that's really dreadful. I desperately need someone to help me!' exclaimed Veronica. Then she looked at John's crestfallen face and realized that his situation was much worse than hers. 'I'm sorry that they have put you in such a position,' she said, trying to console John. 'It's unfair to have made you come all this way first and then tell you that it's off. What are you going to do now?'

'I've found temporary work in a lab in Naboru. They give

me food and lodging in exchange for my participation in a time-experiment.'

'Is that all they give you? Don't they pay you? You're not just anyone from what I remember.'

'What do you mean?'

'Well, aren't you quite an authority in biotechnology? I've been to a couple of your lectures – that's how I know you.'

'That doesn't seem to count for much over here!'

'No, it doesn't. All this must have come as a terrible shock to someone like you! But as you have just found out, over here things are not quite what you were used to back in Europe.'

'Not quite what I was used to!' John laughed cynically. 'What an understatement! I seem to have stepped straight into a parallel sort of world the moment I landed here. Sometimes I think that, if I pinch myself hard enough, I will wake up and everything will return to normal – people, situations, everything.'

'Pinching yourself isn't going to help.' Veronica shook her head. 'Don't expect Africa to adapt to you. It's not going to adapt to anyone. I've learned that either you like it as it is, or you don't. And if you don't, you'd better go somewhere else.' She looked straight at John. 'I would say that Africa is so unlike you that I find it difficult to believe that you are standing here in front of me, though I see you with my own eyes.'

And what incredibly pretty eyes, thought John. They shone like two blue stars in her suntanned face, seeming to burn holes straight through him. He had never met anyone like this girl. She was more than pretty. Life in all its strength and beauty seemed to radiate from her. Was it her life in the bush that had made her the way she was? Was it her mind shining through her eyes, untamed and unspoilt, as difficult to catch as the wind? John shook his head reluctantly, almost unwilling to wake up from the enchantment that held him in its power. He wanted to say: 'If this is a dream, let it continue.' Instead he heard himself say: 'You wouldn't have something to drink, would you?'

His request seemed to bring Veronica down to earth. 'Of course,' she almost stammered. 'How thoughtless of me. You've had a long journey and I'm not even offering you a drink. Please excuse me.'

As he looked at her shapely body while she turned away and

moved towards the house, the long khaki skirt swaying graciously with every step, her golden hair floating around her head, leaving just an inch of her neck visible, he wanted to kick himself. *You triple idiot!* he scolded himself. *You ill-mannered clodhopper! Making the girl feel uncomfortable. How could you?*

After Veronica had disappeared inside the house, John went to the covered veranda and sat down on a homemade wooden bench in front of a table. *How primitive everything is*, he thought as he surveyed the surroundings. There was an open space around the house, some dense growth of trees and low bushes at the perimeter, a few small outbuildings, a shed surrounded by a palisade of very strong posts, a well and water barrel, and a stockade towards the south where he had come from. There had been moments when he had felt pretty lonely in his life but now, here in the bush, he realized for the first time what true loneliness was. This was worse than being an American pioneer setting up a homestead in the West a century or two ago. How could a young woman live here? Alone?

Veronica presently appeared carrying two glasses. 'Sorry,' she excused herself, 'there is only water. And it's not even cold. The fridge has stopped working again. Sorry.'

'It is I who should be saying sorry for troubling you,' John hastened to assure her. 'I barge in unexpectedly and it is you who apologize. That's an upside-down world. Considering the difficult circumstances under which you live, I should be thankful to get anything.'

'May I ask you what you mean by that?' Veronica's voice suddenly sounded a little sharp.

'Well...' John felt embarrassed. *You said the wrong thing again, you ass*, he thought. '...Look, I just mean to say that there isn't much comfort down here, is there?'

Veronica seemed put off. 'This may not be the Ritz in Paris,' she retorted, 'but it suits me fine. And if you're frightened that there's not enough comfort for you, don't worry,' she added with something of contempt in her voice. 'As you're not staying for the job, you won't have to come and live here.'

Just then a little elephant appeared around the corner and when it saw John it rushed forward trumpeting loudly. Presently it began to nuzzle him, dribbling saliva over his neck. John moved away uncomfortably.

'That's Dumbo, my baby elephant!' exclaimed Veronica, suddenly brightening up. 'He's come to say hello to you. Isn't he sweet?'

'Can't you take him away?' implored John who by now had shifted to the edge of his bench and was straining to get away from the exploring little trunk.

'Don't you like him? That's his way of making contact.'

'Can't we just shake hands or something more neutral?' replied John completely confused.

'I see ... you don't like elephants.' Veronica got up, took Dumbo by his trunk and led him away to his shed.

When she came back she seemed distant. She sat down and turned to John. 'You certainly have the educational qualifications for this job...' her voice sounded offhand, '...but if you don't mind me saying so, there are other important factors that count for a job like this. I don't want to criticize you, but I don't think that you are adjusted to life in the bush. Maybe it's all for the best that you're not going to work here.'

John sat there gaping. *I've heard all this before*, he thought. *It just sounds like one of the many job interviews I had in the States. Who does this girl think she is to talk to me like that?*

He felt stung and got up, his face clouding over.

As Veronica looked at him she realized that she had gone too far. He had been kind enough to come all this way to inform her about the bad luck that had befallen both of them. And all she could do was to rub salt into his wounds.

'I'm sorry,' she said. 'I shouldn't have spoken like that, but I can't stand it when people don't like my little Dumbo. He's an orphan. His mother was killed by poachers and I rescued him. Now he looks upon me as his mother and turns to me for protection, and I always worry that he doesn't get enough love. I'm sorry.'

Her words managed to calm John and he sat down again. They both kept silent for a while, staring out over the savannah.

'Wasn't it difficult to bring him up?' John asked finally, interested in finding out more about Veronica's unusual life.

'Feeding him was difficult at first,' she agreed, 'but it wasn't really so bad. And now he is quite independent. He goes out to browse in the bush all by himself like a big boy, and returns to his shed in the evening.'

'Amazing! How you've been able to do all that ... and to

live here? You know,' John admitted, 'you're right about me not being adapted to life in the bush. I find it scary.' Then he added, looking at her with admiration: 'How come you like it so much?'

'Oh! Well ... that's a long story. My great-grandfather was a famous hunter at the beginning of the century – he caught animals for a Swiss zoo. One year, when he took his teenage daughter with him, he was killed by lions. The daughter, my grandmother, buried him where he had died and, being the only European left, she led the expedition hundreds of miles back through savannah and forests till they reached the coast. In the late 1920s she returned to the area where we are now, not as a hunter for she hated killing animals, but to observe the wildlife. She lived alone in a tent in the bush with a couple of servants for months on end. I suppose I inherited my love of elephants and living in the bush from her.'

John sat there trying to imagine the life of a woman alone in the bush some seventy years ago. He imagined a slender woman looking like Veronica surrounded by lions and leopards. *What incredible pluck*, he thought. *No wonder the girl thinks nothing of a few discomforts.*

The shrill sound of trumpeting suddenly woke him from his daydream: Dumbo came storming into the yard followed by a small yapping dog. He made straight for Veronica, bashing into John and knocking him off his bench as he attempted to hide his bulk behind Veronica's back. The young elephant stood there, trembling visibly while Veronica tried to shoo the little dog away, clapping her hands and stamping her feet. 'Go away, you horrid monster!' she shouted at the yapping dog. As the small animal gradually retreated she turned to John who was scrambling to his feet again. 'It's that horrible dog of my manservant Steve. It sometimes accompanies him when he comes over from his village. I wish he wouldn't bring it because it tries to bite my Dumbo's little legs and frightens him.' And she caught Dumbo by his trunk and returned him to his shed.

John almost pinched himself. *This isn't real*, he thought. *This just can't be real. I must be living in a virtual world.* He looked at her as she reappeared, walking slowly towards him: such a dreamlike figure in her long skirt and faded blue blouse with rolled-up sleeves, golden hair waving around her delicate face

... the heat rising visibly around her ... the silence of the afternoon accentuated by the shrill song of a cricket ... the hazy blue of the horizon far away ... *If this is life in the bush, I might like it*, he thought as peace settled in his heart.

His peace was abruptly shattered by a big safari bus appearing in the driveway, music blaring as it crossed the entrance gate and came to a stop with shrieking brakes. Ron jumped out, impeccably dressed in a white safari outfit, teeth flashing.

'Who on earth is that?' inquired John, turning to Veronica.

'Oh! That's Ron. I had completely forgotten! He's taking me into the reserve to make a few observations.'

Ron crossed the few remaining yards with the self-assured air of the man who knows his way in the world, held up his arm in a theatrical gesture and declaimed: 'Here I am, Vee.'

'Just give me a few minutes!' shouted Veronica as she rushed upstairs to change.

Neither of the two men spoke after she had left. Veronica seemed to take ages to get ready, the silence soon became uncomfortable, and Ron went back to his big open-decked safari vehicle. At last Veronica came running downstairs and as she passed John she stopped for a second. 'I'm really sorry about having upset you,' she whispered, her eyes full of apology. 'I have to go now but, please, do come back if you can.' Then she gave him a quick kiss on the cheek and ran off to the safari bus.

They were well into the reserve before Ron spoke. 'Who was that feller and what did he come here for?'

'Oh. That's John,' replied Veronica. 'I know him from my student years. I went to some of his lectures.' She stuck up her chin. 'He's an authority in biotechnology.'

'Well, I don't like him,' commented Ron, changing gears abruptly and manoeuvring the vehicle too rapidly.

But I do, thought Veronica, smiling to herself.

19

John was lying once more on the time machine table while Klaus was fiddling with the dozens of knobs on his remote-control apparatus. He was trying to think very quietly and evenly, but all sorts of questions kept popping up in his mind. What was going to happen to Veronica? Meeting her had affected him deeply. She had upset him but, in spite of that, he had felt strongly attracted to her. Such an extraordinary being she was!

He had pretended that nothing of any importance had happened when he had got back to Naboru, and he was certain that Sam had been taken in, but he had to be careful. Every time a thought about Veronica passed through his mind while his brain was being scanned, he tried to suppress it immediately, somehow fearing that Klaus would see her face pop up on his screen. It was tiring, he was getting utterly bored, and after a while he could stand it no longer. *If only I could engage Klaus in conversation*, he reflected, but there was little Klaus was interested in apart from his time machine. *Ah*, he thought suddenly, *here's a possible subject.*

'How did you come to work here in Naboru instead of in one of those famous American institutions?'

Klaus pondered for a while. 'Well,' he said after some time, 'you know what the world is like.'

'I don't know a lot about it yet, but I'm learning fast. And I dare say you're right.' John nodded vigorously, shaking all the wires attached to his head while doing so.

'*Ruhe!* I mean, keep quiet, *bitte!*' exclaimed Klaus. 'Your brainwaves are swinging all over the screen! How can I work like that? You tell me!'

'Sorry, I forgot.'

'Don't next time,' grumbled Klaus as he began fiddling with the knobs, a concentrated look upon his face.

'Well, what is it like?' asked John after a while, trying to get back to the previous conversation.

71

'What is what like?'

'The world.'

'What are you talking about?'

'You said just now: "You know what the world is like."'

Klaus continued to fiddle with the knobs. 'Why should I say a thing like that?' he finally replied.

John grunted. The fellow was driving him mad.

'Hey!' exclaimed Klaus. 'What's that? I see big brainwaves. Are you under the influence of some strong emotions? I told you to keep *ruhig*. Quiet. Very quiet. Nearly asleep, but not entirely.'

'All right. All right. But we were talking about why you are working in Naboru instead of in the States. If this is the invention of the century, everyone should be willing to fund it.'

'Ha. I see what you mean. But you know what the world is like.'

'There we go again,' sighed John. 'Please, explain in full this time.'

'*Ach ja.* This is the invention of the century as you rightly say. Even of the millennium. But it has no practical use! No commercial or military application. So, not a pfennig from companies or the government.'

'I'm beginning to see the problem,' agreed John. 'But what about universities? What about Germany?'

'Germany! Where you have to send application forms in triplicate to a dozen official channels to get any funding. Where you have to explain in detail the aim and use of the project. Explain the most advanced ideas of science to *Beamten* – to government officials chosen for their political adherence, not their brains! Permit me to laugh.' And Klaus emitted a hollow sort of laugh. He was all agitated now and gesticulating wildly. His gold-rimmed spectacles had slid to the point of his nose and were about to drop off.

After a while he calmed down. 'Would you believe that my time machine, this greatest of all inventions, this glorious scientific advancement, would have been dead and buried but for Sam. He believes in me and backs me unconditionally. He deserves a statue on a pedestal. Though not as big as mine, of course,' added Klaus without the slightest hint of humility.

He now turned again to the machine. 'Let's get on with the

job. We have wasted enough time already. *Ruhe!* No more talking from now on.' He shoved his spectacles back on his nose and with a concentrated look on his face, the tip of his tongue visible in a corner of his mouth, he began fine-tuning the time machine and keying in data.

20

Veronica was completing her notes on different elephants, when she heard the noise of an approaching car and the sound of music becoming gradually stronger. Presently Ron's big safari bus turned into the yard and stopped abruptly only yards from where she sat, throwing up a cloud of dust. The door was flung open and Ron jumped down, his eternal smile on his face, showing a row of perfect white teeth.

'Hi, Vee!' he greeted her in a loud voice, while giving her a peck on the cheek. 'Always glad to see me, aren't you?'

'Sure,' replied Veronica but her eyes didn't really smile a welcome. 'What's made you come out here today?'

'Ah! You're going to be impressed! You told me about the trouble you're having with that project of yours last time, remember? Now, I'm not one to leave a nice girl like you in distress; no, that's not like me. I've been doing some good work since then and I think that I've got the solution to all your problems.' With a theatrical gesture he put his hand on his impeccable white shirt, and drew himself up to stress his importance.

Veronica now pushed her notes aside and began to show interest. 'You've been making inquiries for me? That's really kind of you. Sit down here next to me and tell me about it.'

'You see,' replied Ron who declined to sit down, 'I happen to know some influential people...'

'Yes...' interjected Veronica encouragingly.

'...the Le Telliers. Very important people!' Ron moved his head up and down as if to underline how important they were. 'They have interests all over Africa ... closely connected to a French ex-president ... great political influence...' Ron kept nodding his head vigorously each time he added an item to the list.

'What exactly is their business?'

'Not quite sure. They're trading in all kinds of African products.'

74

Veronica's reply was sharp: 'They're not cutting down forests or killing animals, are they?'

'No, no! Not that I know of. I believe that they're working for the conservation of Africa. All sustainable I hear. Good people. Great political connections in this country too. If anyone can help you with your problems here, it's Jacques Le Tellier. He'll be in Naboru within a short time and I'm going to meet him. I will put in a good word for you and try to interest him in your project. Don't know how far I'll get, though. He's a very busy man.'

Why Ron bothered about her troubles was beyond her, but Veronica was visibly touched by his solicitude. 'Oh Ron, you are a darling!' she exclaimed and spontaneously jumped up and kissed him on both cheeks.

Ron tried to quieten her and patted her on the shoulder, saying: 'Now, now, let's not show undue enthusiasm before the results are in.'

'That's true.' Veronica's enthusiasm suddenly subsided. 'If he's such an important and busy man, it's ten to one that he won't bother. I'm only small fry for him ... nothing but trouble,' she added with a sigh.

'I know, but to me you are important. I can't promise you anything but I will do my best.' Ron nodded gravely. 'Look here, if he happens to take any interest and agrees to meet you, you must promise to be collaborative. He is your best, maybe your only, chance. He has got the money. And if he throws his weight behind the project he may sway government officials. He knows his ways inside the corridors of power.'

Veronica now straightened herself: 'I'm prepared to go to great lengths to save my elephants. I'll give what it takes. Rest assured of that.'

'Good! Excellent! That's what I like to hear. Good girl.' And with a wave of the hand he jumped into his bus and disappeared. A minute later only a cloud of dust indicated that he had been there, then that settled down too, and peace returned to the savannah.

For a while Veronica felt excited, almost elated. Then, little by little she became less confident. While Ron was there she had almost persuaded herself that she would be able to handle this Le Tellier. But now she saw before her mind's eye a man of a certain age, used to ordering others about. She had charm, yes, and conviction, but that wouldn't be sufficient. She would be facing a businessman who would have little time and would want to see all the cost calculations, all the figures. She would need to expose all the ins and outs of the project lucidly and concisely, and she had never made any such computations. She didn't even have the faintest idea where to begin.

Suddenly she was overcome by panic and felt convinced that she would fail abominably. This was no good! She'd do better to count on the World Elephant Fund: the fund's president was touring East Africa and he might turn up any day now. *Don't have any illusions,* she thought. *No businessman is ever going to be interested in elephants. The Fund is my only real hope.*

21

'So your passion is the origin of mankind?' observed John, turning to Sam while the three men were having lunch.

'Yes, I told you,' replied Sam, helping himself to a big slice of pineapple from the fruit dish which the head servant was proffering. 'I'd like to settle the question once and for all.'

'Haven't they got enough information already to settle the question? With all the bones they've unearthed – like Lucy's – and all the tools they've found?'

'You think so? What have we really got to base our theories on? Some fossilized bones and a number of very primitive stone tools – if what they found really are tools, which isn't always certain. No wonder the debate rages on. Any new find, a tooth or two, part of a cranium, reopens the debate. And whoever makes the find invariably tells us that he's discovered the beginning of the true lineage that leads, in an uninterrupted sequence, to us modern humans. There are as many theories as there are people who discovered a few bits and pieces of skeleton. I'm afraid that the debate will never be settled. And it never can be settled as long as we rely on old bones.'

'It's really unfortunate that no soft tissue has survived, otherwise it would be possible to settle the question unambiguously.'

'How do you mean?' Sam leant forward, an interested look in his eyes.

'Well, one of the most startling recent contributions to the origins of *Homo sapiens* comes from my own field, genetics. We can make a time clock based on the average number of new mutations occurring with each new generation and work backwards to see how much time was needed to obtain the genetic variation observed between different modern races today. The conclusions are astounding, to say the least. The study shows that modern man originated in Africa some hundred and fifty to two hundred thousand years ago. Even more surprising is that those who later became Asians, Europeans and Americans left Africa maybe sixty thousand years ago.'

'That's far too recent for me,' objected Sam. 'I'm interested in the much more important question of how mankind originated in the first place. Africa is called the cradle of mankind not because, as you point out so well, modern man may have originated here one hundred and fifty thousand years ago, but because some six to seven million years ago the lineage that gave rise to humans split off from the one that in due time produced the chimpanzees. Then, maybe two and a half million years ago, something extraordinary happened: modern man's ancestors of that far-away era, the hominids, began to use tools. This, really, was the true starting point of mankind.'

'But if, as you say, it's impossible to find out how this happened from the few remaining bones, why bother?'

'But I do bother and I want to find out!' retorted Sam vehemently. 'And there's a way of finding out. If only we could manage to go back in time and see what happened with our own eyes, we would know!'

'That's where my time machine comes in,' intervened Klaus with a look of pride all over his face.

'So you propose to use the time machine to go back a few million years?'

'Yes.' affirmed Sam. 'To project someone's brain contents into a *Homo habilis* of two to three million years ago in order to follow him for a while, and then to bring the brain contents back.'

'But such a thing is unheard of. It's not possible!'

'Klaus believes that he's cracked the problem.' And Sam pointed at Klaus whose eyes were gleaming through his round spectacles. 'And that's why we are here in Naboru instead of in a more convenient location in a civilized country. You'd better explain this, Klaus.'

'Well, if you start from Einstein's equations of general relativity, and apply...'

'I think I'd better explain it,' interrupted Sam. 'The problem, in a nutshell, is that Klaus' time machine can project packaged information such as the contents of a brain a couple of million years back in time, but only over a distance of a few hundred miles. That's why we had to move to Naboru which is more or less the centre of all early *Homo habilis* finds.'

'Got it,' said John. And turning to Klaus who was visibly

disappointed that he hadn't been allowed to give a more complete account of his theory, he added: 'Maybe you'll give me a few details when we do our tuning on the table.'

'I will!' exclaimed Klaus, who cheered up at the thought. 'It will be a pleasure to oblige.'

John now turned to Sam again: 'But what do we gain from being so to speak on the spot?'

'Oh, but that's obvious, isn't it? It would be like sending a TV crew. We would see what the first primitive human beings really looked like, their faces and their bodies. We would see how they lived and walked; what system of communication and primitive language they had, if any; what they ate; what type of shelter they used; whether they lived as couples or were promiscuous and polygamous. Also, and crucially, what technology they had and which tools they used. They obviously must have had wooden tools, for instance pointed sticks which they used as lances or spears. But no wooden objects have survived, so how can we be sure? We don't even have the faintest idea how many of these early hominids there were at that time: a thousand or more? Or only a few dozen?'

'Is that important?'

'Yes, very much so. To give you a modern example: the Zulus. The occurrence of individuals with heavy hips and legs is relatively frequent amongst them. The Bantu ancestors of the Zulus who emerged from the Congo forest about a thousand years ago can't have been very numerous. Maybe there were no more than a few dozen people, and if just one among these ancestors had those very typical characteristics, he or she would have passed them on to a group of descendants that now numbers many tens of thousands. That's why it's so important to go and have a look at the first hominids, to see how our present physical and social characteristics originated. Some may have been essential for our survival, but others might just as easily have been purely accidental.'

'Good heavens! I would never have thought of that.'

'But I have! There are so many intriguing questions about man's ancestors that I'd like to answer, but I'm afraid this experiment will be unable to solve them.'

'Like what for example?'

'Well, take our resistance to certain contagious viral diseases such as the common cold. When it first appeared, people must have died like flies. Maybe only a small percentage survived: those that had a natural resistance to the virus. But they passed it on to all their descendants, to us, and now we are immune.'

'You must be joking? People surely never died from an ordinary cold? And when is this event, this pandemic, supposed to have occurred?'

'No one knows. That's why it would be so interesting to use the time machine for a variety of purposes. And don't look so sceptical. To convince you that such things did take place: you have the unique privilege of living at a time when another kind of great epidemic is happening, similar in many ways to the first outbreak of the common cold.'

'I don't know what you're talking about.'

'It's happening under your very nose and you ask me what it is? AIDS, of course. If it had taken place a few thousand years ago, when there was no medical treatment around and no knowledge of what was occurring, nearly all but a very small percentage of the human population would have died, but the survivors would have inherited a natural immunity and would have peopled the world once again after that dramatic setback.'

'But how can you be certain of what you're saying?'

'Nothing is ever certain unless it has taken place. However, studies amongst the prostitutes here in East African cities reveal that about one per cent remain HIV negative, even after years of unprotected sex. I'm extrapolating from there. But we're diverging. I think that mankind has been lucky, very lucky to survive all the epidemics, disasters and dangers of the last few million years. That's another reason why it's so important to know how many hominids there were. Suppose that at one time there was only a small number, let's say no more than a few dozen hominids, and imagine that they were attacked and eaten by lions. Do you understand that we wouldn't have been here today if this had been the case? Neither you nor Klaus ... Nor me! You realize what a great catastrophe that would have been?'

'It's all right all this talking,' said Klaus who had gradually been getting more impatient, 'but I can't waste my whole afternoon listening to theories while my time machine is just standing idle.' He turned to Sam: 'Mind you, I like your ideas.

But as my father used to say: The time goes *schnell* ... you must use it well...'

He was about to leave when John stopped him. 'I think you said that you don't need me this afternoon?'

'I don't,' replied Klaus. 'I need to check all the settings of the machine and won't need you before tomorrow.' And he left for the laboratory.

Klaus' departure had broken up the conversation and both men sat there for a while in silence. Then John said as an afterthought: 'As I've got the afternoon free I might go into town. Do you think I could have the car?'

'Do you want Kibu to drive you?'

'Not really. I rather fancy going alone. It would be more of an adventure.'

'Haven't you already had enough adventures in town to last you for a lifetime?'

'Oh, but it's different now. That was when I'd just got here. I've gained experience since.'

'Please yourself,' said Sam. 'But be careful!'

A quarter of an hour later John was driving along the northern ring road, looking for the best way to get to the centre, when he suddenly noticed a sign: Bulamonga 30 miles. Before he realized what he was doing, the car had exited the ring road and was speeding north as if it had a will of its own.

This is madness, the realistic part of John's brain kept telling him. *It's a four hours' drive to Elephant Camp and back, and it's half past one already. To go all this way just to say hello and stay for half an hour or an hour at most! And Veronica probably won't be pleased to see me. She may not even be there. It's ridiculous!*

But he kept on driving all the same, pushing the car for all it was worth.

22

As John entered Elephant Camp two hours later there didn't seem to be anyone around. He parked the car, walked slowly through the courtyard and had just begun to circle the house to see if Veronica was there when he heard a shrill sound less than ten feet behind his back. His heart missed a beat, he swivelled around and to his horror he saw Dumbo rushing towards him, his head bent low. John was hit in the stomach and lifted clear off the ground, and before he had time to react he found himself sprawled on the elephant's head in a most uncomfortable position. Dumbo did not seem to mind; instead, he appeared to enjoy the situation. As John hung there helplessly, clinging on to Dumbo's wide ears, he felt the elephant's trunk nuzzling him. This was maybe his way of making contact but John didn't like it a bit.

'Hey! Hey!' he shouted as he felt the little trunk going up his legs and exploring higher regions. 'Stop it, you shameless beast, stop it!' And he started to pull Dumbo's ears furiously, hoping that this would incite him to let go.

Dumbo trumpeted loudly in protest and, alarmed by his calls Veronica, who had been working in one of the outhouses, came running into the yard. 'Hey!' she yelled, seeing a man struggle with her little elephant. 'What's going on?' And she whistled sharply. When Dumbo heard her he spun on his axis and, as he did so, John was flung into the air like a projectile. He landed in a large tuft of rough elephant grass ten feet away, shot clear through the grass, rolled a few feet further and came to rest with his head on a big lump of elephant dung.

John had not anticipated this kind of reception, and he took some time to recover while the little elephant took refuge behind Veronica who was shouting: 'Don't you frighten my Dumbo! Look! He's trembling all over.' Finally he managed to remove most of the dung from his face and sit upright.

'Oh! It's you, John!' exclaimed Veronica. 'I was wondering who the intruder was. Are you all right?'

John began to feel his stomach, legs and shoulders, rubbed them for a while, got up and answered: 'I think everything is still intact. But a bit sore.'

'That's fine then. Listen, you mustn't frighten little Dumbo. He's a very sensitive little elephant and he needs sympathy and understanding.'

John gave Dumbo a look from which sympathy and understanding were totally absent. 'May I strongly suggest,' he said coldly, 'that you keep this Dumbo locked up. If you ask for my opinion, he's a menace to any visitor here.'

'I'm not asking for your opinion!' retorted Veronica sharply. 'And as to visitors, I didn't expect you to turn up!' Suddenly she flung her hand in front of her mouth. 'Oh, but I am expecting someone important. What if he decided to come today? Maybe I'd better lock up Dumbo.' She took the elephant by his little trunk and led him away to his shed at the back of the enclosure.

John stood there gaping. He knew that in his present position it would be unreasonable to expect Veronica to think much of him. All the same, it galled him that she seemed to care so little about him while she thought another man important enough to make sure that he wouldn't be bothered by that menace of a Dumbo.

Presently Veronica reappeared, walking slowly towards him, and as John watched her come nearer, his bad mood dissipated. He was struck again by the sheer beauty of her figure and the grace of her movements. *Such a slender young woman*, he thought. *How she has the courage to run this place is beyond me.*

When Veronica arrived in front of John she suddenly giggled: 'John, you are dirty. Come, let me give you a good scrubbing. Sit down here.' She went inside the house, came back with a wet cloth and began rubbing his face without any further ado.

All John's troubles seemed to fall away as he felt Veronica's hands go over his face in a soothing movement. He closed his eyes and gave himself up to the soft touch of her fingers. He just sat there very still, with an ecstatic expression on his face. After a while the movement slowed and when he opened his eyes he surprised Veronica looking at him with great tenderness. Their eyes met for a split second before Veronica turned away rapidly, blushing slightly. She swallowed a couple of times and then asked, as if making a voluntary effort to break the spell: 'So, how are you, John? What have you been doing with yourself these days?'

Slowly, as if coming out of a trance, John spoke. 'Oh, yes...' His voice seemed to come from far away. 'What have I been doing? Yes ... well ... every morning I lie on the table of Klaus' time machine while he fiddles with a lot of knobs, trying to catch my brainwaves. But of course, you have never met Klaus?'

'Oh but I have.' Veronica blew out her cheeks, made circles with her forefingers and thumbs, put them on the tip of her nose and started limping about. They both exploded with laughter.

'You know, he can be very irritating,' commented John. 'He's the archetype of the mad scientist; but then he is sometimes extremely funny without meaning to be.'

'I don't know him that well but I can imagine that it comes naturally to him.' And she again held her fingers in front of her eyes as if they were spectacles, put her head to one side and yelled: '*Guten Tag!*' in a shrieking, parrot-like voice.

When they had stopped laughing, John carried on. 'Anyway, it's a strange experiment. It was all Sam Goldstein's idea ... I believe you know him. He's pursuing a revolutionary way of probing into the origins of mankind. He seems to think that there were very few ancestors of mankind a couple of million years back, maybe no more than twenty or so, and he wants to use the time machine to test this. I rather like the experiment, but I don't really know what they're expecting of me...'

'How can there have been so few ancestors?' interrupted Veronica. 'Of course we all have the same basic genetic material and so on, but, still, that would make us very close family, wouldn't it?'

'Well, we are more closely related than you imagine. Just to pick an easy example, you and I, for instance, are of the same family.'

'You must be joking. You are an American and I am of Swiss-English origin. I know my family genealogy down to 1800 and I can assure you that there were no Garfingers amongst them!' Veronica spoke the last sentence in a somewhat haughty way.

'Let me tell you that my mother was English! But that's not what I'm referring to. What I'm trying to say is that you're a descendant of Charlemagne, and so am I. Therefore we are of the same family.'

'You are just talking through your hat, John. How can anyone know for sure that he or she is a descendant of Charlemagne? No genealogy goes back that far.'

'I know, I know ... but statistically it's a certainty. All people of European origin are really one big family. Just think. You had two parents, four grandparents, eight great-grandparents, sixteen great-great-grandparents, and so on. Since Charlemagne, twelve centuries ago, counting roughly four generations per century, there have been about fifty generations. So, fifty generations means two to the exponent of fifty ancestors to produce you, or roughly a thousand million million ancestors. And this at a time when the total population of Europe may not have exceeded fifty million. So, each European living at the time, and producing children, must have counted twenty million times over as an ancestor of yours.'

'That sounds like a lot of inbreeding!'

'It was indeed. And in those days powerful people were liable to make a large number of women pregnant and have many children, thereby spreading their genes far and wide. So believe me when I say that we are both descendants of Charlemagne and therefore family.'

'Yes, but what about blue blood? All those nobles?'

'There's nothing blue about their blood. They have all got the same blood as you and me: it's bright red. I can vouch here that we are both related to all those very distinguished noble people. For instance, you and the Queen of England are related. That's for certain.'

'You think so? I'm not so sure that she would be very amused to find me knocking at the door of Buckingham Palace one day, saying: "Hello Auntie, here I am." '

'I guess not.' John chuckled at the idea. 'But who were the ancestors of all those very noble families, let's say a thousand or more years ago? They were crude barbarians just like your forebears or mine. We all have the same ancestors anyway. And the further we go back in time, the fewer our ancestors. If we go back two or three million years, how many hominids were there then on Earth? Maybe no more than a few dozen.'

They sat for a while in silence, John pondering about hominids while Veronica saw in her imagination the surprised face of the Queen of England as she greeted her at Buckingham Palace. Suddenly their attention was diverted by Dumbo who, to their surprise, reappeared emitting shrill shrieks of pure delight. He had noticed the arrival of an important-looking man and now raced across the compound to welcome him, his trunk stuck up like an antenna. The man didn't wait for Dumbo. He turned tail and ran.

'But I locked him up!' exclaimed Veronica. 'I'd better go and see what's happening!' And she rushed off at top speed.

When she returned about ten minutes later, she looked depressed.

'What happened?' asked John. 'Who was it?'

'It was Sir Arthur Llewellyn, President of the World Elephant Fund,' replied Veronica in a hoarse voice.

'Did Dumbo catch him?'

'No. He escaped with only inches to spare. I saw him bolt up a tree surprisingly quickly for someone who must be in his late fifties. By the time I arrived, Dumbo had started shaking the tree to dislodge him but Sir Arthur clung on tightly. The situation was rather embarrassing and, although Dumbo was having great fun, I told him to leave the poor man alone...'

'What did he come here for?'

'I had invited him over. It took many letters to convince him, but he finally came. I had drawn up a list of all the problems the project is facing and I'd hoped to persuade him to help me out.'

'And did you manage to talk to him?'

'My important visitor did not speak a word while I sent Dumbo away. His eyes just went from me to Dumbo's retreating shape in a shifty sort of way. So, to break the ice, I congratulated him on his agility, but that did not seem to brighten him up. He just snorted and remained up there on a high branch.'

'But didn't he say anything?' Suddenly John looked up. 'He's not up there still, is he?'

'No.' Veronica sighed deeply. 'He's gone. When he finally descended from his tree all he said was that he wasn't very impressed with the project, and in particular with the reception committee. I noticed that his trouser seat was ripped and that his pink-striped underpants showed through. I imagine that he did not quite feel his dignified self under the circumstances. He added that he was not going to risk spoiling any more of his wardrobe, went to his car and told his driver to take him back to Naboru.'

'Maybe he'll reconsider when he has calmed down? He's sure to come back,' ventured John, trying to cheer her up.

Veronica stared at him in disbelief. 'Of all the bad luck!' she suddenly burst out. 'To have my attention distracted when he finally came here!' She seemed thoroughly upset and ran off into the house.

Now that he was alone John noticed that the sun was already low on the horizon. He looked at his watch: 'Half past five!' he exclaimed. Night would fall in half an hour and the drive back took two hours in broad daylight. Just then Veronica came out of the house again, a sombre expression on her face. *I don't know whether I dare*, thought John, but looking again at the fading light, he made up his mind.

'Veronica,' he said hesitantly, 'it's getting very late. I don't know whether I can face driving all the way back at this time and I thought that ... Well, if you don't mind I would like to ask you if it's possible to go back tomorrow morning rather than now?'

When Veronica understood that he proposed to spend the night she exploded. 'What! First you arrive here late in the afternoon and hang around babbling about all sorts of philosophical questions as if I had nothing else to do. Wonderful for me, isn't it, to have people like you turning up here? You just sit there talking as if that was all I needed. Sorry, but I have more important things to do. I have to think of the survival of my elephants. And when finally someone comes to help me, you ruin it all! Don't look at me like that! It's all your fault!'

'But ... but...'

'Yes, it is! Your being on the premises and distracting me has ruined what was maybe my only chance to enlist help for my project. And after that you have the cheek to tell me that it's too late to drive back to town, and expect me to put you up for the night! In case you hadn't noticed, this is not a hotel with plenty of rooms and staff to serve unexpected visitors. I have no staff to serve visitors, no spare rooms and no budget. This is Elephant Camp! Not Elephant Wildlife Lodge!'

Her words hit John like a whip, and as he got up he stammered: 'But ... but ... I thought you enjoyed my visit and the conversation. I do apologize for having stayed so long. I didn't realize ... You should have told me ... And I'm especially sorry about your project not going well ... I wish I were able to do more for you, but I seem to cause you nothing but trouble...'

He gazed hesitantly at the setting sun and the shadows of the acacia trees which were lengthening with each passing minute. This was the time lions started to hunt and hyenas crawled out from wherever they spent the day. He did not fancy driving back at night over a bumpy track that was easy to lose even in the daylight, but there didn't seem to be much choice. 'Well, I'll be off then...' he stammered, and turned, ready to go.

As Veronica looked at his despondent figure she began to regret her outburst and felt a pang of remorse mixed with shame at her failure to honour the bush code. You did not send visitors away into the African night. It simply wasn't done. What if the poor fellow had an accident in the dark or got lost in the bush. It might easily happen and she would be to blame.

'I'm sorry,' she said. 'Stay if you like.'

John turned around and brightened up visibly. 'Can I really stay? Oh thank you so much, thank you!'

'There's nothing to thank me for,' replied Veronica. 'This is just normal bush hospitality. But I am in a bit of a fix. You see, the servant has gone back to his village and I'm alone tonight. I'd better go and see if I can knock up something to eat.'

'Let me help you,' offered John, all pleased now.

As he moved towards Veronica in the growing darkness, eager to assist her, he tripped over a low bench and shot forward, his arms milling to regain his balance. He yelled as he toppled over and, groping for something to hold on to, his hands caught Veronica's skirt and pulled it down. He fell to his knees, his arms tightened around Veronica's thighs and, pinning her against the wall, his face came to rest on the v-shape of her panties.

For a few seconds that seemed an eternity to Veronica neither of them moved. It was as if John had been glued to her body. She felt dazed, unable to do anything. Then, almost mechanically, she pushed John's head away, removed his hands from her legs and pulled up her skirt. In her agitation she didn't notice that the zip and buttons had broken and, as she turned to go into the kitchen, the skirt slid down again, this time revealing the backside of her white underwear. A rude word escaped from her lips as she pulled up her skirt and, holding on to it, disappeared inside.

She found matches and a petrol lamp, which she lit with shaking hands. She didn't know what to think of this unexpected attack. Had the fellow gone mad? Was he a satyr, unable to control himself when alone with a woman? And this was only the beginning of the evening. She should have sent him away. Definitely! She looked at her skirt: buttons ripped off, the zip ruined, damn, damn! That idiot of a John! She hunted around for something to fix it quickly and finally found a safety pin to fasten the skirt.

By the time she reappeared on the veranda with the lamp John seemed to have recovered his senses. 'Sorry, sorry, so sorry,' she heard him stutter. 'I think I fell over something. Sorry. It's a bit dark here. No offence meant. Sorry.'

As she stepped onto a stool to hang the burning petrol lamp on a hook overhead, John came forward again, arms outstretched, saying: 'Can I help ... do something?'

Veronica stiffened. 'Stay there!' she hissed, wagging a finger at him. 'Just sit down there and keep quiet. Don't you dare move!' she added as she went inside again.

John sat down on a bench and closed his eyes. As he did so the image of him on his knees came back in waves of intense emotion. He again felt the silkiness of her panties on his face, the springy softness of her lower belly and the warmth of her thighs. And in his nose lingered the faint scent of all that was feminine. He was aware of strong currents going through his body, his muscles seemed to go into a kind of spasm, his pores opened, his hairs stood on end and his senses became alive as never before. The unexpected intimacy, the closeness of the most hidden secrets of the female being, had catapulted his senses into another dimension. Veronica's body ... all the warmth he wanted to embrace and into which he wanted to surrender. He felt like one who had perceived a glimpse of Nirvana, and knew that from now on his life would become a quest to be united to Veronica.

Veronica, who had begun to rummage inside, suddenly appeared in the doorway to check on his movements. He seemed to be sitting quietly on a bench with an idiotic smile on his face, staring in front of him with bulging eyes. The fellow was definitely not normal. Just to show that she was prepared to defend herself she wagged a big ladle at him, repeating: 'Don't you dare move!'

John hardly noticed her defensive attitude. His thoughts were in another world, a world with a Veronica who was sweet to him, lying in his arms, loved by him and loving him in return. *What a privilege*, he thought, *to spend the night here with Veronica, alone in the African bush, far away from everyone.*

After a while Veronica reappeared with some heated maize cakes and sardines from a tin and slammed them on the wooden table. 'You sit there,' she said, motioning towards a bench on the opposite side of the table. Her attitude was still defensive, but she had somewhat calmed down. 'That's all I've got,' she mumbled sort of apologetically. 'We'll have to make do with it. And there's also some filtered water to drink. Better than nothing, isn't it?'

'Wonderful!' exclaimed John as he downed a sip of tepid water. 'You have produced a most delightful supper. Thank you so much for your kindness.'

Veronica looked at him, wondering. What was this now? Overflowing with politeness? She didn't trust it. Was there some hidden plan behind it?

Conversation was difficult. The few times Veronica looked up and caught John's eyes, she found him gazing at her with an absolutely daft expression on his face. His eyes had a strange look in them, as if he were seeing an apparition. It made her feel uneasy and they ate their stodgy maize cakes and sardines in almost complete silence. Only the chewing on the overcooked and slightly burned maize was audible above the chirping of nocturnal insects.

Supper over, Veronica coughed embarrassedly. 'I've only got one bedroom,' she remarked in a strained voice.

'That's all right!'

'With only one bed.'

'Oh, I don't mind'

'But I *do* mind!' she exclaimed suddenly. 'I mind most definitely! If you don't want to drive back tonight, you'll have to sleep outside.'

Her words brought John down to earth with a bang. 'Do you mean that I have to sleep outside, alone in the dark night?'

'Well, what's wrong with that? Animals sleep outside all the time. Elephants sleep outside.'

'But I'm not an elephant!'

'I wish you were. I might like you better,' she sneered in a decided attempt to hurt him. 'But you won't have to sleep alone. You can sleep with Dumbo in his little shed over there.' Veronica pointed her thumb towards the somewhat ramshackle shed further down in the yard.

John recoiled at the idea. 'You can't be serious. You don't really want me to sleep with Dumbo, do you? I couldn't possibly do that.'

'What's wrong with sleeping with Dumbo?' snapped Veronica who was beginning to get really worked up. 'He's a truly decent little fellow. He might even take a liking to you if only you gave him half a chance. But you don't like elephants! That's your problem!'

'I don't want to sleep outside,' pleaded John. 'Please let me sleep inside, please...' And seeing the suspicious look in her eyes he continued: 'I promise that I'll behave. There is nothing to be afraid of.'

Veronica was not to be moved. 'I don't want you in the house! Staying here was your idea, not mine! If you want to spend the night here, you'll have to go outside!' she shouted while quickly running upstairs and disappearing into her room before John could do so much as open his mouth. He heard the door slam, the key turn in the lock and a bolt fasten from the inside.

Shame, he thought, *what a shame. When everything could have been so wonderful.*

23

John stood there for a while in silence, hoping for the impossible, but when after a few minutes nothing moved, he dragged himself away from the house and crossed the dark yard. He inspected the shed by the light of a small torch, found some relatively fresh and not too smelly hay, used it to make a bed and installed himself as cosily as possible.

This wasn't quite what he had imagined. It would have been so different had Veronica wanted to share her room with him. As there was only one big bed – he saw it in his mind's eye with a mosquito net overhanging it – she would have offered to share the bed with him. Everything would have been above board, there would have been no strain and he would have respected her, of course. How could he not respect her when he loved her? They would have been lying there, both naked under a thin sheet, but well apart.

Lying there in the dark of the African night they would have heard the chirping sound of insects outside, maybe even the distant roar of a lion. Was there anything more romantic, anything that stirred the heart more than the sound of a lion roaring in the night? Her heart would have softened, and the waves of love which had been emanating from his soul, from his whole being during all that time, would gradually have enveloped her. After a while she would have been unable to resist, she would have stretched out her arm and softly touched him. And before they would have realized it they would have been in each other's arms, and he would have sunk into her like a body into a warm sea.

As he was dreaming away he had forgotten where he was, but suddenly he was fully aware that an essential element of his dream was missing in his present condition: the mosquito net. The voracious little devils were now coming upon him by the hundreds, buzzing around his ears and trying to eat him alive. Then he heard something else: the distant roar of a lion.

It did not inspire romantic feelings as he had imagined. Instead, he was suddenly paralysed with fear. Any predator could steal in at any moment to kill him and eat him! And where was that horror of a Dumbo? If he were here he might at least sound the alarm.

John sank as deeply as possible into the hay, attempting to forget about mosquitoes, lions and other unpleasant inhabitants of the African night, and tried to return to the pleasant scenes of his imagination. Just as he settled down again to dream about what might have been, and got to the part where Veronica's hand made contact with him, expressing all the yearning of a lonely heart in one soft touch, he felt something damp touching his face. It frightened him out of his wits, and as he jumped up he banged his head against something hard. He grabbed wildly for his torch, found it and switched it on. There was Dumbo, standing over him. He had begun to grow tusks and that was what John had hit.

What a dreadful little terror this Dumbo was! John hadn't even heard him come in. If a bulky thing like Dumbo could enter the shed unnoticed, what about sneaky vicious creatures such as leopards that are prowling about in the night, out to make a meal of unsuspecting innocent fellows like himself? John shuddered.

Dumbo continued for a while to feel around with his little trunk, sniffing and breathing heavily. Then, suddenly, he gave John a shove that catapulted him out of the hay and threw him against the wooden wall of the shed.

'Hey, hey, what's that!' shouted John trying to get back into the hay, but Dumbo had already sunk on his knees with a surprisingly quick movement and occupied the place where John had lain.

'Hey, that's not fair!' he yelled, but the elephant didn't move. In his overworked state of mind John began to talk to Dumbo as if he were a young, somewhat dumb child. 'I know this is your bedroom,' he said apologetically, 'but it's not my fault that I'm here. I would by far have preferred to sleep in your mistress's bedroom but she didn't let me, see. She told me to go out and sleep here with you. So do show some hospitality. There is such a thing as sharing and it would help a lot if you had some consideration for others.'

His well-meant speech didn't have any effect on Dumbo. John now tried to push the animal away but found that he was unable to shift the little elephant a single inch. As he pressed against its bulky body, it pressed back and John finally found himself wedged between the elephant and the wall.

'Stop it!' John shouted. 'Stop it!' He banged his fists on the little elephant's rump, but the animal didn't seem to feel anything and just sighed contentedly.

When John had crawled out from between Dumbo and the wall he began to survey the shed by the light of his torch. Dumbo was still a youngster, not a fully-grown elephant of five or six tons; he weighed maybe no more than six or seven hundred kilos, but he took up a lot of space for an adolescent. He was sprawled out all over the place and there appeared to be standing room only in the shed.

There is no need to take up all this space, thought John, *getting more upset every minute. If I am to spend the night in this shed, this little fellow jolly well ought to leave me sufficient room, bulky though he is. That's the least one would expect. But no! He pretends not to notice!*

John finally managed to half sit, half lie down in a corner, pulled his shirt over his head to protect himself from the mosquitoes and tried to doze off, thinking: *I hope he doesn't roll over while I'm asleep, or I'll end up as flat as a pancake.*

John had just dozed off when the elephant moved and, with a start, woke him up. This appeared to be his set plan of campaign for the rest of the night. Dumbo kept shifting every quarter of an hour or so, or else his little trunk moved around, nuzzling John and sniffing him.

It must have been the middle of the night when without warning Dumbo got up on his legs and then sank down again just as suddenly. John barely had time to crawl out of the way before being squashed. After that he no longer dared close his eyes. *Do elephants never sleep properly*, he thought as he waited for this dreadful, interminable night to end.

At last the deep darkness of the night turned a lighter shade of black. Day was about to break and the ordeal would soon be over. John moved around Dumbo who was breathing deeply and evenly by now. He was about to leave the shed when revenge flashed red in his mind. He gave the animal a good kick, saying:

94

'My turn to wake you up,' but the little elephant didn't even move and just kept on sleeping. *He's too tired after a night of pranks, the horrid creature*, concluded John bitterly.

He emerged from the shed feeling grubby, smelly and utterly exhausted. *I can't face Veronica like this*, he thought, picking some straws of hay out of his collar. *I'd better drive back to town.*

As he walked out in the first faint light to where the car was parked he looked up: stars were still shining brightly overhead but towards the east, low on the horizon, a pale glow had begun to appear. Fresh air penetrated his lungs and suddenly an exhilarating feeling took hold of him. The forces of darkness dissipated as coloured flames streaked through the eastern sky. It was a most glorious morning, perfect as daybreaks in Africa can be. Everything felt fresh, newborn. There was a strong scent of flowers and a chorus of birds in the scattered thorn trees; a milky mist was still floating just above the surface of the savannah while the sun rose behind it like an immense red ball. Soon its heat would dissolve the curtain of mist and its light would paint the plains in brilliant colours.

John started the car and turned up the track towards the rising sun, into the open savannah and towards the infinity of space. He felt liberated. A new life was surging up in him, and as he set off he spontaneously burst into song.

24

'You wouldn't have a cup of coffee for me?' asked John a couple of hours later as he strolled into the dining room where Sam and Klaus were about to finish their breakfast. 'And a bite of something? I'm literally starving.'

The two occupants, who were both munching their last pieces of toast thickly smeared with homemade jam, looked up at John in surprise, shocked at seeing his dishevelled figure.

'You didn't come back last night,' said Sam with disapproval in his voice. 'Where have you been?' Then, as a strong smell hit his nostrils, he added: 'And you seem rather smelly. Don't come too near.'

'It's not my fault that I smell so bad,' replied John defensively. 'I left Elephant Camp early this morning and had no time to wash.'

'I would never have thought that anyone could stink so much after one night,' commented Klaus, pinching his nose, 'simply because he hasn't washed. Just think: if all the people on long-haul flights were like him, the air would become impossible to breathe after a night on the plane.'

'You are worse than usual when you try to be witty!' retorted John, giving Klaus a venomous look.

'So you've been to see Veronica,' concluded Sam, looking very displeased. Then, feeling instinctively that it was better to avert a quarrel, he changed his tone. 'And ... did you get on OK with her?'

'Oh yes...' John was pouring himself some coffee and didn't seem to have noticed Sam's disapproval. 'Yes, yes, we spent a pleasant hour talking about hominids and such matters...'

'Extraordinary! I didn't know she was interested in hominids. I always thought that she was strictly limited to elephants.'

'You'd be surprised how broad-minded she is. Anyway, then this important man interrupted our conversation...'

'You mean that an important man turned up?'

'Yeah, and he ripped his pants.'

'He ripped his pants?'

'Yeah, up a tree.'

'Really?' Sam looked sideways at Klaus with a big question mark in his eyes.

'And what with one thing and the other, it was getting late and I asked her if I could stay for the night.'

'You mean, together with the important man with his ripped pants?'

'No, he just ripped them and then left. You see, he went up a thorn tree and Veronica tried to make him come down. It was strange! One would have thought that he would have liked the little elephant because he was an important elephant man himself, but no ... Anyway, after all that, Veronica proposed to make supper and then something unfortunate happened...'

'Yes...?' Sam and Klaus were completely at sea by now.

'As it was getting dark I suddenly fell upon her and, before I realized, I had pulled off her skirt...'

'You don't say!' Sam stared at John, his mouth wide open.

'Well, I couldn't help it, could I? It all happened so quickly. Before I had time to control myself, her skirt had come down and I found my face buried in ... well...' John blushed visibly, '...in some more intimate ... Well, it was all quite innocent, you see, but Veronica seemed to have misinterpreted my intentions.'

'And what happened then?' asked Sam, spellbound.

'I was forced to sleep with the little elephant,' said John with a long face.

'Well, well!' exclaimed Sam, a little breathless. 'They say that there's a key to every woman's heart, but who would ever have thought that this was the right way with Veronica, eh? It just shows that it takes all sorts!' He shook his head in disbelief. 'So you just jump on her, pull off her skirt, bury your face in her ... well ... more intimate parts and hey presto! It's as if you pressed a button and she's turned on. Incredible! But why such a long face then? And why call her an elephant? Was she a bit rough with you after that? Out of control?'

Klaus too wanted to contribute to the general fun. 'Maybe he simply means to say that she disguises herself as an elephant at night,' he suggested. 'Just imagine that! It demonstrates that anything is possible when someone is so besotted with those animals as that girl Veronica. Still, I don't see how she's able to do a good impersonation of an elephant.' His eyes bulged and he held up a finger. 'She lacks the bulk for that, wouldn't you say?' And he laughed so much at his own wittiness that his round spectacles slipped off.

By that time John's face was looking like thunder. 'How disgusting you lot can get when you put your minds to it!' he growled.

It didn't stop Sam who went on: 'So, tell us about your wild night with the little elephant,' winking at Klaus in a very obvious way.

'Mind your own business!' snapped John.

The African manservant had just come in and John ordered breakfast and more coffee. 'And make it strong,' he added. He retired into the bathroom and for a while the two other men heard sounds of splashing. He reappeared just as the manservant came back with a tray laden with goodies, and he straightaway began to wolf down his breakfast without uttering a word.

After a while he sighed, feeling visibly better, and leant back in his chair. Sam had waited for this moment. 'Come on,' he said soothingly. 'We're pals, aren't we?'

John didn't answer but kept staring straight in front while sipping his coffee.

'You must be able to take a joke.'

Suddenly John blurted out: 'That *wasn't* a joke!' And he added: 'And I don't appreciate you talking about Veronica in such a disrespectful way!'

'Oh!' exclaimed Klaus. 'So that's how things stand. One is in love, *ja*? One is smitten?' He looked up at the ceiling and started whistling.

John didn't answer. He got himself another piece of toast and munched on it for a while. Finally he said: 'You don't seem to understand what an extraordinary girl she is.'

Sam looked at him, feigning surprise. 'What makes you say that?'

John stuck out his chin. 'Let me just give you one example: do you realize that she spends the nights alone in the bush, miles away from anywhere, from any help?'

'What! I wouldn't dream of doing that. What a brave girl!'

John brightened up at this remark, which seemed very much to his liking. 'Yes, she is brave. Apparently it runs in the family.

Veronica told me that her grandmother stayed for months on end in the same area, alone in a tent in the middle of nowhere. That was in the late 1920s or somewhere around that time when there were hardly any women travellers about in East Africa, let alone ones who enjoyed living with the wild animals in the bush. The grandmother seems to have been particularly interested in elephants.'

'I see,' nodded Sam. 'That explains why Veronica is so keen on elephants. It's all in the genes.'

'Yes, but she's not only interested in elephants. She was fascinated by the hominids and by your idea of using a time machine and before I realized, night was falling and I thought it better not to drive back in the dark. I might easily have had an accident, and I didn't want to risk damaging your servant's car, you understand...'

'Very considerate to prefer to stay over there, rather than risk the car!' replied Sam. 'That *was* thoughtful.' In his eagerness not to upset John again he was laying it on a bit thick, but John didn't seem to notice and just continued.

'...And naturally, Veronica proposed to cook a meal, sweet girl that she is. And then that unfortunate accident happened.'

Sam was about to say: 'Yeah ... after you found out that she was alone you were unable to control yourself. The beast in you popped up and you jumped on her.' But he abstained in the last split second.

'Obviously,' continued John, unaware of Sam's near slip of the tongue, 'after this her confidence in me was somewhat shaken, and conversation did not proceed well during supper.'

'Obviously,' agreed Sam, just about able to speak without bursting out into uncontrollable laughter.

'And then she told me to spend the night in the shed where that little pet elephant of hers sleeps. One can well understand the misgivings of the poor girl after I upset her modesty so badly. But there you are. These unfortunate things do happen.'

'And did you enjoy your night in the shed?'

'Not in the least, particularly after that menace – she calls him Dumbo – turned up. Would you believe it? He didn't show the slightest consideration for a guest in his shed; shoved me out of the hay; took up all the space for himself; and worse, kept moving the whole night.'

'Did you tell Veronica about it in the morning?' asked Sam.

'No. I didn't wait for her. I got up at the crack of dawn and drove back. I just couldn't face her.'

'Lucky for you,' said Sam. 'I don't think she would have been impressed. When you came in a while ago you looked like something the leopard had just found in a ditch and didn't want to touch, thinking it unfit for consumption.'

'And you smelled like it too,' added Klaus.

'That's not nice of you,' muttered John. 'I think you're both perfectly repulsive.' And he left the room, slamming the door.

After he had gone the two other men remained seated, staring fixedly in front of themselves. At last Klaus broke the silence. 'Did you hear that? He's in love.' He sounded worried. 'That's really bad news. He'll never consent to be the pig now.'

Sam didn't reply but kept on pondering for a while. 'A most annoying occurrence,' he finally admitted, pursing his lips. Then he spoke, more to himself than to Klaus: 'His imagination has been stirred and that's always dangerous. We mustn't let this get out of hand. But let's not become too alarmed for the moment and just wait and see. We've still got some time before day zero, haven't we, and this infatuation may well have petered out by then, especially if there's no encouragement from the girl's side. I don't think there is any great danger that he'll get his way with her after what's happened. She seems a tough cookie.'

'Lucky for us,' agreed Klaus as he left for his laboratory.

25

Veronica had been tossing and turning in her bed through most of the night. Scattered images kept popping up in her mind between short periods of disturbed slumber: Sir Llewellyn up a tree with Dumbo trying to shake him out of it. Sir Llewellyn climbing down the tree with his striped underpants showing through the hole in his trousers, and making an ungraceful exit. When she had finally managed to suppress these images, worries took over. How was she to carry on without the support of the World Elephant Fund? What had happened was dreadful. Truly dreadful! After all her efforts to make someone from the Fund come to visit her. And it was all John's fault! That bungler of course had to turn up on the one day Sir Llewellyn came. Just her luck! She boiled internally. She had told John in no uncertain words what she thought of him, but he deserved worse: she should have kicked him!

After imagining herself hitting him a few times she quietened down somewhat. Thinking more calmly about yesterday's happenings, she had to admit that she had not expected Sir Llewellyn that day. In fact, she had forgotten about his possible visit until John's encounter with Dumbo had reminded her of it. Also, when she had put Dumbo in his shed, she obviously must have failed to lock it properly. Maybe it hadn't all been John's fault then?

Still, strange things did happen when he was around. She had tried to be nice to him in spite of all the upsets and had offered him hospitality for the night. And what had been his way of thanking her? He had just jumped on her, pulled down her skirt, and held her against the wall while pressing his face upon her lower belly. It had been so unexpected that she had remained in a state of shock for the rest of the evening! No wonder she hadn't wanted him in the house for the night.

It was nearly dawn before she fell into a deep sleep, and it was already eight o'clock when the voice of her manservant,

101

calling from outside the house, woke her up with a start. For a few moments she was unable to piece her thoughts together. Then everything came back to her. She flung a gown around herself and ran downstairs where she found Steve Mutele and his wife Faithful waiting for her, looking surprised that she had remained in bed so long. She rushed to Dumbo's shed to see what had happened to John, but there was no trace of him. The little elephant was alone and profoundly asleep. *You, at least, have slept peacefully through the night,* she thought.

She went back to the house in a pensive mood, and as she stepped onto the veranda, she suddenly noticed a small overturned bench near the wall where John had attacked her. In a flash she understood that he had spoken the truth: he really had stumbled and fallen upon her accidentally. *Gosh,* she thought, *and I accused him of base intentions. He must have been very upset and left the same evening. I do hope that nothing has happened to him. I would never forgive myself.*

She entered the house, washed and, as she dressed, looked in the mirror. Several times these last days she had found herself standing in front of the mirror, thinking that she would soon be thirty and wondering how long she could remain attractive. And now she realized that she had been thinking of John while doing so. She had been looking at herself as though John had been looking at her, and wondering how he saw her, whether he thought her seductive.

He seemed so vulnerable at times. It awakened in her an impulse to protect, to be kind and loving. Yesterday, when she had cleaned his face, she had known for certain that he liked her too. His face was like an open book. He had looked so trusting, so innocent that she had had to control herself not to kiss him, and had nearly given herself away.

But then, at times, he was so strange that she could make neither head nor tail of what he said or did. Still, you couldn't say that he was one of those stuffed shirts. He was real and funny, and he stimulated her. She wanted to shake him, tease him, play with his feelings, excite him!

Then she thought again of his face pressed so suddenly against her lower belly. She felt perturbed but also thrilled. A deep warmth went through her as she wondered how he had reacted to the intimate contact. He had looked like someone quite lost

102

after that. She was certain that it had stirred up a whirlpool of emotions in him, and was strangely pleased that it had happened.

She was attracted to him, she had to admit it. Then she sighed and turned away from the mirror. 'I know, I know!' she spoke to herself. 'Don't even think about it!' She looked outside at the savannah. It reminded her of the almost impossible task she was facing. She couldn't afford to have her attention distracted by daydreaming about John; she had to concentrate on her work, on the elephants. No, this was not the time to fall in love again. She had loved someone before, someone rather like John; it had been disastrous. She had discovered that he had lied to her and was married, and she had suffered so much that she had left Europe and buried herself here with the elephants to be far away from it all.

No, no, you stupid girl! she thought. *Don't let your heart run away with you again. Be careful this time.*

26

'Would you mind very much if I took the old car to go and see Veronica this morning?' John asked after breakfast a few days later.

'Don't you need him, Klaus?' inquired Sam.

'Not really,' replied the scientist. 'I have to go through all the tests we've made so far, see what's missing and make new circuits. No, I'll be busy the whole day. John can do what he likes as far as I'm concerned. In fact, I told him so yesterday.'

'Hmm ... I see. But maybe Kibu will want the car.'

'Well no, I've asked him already,' replied John. He looked Sam straight in the eyes. 'If you don't want me to go and see Veronica, Sam, just tell me.'

'Oh no. That's not it at all. No, no,' denied Sam, turning his eyes away. 'If you've got a day off and the car is free, go by all means.' And shaking his head he repeated: 'By all means.'

'Thank you. I thought it would be courteous to go and apologize to Veronica for last time. Have a nice day all of you.' And he turned and left the breakfast room in a cheerful state of mind.

Sam remained behind in a sombre, pensive mood. 'Hell!' he exclaimed. 'I thought that his "sleeping with the little elephant" had ended the story, but the guy is smitten by her and there's no knowing what's going to happen next. This is bad for the project. A man in love wants to live as long as there's hope. He doesn't want to risk his life being the guinea pig whom you try to zoom back to the past. I hadn't realized he had caught it so badly. This is likely to throw a big spanner in the works. I honestly hadn't expected this to happen.' He turned to Klaus: 'What can we do? Why didn't you keep him here today?'

'That's your job, not mine,' countered Klaus grumpily. 'I told you that I've got enough work to do today without him. Do I have to repeat this?' Then he stared defiantly at Sam. 'If you didn't want him to go, why didn't you stop him?'

'I thought it better not to object openly. He's getting suspicious. We've got to act in subtler ways.' Then he added, his face contorted: 'I hope he doesn't make it up with that stupid girl. I mustn't let that happen.' He banged his fist on the table. 'That would be the end of my project!'

27

'Good news!' shouted Ron as he jumped out of his safari bus. 'I've seen Jacques Le Tellier. He's interested!'

'But that's wonderful!' exclaimed Veronica. 'How did you manage that?'

'Oh, you know...' Ron put his hand on his shirt, puffed up his chest and patted it.

Suddenly Veronica became flustered. 'But I haven't prepared anything for him yet!'

'What do you mean by: prepared anything?'

'Well ... accounts, costs, financial calculations...'

'Oh that! Pfft...' Ron made a gesture of derision. 'He doesn't want to see that! He's a capable businessman. Always does his own sums. No. What he wants is something else. As he's going to put up the money he wants to be in charge. Not officially, of course. That would entail changing international agreements. But in practice.'

'What? Are you implying that he's going to be the boss and make the decisions? That he would be the one deciding what's going to happen to my elephants?'

'I wouldn't put it in such strong terms. But he'll want the reserve to turn out a profit. If he puts up all the money he wants to be sure that it's well invested. That's only natural.'

'I'm not convinced,' said Veronica in a defensive tone. 'This is not what I imagined. Tell him that I'll have to think about it.'

'But, Vee!' Ron spoke as if to a stubborn child. 'You're not living in the real world! You have to face your problems, find solutions and then make up your mind. You can't just play about and keep putting things off.'

Suddenly Veronica's face contracted and she hissed: 'The real world, eh! I don't think I want to live in the real world!' She stuck up her chin. 'And I don't think I want to leave the fate of my elephants in someone else's hands.'

'But I need an answer! I can't keep Le Tellier waiting forever. I told you that he's very important and that he expects a reply right away. He's not used to being kept waiting like ordinary people. Listen, this is a unique opportunity. He's ready to help you if you make a satisfactory arrangement. And you need help! You need financial backing! Just trust him. You can't go on alone like this anyway.'

Veronica strode agitatedly back and forth. She wasn't going to trust blindly someone she didn't know. And she didn't want to make up her mind there and then. 'I just can't think for the moment,' she said evasively. 'Don't keep pressing me. It confuses me so!' She wished that Ron would go away and leave her alone. He, who was always in such a hurry, just kept hanging around today, pestering her. How could she get rid of him?

Just then an old green car turned into the yard, stopped, and the door opened. John's head appeared slowly, his face uncertain of the reception he was going to get. Then, hesitantly, the rest of his body followed. During his two hours' journey he had been thinking of everything he was going to say to Veronica to excuse himself for the clumsy behaviour of his last visit. He had made up a little speech and felt that he might be able to pull it off; that with luck he would manage to put her at ease this time. Then he noticed the big safari bus and when he realized that this hateful fellow with the flashy teeth was there, and that he would be listening to everything he was going to say with a sneer on his face, his mind went blank.

He couldn't remember a single line of the speech he'd prepared, and was ready to disappear into his car again when Veronica came running towards him, calling out: 'John! John!' She flung her arms around his neck, gave him a big kiss on the cheek, and said: 'How nice that you're here. Come along!' And she took him by the hand and led him to the veranda where Ron stood waiting with a long face, unable to hide his displeasure.

'Sit down,' motioned Veronica to John. 'And let me offer you something to drink.'

Ron made one last attempt: 'Think about it, Vee!' he insisted, but she had already disappeared into the kitchen. 'I'd better be going,' said Ron glumly as if speaking to the wall. 'Got lots of things to do.' Then he swung round, stormed off towards his safari bus, crawled behind the wheel, slammed the door hard and was soon gone in a cloud of dust.

John couldn't believe his luck. He had thought of maybe a dozen different receptions. He had been prepared for the worst, but he had not been prepared for this: Veronica positively overflowing with welcome! And that pompous fellow exiting with his tail between his legs! The heavy black cloud of worry that had weighed him down for several days seemed to have lifted and he suddenly felt euphoric. He was unable to hide his joy and when Veronica reappeared with two glasses of water shortly afterwards, she found him sitting there as if in a trance with a big silly grin on his face.

'Ahem,' she said hesitantly, afraid that a too sudden shock might unbalance him. 'Is water all right? It's cold this time. The fridge is working you see.'

'Eh? Oh? Yes, of course. Thank you so much. Yes. Water. Cold water! I like cold water.'

The unforeseen reception had made his spirits soar, and even the sight of Dumbo who now appeared around the corner failed to upset him; he was in the kind of mood where he was ready to accept anything.

Dumbo was balancing a little stick on the tip of his trunk. Suddenly he threw it up in the air and caught it again, balancing it upright.

'Look at that!' exclaimed John. 'How clever he is!'

'Isn't he?' consented Veronica, delighted at the praise heaped upon her little elephant. 'He's a real juggler. You've never seen anything like it.'

'What's he doing now?' asked John, pointing at Dumbo who had sucked up some dust and blew it over his back in a big cloud.

'Oh! That's how elephants protect their skin from the sun. It's their sun cream if you like.'

'I didn't know that elephants could be so interesting and amusing.'

'You'd be surprised. You know what? The Land Rover has been repaired and the driver is going to take me into the reserve to observe the elephants. Why don't you accompany us?'

'I'd love to!'

The conversation had distracted John's attention from Dumbo, who meanwhile had gone to a big open barrel and sucked up a huge quantity of water. Suddenly John heard a sound behind his back and as he turned around he saw Dumbo not a yard away with his trunk pointed towards him, and received a blast of cold water straight in his face!

He began to swear aloud, shaking off the water like a wet duck and brandishing a fist at Dumbo.

'John! Behave yourself!' yelled Veronica. 'Don't you dare threaten little Dumbo!'

'But look what that monster has done to me!'

'I thought you liked cold water,' said Veronica, biting her lip not to laugh. Then she turned and went upstairs to change.

John stood there for a while, dripping and staring at Dumbo with loathing in his eyes. The little elephant didn't seem to show the slightest remorse. Instead, John was certain that he saw a grin on his face.

You horror, thought John, *I wish I could scare the wits out of you as you do to me! But you're a thick-skinned little fellow, aren't you? Nothing appears to frighten you.* Then he suddenly remembered the episode of the little yapping dog during his first visit. *Ah! I've got it,* he thought. *You wait for this surprise!*

After having dressed for the drive through the reserve Veronica was just about to leave her room, when she heard loud barking below. She rushed to the edge of the landing ready to chase the dog away when she saw John standing underneath her, going 'Waf! Wafwaf! Woof!' with a diabolical expression on his face.

Gosh, she thought, *he has gone bonkers! Maybe he's been bitten by a mad dog and is now suffering an attack of rabies?*

'Are you all right?' she called from above, thinking that she might as well remain at a safe distance if he had become crazy.

'Oh! Eh!' stammered John, looking up.

'Why are you barking like a mad dog?'

'Oh! Was I?'

'Yes you were! I saw you.'

'Oh, well ... I suppose these things happen every now and then,' said John evasively while he became more and more confused. Then he brightened up: 'Don't you ever feel the urge to bark?'

'No. I don't!' Veronica barked at him. 'And I wish that you would behave normally every now and then!'

John stood there, not knowing what to reply, just trying to look good.

'All right then,' said Veronica. 'I'll go to Steve and tell him to get the car ready. You still want to come?'

'Yes ... if I may?'

'You may. But only if you promise not to bark when we're in the reserve and you see animals.'

28

As they were driving over the open savannah, Veronica was enthusiastically talking about elephants. She was wearing a safari hat from which sprang her unruly golden hair, and her eyes shone as she turned towards John: 'You'll be surprised to find out how nice they are, and how different they are from one another when we get nearer.'

'I thought they were just dangerous animals and you had to keep out of their way.'

'Contrary to rumours, and to what you believe,' countered Veronica defensively, 'it's rare to find some really nasty individuals amongst them. They only attack when they feel threatened, or because they have had an unfortunate encounter with our bipedal species. Elephants remember well, as you must know, and they don't take any chances the next time. If there is one species that can be really nasty,' she added, 'it's the human species.'

'All right, I'm not going to argue with you. Basically then, elephants are not nasty. But when you say they're all different from one another you surely mean that some are taller or fatter than others?'

'No, silly, that's not what I mean. Although, obviously, they all differ physically too.'

'I must say that they all look the same to me.'

'That's because you're a human. I bet that we humans all look the same to elephants.'

'Permit me to doubt this,' interrupted John in the pedantic voice of one used to discussions amongst scientists. 'We, humans, are all clearly and obviously very different from one another. I would recognise you, for instance, amongst a million other people.'

'That's because I'm so strikingly special,' teased Veronica, taking off her hat and passing her hand over her hair in a film star-like fashion. 'And, of course, you're in love with me, that's why.' She looked at John from the corner of her eye, all smiles and seduction.

John's face turned a bright red and he swallowed hard. 'Look,' he finally managed to say. 'What I wanted to convey is that, if you put ten humans next to each other, you distinguish immediately among them. It's not just that some are taller or fatter, but they all have different faces, a different gait, different everything. While if you put ten elephants together, they all look alike.'

'Tchh, tchh,' went Veronica, 'do you mean to say that you wouldn't even be able to distinguish between male and female elephants? You? A biologist. Fortunately elephants don't make that mistake. A male elephant is capable of zooming in on any female in heat. Just as you, John, will inevitably be drawn to any pretty female,' she added mischievously.

John bit his lip and didn't answer. All one could hear was the sound of the engine as the jeep wound its way over the savannah. After a while the silence between them became heavy.

'Oh John, don't sulk,' pleaded Veronica at last. 'I was just teasing you.'

'You're not teasing me! You're ridiculing me! You've always done so and you always will. I think you just can't help it. It's second nature with you!'

'I'm sorry to have upset you, John.' She softly touched his arm. 'Look, all I wanted to say is that elephants, when you get used to them, become quite easy to single out. Not only do they have different physical characteristics; once you have observed their behaviour and get to know them, you realize that their characters differ just as much as those of humans. Do you know that I've given all my elephants names to stress the fact that they are individual beings?'

John was surprised. 'What do you call them then?'

'Oh, Sylvia, Jessica, Melanie … Some I've even given names of girlfriends or women I know,' said Veronica, warming to her pet subject.

'Do you mean to say that they somehow resemble them?'

'Oh yes, of course. Take Emily, for instance. She's the matriarch of one of the herds. Matriarchs can be quite bossy, and this one is a real platoon sergeant. She reminds me of Miss Emily, the head mistress of the boarding school where I had the dubious privilege of spending far too many years of my girlhood.'

'Nice way to get your own back.' John nodded approvingly.

'Or take Isobel,' continued Veronica. 'She's like a girlfriend of mine: all prim and proper; tries to be the little lady; and is easily shocked. And the other elephants know it and believe me, they don't miss an occasion to upset her dainty feelings.'

'I find this a bit hard to believe!' interrupted John. 'You seem to imply that elephants have feelings like us.'

'Of course they have feelings like us!' Veronica stared at him as if he were a slightly backward pupil. 'And their characters read like an open book. They have not learned to hide their intentions or to deceive like we humans do. They show themselves as they are, without clothes to cover their defects so to speak.'

John felt snubbed by her reaction. *She is pushing things a bit too far*, he thought, but Veronica didn't notice and continued enthusiastically.

'They tend to be a little destructive when they play about because of their bulk, but they are certainly not nasty as you thought. Some are real goodie-goodies, others quite spirited. But more than anything else they are playful, even mischievous, especially when they are young.'

'Yeah, I've had the pleasure of meeting such a mischievous little elephant ... your Dumbo.'

'Oh, isn't he amusing? Such a sweet little thing!'

'A sweet little thing? A real nuisance you should say. I wonder if elephants are like dogs?'

'What do you mean by that?'

'Well, isn't there a saying that a dog takes after his or her master?'

'Haha! You really make me laugh. How witty you can be when you try.' Veronica sounded sarcastic. 'I'm explaining a very important subject for your benefit and all you can think of is to make senseless remarks.'

'Sorry,' said John. 'Please carry on.' And to encourage her he inquired: 'Do you only give names to females, or do males also get the benefit of being named after your friends and acquaintances?'

Veronica looked at him as if in doubt whether to continue or not. Finally she replied: 'Of course males get names too. What a silly question!'

'Like what?'

'Well, for example, there's one I call Ron.'

'Why is that?' asked John in a cold voice. 'Because you like him?'

'That's not it! It's because that particular elephant walks like a pompous fellow.'

John laughed heartily, saying: 'I like that. That's a good one!'

Veronica carried on, unstoppable now: 'And there's another one I've called Klaus.'

'Explain, please.'

'Well, he's got a slight limp and a bulging forehead, and if you could put spectacles on his nose, he would look just like our mad scientist.'

John now roared with laughter, exclaiming: 'Wonderful, wonderful!' Suddenly he stopped and looked at Veronica with suspicion in his eyes. 'There isn't one you've called John, I hope?'

Veronica began to move uneasily in her seat. 'Well, as a matter of fact, there is one called John,' she reluctantly admitted.

'This can't be true! An elephant...' he mumbled. 'I would never have dreamt that one day I would be compared to an elephant. I think you are pushing your humanizing of elephants too far! And are we allowed to learn why you christened an elephant with this particular name?' he asked in a not too pleased voice. 'At least, I hope that you called him John because of his outstanding intelligence? Or his proud bearing?'

Veronica seemed ill at ease. 'No, it's not really like that. He's actually quite ordinary.'

'Then, why call him John?' retorted John, offended.

'Well, I just wanted to call one of my elephants John, I suppose,' replied Veronica, avoiding John's gaze.

'That's not the whole story, is it? I'm sure it's got something to do with me! There's something particular in its character or behaviour that reminds you of me, isn't there? I want to know. I insist!'

Suddenly Veronica got annoyed. 'Well, if you absolutely have to know, I'll tell you. But remember, you asked for it: he's the one that can never leave the females alone.'

'What!' John's breath escaped him like air out of bellows. 'That's a bit thick! What do you take me for? That's highly unfair.'

'I see. That's unfair? Do you mean to say that it wasn't you then whom I saw one evening during the 1996 International Biotech Conference in Bulgaria, about to step out of the elevator of the hotel where you were staying? And you found waiting for you, sitting on a bench on one side of the lobby, a girl I believe to have been Polish with whom you had been going out at night; and facing her, on a bench on the other side, a girl whom I think was Romanian, and with whom you had been going out in the daytime. They obviously didn't know each other, and did not in the least suspect that you were leading a double life. Fortunately for you, you must have been a quick observer because as you were about to follow the other people out of the elevator and step into the lobby, you noticed them both. And you withdrew like lightning and promptly went up again.'

John's jaw dropped. 'How do you know all this?'

'Because I was sitting there too, and I saw the look of horror on your face. Someone else told me the rest of the details. Apparently neither of the girls had seen you. At least they kept the illusion that they were special to you. The poor things!'

'So you were there and knew me?'

'Yes, I was at that international conference too and you hadn't even noticed me. Didn't you say just now that you would recognize me amongst a million others? It didn't seem like that at the time. But maybe that was because you didn't see much of me. You were too busy having fun, I suppose. Unlike you, I attended the meetings during the daytime and slept at night, as all serious participants were doing. So you hardly ever saw me. But your reputation spread. No wonder they didn't renew your contract at the university when it ended a few years later.'

'Did you give me away?' asked John in a voice that would have suited a pallbearer at a funeral.

'Nothing to do with me. I was a young postgraduate then and had just started specializing. I don't know why they sent me there. I tried my best but it went all a bit above my head. But you were certainly the talk of the town during that conference. What a reputation you had! Beau John they called you. There were a number of scientists who were muttering about unethical behaviour but who were, I suspect, quite jealous. Someone must have reported back to headquarters, but it wasn't me! I was too insignificant. And I don't inform against other people. I mind my own business. But do tell me what happened afterwards, I mean to these two girls? I left minutes after and I've always wondered.'

John kept dead quiet, his face scarlet and his lips tightly pressed together. The sudden realization that he had been found out, that his darkest secrets were known and his private life was discussed around coffee tables all over the place, had shaken him to the core. He might just as well have been on the front page of the tabloids! Waves of shame swept over him as he stared out of the window of the jeep. The vehicle moved slowly over the open grassland, bumping and bouncing. Nearby were some scattered thorn trees and far in the background one could just make out the hazy outline of mountains against a pure blue sky. But John no longer saw anything. His gaze was turned inwards.

Finally Veronica broke the silence. 'John, what happened to those two girls?'

Her voice awoke John from his stupor. 'Christ, do you really want to know? I don't like telling the story. It's kind of ... well, it's not one of my best memories.'

'Never mind. I shall enjoy it.'

'But I won't!' objected John and withdrew further into his seat.

Veronica looked at him attentively. Her hand moved slowly towards him, until it touched his arm. 'Sorry to have upset you again.' She spoke softly, as if to a child. 'Honestly, I don't mind what you have or haven't done in your life, or how many girlfriends you've had.'

John still stared in front, a sullen, absent look on his face.

'Come on, John,' Veronica insisted, 'let's be friends. If only you accepted me as your friend, things would be so much simpler. You can tell me everything. I really don't mind.'

'Don't you?' asked John sceptically.

'I must admit that, at the time, I may have thought: *See what happens if you let men out of your sight? You can't trust them for a minute, especially married men.* But I'm not judging you. On the contrary, I'm fascinated by the kind of life you've led. But I do wonder how you managed to combine all that with your scientific career and, on top of that, with your married life – by the way, are you still married?'

'I won't be for much longer, thank God. The divorce should be finalized within a few weeks.'

John had gradually begun to relax while Veronica spoke. *Fine,* he thought, *if Veronica knows everything, there's no need to pretend.*

'So you know the worst?' he asked finally.

'I don't know about the worst, but some stories happened to pass my way.'

'But you weren't even at the same university as me!'

'That just shows how your fame spread.'

'Good heavens! If only I had known.'

'Then what? Would you have behaved differently? I hope not.'

John reflected for a while. 'No,' he said at last. 'No. I don't think it would have made any difference. If you have to live according to what other people think of you, you might just as well be dead. Or become a politician or something like that. No. I don't really care.'

'That's what I want to hear. I can approve of that.'

They sat for a while in silence, each enveloped in their own thoughts, while the driver constantly had to tug at the steering wheel as the jeep wound its way through the bush.

29

They had been driving through the open savannah for an hour or two when they made contact with a herd of about twenty elephants near the edge of a forest. As they approached, the elephants moved into the dense undergrowth and soon their bulky shapes began to vanish amongst the thick foliage.

Veronica and John got out but by the time they reached the first trees the elephants had gone. There was plenty of evidence that they had just passed that way: they had broken down a lot of branches and large bamboos had been uprooted and flung about half devoured. Puddles had formed in the elephants' footprints, they had left piles of droppings on the forest floor, but they themselves seemed to have been swallowed up by the forest.

There was no point in hanging about and the jeep now returned to the plains where it came upon a large herd of black buffalo, standing up to their knees in the long golden grass of the savannah.

'Don't go too near,' warned Veronica, turning to the driver.

'Why is that?' asked John. 'They can't be very dangerous. They look just like cattle to me.'

'The buffalo is one of the most aggressive animals in the whole of Africa,' contradicted Veronica, 'and one of the most cunning too. It's better to give buffaloes a wide berth.'

'How do elephants get on with them then, and with all the other animals?'

'Elephants and other large herbivores don't bother each other; they all live together in harmony. Their law seems to be: live and let live. As a matter of fact, elephants are timid creatures despite their great size. They are really peaceful and are very intelligent animals.' Veronica looked intently at John. 'I wish you would like them,' she said pleadingly.

John didn't want to upset her again and avoided her gaze. Instead, he remarked: 'You say that elephants are very intelligent, but how can that be? They surely don't have the brain size for that, unlike us humans?'

'You'd be surprised! Some theories have it that the brain development of hominids, in which you seem so interested, is linked to the use of their hands. Elephants had a similar sort of evolution of their brain, but linked to their trunk. The tip of their trunk is capable of a vast number of manipulations. Its function is in fact similar to that of the human hand. Elephants can pick up sticks to rub their bellies, pull up grass and shake the dust out of it, handle fragile objects with the greatest care ... you just name it. And as an elephant baby develops and learns to use his trunk, his brain grows, just as the brain of a human child keeps growing. Young elephants also have to learn and memorize a vast amount of things and by the time they've become adults their brain volume has tripled. Their brain-to-body ratio is lower than that of humans of course, but because they are such big animals, the brain of a big adult can weigh five times as much as a human brain. And this permits them to have a highly developed social structure and a sophisticated communication system.'

'So they *are* intelligent!'

'Yes. And there's more: do you realize that elephants are amongst the very few animals that recognize themselves in a mirror?'

'Are you implying that they're self-conscious like humans?'

'I don't know. If we could communicate with them we could ask them but...'

'Hey! Something over there!' exclaimed Steve suddenly, pointing at vultures circling overhead less than a mile away. 'We go and see.'

When the Land Rover got nearer they saw a big dead animal surrounded by lions and dozens of hyenas and vultures.

'Oh no!' exclaimed Veronica. 'No...' She gave a gasp of horror. 'It's one of my elephants!'

As they got to within fifteen yards she screamed: 'It's George. They've killed George!'

Its tusks had been hacked away and the scavengers were ripping pieces out of the elephant's sides. It was a ghastly mess.

'Make them go away!' screamed Veronica. 'Look what they're doing! It's horrible!' She opened the door ready to jump out and chase the lions and hyenas away, but John and Steve held her back. She started hitting them with her fists trying to wrestle free, but they wouldn't let her go. Then she broke down and started crying hysterically.

'Let's go,' said John to Steve. 'Let's get away from here quickly.'

Veronica cried her heart out all the way to Elephant Camp, curled up in a corner of the jeep. When they arrived at the camp the two men led her to a chair and made her sit down. Her sobbing had subsided by now, but she just sat there staring blankly in front of her. Then they heard her whisper: 'It's so unjust ... so unjust they killed *George*.'

'Why, Veronica?' John spoke very softly.

'Only a few weeks ago I stood there alone in front of him. He looked so strong then, such a mighty being. He could have killed me if he had wanted to, but he didn't. He spared me. And now they've killed him! Why him?'

'We can't do anything about it now, Veronica. We must accept it,' said John, trying to reason with her. 'After all, it's ... well ... it's only an elephant.'

Veronica stared at him in disbelief. Then she flared up and screamed: 'You heartless monster! Who are you to say such things? I don't want you here! Go back to your cheap affairs and your silly women. That's about your level. I hate you! I never want to see you again!'

30

John got back to Naboru in a depressed mood. This was bad, very bad. Of course Veronica had gone berserk when she had discovered the dead elephant. He should have realized how much she cared about elephants and not made such a stupid remark, but he had just said anything in an effort to put some perspective into the situation and de-dramatize it. Maybe he would be able to make up for it another time, show himself very interested in elephants...

The worst, maybe, was that she seemed to know all about his past love life. He sighed as he went inside Sam's house, shaking his head. It was beyond him how his private life could have become public knowledge. These things simply shouldn't be allowed. Veronica had pretended not to mind his love affairs, but her violent reaction at the end showed that deep down she considered him unworthy. It was really bad that she had seen him in one of the most shameful situations of his entire life. Fancy Veronica being there right at the moment the elevator came down in that hotel in Bulgaria! It was incredible that she should remember the look of horror on his face and all the rest of it. That's a kind of image a girl will never forget. That just about ended his chances with her. Damn!

He blushed as he entered the living room and nearly collided with Sam who was standing there.

'Hey,' said Sam. 'Red cheeks and a grim expression on the face. And you don't even notice me. What's the fuss? What's on your mind?'

'Oh ... well ... oh ... nothing,' replied John evasively.

'Look here, I'm not stupid. I can see when something is wrong. Anything to do with Veronica?'

'How do you know that?'

'Elementary, my dear Watson. First of all, you asked for the car this morning to go and see her. Secondly, you're in love with her. Thirdly, you look deeply unhappy. Has she discovered some unsavoury secret about you?'

'You're not clairvoyant, are you?'

'Maybe more than you think. What's the matter?'

'I don't know whether I should tell you. It's all too embarrassing.'

Sam's curiosity was really awakened now. 'Come on, John, we're friends, aren't we?' he said soothingly. 'If you can trust anyone, it's me. Maybe I can help you. You know that I'm always ready to help you.'

John thought that maybe he could do with some advice. 'Do you realize', he began, 'that Veronica saw me during the 1996 International Biotech Conference in Bulgaria?'

'That sounds quite normal to me. I'm sure lots of people must have seen you during that conference.'

'You don't realize. She saw me one evening...'

'Yes...' interjected Sam encouragingly. He felt that the story might become interesting.

'...When I was about to step out of the elevator as its doors opened onto the lobby of the hotel where I was staying. Imagine my horror when I realized that a Polish girl with whom I had been going out at night was sitting on a bench on the left, waiting for me; and facing her, on a bench on the right, a Romanian girl with whom I had been going out in the daytime.'

'Did they come to blows when they saw each other?'

'No! They didn't know about each other's existence and hadn't noticed me. But I spotted them both as the elevator emptied and quickly drew back. I was able to hide amongst the people who entered the elevator and went up again. It was a really narrow escape.'

'How come Veronica saw you there?'

'She was sitting on one of these benches too and she, at least, noticed me. Apparently one look was sufficient for her to understand the whole situation.'

'She told you this today?'

'Yes.'

'That's embarrassing. Difficult to make a great impression on her after that sort of thing. What happened after that in your Bulgarian hotel? Did you tell Veronica?'

'She wanted to know, even insisted, but I wouldn't tell her.'

'Quite right. That was the correct decision. The less you tell girls, the better. But you can tell me.'

'Why should I?'

'Don't you trust me? I'm like your lawyer, ready to defend you always in all circumstances. You trust your lawyer and tell him everything, don't you?'

'Of course I trust you, but...'

'There's no but. Either you trust me, or you don't. Come on, John, out with it!'

John felt cornered. He swallowed a couple of times and then started: 'Well, it was like this. I had been going out with these girls. I'd just got back from the States where I'd seen my wife...'

'So you were married then?'

'Well, as a matter of fact, I am *still* legally married, but the divorce has been processed and will take effect very soon. But let me continue. I sorely needed a buck-me-up after my return, and there it all was, or seemed to be: late spring, the sea, everyone carefree and lots of pretty Eastern European girls in bikinis. They hardly spoke a word of English, though. It kind of limited conversation to such exchanges as "Where you from?" or "Dance, yes?" But I didn't ask for more. All I wanted was a bit of fun to take my mind off that bitch of a wife, and a bit of affection, which I was yearning for. Mind you, I didn't try to be one of those Casanovas, going all out for the girls, putting their arms around their waists whenever they could with one clear intention: to get them into bed. I remember that there was an American biologist who thought he was clever. He had taken off his wedding ring because he feared that it might ruin his chances with the girls, but the sun had tanned his hands and had left a thin white strip around his finger where the ring had been. And those Eastern European girls were no fools. The white strip around his brown finger gave him away. So he had no success whatsoever.'

'Served him right I think!' interrupted Sam.

'Worse than that, he had nothing but worries in the end. His wedding ring disappeared one day from his bedside drawer in his hotel room. It was a big valuable golden ring with some inlay – a present from his wife; it had been an heirloom in her family. He was in a terrible state when I last saw him. He dreaded returning to America and having to face his wife. She was a lawyer too!'

'He ought to have been more careful! But *you* were still married as well.'

'Although I was still legally married, I had in fact taken off my wedding ring years before. My wife had never given me any true affection during the few years our marriage, properly speaking, lasted. I was married and well and truly caught before I understood that she was incapable of it. When I lost my job with the biotech company in Chicago and found a position in Europe, she declined to follow me and from then on I no longer considered myself tied to her. As I told you, I'd gone back to the States just before the Biotech Conference in Bulgaria. I'd had a stormy reunion with my wife: I had asked her for a divorce but she refused unless I paid her a colossal amount of money, which I didn't possess. She was a calculating, egocentric bitch if ever there was one, and I told her so as I slammed the door in her face. But that's another story altogether, and I'm diverging. As I said, I really needed a buck-me-up. One day I met Nadia, the Romanian girl, and before I had time to turn around I seemed to be stuck with her. On the third day, as I lay next to her on the golden sands of one of the beaches of the Black Sea, I rolled over and I suddenly found her in my arms.'

'You mean just like that? You yourself had done nothing to make it happen and didn't even know what was going on till it had happened?'

'It may seem odd to say so but, yes, that about sums it up. I fail to remember how it happened, but there I was, suddenly stuck with her. The problem was that she was a day girl. She went to bed early and, because I felt as if I was on holiday, it left me a bit bored with myself in the evenings. So, one evening … it was just after I had met Nadia as far as I remember … I happened to stroll into an open-air dance space with dozens of young people hopping about or languishing in each other's arms depending on the tune the orchestra was playing. And there I met Danusia, the Polish girl. She was a real night girl – never seemed to come alive before 9 p.m. So that's how I got caught up in two affairs at the same time.'

'How did you get involved with the Polish girl then?'

'At the end of the first night I still went to bed relatively early, at 1 a.m. or something like that, because I had to attend the meetings; they began at 8.30 every morning. When I was about to leave she whispered: "You back tomorrow?" As I said

124

I didn't know, she said: "Please," threw her arms around me and gave me an effusive kiss. The second night there was rather a lot of slow music and suddenly I found her arms around my neck as we danced, and her body glued to mine. It was kind of uncanny. There I was, at the same time going out with two girls who didn't know about each other's existence and I can tell you, I was at a loss as to what to do about it. I told myself that this wasn't possible and that I ought to tell one or the other that it could not be, but somehow I couldn't rake up the courage. I didn't want to hurt these girls, you see. They looked so innocent.'

Sam shook his head but disinclined to make any comment. Instead, he said: 'So your days and nights were filled to the brim with activities. I somehow have a feeling that you can't have put much energy into attending the lectures at the conference after that. What happened next? Two romantic happy endings? A double love life, one for the day and one for the night? With you worn out at twice the normal speed?'

'Stop teasing me, Sam, or you won't hear the rest!'

'I'm not teasing you. I'm your spellbound audience. How did it go from there?'

'It's all a bit painful. I don't really want to talk about it,' replied John who had begun to sulk.

'That's not fair, John. You can't stop your story here. First you get me all worked up and interested, and then you refuse to carry on. It just isn't fair. You must at least tell me how a day girl and a night girl both happened to be waiting for you in the lobby of your hotel at 9 o'clock in the evening?'

'Well...' continued John after a while, 'apparently the Polish girl, Danusia, had come to fetch me. I was supposed to have met her on the dance floor that evening, not in my hotel lobby.'

'So it was all a mistake, and you had simply arranged a meeting with your Romanian girl?'

'Not at all. I imagined her to be in bed by that time.'

'It was a bit of a shock to you, then, to see them both sitting there, waiting for their hero to appear?'

'It certainly was. It gave me a terrible jolt. I hid in a corner of the elevator. The doors seemed to take ages to close; it was agony. But I escaped unnoticed! I ran back to my room and stayed there for a while, the door locked. By 9.30 I thought

125

Nadia would have gone to bed, and Danusia off to dance, so I ventured out again.'

'And the coast was clear?'

'No. Nadia was still sitting there. But at least Danusia had gone.'

'What was your early sleeper doing there at that time of the evening?'

'It turned out to be a very special evening for her: it was her last evening. Her roommate had already left, and she herself had to take the midnight train. Nadia, who had hesitated to take the big plunge until then, had decided that this was going to be the great moment. She flung herself into my arms with a cry of relief and then quickly pulled me along to her own hotel a few streets further.'

'So there was a happy ending after all.'

'Not quite. You see, I knew that Danusia was waiting for me and that she would be very upset if I didn't turn up. She had become more affectionate with every passing evening and the fact that she had come to my hotel somehow indicated that this was going to be the night she would chose to give herself up to love. Instead, I now found myself in Nadia's bed. She had undressed in the shower room and then had rushed to hide under the sheet; only her face showed. It was not really pretty and had an expression of "Take me, I'm all yours" painted all over it. Now, I'm a romantic being...'

Sam sniggered.

'...And don't snigger! You see I'm a romantic being and can't start on a cold engine ... and with Danusia waiting and time pressing because Nadia had to catch the midnight train ... Anyway, I did my best, but things did not perk up for quite a while. When finally they did perk up I seemed unable to enter her and was about to give up when I heard her whisper: "Please, this first time for me; please love." She was still a virgin!'

'Well, well. It's not every day a man gets into bed with a virgin. This must have considerably sharpened your senses and boosted your power!'

'It didn't. Quite the contrary! I was willing but it was a hard, uphill struggle. Not much pleasure there. And then the awful thing happened.' John went red in the face.

'What happened?'

'Well, you know, it does happen sometimes.'

'How am I to know what happened? You were the lead actor.'

John reddened again. 'Ahem ... I'm afraid ... well, I suddenly came outside her. You know what I mean. When she realized what had happened she began to cry. Then she got out of bed, went into the shower, washed, dressed, picked up her suitcase and left.'

'Still a virgin?'

'Still a virgin.'

'And Danusia?'

'It was near midnight by the time I got to the dance floor. I found her in a foul mood and had to explain my delay. It was worse than being married! Anyway, I managed to wriggle out of the situation by giving her a necklace. I told her I'd ordered it especially for her, and that the man who was bringing it to me that night had been delayed. So by 3 a.m. or thereabouts, after the orchestra had finished, we went to her place to have our big first night. It was pitch-dark and her lodgings seemed to be miles away, almost in the countryside. By the time we got to the small cottage on the crest of a low hill where she was staying, I was literally exhausted. What with the emotions of upsetting Nadia and all the rest ... I couldn't stop thinking about Nadia. Anyway, when we got to this impossible sort of cottage we heard strange noises coming from inside.'

'What kind of noises?'

'Well, sounds like "huh huh, hoh hoh," some heavy breathing, and squeaking sounds as from springs that hadn't been oiled for a lifetime. It took me some time to realize what was going on inside, but Danusia needed no more than a second to understand the situation. I heard her exclaim *"Cholerny świat!"* or something of the sort in Polish, and then she turned to me: "Girlfriend in there ... with man!" she said in disgust.'

'Now,' smiled Sam, 'I somehow feel that the circumstances were not very propitious for a romantic night. How did you manage after that?'

'I tried to soothe Danusia and, you know, ever the romantic, I stepped forward and murmuring something like: "I'll carry you anywhere. To the end of the earth if need be!" I put one arm under her shoulders and the other under her knees and lifted her up.'

'Something in the line of the groom carrying his newly-wed bride over the threshold of their love nest?'

'Something like that, I suppose. But I didn't quite pull it off. I was exhausted, she was heavier than I thought, and as I stepped forward I stumbled over something and dropped her. She rolled straight down the steep slope of the hill and disappeared into what I vaguely could make out to be a thick growth of prickly pear cacti. I couldn't see her after that, but I could hear her very clearly. I would never have imagined that there were so many swear words in the Polish vocabulary.'

'And you, ever the gallant knight, rushed down to rescue her?'

'Well, ahem ... I felt that it was more prudent to beat a strategic retreat after that ... the sooner, the better. I got lost several times on my way back, and the landscape seemed one long obstacle course in the dark; I've never fallen into so many ditches in my life. By the time I made it to the holiday resort the day had begun to break, and I'd had my fill of romance. I just collapsed on my bed and must have slept for a couple of days.'

'So that's why you were unable to attend the lectures.'

'Yes, that's why. I shone by my absence during the conference and Veronica thinks that the authorities in my department at the university got wind of it. She also seems to think that it was decisive in convincing those authorities not to renew my contract when it ended two years later.'

'I wouldn't be surprised,' mused Sam. 'I wouldn't be surprised.'

They kept silent for a while, and then Sam inquired, almost casually: 'So how do things stand with Veronica? Did you manage to make up for last time?'

'I thought so at the beginning, but I've ended by making a new, even worse blunder.'

'She hasn't fallen for you then? I really hoped that this time it would be OK.'

John looked crestfallen. 'Somehow I feel that the situation is quite hopeless. Such a pure girl she is. She has such high ideals. How can I ever live up to her expectations, miserable clod that I am?'

'But you go on loving her and hoping?'

'Of course I do! She is all I ever wanted. If I knew for sure

128

that Veronica would never love me, well ... there wouldn't be any point for me in going on living.' And as he said so his head sunk between his shoulders.

'Come now,' said Sam putting his arm around John, 'don't be so downcast.' But his eyes shone with a strange light.

31

There was a knock on the door of Le Tellier's office. He knew who was coming and called out: 'Come in, Mr Luonga.'

A heavily built man came in, his jacket and trousers tight over his body. 'Glad to see you back in town, Mr Le Tellier,' said the man, shaking hands.

'Pleased to see you too,' replied Le Tellier. He gave the man a good looking-over, then he remarked with a reprimanding intonation in his voice: 'You have put on weight since last year.'

'I haven't!' objected the man, pretending to be comfortable in his tight clothes.

'All right.' Le Tellier held up a hand to stop all further protests. 'No offence meant. I just thought ... anyway, how's business? Anything of interest?'

Luonga, who had begun to shuffle his feet, now perked up. 'Well ... for a start we have some precious objects from the Swahili Coast. I can guarantee that they're genuine antiques. Arab. But don't ask how I got hold of them.'

'I'm not asking,' reassured Le Tellier, holding up his hand. 'You know I never do. Anything else?'

'Some nice uncut diamonds – smuggled all the way from the Kasai, imagine. Then there are a couple of rhino horns...'

'I love rhino horns,' interrupted the Frenchman. 'Always sell well. One of my good business contacts, an oil sheik, is prepared to pay a lot of money for them. Over there they believe that the powder of rhino horns has aphrodisiacal qualities. And when I look at that sheik, I dare say that he needs it to get anything moving at his age.' He laughed loudly at his own comment, which he thought extremely droll.

Luonga now carried on: '...And I also have some ivory as always. My men shot a big tusker only days ago.'

'*Bien. Très bien!* All excellent for business.'

'So you are pleased?'

'Yes, yes! But I've been thinking about ways to improve the

cash flow, and I've had a bright idea. Tell me, when your men shot that big elephant, what did they do?'

'They cut the tusks and ran. They weren't going to hang around.'

'Right. And what did they leave behind, Mr Luonga?'

'They left something behind?' Luonga became agitated. 'The assholes! I keep telling them to be careful, to remove all incriminating evidence. And they left something behind. I'll box their ears!'

Le Tellier smiled, enjoying the turn the conversation was taking. 'Yes, they left something big behind. Something *very* big.'

'Very big!' Luonga's eyes nearly popped out of his head and sweat began dripping down his heavy brow. 'I do not understand. The car is back, and the guns, and all the rest. I was certain they had removed everything.'

'They didn't. They left the elephant behind.'

'Oh. Pfft...' The air escaped from Luonga's huge chest like from a deflating balloon. 'For a moment I feared that they had left something important behind. They will not be able to incriminate us on the evidence of an elephant's carcass. Haha ... I see that you're joking. Haha ... they left the dead elephant behind. Did you think they could carry it away on their backs? Haha ... what else did you expect?'

'But of course they could have carried the elephant away. On a lorry with a crane!'

'What would be the use of that?'

'You do not see? You do not understand?'

'Well ... yes ... let me see ... that way they would not find the carcass and would not know what had happened. The elephant would just have disappeared ... yes ... but what an effort! To remove a dead elephant just for that? You would need a big lorry ... and what would you do with the carcass? No. I do not understand.'

'Think, Mr Luonga. Just think! What's the value of a dead elephant?'

'Once the tusks are cut out ... well, very little I would say. On the contrary, it would cost a lot of money to remove the carcass.'

'But the meat, Mr Luonga. The meat! Two to three tonnes

131

of meat which could be sold on at five to ten dollars a kilo at least, if we market it well. Plus the hide, hairs, bone meal and all the rest. We're talking about twenty thousand dollars or more for a big bull, without the ivory. Twenty thousand dollars! That's what you leave behind to the lions, hyenas, vultures and ants. They're devouring twenty thousand dollars! Don't you see?'

'Oh!' exclaimed Luonga, hitting his forehead with a big fleshy hand. 'I never thought of that. But ... how can we get the dead elephant out of the park and into the town to cut it up and prepare it for selling? Everyone would know about it and we would all be in jail before we had time to export anything.'

'Trust me, Monsieur,' said Le Tellier. 'I have my methods.'

32

'What a surprise to see you here!' exclaimed Veronica when the old green car turned into Elephant Camp and Sam got out. 'When I saw the car I thought it was John again.'

'I'm sorry you're disappointed. But considering that everyone comes to see you nowadays, I thought that I too might come and pay you homage.'

Veronica was flattered. 'Well, you're welcome, and I don't quite know what you mean by disappointed.'

'Oh! When you saw the car you said just now that you hoped it'd be John, and then it's only me appearing.'

'Oh. I see what you mean. Don't worry, you're very welcome. It's just that I'm surprised. With all your commitments in town I would never have expected you to come out here. John told me that you're extremely busy working on the question of hominids.'

'Yes,' Sam replied enthusiastically. 'I'm trying out a very novel approach to probe into the origin of mankind. This is a really important question, you see. Hominids are the far-away ancestors of us all, and solving the riddle of how they became true humans is the key to all modern behaviour...' Suddenly he held up his hand as if to stop his own flow of words. 'But you know about this. John told me you're interested in hominids. So how do you feel about it all? About hominids?'

Veronica pondered the question for a while; then she said: 'I'm not really sure if the advent of mankind has been such a good thing. Maybe it would have been better for the Earth if hominids had never emerged. I think I'd prefer a world inhabited by elephants and other animals to one full of nasty people out to grab everything for themselves and destroying the rest of nature in the process.'

She had hardly finished her sentence when she noticed a strange expression of displeasure on Sam's face. It was as if a mask had dropped away and his real self had appeared. Had she not looked up just at that moment she might have missed it. A split second later Sam seemed to be his amiable self again and Veronica was no longer sure whether or not she had observed correctly, but somehow she sensed that the mood had changed. Or was this a wrong impression too? She felt disturbed and didn't know how to continue the conversation. Finally she asked: 'And how is Klaus? Working all the time? And John...' She hesitated. 'Do you think he will have time to come again?'

'You'd like to see him again then? I thought you parted on bad terms last time?'

A forced smile appeared on Veronica's face. 'I was somewhat short-tempered after what happened. I hope he didn't take it too badly.'

'Why should he? From what he says, he likes coming to visit you. But he goes to other places as well.'

Veronica looked up rather sharply. 'Which other places? And what does he say?'

'Oh, nothing special.' Sam seemed evasive. 'Then he added, as an afterthought: 'You seem to like him a lot! He's a really nice guy, handsome and so on, don't you think?'

'He's handsome all right,' admitted Veronica as if with difficulty.

'Yes ... and also a great seducer from what he's told me.'

'What has he told you?' Her breathing came fast. 'What do you know about him?'

'Oh ... not much. Still, I've learned a thing or two about him these last weeks.'

'Such as...'

'Well, his past, his character, what he thinks and so on. But why do you want to know?'

Veronica was at a loss for words. She twisted her hair around one of her fingers while thinking of something to say. 'I'm not interested in him!' she suddenly exclaimed. 'He doesn't like elephants and I think he's unreliable.'

'You mustn't judge him harshly just because of a few unfortunate incidents.'

Veronica's voice trembled slightly as she asked: 'Which "unfortunate incidents" are you referring to?'

'Well, didn't something unfortunate happen that time he spent the night here? Nothing important of course, but he ... well, he pulled your skirt down, didn't he?'

'How do you know that?'

'He told Klaus and me all about it.'

'Oh, did he?' Veronica's face looked grim. 'Has he told you more about our meetings here?'

'I ... well, I don't know whether I should tell you about it,' said Sam hesitantly.

'Has he told you about the reserve? The elephants. And Dumbo?'

'Oh, your little elephant? We were roaring with laughter the other day. He told us that you were besotted with that little fellow and he imitated you talking to him. It was quite comical. Oops,' he said suddenly, seeing that Veronica's face looked like thunder. 'I shouldn't have spoken.'

'You do well to tell me these things,' replied Veronica in a cold voice. 'At least now I know where I stand.'

'Oh, but you mustn't take it personally.' Sam seemed keen to put Veronica in a better mood. 'John talks a lot you see, and I'm not certain how much of it is true. He likes to play to the audience and brag a bit.'

'I don't know if he's got much to brag about. An outcast like him!' she said, moving her hand derisively.

'Don't judge him badly because he looks like an outcast – old clothes and all that.'

'Actually,' admitted Veronica reluctantly, 'that was one of the things I liked about him: his casual dress and manner.'

'Don't you like nice new clothes on a man, then?'

'I absolutely cannot stand well-dressed men. Peacocks I call them. When I see one dressed up in expensive clothes, strutting about to make a big impression, it puts me off forever.'

Sam thought for a while. Then he spoke: 'How strange that you should say that. John was thinking about coming here next time in brand-new expensive clothes so as to make a really big impression on you.'

'That can't be true! He hasn't got any money!'

'But of course he's got money. Where on earth did you get the idea that he hasn't?'

'He's been lying to me, then!'

'Maybe he wanted to keep it secret. But he wants to be irresistible. He's been talking about suddenly turning up here in a brand-new outfit to spring a big surprise on you.'

'He has already sprung a surprise on me once and I don't fancy a repeat performance!'

'So you prefer him as an outcast?'

'I don't know whether I prefer him either way.'

'Oh but he's really interesting, you know. He can be very entertaining when he begins to tell his stories. He's had a very active life.'

'Active! I see! Does he call it that? I've seen some of his activities! Trying to lay two girls at the same time!'

'Two? He talks about many more!'

'Does he?'

'Well … yes. You must admit that he has a certain way with the girls. He sort of goes for them and he gets away with it. From what I heard he could never keep his hands off any pretty girl student. He likes them young and crisp. Didn't help his scientific career it seems.'

'The pig! That's really him. And to think that I was nearly taken in by his charm!'

Sam now seemed to hesitate. 'I shouldn't have been saying all this!' he suddenly blurted out. 'It'll really upset him if he hears about it. He'll say that it's my fault that he didn't get you.'

'Get me?'

'Well … yes. He's been fairly bragging about it for the last week or so. Apparently he keeps track of his successes – I don't know how he does it – and he has kept on about you going to be number twenty-one. Twenty-one … lucky number, he keeps saying.'

Veronica almost froze at hearing this. 'Oh, that's what he says, does he?' came her voice, icily. 'That's how things stand. I'll show him his lucky number if he dares turn up here again!'

33

'Memsabu, I not trust,' said Steve Mutele as Veronica was having her breakfast on the veranda.

'What is it, Steve? You don't trust me?'

'No, no. You I trust. It is the situation.'

'Could you be a bit more explicit?'

'What is explicit?'

'Well, tell me everything.'

'Ha! I understand. Yesterday Faithful, she see man around.'

'What kind of a man?'

'One like us, Memsabu.'

'Do you mean one like you, or one like me?'

'Haha, Memsabu, this joke. You are not man. You are woman!'

'She saw a man like you then?'

'No. Not like me. Not as big. Not as beautiful.'

'Right, but an African?'

'Yes.'

'What was he doing?'

'That not certain. He keep hidden in bush looking at Faithful.'

'Did she go to him to ask what he was doing there?'

'No, Memsabu!' Steve stepped back in horror. 'Faithful is good wife. She no go to no man when I not there. I went after with big knife, but man had gone.'

'This is worrying. What can we do?'

'Put armed guard around house!'

'Ha-ha!' Veronica laughed sarcastically. 'As if we could pay for one.'

'Then I not know, Memsabu.'

Veronica sat there thinking for a while. 'I've got it!' she exclaimed suddenly.

'What you got, Memsabu?'

Veronica sighed. Steve was strong and reliable, but he could be trying. 'The solution!' she said. 'We're going to install an alarm system.'

'What is alarum system?'

'A booby trap.' And seeing that Steve still did not understand, she explained: 'Something the man does not know or see, and falls into.'

'Ha! I understand. Like animal that does not know. Comes along...' and he imitated the animal, a leopard or something, but a two-legged one, walking along without giving a single thought to danger, sniffing this flower, then that one and whistling to itself, '...and suddenly: bang! Falls into hole.' Whereupon he sank through his knees and collapsed into an imaginary hole, emitting loud wails.

'That's it! I'll think of something original. Will you help me?'

A big smile split Steve's face. 'Naturally I help, Memsabu. This very great fun. I very good at making alarum system. I make many when boy. My father he teach me. This I like, Memsabu!' And he went away contentedly, laughing all by himself while clapping his hands.

34

Sam stuck out his chin. 'You know what's wrong with you?'

John reddened. 'What do you mean? There's nothing wrong with me.'

'Well … you look like a hippie who missed his era by a decade or two.'

'You have no right to call me a hippie just because I wear casual clothes. Don't look at me like that! I'm a clean person, brush my teeth at least three times a day and wash regularly. The fact that I came in unwashed a week ago doesn't mean that I'm a regular pig.'

'As far as I can see, you always wear worn-out jeans and old shirts.'

'But that…'

Sam raised his hand to stop John from making an objection. 'You may feel comfortable in those sort of clothes, but I can tell you that it doesn't impress the girls and…'

'If you really know all this so well, then how come you haven't got a girlfriend yourself, eh?' interrupted John defiantly.

'Don't interrupt me! For the time being I'm dedicating my life to a grand scientific goal and sacrifice all for it – unlike someone else, here present. But I know what girls like.'

John felt put off. Then he thought of Veronica, of how little she considered him. Could it have something to do with the way he dressed? 'Well, what do girls like, according to you?' he asked finally.

'If you want to impress a girl, I mean really impress her, you need to be properly dressed. That ought to be clear to anyone. I don't mean dressed in a suit and tie. What I want to say is that you need clothes that show your personality at its best; that bring out the man in you; that will make women turn their heads as you pass by and follow you with their eyes. Those are the sort of clothes I'm talking about. What you need, I think…' he got up and looked at John through half-closed eyes, 'is a safari outfit. The irresistible adventurer! That's what you ought to look like.'

John, who at first had almost refused to listen, now began to show some interest. 'Do you think that Veronica would be impressed if I showed up looking like the irresistible adventurer?' he asked, still somewhat in doubt.

'She most certainly will. There's no doubt about it. What you think, Klaus?'

'I have no idea, man,' replied Klaus who looked his usual self: something like a slightly distracted owl. 'I don't know much about being well dressed and girls. I'm more at ease with my time machine.'

'Maybe you're right, Sam,' said John at last. 'I don't know whether you've ever met a horrible, slimy guy called Ron, who has a safari bus. He turns up a lot at Elephant Camp, always impeccably dressed, and Veronica seems to think the world of him. Maybe I should get myself a decent outfit. But how do you go about this sort of thing in a place like Naboru? Where do they sell well-fitting safari clothes?'

'Ha!' exclaimed Sam. 'That's the whole trick. They don't sell ready-made well-fitting safari clothes. But they can make them for you if you like. Wait a minute...' He turned towards the door and shouted: 'Kibu!'

A few seconds later the head servant appeared, dressed in the loose bright garments they wear on the Swahili Coast. 'Yes, Sahib?'

'Kibu, who's the best tailor in town? I'm asking for someone who could advise this gentleman here on how to dress, has a wide choice of materials and could produce an outfit in a day or two.'

The head servant thought for a while. 'Shillingi Mingi in Koi Avenue has a good reputation, Sahib.'

'Thank you, Kibu. That's all.'

'There you are, John. You go to Shillingi Mingi. I remember now. He's a trader from the coast who has a large workshop. He produces top-quality clothes.'

'What a strange name that man has got,' interrupted Klaus.

'It's not actually a proper name but a nickname. I gather that it's Swahili for "Many Shillings".'

'See!' exclaimed John. 'However much I appreciate your advice, Sam, and agree with you, it's not possible.'

'Why ever not?'

'Don't misunderstand me. I wouldn't mind having a beautiful safari outfit. But I see an insurmountable obstacle to getting it.'

'Which one?'

'I haven't got a shilling left, not even to pay for essentials. So how can I pay for a safari outfit made by your very expensive Shillingi Mingi?'

'That's no problem.' Sam waved his hand. 'I'll advance the money. You know that I dearly want you to help me and Klaus with the realization of our experiment, but if your destiny lies somewhere else and you love Veronica and need to impress her, who am I to begrudge you your happiness?'

John felt deeply moved. He stepped forward, took Sam's hand in his and said: 'Sam, old man, I'll never forget this. If ever you need me, you just call me and I'll help you.' Then he turned, smiling, and said: 'Off then to this Shillingi Mingi! Let's not waste any more time.'

35

That same afternoon Sam's head servant drove John to Shillingi Mingi's shop. As the car was winding its way through the traffic, John felt rather pleased with himself. Sam's advice had been good. He would soon be a new man, dressed properly, his past life behind him. Now he knew what to do. He would be the man of action. Action, yes, that's definitely what was needed. He would move in like the marines and conquer all before him. Leave Veronica no time to think. Be the strong man! And she would follow him like a lamb.

'Are you all right, Sahib?' inquired Kibu as he heard John mumbling to himself.

'What? Oh! Yes. I feel just fine.'

John indeed felt on top of the world. No more surprises for him. He had seen it all. He had even survived a visit to the American Embassy! Nothing untoward could happen to him now. And as for women: he had been the victim of fate long enough. Too weak, that's what he'd been. But now he was strong. The road was straight from here onwards. He'd had his fill of senseless adventures. They could dangle any temptation in front of his eyes now, and he would just look at it with scorn. Veronica was the one for him, and he was going to sweep her off her feet. He was firmly in control of his destiny!

He was interrupted in his reveries by Kibu pulling in and saying: 'Here we are, Sahib. Shillingi Mingi's shop. I'll wait here in the car for your return.'

As John entered the shop, a somewhat corpulent man with a shiny round face came forward. 'Come in, Sir,' he said, bending low. 'What can I do for you, Sir? A new outfit, you say, Sir. Everything totally new? All made to size ... You want the best materials? No expenses spared? Wonderful ... wonderful!' The owner rubbed his hands, visibly satisfied. Suddenly he stood back and eyed John like someone sizing up a problem. 'You want my advice, Sir? A safari outfit is what would really bring out your personality.'

They went around racks with materials, some for shirts and others for trousers. Shillingi Mingi pulled them all out and as he praised their quality and durability his voice became almost authoritarian. 'I can assure you that these materials are so strong that they will outlast you, Sir! And let me add that quality always speaks for itself, Sir. If you permit me to say so, Sir, a well-dressed man invariably makes a great impression on the ladies.'

The choosing done, he made a sign to an African assistant who had been leaning against a wall. 'Mbungi,' he ordered, 'take this gentleman to the dressing room.' And, turning to John: 'Please undress there, Sir, and the assistant will come and take your measurements.'

'Undress? Completely?'

'No, no. Of course not, Sir! You keep your underwear. But to take all the necessary measurements we need to get as near to the skin as possible. I'm sure you understand, Sir.'

Mbungi led John to the back of the workshop and into a corridor. 'You go in there behind curtain, Sah,' he said, pointing at a curtain further down the corridor, 'and undress and wait.'

As John lifted the edge of the curtain, bending low to pass underneath, he collided with the back of a voluminous African woman inside. She was naked but for tiny purple briefs with frilly white edges, which were drawn tight over her huge bottom, and as she turned around surprisingly quickly for someone of her bulk, one of her enormous breasts hit John plain in the face. John retreated with a yell and ran out of the corridor and into the shop, shuddering like a jelly. He caught up with the man named Mbungi, shouting: 'Hey, hey, there's a naked woman in there!'

'Oh! Sorry, Sah. This is unfortunate accident. I forgot, Sah. The dressing room of the ladies' department is out of order. Mirror broken, Sah. Today women are obliged to enter from the other side of corridor and use men's dressing room. Sorry. Wait a minute in workshop, Sah. You sit on this chair, Sah. I tell you when dressing room free.'

John sat there for a while, rubbing his face until he had calmed down. He now began to look around: at least a dozen men were cutting materials for clothes, while another dozen were bent over their sewing machines. *Isn't it strange that men should be doing the sewing?* he thought. *But everything here is the other way round. Look, here I am, only a few weeks in Africa, and I'm no longer surprised at anything. I've seen it all; I've analysed it; and understood it all. If there is a problem, you reason logically; find the solution; and then you do exactly the opposite. It's as simple as that. Just remember to do the opposite of what you would normally do in America or Europe and you'll be on top of everything.* And suddenly he felt very sure of himself. *I can handle any situation now*, he thought. *I'm in control.*

Presently Mbungi returned. 'It's all right now, Sah. But I go with you to make sure, Sah.' He led him into the back corridor again, lifted the curtain to ascertain that there was no one inside the cubicle, and motioned John to enter. 'You undress, Sah. The assistant will be with you shortly.'

John had only just managed to undress and sat down on a stool in a corner, naked but for his boxer shorts, when he heard steps outside. *That's quick service*, he thought. *Rare for Africa. It just goes to show that one must never judge.* Then the curtain was lifted up and a young African woman appeared, carrying a few dresses. If she was surprised to find an undressed white man sitting in the corner, she didn't show it. Instead, she glanced at him from under her long, curved eyelashes. Was there a slightly mocking, mischievous expression in her eyes? Was it daring, challenging?

She looked at him a mere instant; then she paid no more attention and turned towards the mirror. She now picked up the bottom of her long dress and, slowly, lifting her arms, pulled it up. *I don't believe this*, thought John, *this cannot be real.* He sat there holding his breath, staring the way a hypnotized rabbit stares at a snake, as the raised dress revealed a pair of long slim legs. Gradually, as the woman wriggled her body to get out of her tight dress, her small creamy briefs became visible, then a muscular belly, and finally a pair of firm breasts. As the woman slipped off her dress, her strong body odour fully hit John's nostrils. Suddenly he was confronted by all the deep sensuality of Africa and felt utterly defenceless. This was like an invitation into Africa's mysterious world – a promise to fulfil a man's hidden desires.

The young woman now tried on one of the dresses she had brought with her, and as she struggled to pull it over her head and it covered her face, her knee touched his. An electric shock seemed to go through John's body and a primitive, almost irresistible attraction welled up from the deepest recesses of his belly. Thick droplets of perspiration rose to his forehead and ran down his face as he stared at the curves of the woman's body, at the sensuality of her movements, at her thighs, rubbing over each other and then opening slightly as she twisted the dress over her head. Then his eyes were irresistibly drawn to her slightly transparent briefs suggesting the dark outline of the pubic hair, not two feet away from his bulging eyes.

Lord almighty, he groaned. *Don't do this to me! Please, please, do not tempt me like this. Please make me keep myself under control.* He closed his eyes tightly, but his imagination was racing away inside him. He could not shut out the strong female odour; he still heard the rustling of the woman's dress and sensed the incredibly strong waves of sensuality emanating from her. Finally, after what seemed to be an eternity, he heard the curtain move and the woman was gone, but her body odour still lingered. John sat there thoroughly shaken, in a state of strong emotion.

Moments later an assistant dressmaker entered with a tape measure. 'I've come to take your measures, Sir!' He spoke with a forced but polite joviality. 'We will first do the trousers, Sir. Will you stand up, please, so that I can measure the inside of the leg?'

No, no! thought John. *Not the inside of the leg!* He still had not been able to get his emotions under control, and it showed. As he stood up hesitantly, the front part of his boxer shorts bulged conspicuously and embarrassingly.

The assistant took one look at it and recoiled, startled. 'Sir,' he exclaimed, 'please! Don't! I'm a man. Please. You mustn't! Please. This will cause great scandal. I will lose my job! Please, Sir, I have five children to feed.'

Christ, thought John. *Why, oh why does this have to happen to me?* He sat down again and groaned, covering his face with his hands.

'You not upset, Sir? I'm sorry, Sir,' he heard the assistant say. 'I'm only poor man.'

The plaintive protests of the assistant seemed to have broken the spell the woman had cast over John. As her image receded, he felt everything returning to normal, and he stood up saying, 'Come on, measure,' with a still somewhat shaky voice.

When John was about to leave the shop, Shillingi Mingi suddenly reappeared from nowhere, a big smile pasted on his round face. 'I trust that you have been pleased with what we offer, Sir,' he said while he opened the front door.

John didn't answer but just stood there like someone who had seen an apparition. The shop owner stared at him, visibly worried, and asked with disbelief: 'You didn't like what you saw, Sir?' As there was no reply, his smile disappeared, his face took on a painful expression and he spoke with concern: 'You have not seen enough? You like to see more?'

John was about to make a comment, but he abstained and just replied: 'No, thank you. I think I've seen plenty.' Then, as he crossed the threshold, he couldn't help adding: 'I do want to tell you, though, that this is the most incredible shop I've ever been to.' His remark left the owner completely gratified and smiling with satisfaction.

36

John breathed a sigh of relief when he opened the door of the waiting car and sat down. He had escaped: the woman had gone and nothing had happened! But his self-confidence was shattered. He was conscious that there was a lot he hadn't yet understood about Africa. Was there a missing dimension in his perception? Or several missing dimensions? Maybe he didn't know anything about Africa, not even where to begin? He was in a pensive mood while Kibu drove him home, and remained silent all the way.

When he got back to Sam's house his feelings were at low ebb and Sam noticed it.

'What's wrong?' he asked. 'Didn't you find the clothes you wanted?'

'No ... that's not it. You see, I've had a terrible shock. I don't know why but I just seem to get into the most improbable situations. This has happened all my life, but this morning I felt so certain that nothing could possibly go wrong. And there it was again, and worse this time.'

'I don't know what you're talking about.'

'Tell me,' said John as if thinking aloud, 'have you ever made love to an African woman?'

'My God! Is that what you've done? I can't believe it! I let you out of sight a minute and there you go, getting mixed up with African women this time! You're not to be trusted! I think you should not be let out unless you're on a leash with a dog collar around your neck!'

'Take it easy, man!' barked John. 'Don't jump to conclusions before you know what it's all about!'

'Then tell me what it's all about!' retorted Sam impetuously.

'It happened through no fault of mine, I assure you. It occurred all by itself. It's always like that. Before I have time to shut my eyes and open them again, it goes bang! And it's happened.'

'It goes as quickly as that!' exclaimed Klaus who seemed visibly impressed. 'Man! We must write to the *Guinness Book of Records*.'

John flared up. 'Klaus, you're an ass! Can't you let me finish what I'm saying? You are muddling me all up. How far have I got?'

'You got to where you went: Bang!' replied Klaus, offended.

'No, no! I went into Shillingi Mingi's shop and retreated into a sort of cubbyhole at the back, and as I sat there undressed, an African woman joined me. No, I forget. First I was hit by another African woman. She hit me with a naked breast ... it was painful, I can tell you,' he said rubbing his face. 'She had huge breasts! And then this other young woman undressed right in front of me. Would you believe that?'

Sam put his forefinger against his temple and raised his eyebrows as he looked at Klaus. 'And all this happened in a cubbyhole?'

'Yeah, in front of the mirror. She had a most beautiful body. No, beautiful doesn't cover it. It was feline, sensual, incredible! I've never seen anything like it.'

'Good heavens! You pretend to be in love with Veronica, I send you out to get a set of expensive clothes and there you are, having sex with an African woman in a cubbyhole!'

'I didn't have sex!' protested John vehemently. 'I shut my eyes not to see anything!'

'I must confess that I can make neither head nor tail out of your story,' said Sam, visibly annoyed.

'Oh! Drop it. I want to forget it anyway. It's just that it came upon me so unexpectedly.'

'So where do we stand? You still love Veronica?'

'Of course I love Veronica! Why do you ask?'

'Because you're confusing me completely!' Sam held his head between his hands. 'I really wonder sometimes. So are you getting a new outfit or not?'

'Yes, all the measurements have been taken and everything will be ready tomorrow afternoon. I must admit that Shillingi Mingi is the top for service. Although the goings-on in his shop are somewhat unusual, as I told him.'

'Somewhat unusual,' mimicked Klaus, rubbing his face. 'I dare say! Women hitting you with breasts! And...'

'Stop it, Klaus!' interrupted Sam. 'Let's not go into that again. Right then, John! The day after tomorrow you leave for Elephant Camp first thing in the morning. And you take my big car. I want you to really impress Veronica.'

'That's very generous of you, Sam. Most generous!' exclaimed John as he turned and went up to his room.

'Why do you send him off to Veronica?' asked Klaus in disbelief when John had gone. 'This I find really incredible. I thought you wanted him for the experiment? I work for three weeks on John, set up everything, and just when I'm ready you send him away to that girl. You astound me!'

'Trust me,' countered Sam. 'I have my ways. I'm like the Lord.'

'How do you mean?'

'My ways are like the Lord's. They are inscrutable. But they lead to our goal, believe me. So you are ready?'

'Yes, in a day or two if you like.'

'That's what I call perfect timing.'

37

Two days later John got up at the crack of dawn and after a quick breakfast he set off in Sam's car. As he sped north towards Elephant Camp he began to feel ever more confident. The previous times he had driven an old, small car, feeling every bump in the dirt road, and having to pull on the wheel constantly to avoid the deep ruts. This time he was steering a powerful, comfortable four-wheel drive vehicle and it made an enormous difference: he advanced smoothly, effortlessly, and his spirits soared.

He had felt rather low the last two days. Had the African woman bewitched him? Although his scientific mind refused to consider such a possibility, they said that witchcraft was alive and well in Africa. Anyway, it was certain that many and, maybe, most Africans believed firmly in witches and all their dark doings.

The night after his visit to Shillingi Mingi he had hardly been able to sleep, and when he had dozed off he had had the wildest dreams of Africans hitting tom-toms in the depth of the forest, and of naked women dancing around a fire. He himself was tied to a tree while one after the other the women danced towards him, rubbing their oiled bodies over his with sensual movements. He had woken up with a start, wet with perspiration and out of breath, and had hardly dared go to sleep again because he knew that he was going to be sacrificed after being raped by all the women.

He had felt weak and exhausted the next morning, and even when his new outfit had arrived and he had looked at himself in the mirror, he had not been able to regain the confidence with which he had set out the morning he had gone to Shillingi Mingi.

But today was different. He had slept like a log and the spell seemed to have receded. John felt that everything would be all right from now on. Sam had briefed him. 'Forget witchcraft,'

150

he had said. 'It doesn't exist. Be a man. Just go ahead and impress Veronica.' And he was right, yes. He was going to impress Veronica. The car was magnificent, big and shiny. And he himself! He cut a stunning figure in his safari outfit, his new shining shoes and broad-rimmed hat. Sam had shown him how to walk: like the real adventurer, the man who comes to conquer.

As he manoeuvred the car along the dusty track, he mused about Veronica and how smoothly everything would go. She would be lonely, thinking of him. He could see the pleasant surprise in her eyes at his turning up unexpectedly. He would look his very best. They said that nothing impresses a girl so much as a well-dressed, clean man, and he was going to be that man. He would be very amiable, of course, and even appear to be interested in elephants, but he would be in command, most definitely. This time he was not going to be meek and mild and accept everything. He would be firm and tell Veronica to remove that terrible nuisance, that Dumbo; maybe they could put him in a zoo or somewhere far away. Then, when Veronica had been listening to him for a while, impressed by his manly presence, he would suddenly take her hand and tell her that he loved her. And she would put a hand in front of her mouth, overcome by emotion, look up at him and whisper: 'Oh yes, I'm yours.'

38

Veronica had got up early that morning, had taken Dumbo out of his shed, organized the work for the day, and then sat at the table on the veranda where Faithful had laid breakfast for her. She had plenty to do, yet when she went up to her room to dress properly, she sat down on the bed and remained there in a pensive mood. She had been thinking a lot in the last few days, in fact since Sam's visit. Why had he come? Sam was not the kind of man who would waste his time on an impromptu visit. The more she thought about it, the stranger it seemed. But she did know that something had changed since that visit. Sam's words had turned her against John. Her feelings had been unable to resist the poison that had been injected into her mind.

Yet, deep down she was unwilling to believe that John had just been lying and bragging. He was not like that. His mind was not tortuous and deceiving. He was too innocent for that! And he was fun. He may have had many adventures – *that*, yes: he had the reputation of being a woman's man. But that made him all the more interesting to her. It was a challenge. It just showed that so far he hadn't met the woman he was destined for. She was sure that things would be different with her, that she would be able to change him and keep him from straying.

As she was staring out of the window, not knowing what to think, an image flashed onto her mind: she remembered the expression of displeasure that had clouded Sam's face for a short unguarded moment because she had opposed him. Suddenly she understood the reason for Sam's visit. He wanted John for his experiment. He wanted him to end up on Klaus' time machine, not in her arms! *That must be it*, Veronica thought. *That would explain it all!*

Sam had noticed John's affection for her and, if it were answered, John would certainly not be willing to risk his life having his brain twisted out of him. Sam had not counted on

John being attracted to her, and on the possibility that she might respond. Their mutual attraction had become an unexpected obstacle, a spanner in the works. Sam's visit had not been casual! He had planned it all carefully. How diabolical that fellow was! The only thing that counted for him was his experiment. The fact that John risked his life wasn't of the slightest concern to him. He was to be led to the altar to be slaughtered, like a sheep trusting his butcher. Veronica was shocked at her discovery. She must warn John!

Just then a big shiny red car stopped outside the compound that surrounded the wooden two-storey house. The driver got out, straightened the creases of his trousers, adjusted his shirt collar and safari hat, and started walking towards the house like someone who wants to show the world that 'here he comes'. One casual glance through the window was sufficient for Veronica to make up her mind. *Look at that strutting peacock*, she thought. *Just look at his clothes! And his stupid car! He thinks he is going to impress me. That is clearly someone I don't want to see.* And she turned away and deliberately stayed inside.

John was now close to the house. There didn't seem to be anyone around but he hesitated. He remembered treacherous Dumbo who was in the habit of sneaking up behind innocent visitors to scare them out of their wits with his loud trumpet calls, and glanced around quickly. This time he wasn't going to let himself be caught unawares: he came prepared. No hidden dangers would catch him this time. Not him.

As he looked around left and right, scanning for the Dumbo menace and advancing slowly, his foot suddenly got hooked behind a wire, and before he could utter a single word a load of brown, smelly stuff emptied over his head.

He swore aloud, and as he rubbed the sticky stuff out of his eyes, Veronica's pretty tanned face appeared in the upstairs window.

'Hey, what's happening?' she shouted to the mass of brown muck below. 'Who are you? And what do you want?'

John had been prepared to be as sweet as he possibly could, but no man likes this kind of reception. He surveyed his expensive new clothes, all splattered, the stinking sticky stuff running over his shirt and trousers and staining them a foul brown.

He exploded: 'What do you think you're doing! Are you mad?'

'Oh it's you, John,' Veronica's voice came soothingly from above, 'I didn't recognize you.'

'Of course you didn't recognize me! How could you recognize me if you first dump dirt all over me!'

Veronica suddenly giggled. 'You look positively filthy.'

'What the hell is this stuff you dumped over me?'

'Oh that. It's nothing. It's not as bad as it looks.'

'It stinks!' exclaimed John in disgust. 'What is it?'

'Oh, it's a mixture of all sorts of leftovers we could find, some excrement too, but mostly fresh elephant dung.'

'Isn't it wonderful', said John in a theatrical voice, 'to know that one is going to be received with all due regard to rank and position? This is sure to set new standards in the matter of welcoming visitors. I can see a new style taking off right here! This beats cream tarts by a long way. Now there's a new line of business for you. You'll get rich by exporting elephant dung. This latest fashion will take off like wildfire the world over, especially in America and the UK where they want to receive people in style and are always on the lookout for something new to impress their neighbours.'

'Don't be silly,' replied Veronica. 'This is my new alarm system. It's made to scare away unwanted intruders. You know you set it off yourself? You must have hooked your foot behind the tripwire. The wire is linked via pulleys to a big bucket hanging overhead that has just emptied its contents on you. Clever, isn't it? I thought it out all by myself.'

John remained speechless. He just stood there gaping at her.

Veronica giggled again. 'I'm afraid I can't let you come in. You look too filthy.'

'How clever women can get if they really set themselves to it,' sneered John, really upset now. 'You'd better patent your system. The world is full of idiots. Who knows, you might find plenty of followers.'

'You're getting very personal, John Garfinger. Watch your words.'

John fumed by now. 'You're getting very personal,' he imitated in a high-pitched voice. 'How can you not get personal after this? You arrive all nicely dressed in new clothes and before you can do so much as say "Hello" a scatterbrained female transforms you into a pile of elephant dung. Of course, I forgot that you are besotted with elephants. Maybe you find their dung attractive.'

The successful effect of her alarm system upon John had made Veronica forget that this was the man who had come strutting inside the compound in new clothes; and that John also had a new car. His unpleasant reaction suddenly brought her back to reality. So Sam had been right after all. He had told her that he would turn up to visit her in a new outfit. And there he was!

Veronica now stiffened. 'Oh, that's how you take it?' she replied in a cold, haughty voice. 'I thought you were above such little upsets. You, the great philosopher! Pfff ... maybe you only pretended to be one. Maybe you do nothing but pretend. If you ask me for my opinion, you've had it too easy. It's about time you learned that you don't always get what you want.'

'I'm not asking you for your opinion!' retorted John. 'And what do you mean by: I've had it too easy?'

Veronica didn't answer his question. Instead, she replied: 'You'd better wash. I'll come down.' Her voice seemed distant, impersonal now.

There was a clatter of steps on the wooden outside stairs, and then she motioned him to follow her. Around the corner a typical African contraption stuck out from the wall: an iron pipe with a showerhead attached at the far end. The other end ran up the wall to a huge open tank on top of the roof. Water was pumped manually into the tank every morning, and by the afternoon the sun had heated it sufficiently to provide a hot shower.

'Here's your shower, and here's some brown soap,' she said as if speaking to a stranger. 'You'd better strip. I'll call the servant to take your clothes and wash them.'

'Strip?' John suddenly looked very hesitant. 'Here in the open? In front of you?'

This was not what he had imagined. He had gone through several possible scenarios. In all of them he had appeared in his beautiful new clothes, and in all of them Veronica had been duly impressed by his good looks and impeccable appearance. In some of these scenarios she had, for a while, tried to hide being impressed, but in the end her admiration had shown through. In others he had been the irresistible conqueror from the start. But in none of these scenarios had he ever considered the possibility of standing in filthy clothes and having to strip outside in front of Veronica's eyes. The indignity of it all was almost too much.

A spark of disdain now showed in Veronica's eyes. 'Are you shy or what? This is certainly not the first time you've stripped in front of a woman, is it? A great womanizer like you must have been seen naked by dozens of silly, worthless women. Or maybe,' she added, 'you have something special to hide? A deformity?'

John was now deeply stung. Through clenched teeth he hissed, 'Please yourself,' and switched on the shower as he began undoing his shirt, then his shoes, his trousers, and finally his boxer shorts.

It was still early in the day and the water was bitterly cold. As he stood there under the shower, slightly bent and shivering, trying to hide his private parts with both his hands from Veronica's critical look, a loud hooting became audible and a big, gaudy safari-tour vehicle turned up, music blaring from the cabin. Out jumped Ron, impeccably dressed in white flannels, teeth flashing as he saw Veronica. He moved forward and then he noticed John, the brown dung running in rivulets off his naked body, his dirty clothes lying in a heap on the grass.

'What's that?' motioned Ron, his thumb pointing at the naked man who tried to turn away.'

'That's John Garfinger,' replied Veronica in a malicious voice. 'He came to visit me but he was too dirty to be let into the house. I told him to shower first.'

'That man needs to learn good manners,' commented Ron. 'One doesn't visit a nice lady like you unless one is impeccably dressed.' And with a gesture that left no doubt as to whom he thought the example of the perfectly turned-out man, he put his hand ostentatiously on his chest and patted it. He stood full in the sun, the light reflecting on two big signet rings on his hand and on his shining teeth.

I hate him, hate him! thought John. *I wish he would sink into a deep hole with his flashy teeth, his safari bus and his affable manners.*

Veronica, on the contrary, seemed to enjoy the latest development. 'Quite right, Ron!' she said, making sure that John

156

could hear her. 'But the worst is that some men are like butterflies, flitting from one pretty flower to the next. There're not serious and never will be. They just brag and lie. But the saddest thing, maybe, is that, however much you exert yourself to make them love elephants, it's no good. They never will. Just look at this one,' she added, pointing at John.

'Oh, let's not talk about him,' interrupted Ron impatiently. 'Vee, I want to discuss some business matters with you. Shall we go for a ride?' And moving aside with an exaggerated gesture, his arm stretched out, he bent down and invited her to step into the open-roofed safari bus.

Veronica jumped inside, shouting: 'Let's go!'

Ron got behind the wheel, turned the vehicle around and off they went in a cloud of dust, leaving John alone under his shower.

He stood there for a while, eyeing the disappearing bus, the cloud of dust, and the umbrella-shaped thorn trees silhouetted against a hazy-blue sky. A bird made a shrill, regular sound, accentuating the silence and his feeling of being left behind. A heavy black cloud seemed to have settled over his brain. He was unable to think, his lower jaw had dropped and the water was running down into his mouth.

The cold water finally brought him to his senses. He began collecting his clothes, rinsed them as best he could, put them on wet, and wandered back to his car in a daze. By the time he reached it his blood was throbbing in his ears. Images of him under the shower, of Veronica ridiculing him in front of that hateful blown-up frog, kept returning to his mind and made his cheeks burn. 'Oh, the indignity of it all!' John exclaimed to himself. 'This is the limit!'

Little do we, mere mortals, know that the limit is much further than we can possibly imagine. John took the car keys out of his pocket and unlocked and opened the door. The car had stood in the full sun, it felt stifling inside, and John decided that it was better to turn the driver's window down before getting in. He was standing between the open door and the car, busy turning the handle while holding his keys in the other hand, when suddenly a loud blast close behind scared the wits out of him and made him throw his arms up in the air. Before he was able to turn around he was bashed in his lower back and pressed hard against the car door, which emitted a plaintive cracking sound.

As he hung on the door in an awkward position he saw Dumbo from the corner of his eye. Elephants do not smile, but John could have sworn that Dumbo had a mischievous smirk on his face. *Of all the rotten dirty tricks!* he thought. He would gladly have administered a series of firm kicks to the little animal's butt, for this time and for all the previous times when Veronica's presence had prevented him from giving full vent to his feelings, but he was hanging limply on the open door, gasping for breath, and seemed unable to move. After one more look at the victim of his pranks – a look of satisfaction, John was certain of it – Dumbo turned and walked away.

There he goes, the miserable little horror, thought John. *Just look at him. I hate this Dumbo! I hate elephants! I never want to come near an elephant again in my life. Or even see one. Ever! That's it for me. On the road from here to death a lot will happen, I will see many things, but I want to make sure that there's not a single elephant amongst them. No more elephants for me. I'm through with these horrible, treacherous animals. Veronica can have them all. And to hell with her too!*

John now straightened his back. His ribs were terribly sore and he found breathing difficult. Any movement was painful, but he didn't seem to have broken anything. He next tried to move the door, but it hung down slightly and no longer shut properly. *Damn, damn!* John swore internally. *Sam isn't going to be pleased when he sees the state of this door. Let's get out of here before anything else happens.*

As he climbed in he realized that the car keys were not in the ignition. Where the hell were they? Suddenly he remembered. They had been in his hand when he flung his arms up in the air. He got out again and stared along the track but couldn't see anything. Then he looked at the scattered thorn trees and dense prickly bush lining the track. They could be anywhere in there. 'Oh God!' he exclaimed. 'This really is the limit.'

He went down on all fours and started exploring the bush. It was terribly prickly stuff. Every branch, however small, seemed to be covered in thorns, and the thicker the branches, the longer and harder the thorns were. After some ten minutes of exploring the patch nearest to the car he was already covered in scratches but still hadn't found the keys. He dared not think what would remain of his clothes. He now ventured inside the denser undergrowth, crawling along, sticking an arm forward and feeling around as far as he could. Suddenly an agonizing pain shot through his hand and, as he quickly withdrew it, the air was filled with the buzzing of angry bees.

African bees are not to be messed about with, and John tore himself away from the nest into which he had so carelessly stuck his hand and made a dash for the car. As he charged through the bush, his foot got stuck between two protruding roots, his shoe was torn off, and he fell flat on his face. But he had no time to loiter. He crawled up again, shot out of the bush like a cannon ball, dived into the car and pulled the door behind him as best as he could. He started cranking up the open window, but before he had time to shut it properly dozens of bees had got in and were going for him.

As he tried to ward them off, his arms flailing wildly, he hit the rear-view mirror which came down with a crash. The bees now went for his face, and he started slapping himself trying to kill them as they landed on him. When the last intruder had been eliminated he sat still, gasping for breath.

His twisted ankle throbbed painfully, his scratches bled and hurt, his clothes were in tatters and one of his shoes was somewhere in the bush, guarded by mad African bees. He had to pull the door towards him to prevent it from opening and letting in more bees, which were still swarming angrily around the car. He was stuck inside, it was stiflingly hot, and he had no keys.

While he sat there holding on to the door, thirsty, sweating profusely and numb with pain, waiting for the bees to quieten down and fly off, his face started to swell. He began to search for the rear-view mirror to look at his face, but it lay broken on the floor amongst scattered dead bees. Even without seeing his face, he felt that it would not be a pretty sight. And it was rapidly getting worse. By the time the last bee had flown back to its nest, the area around his right eye had already swollen so much that the eye had disappeared, and his left cheek felt like a balloon that had been inflated to grotesque proportions. This was no longer a human face; not even a distorted caricature of a face; this was the stuff nightmares were made of.

The sun was now much higher in the sky, and as it moved

overhead, something began to sparkle not far from John's single open eye: the car keys! They were stuck between the windshield and the bonnet. How had he not seen them before? He looked carefully: there was not a single bee in sight. He turned around as much as his swollen head permitted, just to make sure: no Dumbo either.

Then, with a quick movement, he opened the door, leaned over the windshield, grabbed the keys, disappeared inside shutting the door as tightly as possible, started up, threw the clutch into first gear and was off with a jerk.

39

Ron had barely left the camp when he brought up the subject of the French businessman.

'Great news!' he burst out, bestowing a flashy smile on Veronica. 'Le Tellier has decided to come to Elephant Camp and visit you. But remember what I told you: he's very important and wants a clear answer. Have you made up your mind yet?' As she didn't answer, Ron kept pressing her: 'You must accept, Vee! You can't refuse such an offer.'

Soon the atmosphere became strained, and Veronica longed to be away from Ron's overbearing presence. After a mile she'd had enough and told him that she wanted to get out. He dropped her in a huff, revved up and rushed off, leaving an angry cloud of dust behind.

Veronica breathed a sigh of relief. She sat for some time on a boulder, then got up and turned towards the savannah. A stroll through the open grassland always had a soothing effect on her and, as she walked along, she calmed down. After a while her thoughts turned to John, and she began to feel uneasy: maybe she had gone too far. But then, it wasn't her fault that he had set off the booby trap. Suddenly she boiled over. The liar! The womanizer! It served him right! Coming here in new clothes and his big car to impress her! Going to add her to his list of conquests! Today he had been taught a lesson that he would not easily forget. He had got what he deserved and would probably have returned to Naboru by now.

When she turned the last bend of the narrow path along which she had walked and joined the track not far from the camp, she noticed the parked red car. *Isn't that the car John came in?* she thought. *But where is he himself?*

Just at that moment some indescribable being with a grotesque face and clothes hanging around him like torn rags popped out like a Jack-in-the-box, grabbled wildly about him, disappeared inside again, started up and veered around. As she stepped

161

aside into the bush to let the car pass, she got a glimpse of the driver. *That must be John,* she thought, but she did not recognize him. His face was monstrously deformed and there seemed to be a demoniacal light in his one open eye as he whizzed by, clinging with one hand to the steering wheel. Mad! He looked absolutely and totally mad! She couldn't understand how this could have happened and felt greatly disturbed. Was this reality or an illusion?

Somehow she was not certain that everything was what it seemed. Suddenly she thought: *It's not the first time I've got it all wrong. I should at least have given him a chance to explain himself. But I'll probably never see him again. After what's happened he is unlikely to ever come back.* And somehow she felt very sad.

40

As the car rattled over the track, John began to feel sick with pain. His sprained ankle had swollen dangerously by now, and he could hardly keep it on the accelerator. The door jolted open with every bump, and he nearly crashed into a tree a couple of times as he was no longer able to judge perspective and distance with his single open eye. After a while he had to stop, and he lay down on the seat as best he could. The bee poison in his blood was doing its job and suddenly it came to him: *I'm going to die of blood poisoning here in the middle of the bush. What a tragic end to my life! What an early exit, long before I have had the pleasure of getting older surrounded by loved ones and been able to enjoy the peace of old age.*

But then, again, he felt that an early exit was maybe all for the best. What good had been the thirty-nine years he had spent in this world? *Look at the mess I've got myself into*, he thought. *And I managed to do it all on my own without anyone's help.* His poor parents had been so proud of him and his brilliant achievements. But look at his ruined career: the efforts of years of study gone to nothing and his intelligence squandered! And his disastrous marriage followed by a few extramarital affairs without a spark of love, just quickly consumed sexual attraction. The emptiness of it all!

And now, stranded here in Africa without so much as a cent and no prospects beyond the next day. So far he had survived on the support of Sam who had lent him money and supplied all his needs generously. But surely, there had to be an end to that. How was he going to explain to Sam that he would be unable to pay back the money he had lent him for his new clothes; that the new clothes in which he had set out so proudly this morning were now mere shreds; that the door of his posh new car no longer shut properly and the rear-view mirror was lying on the floor. He looked at the broken mirror. *This is the image of my life*, he thought. *This is my life lying there on the floor, smashed to pieces.*

He shook his head. It felt painful. *I don't know where to go from here*, he told himself. *This time I really have come to the end of my tether.* Thoughts continued racing wildly through his swollen head: *I seem to make a mess out of everything. I'm not fit for this sort of life. It's too uncertain. I want to quit. To get out of it now!*

Then he had a sudden inspiration. If he survived the poison and managed to reach Naboru, he would propose to be the human guinea pig Sam wanted for the time-machine experiment. If he had to die, he might as well die in the service of science. Yes, that was a good idea. It gave him courage. He had a mission to fulfil. He could not let himself die here in the bush. He had to make it back to Naboru and to Klaus' time machine. He forced himself to sit upright, let the clutch into first gear and slowly, very slowly, touching the accelerator as little as possible, he started the grinding return journey over the dirt road.

Night had fallen by the time the bright city lights announced that the end of his long quest was near. Driving in the now dense traffic was painful, but his blood felt less poisoned. His spirits had just begun to lift when the car engine appeared to have hiccups and suddenly stopped. He had run out of petrol! Fortunately, the car had come to a standstill against the edge of the sidewalk and he was no more than a few hundred yards away from Sam's property. He got out with difficulty and started hopping on one leg while the other shoeless foot swung limply along. As he hopped by, the Africans made way for him. There are many poor people in rags in African cities, but rarely do they appear so down and out as John looked now. And they were, almost invariably, black, whilst this was a white man. After what seemed an eternity John reached Sam's house, rang the bell, and collapsed in a heap against the big iron gate.

41

'How far back can you send the contents of his brain?' asked Sam, pointing at John who was lying on the table of the time machine, probes on his head from which a jumble of wires led to Klaus' control unit.

'Three million years at most. It's the furthest I can go with this version of the time machine. But I have all the calculations now. And the experience. If you give me a few months I can build you a machine that may be able to go back to the time of the dinosaurs. Just imagine! Don't you think that it would be nice to send John's brain back to the dinosaurs?' Klaus smiled encouragingly at Sam, his round spectacles shaking on his nose.

'I'm not interested in dinosaurs!'

'Oh. I just thought that maybe...'

'Let's stick to what we set out to do, shall we?' said Sam in a commandeering voice that didn't tolerate any opposition. 'Three million years is plenty. In fact, *Homo habilis* only appeared about two and a half million years ago. Can you set it for that time?'

'I have done so, *mein Freund*, I have done so,' replied Klaus rather coldly. 'Remember, you asked me to.'

'Ah, yes. Good! What's the search radius again?'

'With that time displacement goes a maximum range of about five hundred miles. The machine will search within that radius for a suitable receptacle in which to dump John's brain's contents. And once it's found one, whizz...'

'OK, are we ready for the great moment then?'

'Are you ready, John?' asked Klaus.

John was lying immobile now, holding his breath, and emitted a faint groan that Klaus took for a 'yes'.

'Here we go then,' said Klaus and pressed the handle.

Suddenly, in rapid succession, John saw images of the past weeks, of last year. In a flash he glimpsed his wife's face as

165

they stood before the altar; then came more and more images, ever more rapidly. He was at university now, then at school, then a boy. He saw the moment when he had nearly cut off his thumb playing with the bread knife when he had been left alone in the house; he suddenly felt the pain and saw the blood ... The memories were being sucked out of his head, he felt it emptying, he was going, his mind was leaving him, no! His body shuddered and he lost consciousness.

PART TWO

1

When John regained consciousness and opened his eyes he was in for a nasty surprise: he was surrounded by elephants! He quickly closed his eyes hoping the nightmare would go away, but when he opened them again, very slowly, those ghastly animals were still there. Then he noticed that a big trunk was sticking out right in front of him where his nose was supposed to have been. He turned his head swiftly to look at his own body and just couldn't believe what he saw: he was an elephant!

Of all the lowly, dirty tricks played on me this is the worst! he raged. *Klaus! You miserable, sneaky, lying worm. If ever I get out of here I'll kick your ass all the way back to Germany and boot you up a tree in your Black Forest where you can sit with the other stupid owls! You, the greatest physicist on Earth! Prattling about relativity and space–time transformations! Your so-called time machine! And all you've been able to do is put my brain into one of the elephants in Veronica's reserve. I wouldn't be surprised if she suddenly arrived in her Land Rover. I can already see her look at me with those silly big eyes of hers. With tenderness because I'm an elephant! There really is a John the elephant now. It's sickening. This tops it all!*

Suddenly he heard a sound behind him and, as he turned round, he saw that it wasn't Veronica's jeep that had arrived but a huge bull elephant. It seemed extremely agitated as it came rushing towards the herd. Then John noticed something else and became alarmed: *Look at that enormous thing dangling underneath him! It's repulsive. Males shouldn't walk around with a thing like that hanging about. They should keep it tucked inside their trousers!*

The bull made directly for John and, as the latter realized its intentions he turned, ready to flee, but he ran straight into a clump of trees. His head got stuck between two close trunks and his back part was exposed to the raging bull which had come up just behind him. The bull's trunk now began exploring John's hither parts, touching and sniffing them, and as it did

169

so it got more and more excited. Suddenly it lifted itself up on its hind legs and put its front legs on John's back.

Hey! John wanted to shout, *I'm a man. You can't do this to me! You can't stick that big thing of yours inside me. It's disgusting! I don't want it. Stop it!* but he could no longer speak or shout. Then, as the big thing was shoved inside him, he realized that the bull had made no mistake. He was not just an elephant. He was a female elephant!

He wriggled and pushed to get the male off his back but he was pinned between the trees and the male's body, and all he managed to do was emit a weak protesting trumpet sound. This was dreadful! Why didn't anyone intervene to stop this hideous aggression? Where were the other females? He glanced around as far as his head could move and saw that the other females were just standing close by, looking on with interest. *Don't just stand there!* he tried to shout. *Do something! I'm being raped. Raped! Do you hear me?* But none of the other elephants came forward to help him and he had to resign himself to his fate. He was powerless to do anything and felt waves of despair going through his mind. The bull was now shaking above him, nearly breaking John's spine. He finally discharged his liquid load while trumpeting loudly, got off John's back, turned and walked slowly away.

There he goes, the rapist, John thought with anger after he had extricated himself from the trees. *Just look at him. Look how he swaggers! He's proud of his foul deed, the repulsive fellow! The big macho! I wish a poacher would come along and shoot him. That would serve him right. Or he ought to be locked up for a lifetime behind bars in a zoo with females all around in another cage just out of reach, enticing him till he rages with frustration.*

Then he looked at the female elephants which were clustered near him. *Those females,* he thought with resentment, *they're just as bad as the males, or maybe even worse.* One would expect the worst from brutal males who have nothing but sex on their minds, but one would have imagined that there would at least have been some group solidarity amongst the female gender. Forget it! All they did was to look on and get a kick out of the scene. John wanted to hit them. *They ought to be punished for non-assistance to a person in distress,* he fumed. *Peeping Toms at least hide their degenerate behaviour, but these females don't even try to hide their perverse nature. They practise voyeurism openly. It's a group activity with them! I'm sure they would be commenting on the juicier bits of the action if they were able to talk.*

John had always believed that having sex was a private activity, only done between two people who had agreed to enjoy it. And there he was, having been forced to undergo it before a crowd of onlookers. He felt ashamed, humiliated. The elephant world was a world of vice. *Damned Klaus!* he grumbled to himself. *You might at least have put me inside a lion but no, of all animals you had to choose an elephant. I just can't stand elephants! I loathe them intensely. How Veronica can like those brutes is beyond me.*

2

The herd now started to move, baby elephants almost glued to their mothers, and John found himself pushed along with the other females. They were so close together that John had his trunk, that long outgrowth of the elephant's nose and upper lip that also serves as a sensitive smell organ, nearly stuck in the backside of a female in front of him. The aroma was far from pleasant.

He had always been such a clean fellow, intolerant of body smells, using deodorants and essential oils in profusion. *And now this!* he thought. *I have to walk with my nose nearly stuck in the arse of a smelly female. This is just as bad as having a pile of Dumbo's dung dumped over you. Revolting elephants! And the insects that go with it!* There was a buzzing as of a million flying horrors, whole clouds of them.

Suddenly the big belly of the elephant in front of him produced rumbling sounds and John received the full blast of fermented gas straight in the face. *Pfooh*, he went, trying to get away from the cloud of stinking gas that enveloped him. *This is truly awful. It's disgusting!* And he cursed Klaus again wholeheartedly for having put him in such a position.

I must get out of here, he decided. *The sooner, the better.* And he started moving away from the centre of the herd, bumping now into this female, then into that one, and nearly treading on a couple of babies. He finally made it to the edge and was about to trail behind when he felt a strange presence opposing him. At first he couldn't understand what was happening. It was as if an invisible string was pulling him back towards the herd, and the more he struggled to get out, the stronger the opposing power became.

Then he felt something even stranger: a hostile force was trying hard to push him out of the elephant. Suddenly he realized that he was not alone inside the elephant's brain. Of course! Before Klaus had projected him inside this new receptacle,

172

the brain had been home to the elephant's personality, its feelings and memory. The shock of the arrival of the concentrated package of human memory and knowledge that represented John had pushed the elephant's mind to the fringes of the brain. Now it struck back in full force, attempting to regain control over the huge lump of bones and muscles whose brain housed both a female elephant and John.

This cannot be true, thought John. *Klaus! Damned asshole that you are! You nitwit! You second-rate screwball scientist! The lousy trick you played on me sticking me into an elephant. And as if that weren't bad enough, I'm schizophrenic. I've got two personalities: half of me is male whilst the other half is female!*

While John was thinking his thoughts and battling the female inside the brain, he felt a brusque push in his rear. He swung around, upset at such rudeness, and found that he was facing the matriarch, the leading elephant of the herd. She was the one who had stood close by while he was being raped, and John remembered that she had even encouraged the bull during his dirty deed instead of protecting the females in her charge as should have been her duty. He felt enraged when he thought again of the humiliating scene that had happened so recently and was about to pay the matriarch back for her despicable attitude by giving her a good kick; then he noticed that she was much bigger and stronger than the elephant in which he was stuck, and wisely abstained.

Unaware of the upsets she was causing, the matriarch kept nudging John along, and everyone now got going at a good elephant's speed. *So that's it*, John mused. *Walking at a brisk pace all together! Just like in primary school. Or like boy scouts; or rather girl scouts in this case. I'm not going to take this! What about my personality? Freedom of choice and movement and all that, guaranteed by the Constitution! I'm not going to let a bunch of tyrannical females boss me about. I'm a man and an independent individual and I can go as and where I please.*

But the matriarch kept an eye on him and the elephant inside pulled the body along with the rest of the herd, however much John wanted to step out of line. After a while he gave up struggling and went along with the others. *We'll see*, he thought. *I'll manage to escape later when they have their attention turned elsewhere. Or maybe at night.*

173

Suddenly he remembered George the dead elephant, and the poachers. He'd forgotten all about them. *God*, he thought, *if I stumble upon poachers they'll kill me! I'll end up as a dead carcass eaten by lions, hyenas and vultures.* A feeling of despair now took hold of him. *Please, Klaus*, he prayed. *Please, please, call me back. Get me out of this elephant! I want to be a human again. Please, make me human and I promise that I will never ever be displeased again with my fate. I will be the most contented, easygoing man on Earth – or woman. Whichever. Just as you wish*, he added, *but a human.*

He waited for a miracle, but nothing happened. He seemed well and truly stuck inside this new body. He was an elephant now, and that elephant kept following the herd to which it belonged ever further into the open savannah.

3

'It's all very well letting non-governmental organizations run projects, Minister, but don't you think that they are trying to punch above their weight?' Jacques Le Tellier stopped a second or two, looking the Minister straight in the eyes. 'What I mean is: these people talk a lot, argue, impose rules and restrictions, but what do they bring to the government? To your country?'

Mamabeka, Minister of Home Affairs, reflected for a while. He was a large, thickset man with greying hair who had temporarily taken over the Wildlife Department after Kimbabe had fallen out with the government. Finally he replied: 'Isn't it important that we collaborate with international organizations? That we all work together for the common goal? Doesn't this bring international publicity and create a lot of goodwill abroad for my country?'

'That all sounds very fine, Minister, but at the end of the day, when you do your sums as every government department has to, does it add up to anything? I mean: where's the business aspect? Where's the money? You need money to run everything, don't you? You need money to live. What I want to draw your attention to is this: does it pay?'

'But what about the satisfaction that doing something for the environment brings? Isn't conservation an aim in itself?'

'Minister...' Le Tellier shook his head disapprovingly. 'While I admire your high ideals, I cannot at the same time fail to be worried by the total refusal of these non-governmental organizations to consider the wider implications of their attitude. How can one conserve anything when there's no money? A conservation project, like any project that is well thought out and run properly, ought to pay for itself.'

'My dear man,' replied the Minister who was not accustomed to being lectured and did not like it, 'how can you expect an elephant conservation project to pay for itself? It simply cannot be done. It costs money instead. And that's a real problem when already we don't have enough revenue to pay for the many urgent social programmes. People in towns are becoming restless. Villagers around the elephant reserve complain about their gardens being destroyed by elephants. But there is international pressure. Our hands are tied. The African elephant is a kind of symbol. It is the biggest animal...' he held up his hand as Le Tellier was about to say something, '...and no one wants it to become extinct. As it is, the whole world is watching us ... Yes, you wanted to speak?'

'Minister,' said Le Tellier, 'you mention that the elephant is the biggest animal. It is indeed, but on land. There are bigger animals in the oceans: the whales. And I think that we could learn a great deal from the practices applied in the conservation of whales. Do you know that countries such as Norway and Japan kill a number of whales every year as part of their scientific programme? And that afterwards they sell the meat? It's accepted practice. And it pays for their scientific studies and conservation programmes.'

'Is that right?' exclaimed the Minister. 'But that's a really bright idea!'

'It's conservation and business combined,' lectured Le Tellier. 'It's the only sensible long-term attitude.'

'Mr...' the Minister looked at the paper lying in front of him on his large desk, '...Le Tellier, you are introducing a new dimension to conservation,' admitted the Minister with something like admiration showing on his face. 'I believe we ought to inform the director of the elephant reserve of this new approach. I shall contact the project leader and strongly suggest something along these lines. The governments' coffers are empty and we could do with some money coming in.'

'Minister...' Le Tellier shook his head again. 'I happen to know who the present project leader is. It's a young woman, a Miss de Ville. I have the greatest respect for her youthful enthusiasm but, alas, youth does not compensate for lack of experience.' Seeing the Minister shake his greying head in agreement, he waited a few seconds to let his words sink in. 'I am of the opinion that she will fail to see the sensible attitude you are suggesting. I have tried to contact her in order to see whether she would be amenable to rational arguments and be willing to run the elephant reserve on a business basis, but she has declined to consider that aspect of the matter. She is no doubt a good person but, being young and a woman, I fear that her actions are ruled by sentiment rather than reason.'

Minister Mamabeka suddenly rose from his chair. 'She refuses to listen, you say? She must be relieved of her responsibilities immediately! It is intolerable that a young foreign woman permits herself to lay down the law in this country.' His face had become angry and contorted as he spoke.

'That would be best for everyone, Minister. I admire your straightforward approach. Unfortunately the President has signed a contract with the World Elephant Fund, giving them control over the reserve, and they have appointed Miss de Ville as project leader. It will not be so easy to remove her, which is really a shame because I am sure that my company would be capable of running the project to everyone's satisfaction.'

The Minister sat down again, his face clouded over, and he didn't speak for a while. Finally he asked: 'So, how would you propose to run the project?'

'Well, Minister, seeing that Miss de Ville didn't seem to be open to considering the business aspects of the project, I have not really worked out anything in detail...'

'But if you could run the elephant reserve, how would you do it?'

Le Tellier rubbed his chin and pretended to give the matter some deep consideration. At last he spoke: 'Well, it would be something along these lines ... Every year part of the herd would be culled, and the dead animals marketed just like cattle. An elephant is worth approximately twenty thousand dollars, I would say. The exact value depends on the marketing of the meat and other products, but let us accept that number as a rough working base. There are some five hundred elephants in the reserve, so their commercial value would be of the order of ten million dollars. Of this you, as Minister of Wildlife, would receive one-tenth to cover your expenses, and the rest would go towards the running of the project, the marketing and commercialization.'

The Minister's eyes suddenly bulged. 'One-tenth, you say? That would be...'

Le Tellier completed the sentence for the Minister's benefit. 'Yes, that would be a million dollars...'

The Minister's fingers closed and opened a couple of times while he swallowed hard. 'I need that money...' He sat there for a few seconds, staring out of the window, then he carried on as if speaking to himself: 'I have great plans for...' he suddenly seemed to notice Le Tellier, 'yes ... ahem ... for my ministry. Yes, that would be much better than having to spend money on the reserve. My ... ahem ... ministry could certainly do with some financial help,' he commented in a hoarse voice.

Then he was again in control of the situation, got up and stretched out his hand. 'This has been a most interesting interview, Mr...' he looked at his paper, '... Le Tellier. I will do what I can to improve the running of the project to everyone's satisfaction. I shall contact you and call upon your services as soon as there are any developments, which, I trust, will be relatively soon. I am pleased to have met someone who so clearly understands the needs of my ministry and my country.' Presently he led Le Tellier to the door, holding his arm in a sympathetic grip.

As he was about to depart, Le Tellier turned towards the Minister one last time, saying: 'It is very generous of you to have wasted your precious time on what must be no more than a minor problem in your busy schedule.' And with eyes expressing esteem he added: 'And I feel fully confident that you will solve this problem to everyone's satisfaction and that I shall have the honour and the pleasure of collaborating with you in the near future.' Then he left, already thinking of the next step to be taken.

4

Le Tellier felt mighty pleased with himself as he drove to Elephant Camp on the following afternoon. Yes, Ron had done a good job putting him on to this. Obviously, Ron wanted to be the one bringing the tourists into the elephant reserve the moment everything had been arranged to everyone's satisfaction, and he would get the monopoly. He deserved it. *They will be called tourists,* thought Le Tellier with a smile, *but they will be a special sort of tourist, bringing guns rather than cameras.*

All he had to do now was to neutralize that obstinate female project leader, and he had devised an elegant plan in case the Minister was unable to come up with a successful scheme. He had taken one of Luonga's men, a certain Bongo, with him. Bongo was to pretend that he was a deputy director of the Wildlife Department, and that plans were on foot for rules and regulations to become much stricter, resulting in driving up the cost of running the project to astronomic heights. After the fake government official would have put this across, that bothersome woman was sure to break down saying that she had no money, and then Le Tellier would magnanimously come up with the proposal that he would take care of all the expenses.

Instead of driving straight into the camp, Le Tellier parked the car some distance away. Bongo was a huge man but he was a bit slow on the uptake, and the Frenchman thought it safer to go over the instructions once more while they walked the last two hundred yards. As they did so, Le Tellier noticed that Bongo was moving uncomfortably.

'Why are you walking like that?' he grumbled. 'You look like a log on thick wooden legs. Just try to walk naturally, man. You must appear to be at ease – to be used to giving orders. You're supposed to exude confidence. It is essential that the horrible woman we are going to visit believes you to be an important government official. If you walk in like that she'll see through the whole set-up in no time.'

179

'It's difficult, Boss. I'm not comfortable in this suit, Boss,' replied Bongo in a plaintive voice. He was indeed a muscular man and seemed to be bulging out of his clothes on all sides.

'Why the hell did you have to wear such a tight suit?'

'This isn't my suit, Boss. I haven't got a suit. It belongs to my boss, Boss. He lent it especially for the occasion. I'm sorry, Boss.'

'And to think that I picked you amongst Luonga's men because you talk English more or less properly and have an impressive figure!' Le Tellier shook his head. 'All right! But you must perform better. Look here, this is how you're supposed to walk.' And he gave an imitation of the perfect gentleman, strolling leisurely into someone's house. 'Got it?'

'I'll try, Boss,' replied Bongo eager to please, and he moved forward as well as he could.

'Is that what you call trying?' exclaimed Le Tellier. 'You're walking like a dressed-up scarecrow from which they have forgotten to remove the broomstick. Relax your back, man! And look how stiff your arms are. Just let them go. And put a bit more spring in your step!'

Bongo now let his arms hang down and started bouncing forward.

'*Mais qu'est-ce que c'est que ça?*' shouted Le Tellier. 'What is this? You are giving *l'imitation* of the mad gorilla or what?'

'Not good, Boss?' Bongo shot a worried glance at Le Tellier.

'Not good, Boss?' imitated Le Tellier in a shrill voice. 'I'll give you a "not good, Boss" in the pants if you don't do any better soon. And stop calling me boss! Remember that you are a deputy director, got it? And button up your jacket!'

Bongo buttoned up his jacket, and hoping that this time he would meet with approval he looked at Le Tellier. 'Is this all right, Boss?'

'*Mais quel crétin! Mais ce n'est pas possible!*' Le Tellier hit his forehead hard with his hand. 'Damn it all! How you think you are ever going to pull this off is beyond me. Don't you understand? If that awful woman hears you call me boss, she'll become suspicious. Don't call me boss!' he yelled.

It confused Bongo totally. 'All right, Boss,' he stammered. 'I won't call you boss, Boss. I am an important government official and the Minister is my boss. Which minister would that be, Boss?'

Suddenly someone exploded with loud laughter just behind their backs. Bongo screamed with fright while the buttons popped off his jacket, and as he shot away there was a lot of spring in his steps. Le Tellier swivelled round as if bitten by an adder, and looked straight into Veronica's face, convulsed with mirth.

'Who the hell are you?' he barked at her, upset at the unexpected turn events had taken.

Veronica did not answer his question but instead replied: 'If the one who has just run away is an important government official, who then are you? The President of France, I wouldn't be surprised?'

'Mademoiselle,' replied Le Tellier angrily, 'I fail to appreciate your sense of humour, and I have no time to waste on *une jeune femme idiote* like you.' Then he added in a haughty voice: 'I am a very important businessman. I have come to see the director of this elephant reserve, a Miss Veronica de Ville.'

'Don't say any more. I've got it!' Veronica pointed her finger at the angry man in front of her. 'You must be the very important Le Tellier. The one I had to trust blindly. It's always a pleasure to meet people when the masks are down. You see, I'm the one you just called "that awful woman". And for your benefit I want to inform you that I understand French perfectly.'

'But ... but...' stammered Le Tellier who had lost some of his cocksureness, 'you overheard me talking to the government offi... to the African man?' He stood there for a few seconds lost for words. Then, as if by magic, he seemed to have recovered his aplomb and said in a reprimanding voice: 'So you sneak up on innocent people like me, eh? But that's very naughty of you!' And he laughed in what seemed to be a hearty way. His tone now changed and became almost confidential: '*Mais je vous pardonne.* It is not every day that I have the pleasure of meeting a pretty young woman like you.' As Veronica did not reply, he believed that he might pull it off after all, so he carried on: 'I am delighted to be able to talk business with you and I am confident that we can come to an understanding that is agreeable to both you and me.' He looked at her with a conciliatory smile and held out his arm saying: 'Shall we move to a more comfortable place?'

Veronica had a good look at the man in front of her: late

forties, well-cut brown hair perfectly fitting his clean-shaven Mediterranean face, sleek manners, gold watch and expensive clothes. Everything seemed designed to pass on the message: 'I am someone important. I have got money.'

She now spoke in a clear, cold voice: 'Would you please call back your important government official and do me the favour of removing your presence from the premises immediately.' Then she turned her back on him and walked towards the camp, leaving Le Tellier gaping at her retreating figure like a fish out of water.

5

Le Tellier was in a thoroughly foul mood as he drove back to Naboru. He didn't look at Bongo, but the poor man felt waves of disapproval emanate from the Frenchman. He shifted nervously in the passenger's seat, trying to make himself as inconspicuous as his great bulk permitted.

'She'll pay for that, the bitch, she'll pay!' Le Tellier was muttering to himself, while jamming down the accelerator as if it were that despicable woman he was squashing under his foot. He pushed the car hard to give vent to his feelings, driving recklessly along the uneven dirt road and avoiding obstacles only in the last split second. Suddenly a deep groove appeared in the middle of the track, and as he swerved brusquely to steer clear of it, the front wheel hit a sharp rock. The tyre exploded with a loud 'bang' and the car abruptly left the road and finally came to a halt near a big thorn tree.

The Frenchman screamed in frustration, and as he got out to survey the damage he started swearing loudly: '*Merde, merde!*' and began kicking the car. Then he flew at Bongo who had clambered out in a state of shock, rubbing his shoulder.

'Don't stand there with that stupid expression on your face, you idiot!' he shouted. 'Get the spare and change the wheel. And be quick!'

Bongo, who was still rubbing his shoulder, sprang to attention, got out the jack and spare wheel and started at once while Le Tellier began pacing up and down. After a few minutes he lit up a cigarette to relieve his nervous tension.

'Careful, Boss,' warned Bongo, moving to where the Frenchman had thrown the lighted match and putting it out. 'This could easily start a bushfire.'

'No one is asking for your opinion!' yelled the Frenchman. 'Change that wheel and shut up!'

'Yes, Boss. I'll shut up, Boss,' acquiesced Bongo.

He had just changed the wheel and got up when he noticed

something bulky and black not thirty yards away. A rhino stood there looking menacingly at them. Its peace had been thoroughly disturbed by Le Tellier's loud voice and the scent of cigarette smoke. Suddenly it snorted and lowered its head from which a massive horn protruded. It was about to charge! 'Quick, Boss!' shouted Bongo while rushing up the thorn tree. 'A rhino!'

'What is it now?' barked Le Tellier who had his back turned to the animal. Then he heard the thunder of heavy feet behind him, swivelled round, and just managed to jump aside while the rhino went straight on and buried its horn deep into the driver's door. The Frenchman did not wait but bolted up the thorn tree like an accomplished acrobat and clambered up to one of its highest branches, well out of reach of the animal. The rhino had freed its horn by now and was looking around in sheer outraged fury, visibly frustrated that the disrespectful intruders had vanished.

'The brute! The savage!' yelled Le Tellier in disgust, shaking his fist. 'Look what's happened to my clothes.' He pointed to his designer clothes: a flap of material hung below one knee, the other leg was in shreds and the back of his jacket was ripped from top to bottom. Then his attention turned to the black rhino beneath them. It was a huge animal with a very large, beautifully curved horn. 'That's the biggest horn I've ever seen!' he exclaimed. 'That must be worth a lot of money.' He now turned to Bongo. 'There's a gun in the car,' he commanded. 'You go down and get it!'

The rhino was still pacing up and down angrily, trying to find the people who had caused its wrath. Bongo took one look at the big animal and began to search for an excuse. 'This is too dangerous, Boss,' he objected. 'You're not allowed to shoot animals here and this is the main road into the reserve. Someone will catch us.'

'To hell with the reserve and the animals!' Le Tellier was completely infuriated. 'Get down!'

'Maybe you go down, Boss,' suggested Bongo in a small voice, staying quietly where he was.

No one moved for a while. Le Tellier and Bongo clung on to their respective branches like bizarre apes, while a bird sitting on another branch made a strange clicking sound and the cicadas kept chirruping away. Below them the rhino snorted furiously and banged into the car a couple of times to vent its irritation. Finally it got bored, turned and moved away at a rapid trot.

'Quick!' Le Tellier shouted. 'It's going to escape. The horn. I want that horn!' Seeing that Bongo did not move he jumped down impatiently from his high branch, his foot hit a stump and he fell in a most awkward position, his leg bent underneath him. Then he began to scream in agony.

Bongo clambered down as rapidly as he could and started to pull the Frenchman inside the car in case the rhino returned, but the animal had lost interest and was removing itself from this unseemly scene at a steady pace. Le Tellier was writhing in pain, screaming: 'My leg! I've broken my leg!' while Bongo stretched him on the backseat.'

'Drive me to Naboru,' urged the Frenchman with a contorted face. 'Quick!'

'Sorry, Boss,' replied Bongo, excusing himself. 'I can't do that. I don't know how to drive, Boss.'

'You're damn well going to!' yelled Le Tellier. 'Get behind the wheel.'

'Boss, there is no room for me there.'

'What?'

'The door, Boss. It goes all the way to the steering wheel. And there's a big hole in it. The rhino, you know.'

'Then sit astride!'

'All right, Boss.'

'Turn the key to start up the engine.'

Bongo did as he was told and the engine started.

'Now put in first gear.'

'How do I do that, Boss?'

'Push the left pedal with your foot and move the big stick in the middle to the left and forward.'

'I can't reach the pedal, Boss. The door is in the way.'

'Damn, damn, you'll have to!'

'Got there, Boss!'

Suddenly the gearbox cracked painfully and the car shot forward and bounced onto the road where it began to move jerkily like a kangaroo. 'The accelerator, fool, push the accelerator with your foot!' shouted the Frenchman. 'No! Awooh!' he screamed as he was thrown off the backseat. 'You idiot! That's the brake!'

After another trial or two Bongo seemed to get the knack of driving and began to enjoy himself, clinging on to the steering wheel, revving up and tearing along in first gear. Half an hour later he had covered the ten miles that separated them from Bulamonga, and, fortunately for the inhabitants who were walking in droves through the main street at this hour near sunset, Bongo managed to bring the car to a standstill against the sign indicating 'Naboru 30 miles', knocking it over in the process.

The last minibus of the day was just about to leave for Naboru. It was crammed full, but ever ready to help, the Africans found room for the Frenchman. They picked him up and shoved him onto the roof rack where they tied him on top of some bulging sacks of maize amid loud cheers from the enthusiastic crowd below.

Having been delayed by these events and by one or two sacks falling off the roof rack while the white man was being secured with a length of coarse rope, the driver now tried to make up for lost time and the nearly springless vehicle proceeded to Naboru at top speed. Bongo stayed behind with the damaged car which belonged to his boss, Luonga, somehow feeling that the latter was not going to be pleased with the present condition of his car.

Le Tellier swore loudly every time a bump in the road shook him. A box full of noisily cackling chickens was tied next to his head, while several passengers sat there with him on the roof rack, clinging on for dear life but smiling cheerfully to encourage him. They reached Naboru by 8 p.m. and the Frenchman was immediately admitted into the main hospital.

6

The next day the *Daily Star* reported under the title: 'Businessman Attacked by Rhino':

In one of our previous editions we had the pleasure of reporting the arrival of the well-known French businessman Mr. Jacques Le Tellier, who came to our country with the intention of making some important investments. Yesterday Mr. Le Tellier decided to spend his day visiting the elephant reserve north of Naboru in order to relax from his busy schedule. Unfortunately his car had a puncture and while the driver was changing the wheel they were attacked by a rhino. The savage beast destroyed the car and, although the driver escaped unscathed, Mr. Le Tellier broke his leg, and his painful evacuation to a hospital in Naboru took a long time. We are happy to report that his life is out of danger and that his condition is improving. However, all business contacts have been broken off for the time being and it remains to be seen whether he is willing to make any investments in our country after the frightening encounter that might have cost him his life. Many jobs may thus have been lost through the impetuous action of one savage inhabitant of the elephant reserve. We want to remind our readership that the reserve is run, if one can call it such, by an obstinate foreign woman without any experience of local conditions. It has been whispered that she prefers elephants to people. Whether this is correct or not, it shows the state of mind that governs the behaviour of certain foreigners.

We have already had ample occasion to draw attention to the contradiction of letting a foreign non-governmental organization run one of our country's animal reserves, and to the conflicts of interest this generates. Indeed, this organization does nothing to prevent elephants from straying beyond the boundaries of this particular reserve. Elephants are savage animals out for wanton destruction, and they cause a lot of harm to people's shambas, thereby ruining their livelihood. This is the inevitable outcome of letting irresponsible foreigners promote the principle that animals are more important than people. Yesterday we had a near-fatal accident – tomorrow maybe the first death of an innocent citizen. Do we have to wait for such a catastrophe before we remove incompetent foreigners and take back what rightfully belongs to us?

7

During the first days he had been inside the elephant, John had lived in fear: fear of poachers, fear of the unknown. He had been in a state of shock, almost paralysed, unable to move, praying that Klaus would deliver him from this prison and waiting for the ordeal to be over. *Surely, by now, they must be ready to call me back*, he thought.

Nothing in his life had prepared him for this, and he was at a total loss as to what to do. He just wanted to get out. There were moments when he revolted and flared up, refusing to accept his condition. *I don't wish to be here!* he screamed from inside the elephant. *I want to get back to my own secure world.* He felt like hitting the walls of this brain in which he had been put against his will, as if they were the walls of a prison, but he couldn't do anything. He was powerless, well and truly caught inside the elephant.

It was clear that he no longer had any say over his destiny. Day after day the elephants kept moving ever deeper into an unknown, hostile world, and however much John's mind refused to go along with them, he was forced to follow. Gradually his willpower was broken and he fell into a deep depression. *This is what young women must feel when they've been lured away from home and then forced to prostitute themselves*, he thought. *Or what being in prison must be like. Quite innocent people are sometimes thrown into prison, even put on death row. It does happen. They know they are trapped, they realize that their situation is desperate and that there's no way out.*

Finally he stopped fighting the female with which he had been forced to live inside the elephant, and let her take over. He retreated into a little corner of the brain, disconnected himself from the outside world, and tried to ignore what went on, unable to cope with what was happening to him. He no longer wanted to live but did not know how to end this existence.

He had been hiding in his corner for some time, only half

conscious of his surroundings, when he felt that he was coming to life again. Every now and then he looked around as if peeping out from a corner of the elephant's brain, and gradually he became interested and puzzled. It was less what he saw that seemed strange to John, than what he did not see. The herd walked surprisingly long distances every day, and it must have covered a vast area during the last weeks. Yet he had not come upon a road or observed a single jeep on the horizon; he hadn't met any poachers, nor seen any tourists or noticed the tracks of vehicles that crisscross parks every day. There was no sign of human habitation or presence, not even an airplane passing overhead. He couldn't understand what was happening. The human world seemed to have vanished, wiped from the face of the Earth without leaving a single footprint. Where had all the humans gone?

The other surprising fact was the presence of huge herds of animals. Wherever he looked, the plains seemed to be teeming with game: elephants, rhinos, buffaloes, gazelles, impalas, giraffes, gnus and zebras, antelopes, elands, ostriches, warthogs, sand-grouse and guinea-fowl ... The savannah was literally filled with thousands upon thousands of larger and smaller animals all intermingling and grazing as far as the eye could see. This was not a modern game park! It was more like a Garden of Eden.

Every day he became more conscious that he was somewhere aeons ago, at a time long before modern humans had appeared. It was frightening: he was lost, marooned in the past, all connections with the human world severed.

Then, little by little, he accepted his fate, determined to make the best out of his new life.

8

The Macauleys' phone had already rung twice that morning, but as Mike was at work and Mary had gone shopping with her daughter, Monta, there had been no one to pick it up. Monta and her mother were just coming into the house when it rang again, sharply and insistently.

'I'll take it,' said Mary, while Monta went on unloading the car.

When she finally entered the hall her mother was just about to hang up. 'Wait!' she heard her say through the phone, 'my daughter – his wife – is just here. She may know more about it. I'll put her on.'

Monta made signs that she didn't want to speak but her mother passed her the phone anyway. She put her hand over it, hissing: 'Who is it?' but her mother had already turned her attention to the shopping bags, and then disappeared into the next room.

'Yes?' Monta spoke defensively.

'Are you John's wife?' a voice thundered through the phone, so loud that Monta had to move the receiver a foot away.

'To whom am I speaking?'

'I'm Angus McDoughal Junior, the boss of Biotech One, the company John used to work for some years ago.'

'What is it you want?'

'I've explained all that already to your mother. Where is he?'

'Why do you want to know where he is?'

'Are you hiding him or something?' thundered the voice.

'It's just that I don't want any trouble.'

'I'm not calling to make trouble! It's about his shares, as I told your mother. I want to buy them from him.'

Monta didn't have the faintest idea what that man was talking about but her interest was awakened: her sixth sense told her that there was money to be got, maybe a lot of it!'

'Oh! Well…' she replied, politely now, '…that's different. So

191

you want to buy his shares. What kind of money are we talking about?'

'A substantial amount of money.'

'How much?'

The man seemed unwilling to commit himself. Then, as if against his will, he said: 'A share in Biotech One is worth nearly two hundred dollars today. And as he's got a thousand shares...'

Monta had gone quiet. 'Oh...' came her voice after some seconds.

'Don't you think that's enough?' shouted the man. 'Look here. I'm open to discussion. But where's John?'

Monta didn't have the slightest idea as to where he was. In truth, she hadn't cared up to this very minute and had counted the days until the divorce became official and she would be free again. She sensed that she had to say something, and for want of anything better she replied: 'He's not here at the moment.'

The man was clearly irritated. 'When will he be back? Or where can I reach him?'

Monta was about to answer that she didn't know when suddenly she had a brainwave. 'He's gone abroad,' she said. 'He's travelling and can't be reached for a few weeks, you see.'

The man's voice sounded loud and upset now. 'But this is urgent! I need to speak to him immediately. I can't wait that long.'

'Give me your number and I'll see what I can do.'

After she had got the information and had put back the receiver, she needed to sit down. She was fuming. That John! The pig! She could still hear him during the divorce settlement, pretending that he was poor and had no job, no money or possessions. The rotten bastard! It was natural that she had believed him under the circumstances. After all these years she had only had one idea: get rid of him. She wanted to start a new life as soon as possible and find another husband, a rich one this time. But her lawyer should have done a better job: he should have found out the truth. He, a man who was supposed to have defended her interests, had accepted John's words at face value. What a let-down! She was angry, not just with the circumstances but for once with herself too. *I should have listened to Minnie's advice and gone to that famous lawyer, that Phil Harriman,* she thought. But he was so expensive and there hadn't seemed to be any money in this divorce case, so she had turned to a second-rate lawyer instead. And see how she had been done in! She was not going to let herself be caught like that again. She picked up the phone book, looked up Phil Harriman's number and rang him, a decided expression on her face.

9

John had no way of knowing how long he had been with the herd but he reckoned that many months must already have passed by. He had long since understood that his herd consisted only of females and their young. Females stayed with the herd till they died, but males left to live in separate groups when they became adults, and became loners when they reached the peak of their power. Sometimes the herd would run into one of these old giants: they were a truly majestic sight, seven tons of concentrated force, and the whole herd would reverently make way and wait for the old bull to move on.

Gradually John began to recognize the other females in the herd. They were quite a collaborative bunch, gentle in their movements and very affectionate; they would touch each other with the tip of their trunks and make encouraging sounds while doing so.

A background of rumbling sounds, low grunts and deep sighs always accompanied the herd, and John finally realized that it was nothing but the elephants' chatter. They seemed to be constantly talking to each other, as if keeping up a running comment on everything and everyone. *Strange*, John thought, *that Veronica never talked about this, and that I never heard anything like it while I was a human.*

It puzzled him, until he understood that the elephants produced infrasounds. Their bulk allowed them to emit very deep sounds and their ears had adapted to picking them up. But humans, who were incapable of producing such low-frequency sounds, were unable to hear them.

Low-frequency sounds travel much further than high-pitched ones, and sometimes all the elephants would abruptly stand still and turn towards a certain direction, their ears stretched out wide. As John did the same and strained to listen, he would vaguely perceive the faint rumbling sounds of another herd. The other elephants might be many miles away, somewhere beyond the horizon, but John's companions invariably managed to identify them. They either started moving towards them if they liked them, excited by the prospect of a meeting, or moved in the opposite direction if they weren't on very good terms. *If only I could tell Veronica about this*, John thought. *She would be so interested in everything I'm learning about elephant life.*

Life in the herd was easy. There wasn't much to be worried about. John realized that he had in fact been quite lucky. His brain might have been projected inside a zebra or one of the other browsers, and then he would have had the lions after him all the time. That would have been really unpleasant, whilst as an elephant he was invulnerable to any kind of attack and had no one to fear. Even better, he was surrounded by care and company and just had to eat, drink and live. This, at last, was a totally carefree existence.

He remembered what Veronica had told him: that elephants lived until seventy or eighty. And the female in whose brain he now resided was still quite young. This meant that he might easily have another fifty years of healthy existence ahead of him. It wasn't such a bad prospect, considering that he could have expected probably no more than another thirty-five years or so had he remained a human.

But what kind of life would that have been? he thought. He would have had to make great efforts to find a job and would have had to give his all to cling on to it, knowing very well that his company would squeeze him until he had nothing more to offer and then discard him like an orange from which all the juice had been pressed. Then he would have had to start all over again, and his prospects would have worsened every year. His life as a human would have been nothing but a long fight for existence to end up in solitude and misery anyway. Would it have been worth it?

It was really rather a relief to have got out of the race. Life with the elephants felt like one long holiday, away from work and the struggle for income and position. Here you just lived the day without a thought for the morrow. Morning followed night and each bright and sunny day was like the previous one. When the sun rose gloriously above the horizon in a fire of red and orange flames and the last bright stars faded, you did not have to rush out into the deafening roar of traffic, to spend the day between four walls and work for a boss intent on exploiting you, amidst colleagues trying to elbow you out of the way.

There was no need to worry about paying the rent or mortgage, or the electricity bill. There were no taxes, and no government that made decrees that were going to regulate your life. There were no lawyers, out to sue you for a rule you had inadvertently broken; there were, in fact, no written laws to obey. The wide world was one huge garden devoid of enclosures, through which John could walk without fear of trespassing on private property. It was his to roll about in, enjoy and explore as he wished.

There was no necessity to store up provisions either: the savannah was an enormous restaurant where there was food aplenty. Meals were free and always fresh. And there was no pollution. You just drank the water at your feet and ate what happened to be within reach of your trunk: fresh grass, leaves, fruit, bark, small branches, in fact anything you fancied that was edible and tasty.

Little by little John settled down to the rhythm of the herd and began to feel at ease with his new life. He felt sheltered and supported, and by degrees, almost imperceptibly, the opposition between him and the female elephant ceased. The thoughts were still John's thoughts, but the feelings, reactions and interests were those of the female elephant in which he now lived. He was no longer a human mind which Klaus had projected inside an elephant. The mind that used to be his had fused with that of the elephant. It had become one single mind, both male and female.

Klaus! He seemed so far away, and his previous life so unreal. He rarely thought of the past now, was not even certain that he wanted to remember. In fact, he was beginning to feel perfectly happy with his new existence, and would have been offended had anyone called him a human.

10

The phone rang in Phil Harriman's office.

'Is that you, Phil?' said a voice on the other side. 'Doug here. I've done some research into what you asked me, and you'll be surprised to hear what I've found out.'

'Tell me, Doug. I'm dying to know.' Phil Harriman congratulated himself on having had the good idea of calling up his broker at the stock exchange. Doug had a reputation for ferreting out any piece of news of interest to the financial world, and he clearly deserved his reputation.

'It's one of the most exciting stories I've heard for a long time, Phil. Listen: there's been a battle going on for the control of Biotech One for weeks now. A rival company led by Merrill B. Camson II launched a hostile takeover bid some time ago but managed to buy up no more than 49.5 per cent of the shares, whilst the CEO of Biotech One, Angus M. McDoughal Junior, was able to hold on to 49.8 per cent.'

'Who's got the missing shares?'

'It appears that the remaining 0.7 per cent is held by one John Garfinger, an ex-employee of Biotech One.'

'So these shares are important?'

'Sure. Whoever gets them takes control of Biotech One.'

'Are we talking about a big company?'

'An extremely promising one, from what I hear. They've got a few patents that are real money-spinners. It's difficult to value the exact worth of the company today, but we could be talking tens of billions of dollars within some years. So you see...'

'So this Garfinger's shares are worth a lot of money?'

'Sure.'

'More than two hundred thousand dollars you'd say?'

Doug laughed heartily over the phone. 'Phil, you must be joking. Where did you get that ridiculous figure from? I'm certain that the two rivals would be willing to go much higher than that. With a bit of pushing we could be talking millions of dollars. Many millions!'

Phil Harriman whistled. 'Thanks a lot, Doug,' he said. And then he added: 'It's very likely that I'll need you soon for some good advice about investments.'

As he laid down the phone thoughts whirled in his head. Millions of dollars! And that woman who had enlisted his services was a real fool. God, this was a unique opportunity! Whatever it took, he would do it. Millions of dollars, think of that!

11

One day John's herd came to a part of East Africa where he had never been before. The elephants had crossed a wide river, swimming to the other side with their trunks just above the water. Many hippopotami were living here, half-immersed, with their pink mouths yawning above the surface of the lazy river, or dozing ashore in the warm mud, looking like fat lumps. As the elephants climbed the opposite bank, dripping wet, treading carefully not to step on one of those bulging shapes, they found themselves in an area of muddy shallows and green woodlands. It was an enchanting place.

The matriarch had been here many years ago at the time when her own mother had been matriarch and she a young female. The memory of all the places she had ever been to was stored deep in her brain, and when she in her turn had become matriarch, she knew where all the waterholes and rivers were. Now, at the height of a particularly dry season, she had led her herd to this permanent watercourse and the rich pastures on the other side of the river.

As the elephants dispersed to graze, John noticed some small dark creatures which vanished into the denser growth as he approached them. At first he was astounded, unable to make out what they were. What intrigued him most was that they were running upright; in all his wanderings with the herd he had never seen anything like it. Suddenly he realized that he had at last come face to face with his ancestors! When he drew nearer to have a better look they recoiled in fright, screaming and brandishing wooden sticks at the intruding elephant before retreating hurriedly into the dense forest. He found their campsite littered with smashed bones and decaying, smelly leftovers of food. The stench was repellent and he soon left.

Since the herd was staying in the area until the beginning of the rainy season, John was determined to see as much of them as he could, and in the following weeks he regularly went along to observe them. Their campsite had been fortified with broken branches that gave them some protection. It was situated on a high, dry spot above the river from which they could look out over their surroundings and observe any approaching predators. They seemed to communicate quite well through shrill cries, and whenever John tried to draw nearer while he grazed, one of the small creatures invariably gave the alarm. As soon as he came too close they would scatter and run.

So these were the hominids: hairy, apelike beings with heavy brows, thick protruding lips and broad noses! When undisturbed and performing some task they sat crouched on their haunches, but at the slightest danger the females would swing the babies onto their hips and the males would shoo them all into the forest while making threatening gestures with clubs and sticks to the approaching animals. He had to admire their courage, considering that they were no more than four feet tall. All the same, he was struck by how filthy and dishevelled they looked.

John had never come across any other band of creatures such as these in the course of his wanderings through the eastern part of the African continent. Were they the only existing hominids? He had no idea how far his herd had travelled since he had been part of it, but he was certain that they had covered a huge area. It therefore seemed plausible that these hominids were the only ones of their kind.

They've found a good spot for themselves, John thought, *near permanent water. Very clever of them.* There was plenty of fruit in the nearby trees which furthermore provided cover. They also fed on small animals which sometimes found themselves trapped in the mud, managing to cut through the skins with the sharp edge of stone flakes. In addition they collected the numerous bones left behind by predators who had killed antelopes, zebras and other herbivores that had come to drink. The hominids had found a way of extracting the marrow from these bones by cracking them with stones that fitted into their fists. They had plenty of rich food, but it was a dangerous way of living.

John now began to understand Sam's concern for these ancestors of mankind. There were no more than fifty individuals in total, including the babies and small children. Fierce though the males tried to look, wielding clubs and threatening intruders with pointed sticks, they were in fact extremely vulnerable: they had no sharp claws or horns that could pierce an attacker; and they couldn't run fast. They were naked and defenceless. How could they possibly overcome the many dangers of the hostile world that surrounded them? Escape the lions, leopards and hyenas that abounded everywhere? He looked at the small babies, carried about on their mother's hips. How could they survive, when even young elephants sometimes fell prey to lions? These hominids simply weren't up to it, even though they seemed clever and cunning. Their battle for survival was so unequal, so hopeless, that John felt for them like a mother for her offspring. What if this group was attacked by predators and disappeared? That would be a calamity: it would be the end of mankind! And he decided to stay around as much as possible.

Now he also understood a question that had puzzled him since the beginning. He had wondered why his brain's content had been dumped into an elephant instead of a hominid, as Sam had expected. The answer had become obvious since he had seen these small beings: they simply didn't have the capacity to receive all the information he, a modern human, had stored into a brain that was possibly three times as big as theirs. Klaus' time machine, while searching for an appropriate receptacle in this area, had found that only an elephant's brain was large enough to receive the contents. At the time he had cursed Klaus for having transferred him into an elephant, but after having seen the hominids he felt a great relief at having been put into such a majestic, invulnerable, peaceful and altogether intelligent animal, rather than into one of those small, filthy, apelike creatures. He now felt great pride in being 'John the elephant'.

12

The smell of bacon mingled with that of coffee invariably ended by drawing Klaus down every morning. The breakfast table was always loaded with food: fried eggs and crisp, curly bacon; there were stacks of warm toast, fresh butter and homemade marmalade; finally dishes of bananas and sweet oranges; and big cups of steaming coffee. Klaus had a vigorous appetite, and it was a miracle that he remained so skinny.

While Klaus was gulping down coffee, Sam, who was always up first, sat staring at him with an exasperated face. Suddenly he said, sharply: 'I want to know what's happened to John's brain.'

'Who knows?' replied Klaus who had already devoured two helpings of bacon and eggs and was now picking up a few pieces of toast. 'We're still at breakfast. It's too early in the day to tell.'

'We! We! Let me tell you that I finished my breakfast some time ago. And in case you didn't notice, it's no longer early in the day. I always thought you Germans got up with the chickens and started working at the crack of dawn, but it's already nine o'clock! How can you sit there munching toast with an indifferent face when there's so much to worry about?'

'I'm not just munching toast,' corrected Klaus. 'I'm enjoying my breakfast.' He now stuck up a thin finger. 'Let me quote my father who used to say: a healthy man needs a substantial breakfast. My father was a great philosopher, and I am a very healthy man.' He took another piece of toast from the rack on the table and smeared it thickly with butter and jam.

'I don't give a damn about what your father was or said! I want to know what's happened to John's brain.' Sam's fingers drummed on the table and his mouth started twitching nervously. 'I'm getting very, very impatient.'

'Tchh, tchh. Impatience will get you nowhere. Leave him a bit more time. The longer he is out there, the more he will

202

have seen, and that's what you wanted, *nein?*' replied Klaus without the slightest sign of concern, shaking his head in disapproval at Sam's outburst and waving his piece of toast in the air. As he did so a big lump of jam flew off, splashed into Sam's face and slid onto his shirt. 'Oh, *Entschuldigung*!' mumbled Klaus, and started to wipe Sam's face and shirt with his napkin, smearing the jam all over him.

'You clumsy idiot, stop it!' shouted Sam, having at last found a good motive for relieving his frustration on Klaus. 'See now! A brand-new shirt! This wouldn't have happened had you been in the laboratory where you should have been concentrating on bringing John's brain back by now.'

Klaus suddenly flared up, his face contorted with anger. '*Was*! Call me a clumsy idiot? *Du Finkelstein*! You dare call me an idiot? A *Dummkopf* like you!' He got up and as he turned around shaking with rage he knocked the coffeepot clear off the table. It fell down pouring its content of piping-hot coffee over Sam's lap, but Klaus ignored the screaming man, went to his laboratory and slammed the door.

13

A quarter of an hour later Sam had changed his shirt and trousers and had calmed down. Only Klaus was capable of ending the experiment successfully, and Sam fully realized his dependence. He decided to play it cool until John's brain was back, but he wasn't about to forget the insult. The moment would come when he no longer had any use for Klaus, and then this mad scientist would find out that one did not insult Samuel Goldstein Jr. with impunity.

He walked into the laboratory saying: 'Hello!' and trying to seem upbeat, but Klaus merely grunted. Sam now tried another approach, pretending that he was interested in Klaus' equipment. 'Nice machinery you got here,' he observed. 'To think that you invented and built it all yourself. It's really incredible.'

Flattery did the trick. Klaus' mood improved visibly and when Sam asked a few questions as to the functioning of certain racks, Klaus mellowed completely and began to explain their use. Then Sam walked over to the table where John was lying, shaking his head as if he were overcome with sadness. 'Poor guy,' he sighed. 'I do hope that he doesn't suffer out there. The days must seem long to him, so far away from everything.'

'Days? You said days?' Klaus raised his arms in disbelief at such a lack of knowledge. 'Years would be more to the point. For all I know, a day or two where we are could easily translate into half a year or even a year where he is now. You see, time is elastic in relativity theory, and with his translation of two and a half million years through space–time...'

'What! Are you saying that he has already spent a year or more in the deep past?'

'That's exactly what I mean.'

'But a lot could happen in a year to the hominid in which John now lives! He might have an accident, be eaten by a lion or God knows what? If he dies, John's brain is lost, isn't it?'

'I'm not God ... at least not yet,' replied Klaus without the slightest hint of humility in his voice. 'My machine can send brains into the past, but alas, cannot resurrect them so far. This is a whole new line of study you're suggesting. A very interesting idea. I shall take it up.'

'Don't take up anything new before you've brought back John's brain,' implored Sam. 'You must return his brain to his body immediately before it dies inside a hominid.'

'Hmm. I've been trying, but I haven't been successful. I can't locate him. He seems to have disappeared.'

'Do you mean to say that John the hominid is no longer alive? And that his body here will remain brainless forever?'

'No. No! That's not what I mean. What I'm saying is that he must be out of range. That he's more than five hundred miles away from Naboru.'

'From Naboru?'

'Yes, from the point that corresponds to the geographical location of Naboru, but two and a half million years back in time of course. He could for example have gone to Ethiopia to see his cousin there. What was she called again?'

'Are you referring to Lucy?'

'Yes, that's her. "Lucy in the Sky with Diamonds". Nice song that was. A Beatles' song. I liked the Beatles. And I liked "Strawberry Fields Forever" … Pity though that they didn't sing in German. Just think of *"Erdbeer-Felder für immer"* … How nice that would have sounded…'

'Stop it, Klaus!'

'You don't like the Beatles?'

Sam held his head between his hands. 'You'll drive me crazy one of these days! Don't be daft. How could John the hominid have gone to visit Lucy in Ethiopia when…'

'On holiday, no?' interrupted Klaus. 'Ethiopia is just next door. I don't see any reason why hominids should not have had the right to go on holiday. Now, I am different of course. I don't need to go anywhere because my whole life is one long holiday. My work is my holiday. But everyone is not as lucky as I.' He looked at Sam, very satisfied with himself.

'I give up,' said Sam with a deep sigh. 'You just keep trying. And make sure that you get John's brain back. The sooner, the better.' And he left the laboratory shaking his head and muttering to himself.

14

There were no dates, weeks or months in the savannah, only the slow alternation between dry and wet seasons. The rains had started and the herd had left the hominids long ago. They were now in an area of bush, scattered forest and large clearings where the lush vegetation which elephants so appreciate grew in abundance. The elephants seemed to be eternal nomads, permanently searching for new grazing. They needed a lot of food and ate almost constantly but never depleted an area, moving on well before that time and not returning until years had passed, giving the land ample time to recover from their incursions. They proceeded according to an established pattern along ancient trails that the matriarch had once learned from her mother. John realized how much the elephants depended on the matriarch. She was the memory of the herd, and her loss would totally disrupt its existence.

He now loved his life in the open plains, the waving golden grass, the low shrub and the anthills sticking up like gnarled fingers in the tree-studded savannah. There was no time to get bored. Lots of activities were going on all around. A family of warthogs would trot along in single file, father and mother followed by a few piglets, their tails sticking up like antennas. At the slightest sign of danger they would dart for one of the many holes they had dug everywhere, and disappear inside backwards. Noisy baboons would run in front of the elephants' legs, deciding to cross the path of the herd at the very last moment. A cheetah would suddenly shoot into view in pursuit of a gazelle; the yapping laugh of ungainly hyenas could be heard in the far distance; and small jackals would quietly slip by like silver shadows.

And then, there were the animals most feared by all: a pride of lions sunning on a cluster of rocks, yawning and stretching themselves; the matriarch would trumpet a warning as she felt them becoming restless and looking for prey. Long-necked giraffes were standing amidst a clump of trees, browsing off the high branches, their heads turning constantly in all directions, watching for danger. Gazelles, antelopes, zebras and other herbivores always kept an eye on them: if the giraffes bolted, the other herbivores would do likewise.

As the last rains fell and the dry season began, the plains turned yellow. Then the long, golden, waving grass of the savannah gradually shrivelled, water became scarce and the herd, led by the matriarch, started its migratory movement towards one or another permanent watercourse or bog area. During the long journey the elephants had to dig for the roots of coarse grass, pulverizing the soil with their toenails, or feed on an ever-declining supply of young branches and leaves as they advanced through plains that slowly turned into a vast expanse of brown-red dust, until they reached a permanent watercourse or a big waterhole where the elephants would retreat into quiet backwaters till the new rains came. After the torrid heat of the savannah the semi-permanent life around a waterhole was great fun for the young elephants who loved to play about, rolling in the mud.

Towards the end of the dry season these places would, however, become very cramped, as more and more animals accumulated there. Several unrelated herds of elephants would congregate around big waterholes or permanent rivers, maybe as many as a thousand animals altogether, but elephant traffic around a waterhole was well regulated. An incoming herd would wait politely until it recognized the signal of approval from the herd that occupied the drinking places, signifying that it had drunk its fill and was about to leave the water.

Other animals behaved very differently. Great numbers of buffalo would suddenly stream out of the forest, rushing down to drink, leaving little room for the elephants. Small baby elephants would sometimes be pushed off the bank during the stampede and get stuck in the mud below, unable to free themselves. Then all the elephants would come to dig a ramp with their feet and push the little ones with their trunks until they were safely back inside the herd. Such situations were extremely dangerous for the small elephants: lions were always prowling around, on the lookout for any animal in trouble, and would swoop in to kill if they were given half a chance.

John, who had become accustomed to the freedom of the open savannah, found it hard to tolerate this overcrowding. He wondered how long they were going to stay there, and whether it would ever rain again. Day after day the sun rose to reveal another cloudless sky, and by early afternoon the heat was almost unbearable. The elephants needed all the water they could get and tried to coat themselves in mud to protect their sensitive skin from the burning rays of the sun and the incessant attacks of ticks and other bugs.

Then, one morning, walls of black clouds began to pile up on the horizon. Soon the sky became overcast and the air was extremely oppressive. Gusts of wind tore through the clouds and suddenly the first flash of lightning split the sky, closely followed by a crash of thunder. The electric storm continued all through the evening and night. Giant zigzagging sparks of lightning lit up earth and clouds, throwing the peaks of several volcanoes into sharp relief, and thunderclaps of great violence seemed to shake the world.

The next morning, finally, heavy drops of rain began to fall, making concentric ripples in the water and drumming against rocks and trees. At first the animals sought shelter under the trees, which gave some protection, but soon the rain was driving hard through the leafy tops until zebras, gnus and other animals were thoroughly soaked, standing still like dark shiny silhouettes, while the earth around their feet gradually turned into muddy puddles. By noon the rain poured down so densely that a wet curtain seemed to have been pulled around the herd of elephants, obliterating the world around. Towards evening the thunder and lightning gradually passed into the distance but a violent wind continued to drive great masses of rain-swollen clouds overhead.

Within hours torrents of water came pouring down the gully. Over the next days, as new storms kept breaking and the deluge continued, the swollen river burst its banks and turned into a wild muddy-brown flood that rushed by with furious strength, carrying whole tree trunks along, bobbing up and down like matchsticks.

John felt insignificant before this show of power. Nature was too strong. It dominated totally while he was merely permitted to live and be a small part of it. He was not the master of his fate as he had so often lulled himself into believing when he was a human. He merely occupied a minute place in a much wider scene that he had failed to recognize. He was a mere speck of life which by accident had ended up on the plains of East Africa, to play its role in the cycle of life and death for a limited time.

He now perceived his irrelevance. The pride he had felt as a human had been no more than a bubble of hot air. All his endeavour, his efforts to stand out and be someone, were meaningless. He was here today, gone tomorrow without leaving a trace. Most of the atoms now inside him and forming his body would reside there only for a few dozen years, to be rejected again, recycled in nature and be taken up by other living beings, plants or animals. Everything was shared. Nothing was isolated. Billions of years ago these same atoms had been created by stellar explosions of unimaginable violence and flung into space as cosmic dust. Now, for a short time, these atoms, this cosmic dust, had combined into an extraordinary arrangement to make up the elephant's body which John's mind inhabited.

Yet he felt immensely happy to be alive. There was a sense of expectation, of renewal, of youth and freshness after the storm had rejuvenated the world. The land was infused with new colours, with new light, and a thousand strong scents flowed into him as he filled his lungs. It was exhilarating. It was glorious!

The rains had turned the savannah into lush parkland. Young shoots sprouted on bush and tree; the green grass was rich with minerals and there was food aplenty for the large herds, which now spread out over the land again, loitering at ease. There was no lack of water at present. Small streams ran through the savannah, and the rains had turned hard pans into shallow expanses of water, blue as the sky and ringed by green grass. The morning mist hung over these new, shallow lakes when the elephants came to drink after the night, dissipating slowly as the sun kept rising overhead. Innumerable colonies of birds came to these temporary lakes: ducks and geese, cormorants, ibis, egrets and many others, their coloured feathers sparkling like fire in the morning sun.

John enjoyed every moment of the day as never before. This was a carefree existence, a life for which there was no equivalent in the world he had left behind. He ate to his heart's content, nibbling anything he fancied, breaking young branches off the trees and gulping down the fruit with all the seeds inside. Everything was organic and nothing was wasted. After digestion the seeds would be ejected and dropped onto the soil miles away from their source, coated in a ball of fertile dung, which would help the seeds to sprout, and the trees and flowers to spread over the savannah.

Passing water was the most natural of functions. Any time was the right time. He remembered so many occasions, lectures, conferences or long drives in the car with colleagues, where he had felt all right at the start but had perceived an increasing urge to relieve himself after an hour or two, while being obliged to pretend that all was well and have to sit still in growing discomfort. And then, when the conference was over, or the car had reached its destination, the rush to find a free restroom. Now the whole world was a free restroom!

All this made John feel part of nature, of a much larger cosmic cycle in a way he would never have expected. It brought a sensation of freedom, not just in the sense of unlimited space, but of following natural inclinations without the slightest inhibition. He felt at ease now with his surroundings, at ease within the herd. Everything was perfect as it was.

For a long time he had no longer thought of himself as being inside an elephant – he *was* an elephant now. But he was not alone, an atom lost in a hostile world. He was part of a whole, intimately and inseparably linked to all else around him. He was the earth upon which he stood, the very grass he ate, the air he breathed. Atoms went into him, became part of his body for a while, to return to nature that had given them. He was no longer just a living being walking about in the savannah. The savannah was inside him. He was the savannah.

15

As the big airliner flew over the Sahara, Monta Macauley closed her eyes and tried to forget where she was. She would never have travelled to these insecure parts of the globe had she had the choice. It was all John's fault again, naturally! Everything that had gone wrong in her life had been his fault.

She had had such a secure and happy youth in a small Midwestern town. Her parents were good American citizens. They went to church every Sunday and flew the American flag from a flagpole in their front garden whenever the occasion called for it. They had three daughters and as they loved their country they had called them after American states: Minnie, the eldest, Missou, the second, and Monta.

The girls were artistically gifted – ballet, music, acting, painting – they were good at it all and their parents pushed them to the utmost. They expected at least one of their daughters to become famous, and all of them to make good marriages and become rich. And rightly so! Known as the three Ms, they were the sensation of their town: long brown hair hanging loose over their shoulders, and a talent for dressing and choosing the right jewellery. No wonder their parents had their hands full warding off poor suitors and other undesirable young men. It was not always to the liking of the three girls, but Monta admitted that they had been right. They always acted in their best interests.

Then, one evening when she had gone to a ball with her sisters, a young man came over to ask her to dance. He was clumsy but handsome, and when she heard that he was a scientist with a good job, she had not minded when he stepped on her feet a couple of times. He had been shy at first, excusing himself for not dancing better, but she was a good dancer and guided his movements without him noticing it. He was surprised that everything went so smoothly and seemed touched by her constant smiles and encouragement. He kept asking her for dances throughout the evening, visibly relieved that dancing was so easy with her. Towards the end of the ball the orchestra played slow tunes and gradually she leaned towards him, and put her arms around his neck and finally laid her head on his shoulder. He had not drawn back but seemed pleased at having such a pretty girl nestling close to him, and when the ball ended he asked her out for the next weekend. That was how it had all begun, and before John realized what was going on they were engaged.

Monta's elder sisters had been extremely jealous because they were still single and John, it had to be admitted, was really handsome. In fact, they had bitterly resented her triumph. She, whom they thought the least attractive of the three, who hadn't had much success so far, had beaten them all! Monta missed no occasion to show John off and rub in how promising his career was, and how well off she was going to be. She would never have to work. She was going to be able to devote her time to developing her artistic talents, and become the most famous of the three. Green with envy her sisters were!

Missou had even tried to steal John from her one day when he had come to the house and she was out. That cat of a sister had snuggled up to him on the divan. John told her afterwards that her sister had suddenly turned around and quite accidentally had pressed her lips on his. Quite accidentally! The viper she was. She'd tried to seduce him, oh yes! But John, the innocent fool, hadn't even realized what her intentions were.

From that day on she made sure that he was never alone with her sisters and that, if anyone's lips were going to touch his, they would be hers. Not that she much liked the physical side of love, but she knew that this was what men expected of girls, and she was prepared to give what it took to reach her goal. She refused to go all the way, though, until they were married. The big prize had to be kept dangling just out of reach as an incentive for him to marry her. It would be the reward for making the final step and putting his fate into her hands. She knew that once married she would have to give herself up entirely; not too often, of course, but enough to satisfy marital duty. She felt sure that she could handle it: she would be master of the situation.

Her marriage had been perfect. The whole town had come to see her wedding. Her two sisters had been bridesmaids and been forced to smile and look happy for her sake. How she had triumphed! Everything seemed to be going her way. They had rented a house not too far from her parents so that she could continue to live in the security of her hometown. And she was able to indulge in her art whenever she felt like it, because John's income was good. Naturally, he was obliged to drive long distances every day to work in Chicago, but he didn't seem to mind.

Supper was a nuisance. She disliked cooking and they often went to eat at her parents or in a little nearby restaurant. For weekends they sometimes drove to his parents, thirty miles closer to Chicago. She hated it. John's father was OK, but she had never felt at ease with his mother. She simply didn't know how to handle her: everything was un-American about that woman, her accent, her manners, her interests; and you could never be sure how she was going to react. Monta sensed that the mother had never really accepted her and it made her feel insecure. She hardly opened her mouth and just waited for the interminable weekend to be over.

She hated weekends for another reason. It was the time when John did not work and she had learned that men, when they have nothing else on their minds, start thinking about sex. She was happy when her periods gave her an excuse to be left alone, and she often managed to pretend that she was suffering from headaches or fatigue, but she could not always wriggle out of it and then she had to undergo the ordeal with her eyes closed, hoping it would soon be over. Fortunately he often had to work on Saturdays and sometimes even on Sundays, and then she was able to spend the weekends in peace with her own parents.

Several years had passed by like this in harmony and satisfaction, when disaster struck: John lost his job. For weeks on end he was just hanging about the house in between job interviews and sending CVs everywhere. It was dreadful! She just couldn't cope with having him around all day long with an unsatisfied look on his face. Soon he started grumbling that she wasn't doing anything, not even any housework to cut down on cleaning expenses. He said that it was a wife's role to keep house and, anyway, he could no longer pay for the Mexican maid. As if he expected her to dirty her hands! She was an artist and wasn't going to lower herself to do menial work. When she refused he became nasty, reproaching her that she did nothing to help him in this difficult situation, and just spent money instead of bringing it in. Why should she? She had married him for his prospects, and it was his duty to assure a decent income.

After a month or two they hardly spoke to each other. He just hung around, sat in his office writing or phoning while she went to her parents as often as possible. Then, one day, he announced that he'd been offered a job at a university in Belgium. In Europe! Where they spoke foreign languages! And ate horrible things! She had been told that they even ate frogs over there. She shuddered. And snails! She certainly didn't want to have anything to do with that, thank you very much. She was totally satisfied with good American food and was damn well going to stick to it.

So she told John that he should consider her happiness before any fancy foreign adventure, and that, if he persisted, she would be obliged to refuse to accompany him. And all he had done was explode, and call her an egocentric, lazy, cold broomstick, too scared to move a foot away from her parents!

She had been on a slimming diet for months because she didn't want to end up being overweight like so many women. She believed in preventive action. And there! Instead of appreciating her efforts he'd had the cheek to call her a broomstick! As to the rest of his accusations, she boiled with anger. She had always done her best to carry out her marital duties. Was that all the thanks she got for it? She had stormed out of the room and run to her parents. When she returned two days later she had found him gone, to Europe she presumed.

It had been a relief not to have to see his face again. The only problem was that he had left her without money and didn't send her any either. Soon she had to leave her house and move in with her parents. They didn't make any reproaches but she could feel that they blamed her for having made a wrong choice, and she now bitterly regretted having believed in John and having married him. She should never have rushed into the arms of the first man who seemed to have good prospects. If only she had been more patient. Shortly after her engagement, when John had had to work the whole weekend, she had gone to a ball with her sisters. It was there that she had met this medical doctor. They had danced and he had seemed quite taken with her, but she had remained distant and had sent him on to her elder sister. And he had married Minnie and was now a famous surgeon. To think that, but for John, it might have been her happily married to a doctor and rolling in money!

Life had been unfair to her. *Look at the condition in which that unreliable man has left me!* she fumed. She, an exceptional artist, had been demeaned and been forced to do housework at her parents. She had become a beggar! And to think that this cat of a Missou revelled in her misfortune! When she saw the smirk on her sister's face, her pride was deeply wounded.

A hand touched her elbow. 'All right, Monta?' asked the man sitting next to her on the plane. 'You're not ill or something?'

'No. Just thinking. How many more hours before we get there?'

'Another four or five maybe.'

'That long? Can't they bring me a drink?'

'I'll get it for you,' said the man, and put up his arm to attract the attention of the stewardess.

So lucky Phil is there, thought Monta. She wouldn't have known what to do without him. Phil Harriman! She had left the matter in his capable hands, and in no time he had found out everything. He fully deserved his reputation as one of the top lawyers. She could rely on him and had followed his advice, even when he had said that they would need to go to Africa.

The things she was obliged to do to find John. That terrible man! Where he had gone to this time was beyond description. As if Europe hadn't been bad enough. She'd had a taste of it yesterday when they had changed planes at Heathrow Airport, and it had been enough. The long, derelict corridors through which they had walked; the ramshackle bus that had taken them to another terminal in the pelting rain, and this was August! So this was the Europe John had liked so much. A couple of years after his departure, when he had returned to the States for a short time, he had told her that everything over there was so small-scale, so quaint, so old and full of history. Old it certainly was, but looking at Heathrow she had felt that *decaying* was more to the point. She was not impressed. She had been right to refuse to follow him to this dump they called Europe! But this time he had beaten everything. By a wide margin. He had gone to Africa! She shuddered at the thought that they would land in Africa within a few hours.

Just then the drink arrived. She took a long swig and as the alcohol ran down her throat she began to feel more relaxed. It would be fine. Phil would do everything, all the research, the dealings and the paperwork. He would find John and make him sign. And she would be rich! Phil had been very upbeat about her prospects. Biotechnology shares were worth a lot in the bull market, he had said, and he had assured her that if John's ex-boss wanted them so much, they might get far more than two hundred thousand dollars out of him. He even thought they could drive him up to a million dollars. A million dollars! That was beginning to look like real money. And although the divorce was to be finalized within a week, Phil felt confident that he could force John to sign over half of the shares and claim damages for deliberately withholding information about his real wealth. That pig of a John! She hoped he would sign quickly and wished it was all over; that she were back in her hometown, rich and independent, ready to start a new life.

16

Several rainy seasons had come and gone, but John had no idea how many rainy seasons there were in a year. He felt certain, though, that he had been an elephant for well over a year already. Then, one day, he felt something move inside his belly. By now he was used to the constant rumblings food made as it was digested and fermented, but this was different. Was it something he had swallowed and was unable to digest? Suddenly he thought: *What if something serious happens to me? I won't be able to see a doctor. There are no doctors where I am!* He tried to forget about it but his condition seemed to get worse. The internal movements were getting stronger by the week and his belly was unquestionably blown up now. It was as if an independent being kept twisting and turning, and even kicking him inside. He was getting almost frantic with anxiety when he realized what it was: he was pregnant. He was going to have a baby!

As his belly extended ever more over the next weeks he was filled with apprehension. How was he going to cope with this? He had never had a baby before and didn't have the slightest clue as to what to do. He was not sure that he could handle the situation. If only he had asked his mother about having babies while he was still a human: she would have been able to advise him on how to give birth and, at least, he would have known how to handle the newborn baby.

Then he realized that he had nothing to worry about. His mother was there, and even his grandmother, who was the stately matriarch. All the other elephants in the herd were his family, his aunts and nieces with their babies and offspring. When he went into labour a few weeks later they all stood round him. It was all over in a few minutes, and when the new baby was lying on the grass the other females assisted him, using their trunks to lift it to its legs, and guiding it gently to its mother's teats between her front legs. It was not easy for the small baby elephant because it had to suckle with its mouth

217

and its little trunk was in the way, but once it had mastered the feeding process it drunk greedily and soon was able to walk with the herd, surrounded by a protective wall of legs.

As they walked away and he looked at his baby elephant, John felt immensely proud. A long, uninterrupted line of creatures going back billions of years linked him to the first living cell. So far he had been the end of that long strand. Now he in turn had procreated to perpetuate the miracle of life on Earth. This was the most glorious thing that had ever happened to him: he had given birth to new life. He was a mother now!

17

Monta Macauley was reclining on her bed in the Naboru Hilton, her eyes closed, feeling slightly headachy. She had spent the two days since her arrival in bed, being served drinks, unable to face the outside world. A taxi had brought her and her lawyer here from the airport, and one look at the town as they drove to the Hilton had been sufficient. This was worse than the Chicago ghetto. She shuddered as she thought about this dreadful town and how people lived here: no hygiene, no comfort and no security. She preferred to stay inside and cursed John wholeheartedly for having put her in such a terrible situation. Who would have imagined it? That awful man had gone to work with an elephant project. 'Elephants!' she snorted. That's how low he had fallen. How she could ever have believed in a man like him and married him was beyond her. Elephants! *Soon it will be pigs; it wouldn't surprise me,* she thought. *Pigs! That's where he belongs.*

But where the heck was he? For two days Phil had been phoning and running about, unable to locate him. Time was pressing: another four days and they would be divorced.

There was a knock on the door of her hotel room, and Phil came in.

'Have you found him?' Monta asked anxiously.

'Probably.'

'What you mean by that? Is it yes or no?' Her voice was shrill. 'I can't stand the tension much longer.'

Phil held up a protective hand. 'Wait. Just let me explain. You know where I've been?' And without waiting for a reply he supplied the answer: 'To the American Embassy. I spent the whole morning trying to worm some information out of them. Hell, what an experience! At times I felt I was up against the CIA and FBI combined. Those fellows don't want to part with any piece of information unless you get it out of them with a crowbar. I had to throw all my legal weight in the scale, threaten

219

them with a court case and with creating a scandal for non-assistance back home before the Chief of Security parted with the information in his possession. Pfooh!' He wiped his brow.

Monta barely listened. She was not interested in the lawyer's methods or problems. She wanted results and was interested only in one thing: 'Where is he then?' she insisted loudly.

'It seems that he's working in a laboratory here in town for an American scientist called Sam Goldstein. I've got his address.'

'Good! At last! Then go over there and arrange everything so that I can go back home.'

'I'm afraid, Monta, that this time you'll have to come too.'

'I can't go out into this horrible town,' she complained. 'And I don't want to face my ex-husband.'

The lawyer now spoke quietly, as if to a child. 'Don't worry,' he said soothingly. 'I'll be at your side. You've got nothing to be afraid of. You simply come and sign the agreement; then we go and it'll all be over.'

18

For several days after John's last visit Veronica had tried to forget about him. Then, gradually, she found herself looking out over the plains towards the south hoping to see his car appear, but the days passed by slowly, one after the other, without any sign of him. Where was he? Just after they had met he had always felt so near, but now he no longer seemed to be anywhere, however intensely her thoughts went out to him. There was just a void; it was as if he had been wiped off the face of the Earth.

After a week she could no longer stand the uncertainty. She had to find out what had happened to him, whatever the outcome. Steve was waiting with the jeep to drive into the reserve after breakfast but she told him that she had some urgent business in town and that he would have to drive her to Naboru instead. By midday she was standing in front of the gate of Sam's house and rang the bell.

'A memsabu to see you, Sahib,' announced Kibu a minute later.

Lunch was just about to be served and Sam, who had his regular habits, did not like to receive visitors at this time of the day. 'Tell her to come back later,' he said.

'As you wish, Sahib, but she seems somewhat agitated.'

Before Kibu had time to turn around, Veronica burst into the dining room looking greatly perturbed.

'Well, well. If this isn't our little elephant lover,' commented Sam, trying to hide his displeasure. 'What a surprise! It's not often that we have the pleasure of seeing you in town. What good tidings bring you here?'

'I want to find out what's happened to John,' Veronica blurted out without any further ado. 'Where is he? Has he left?'

Sam had no intention whatsoever of elaborating on the subject with Veronica and was just producing some evasive noises when Klaus entered the dining room. '*Guten Tag*, Veronica,' he said

221

with an expression of delight on his face. He moved towards her, clacked his heels together and, bowing forward, repeated: '*Guten Tag!* Are you lunching with us? How very, very nice! We eat first and then I show you my laboratory, *ja?*'

Sam was making wild gestures behind Veronica's back, but Klaus didn't seem to notice anything as he sat down, motioning to Veronica to do the same, while he went on: 'You will be surprised. We have your friend John there on my time machine. You can say hello to him if you like, but he will not be able to answer. He is brainless.'

'What! You mean to say that he's lifeless?'

'Let's take this calmly,' intervened Sam, shooting thunderous looks at Klaus. 'Of course he's not lifeless. He is in fact full of life! The only part that's missing is the content of his brain. So it's no use making a fuss or trying to see him right now. You'd better come back later.'

When she heard this, Veronica looked completely dispirited. 'It's all my fault,' she lamented. 'If only he hadn't turned up in a flashy car and brand-new clothes. Where he got those new clothes from is beyond me.'

Sam looked the other way mumbling evasively: 'New clothes … I don't know…'

'But of course you do!' exclaimed Klaus with a bright face. 'He got them from that expensive shop in town. What was it called? … *Ja!* Shillingi Mingi, that's it. You surely must remember: you sent him there yourself. You cannot have forgotten that? But I perceive that you don't want to admit to your great generosity,' continued Klaus while Sam was making frantic signs. He now turned to Veronica. 'You see, John was very much in love with you but he thought that you would never look at him. However, Sam here, whose natural modesty prevents him from admitting it, wanted to help. He told John that new clothes were sure to impress you and paid for everything. It just shows what he really is: a great romantic like me. I was strongly touched by this generous gesture, considering that it might have ruined any chance of John wanting to go on with the experiment…'

Sam, who had been listening with growing concern, suddenly flared up: 'Klaus, you witless fool! Shut up! No one is asking for your opinion!'

Veronica now turned to Sam. She seemed icy-calm, but her

face looked like thunder. 'That big flashy car in the front garden is yours?'

'Yeah. Nice car, isn't it? Pity that ass ... pity it got somewhat damaged.'

Suddenly Veronica exploded. 'You scheming snake!' she screamed. 'So you tricked him into this! You deceitful devil!'

'My dear girl...' Sam spoke in a haughty voice. 'I don't see what the fuss is all about. What's so special about this John anyway? Simple and clumsy, that's what he is. It's lucky for you that you got rid of him, if you ask my opinion. You'll end by thanking me for it. And as the saying goes: you lose one, you gain ten. I'm certain that plenty of men, more worthy of you than that John, are waiting in the wings.' He seemed pleased with his little speech and sat there with a self-satisfied smirk on his face.

Veronica gave him one scornful look and advanced threateningly towards the table. Then, with a quick gesture, she picked up the steaming soup tureen which had just been brought in, emptied it over Sam's head and rushed out.

19

'Two people who would like to see you, Sahib,' announced Kibu at this very moment. He looked somewhat surprised when he saw his employer sitting there with the soup tureen on his head and soup leaking over him. If he disapproved of the practice of wearing soup tureens in lieu of hats, he did not show it and turned around in search of a servant to clean up the mess.

Phil Harriman was a man of action who abhorred having to wait. When he noticed that Kibu had left the front door open he didn't hesitate a second and entered the house, followed close upon his heels by Monta. 'It's best to catch John by surprise and make him sign before he gets over the shock,' said Phil. Then, seeing a half-open door at the end of the corridor and hearing voices behind, he pushed forward.

The scene that unfolded before Phil's and Monta's eyes as they entered the dining room seemed to come straight out of a horror movie. Two men were sitting opposite each other at a large table. One of them, a skinny fellow with a big forehead, gold-rimmed spectacles that were nearly sliding off his nose, and a pointed chin, seemed extremely displeased: he was looking at the other man with a face distorted by anger and eyes that were spitting fire; then he bent down, stuck his head into a plate piled high with potatoes and began to gobble them up. The other man was even more bizarre: he was lifting a soup tureen off his head with both his hands. A few strands of vermicelli were stuck behind his ears and a bit of greenery and some meatballs were balanced precariously on the top of his head. Some of the soup had disappeared down his shirt collar, but most of it had run down his clothes and now formed a big puddle around him on the floor.

'Eeek!' screamed Monta, attempting to hide behind Phil's back.

This is the strangest way of partaking of food I've ever come across in my whole career, thought Phil, who had been to a number of out-of-the-way places during the pursuit of those who had in vain tried to escape the long arm of the law. He had been witness to some very odd dinner customs in the process, but never had he seen anything like this.

'Who the hell are you and what are you doing here!' shouted the man with the tureen, visibly disturbed at being interrupted during what was probably a critical phase in the feeding process.

'I'm looking for a John Garfinger,' said the lawyer, 'but carry on. Don't let me disturb you and please finish your ... er ... feeding. We'll keep looking around.'

'You'll do nothing of the sort!' yelled the man, rising from his chair. And if anyone pronounces that name again in my presence I'll hit him over the head with a tu ... with a ladle!'

'Are you referring to John Garfinger?' uttered the lawyer, astonished. 'I would never have believed that his name alone could have such an effect on people. He seems quite an inoffensive fellow from what I've heard about him.' He turned to Monta, repeating: 'John Garfinger, John Garfinger. See!' he said. 'It doesn't do anything to her and she's his wife.'

'Stop it!' screamed Sam, putting his fingers in his ears and leaking soup all over the floor. Then he looked up: 'What did you say?'

'John Garfinger?' repeated the lawyer.

'Nooo. After that.'

'That Monta is his wife?'

'You mean that the woman there behind you is...'

'Yes, she is John's ... sorry! Yes, she is Mrs Garfinger ... and I'm Phil Harriman, her lawyer.'

'You're a ... you're a...' A nervous twitch began to develop around Sam's mouth. 'And she's his...'

'That's right. And whom do I have the honour of talking to?'

'I'm Samuel Goldstein, the director of this house ... er ... I mean of the laboratory.'

'I see. I've been told that Jo ... I mean, my client's husband is working here and we've come especially from America to see him about a very important matter.' The lawyer opened his attaché case and, like a magician in front of a stupefied public, produced a few sheets of paper as if he were pulling a rabbit out of a hat. He held them up in the air, thumped them with a finger and declared: 'These are extremely important documents!

Mr Garfinger has to sign them.' And he kept thumping the papers for greater effect, adding: '*Immediately!*'

Klaus, who by now had worked his way through most of his potatoes and the big sausage that went with these while listening to the conversation with the greatest interest, could contain himself no longer. 'Hahaha!' he laughed loudly. 'Hahaha! He wants John to sign papers. *Das ist doch nicht möglich.* He's a hominid! And hominids cannot read or write ... hahaha!'

'What's that idio ... well ... that person over there jabbering about?' inquired Phil, turning to Sam. 'I can't make sense of his babble.'

'Don't pay any attention to him!' snapped Sam.

But Klaus was not to be stopped. 'Make him sign immediately? Hahaha! He cannot sign. Not today. Not tomorrow. Maybe never. He is lying on his back in the laboratory. We've taken his brain away!' And he laughed so heartily that tears rolled down his cheeks while he was holding his stomach, bloated by the large quantity of potatoes he had gulped down.

'What!' exclaimed Phil. He now turned to Sam. 'What have you done to Mr Garfinger?' he asked in a threatening voice. 'I demand a clarification of the situation this very instant!'

Sam began to perspire. 'It's not really so bad,' he replied, trying to minimize the state of affairs. 'There's no need to dramatize.'

'I haven't dramatized anything yet,' snapped the lawyer, 'but I request to be introduced to Mr Garfinger without any further delay.'

Sam looked shifty. 'I'm afraid that's not possible.'

'His wife has a legal right to see him,' stated Phil Harriman in a cold, professional voice, 'and you are obstructing the law! But I believe that you are hiding much darker deeds, and that my client's husband has been killed.'

'No, not killed!' protested Sam. 'It's just that ... that he's been used for an experiment.'

'Do you have his written consent attesting that he agreed to the terms of the experiment?' asked the lawyer in a stern voice. 'Did you inform him clearly of all the risks involved and was he aware of these?'

Sam removed some vermicelli from his face and looked away while his mouth began to twitch nervously.

'I see! There are no signed documents. This is a clear-cut case. You haven't got a leg to stand on!' barked the lawyer at Sam who stood there in silence while the puddle of soup started to congeal around his legs. 'I'm going to start legal proceedings against you at once and sue you for an astronomical sum in the name of my client here present.' He looked around: Monta had gone!

20

After Veronica had left the house she searched for the lab, determined to find John. She discovered a long low structure in the back of the garden and went over. *This must be Klaus' famous lab*, she thought. As she entered the cool, gloomy building she noticed racks full of equipment and wires trailing everywhere. She advanced in the semi-darkness, her throat dry, and suddenly her heart began to throb wildly: in the middle of the room, on a long table, a human body was lying. John! He lay there so still, so peaceful.

Hesitantly she drew nearer until she stood next to him in shocked silence, looking at his inert body. Then, shaking her head in despair, she uttered in a choked voice: 'What have they done to you? But what have they done to you?'

Waves of desolation overwhelmed her, and as she touched his hand her eyes filled with tears. She stroked his cheek with infinite tenderness and thought of the love that was lost before it had even begun.

'John, please don't die,' she pleaded overcome with grief. Words of regret suddenly welled up in her throat: 'Please forgive me. Forgive me for not having had faith in you ... for having sent you away. Wherever you may be now, if you can hear me, please forgive me...' She knelt down beside the table and her body started shaking uncontrollably. The sorrow of losing John was too great to bear, and tears began streaming down her cheeks.

She remained there sobbing, her head against the table, until there seemed no tears left inside her. Finally she got up and, kissing John softly, whispered: 'I love you.' Looking once more at him, she turned away and left the laboratory.

As she approached the house she heard unknown voices. She didn't want to see strangers, she didn't want to see anyone; she wanted to be alone with her sadness. She retreated into the garden, found a small door in the back wall, and slipped out quietly.

21

Monta had felt very uncomfortable from the moment she had set foot in that strange house. How Phil had dared step inside without being invited or knowing the people was beyond her. She had stuck close to him, but even so the sinister atmosphere made her hair stand on end. She felt certain that unspeakable things were going on in there. Then they had stumbled upon a most horrible scene: a man covered in soup with a tureen on his head, and another one with gold-rimmed spectacles on his nose, his face stuck in a heap of potatoes.

The sight of these two men made her stomach turn. *Who knows what strange ceremonies go on in here?* she thought. She remembered a book she had once read about the primitive rituals and human sacrifices that went on in Africa, and shuddered. Then the madman with the gold-rimmed spectacles laughed hysterically, admitting that John was lying in what he called 'the laboratory' and that they had taken his brain out. He had been sacrificed! She felt like an ensnared animal. Waves of panic ran through her body when she realized that she could well be the next victim. Why the hell had she consented to come to Africa?

She had only one idea: to get out of this death trap; to be out in the street where it was not safe, but where at least she didn't risk being sacrificed. She began to retreat, foot by foot so as not to attract attention, until she was outside the room. Then she quickly slipped along a corridor and found herself outside. But where was she? This was not the way they had come in: this was a garden. She wandered around looking for the exit when suddenly she noticed a low structure. As she passed by she peered inside the open door, and then she realized: this was where the sacrifices took place! This was where John's body must be.

She stood there, frightened but at the same time irresistibly drawn inside. At last she entered hesitantly, and as her eyes grew accustomed to the dark she saw a table in the middle with a body lying on it. She came closer, pushed along by morbid curiosity, until she stood at the side of the motionless body and looked at it. *So this is what has become of you,* she thought, looking at all the wires attached to John's head. *No more brain, eh? You the bright intelligent fellow who never missed an occasion to show other people how dumb I was. You the great adventurer who always laughed at me for not wanting to follow you to dangerous places. See where it's led you? Serves you right!*

There he was then, lying on his back. The great John! The promising scientist she had married, only to be dumped unceremoniously a few years later. Her whole life had gone wrong because of him. Everything was John's fault. How she had suffered because of him. She, a unique artist, was obliged to live from the handouts her parents gave her while he was hiding a fortune!

Suddenly all the suppressed anger of the last years, all the suffering and indignity he had inflicted on her flared up. Revenge! This called for revenge. Her lips tightened, she bent forward and her hand reached for the wires attached to John's head.

22

Veronica had been unwilling to face anyone after she had left Sam's property via the back door. She sat down on a low wall a few yards further, staring in front of her with unseeing eyes, unable to think or do anything. After a while she began to feel very hot and became aware that she was sitting in the full sun without her hat. *Where's my hat?* she wondered. Then she realized that she must have left it in the house and would have to retrieve it. As she slipped through the back door she perceived a movement at the entrance of the lab and vaguely glimpsed a human shape, vanishing inside. Veronica was puzzled. *That looked like a woman*, she thought. *What is she doing in there with John?* She moved to the door and entered silently. A woman she didn't know was standing in front of the table on which the body was lying. Her attitude was hostile and Veronica, who was approaching quietly, eyed her with distrust. Just as Veronica crept up behind her, the woman bent forward and grasped the wires that came out of John's head.

Before she had time to pull them out, Veronica's hand closed around her wrist like a vice. The woman screamed in panic and let go, and suddenly Veronica's deep grief turned into furious anger. In a wild rage she twisted the woman's arm behind her back and forced her down.

The lawyer, who by now had left the house in search of Monta, suddenly heard screams coming from the low structure in the garden. He ran forward, followed by Klaus, and as he burst into the lab he saw Veronica, her knee dug into Monta's back, pressing her to the floor.

'Hey!' he shouted storming forward. 'What's this? Let go of her immediately! This is an unprovoked attack upon an innocent person.'

'Innocent!' screamed Veronica. 'She was about to pull out the wires and kill John!'

'Are you accusing my client of wanting to murder her husband?'

'What? Is this his wife?' yelled Veronica giving an extra twist to Monta's arm, making her scream with pain. 'This bitch?'

The lawyer did not seem willing to clarify the situation. Instead he said in a stern voice: 'You are assaulting my client in front of witnesses. And you are accusing her of criminal intentions without any proof. I must warn you: you'll go to court for that. I'm going to sue you for inflicting mental and physical suffering on Mrs Garfinger.'

'Sue me, eh!' yelled Veronica, giving another twist to Monta's arm. Then, before anyone had time to react, she jumped up, rushed around the lab, saw a bundle of cables about ten feet long, neatly tied together, which Klaus had been preparing for a new experiment, grabbed it and whirled the bundle over her head like a whip.

'Hey, careful!' shouted Klaus. 'My new set of cables.'

She now advanced upon the lawyer like a fury, cracking the cables on the floor in front of his feet. 'If you want to sue me I'll give you some good reason for it!' she screamed.

The lawyer didn't dally. He was unequalled when it came to verbal duels, but never in his career had he had to face a female fury who'd gone berserk and attacked him with a whip. He leaped up as the cables hit the floor under his feet, dashed to where Monta was lying, hissed: 'Let's get out of here,' yanked her up by the arm which made her scream again in agony, and pulled her along to the exit while the whip was cracking on the floor behind them.

Just then Kibu appeared in the doorway holding up some objects. 'I think you forgot your briefcase and documents, Sir,' he said with an impassive face. The lawyer grabbed them from Kibu's hands without stopping and rushed towards the house and out of the property, dragging Monta along with him, deaf to her screams.

A few seconds later Sam entered the lab. He had cleaned most of the soup from his face but still looked a sorry sight. 'Where's everyone?' he called. Then he noticed Veronica and saw red. 'You little idiot!' he yelled. 'How dare you! Get out of my house!'

Veronica flared up. 'You ... you bastard! You criminal! I'm going to denounce you to the police for premeditated murder. But I'll kill you first!' And like an enraged lion tamer she went for him, cracking the cables in front of his feet and making him run for his life.

Klaus was the only one left now. He stood there trembling and remained at a respectful distance until Veronica had quietened down. Then he asked deferentially: 'What are you going to do with these?' pointing at the bundle of cables like a child at his toy that has been taken away from him. 'Can I have them back, please?'

'No! I'll keep them for a while,' said Veronica with a resolute look in her eyes. 'They're very efficient. I'm going to stay here to guard John and keep the human vultures away from his body.' Then she commanded: 'You go and tell the servants to bring me some food – I'm literally starving. But return immediately and get to work. I want you to bring John's brain back before further disasters happen to him.'

23

Meanwhile, two and a half million years back in time, John was moving slowly over the plains with the other elephants, unaware that his mindless body was stirring up such passions in Naboru. For several seasons already he had not given much thought to his previous life as a human, but since he had become a mother his past seemed totally irrelevant. Now he just wanted to take care of his baby, a little male, growing stronger and more playful by the day.

At first the baby elephant had been surprised at having a little trunk where his nose and upper lip were supposed to have been, and hadn't known what to do with it. When he started eating solid food he had been unable to learn the trick of using his trunk to pull out grass however much John tried to teach him, and in the end he had sunk on his knees with his head in the grass to browse in a most ridiculous fashion. It had taken two rainy seasons for him to master the art of controlling his trunk, but now, what a little show-off he was! He would pick up a stick and balance it on the tip of his trunk, or play with anything he could find, then break into a wild trot and try to hide.

Such moments could be dangerous because he might stray into a pride of lions, but John was not alone in keeping an eye on his baby. He could count on the assistance of all the other females of the herd. They were constantly on the lookout, talking to the little ones and calling them back when they moved too far away and might get into danger. They were very concerned when one of the young elephants was in trouble and always touched them to reassure them.

Mothers had to teach their offspring everything about elephant life: what to eat, where to look for the minerals their diet lacked, and how to pulverize the soil to get at these essential supplements. They also taught them how to keep clean, take a bath every day if they could, and coat themselves in mud to protect their skin from the burning rays of the sun and rid themselves of parasites. In the beginning John hadn't had a clue about all this, but to his relief he found that he could count on the unfailing support of the other mothers to educate his little elephant.

John now lived with and for the herd, and the interests of the other elephants were his. When one of the females was in heat, the whole herd was on the alert and appeared to be discussing the subject endlessly. This was one of the most critical moments of a female's life, and the other elephants seemed to be feeling for her. At any one time several bulls were in must – that frenzied state when the blood of male elephants is infused with sexual hormones; when they feel virile and full of fight, and go nearly crazy with lust. Females could smell males in must for miles, and the herd wanted a female in heat to attract the strongest of the bulls to produce healthy offspring. When the female had found a bull to her liking she would pretend to run away from him, with the bull in hot pursuit, until she finally surrendered and he mounted her.

The herd surrounded her in this difficult moment, and John had learned to make encouraging movements and sounds so that the cow elephant would feel the support of the others. Like all the other females in the herd, he took a healthy interest in such vital matters. Copulation was not simply a private affair between a bull and a cow. It was the concern of the whole herd, which was one large family and would collaborate for years to educate the baby once it was born.

John no longer felt alone as he so often had in his previous life. The other elephants surrounded him with care and affection and he felt secure as never before. He loved his life: the rising and setting of the sun, the endless succession of sun-drenched days followed by starry nights, the infinity of the universe above the wide-open space of the savannah. He was immensely happy now. He no longer wanted anything else. To live with the herd, educate his little elephant and have more babies was his role in life. Being a mother was total fulfilment.

24

Joseph Polepole, the new handyman at Elephant Camp, was standing at the top end of the landing of Veronica's two-storey house. He was working on the rail where the wood was rotten and had already lugged a big bucket full of white paint up the stairs to repaint everything when the repairs were finished. He had removed the rotten part and was about to hammer a new solid plank in its place, when he sat down, his mind absorbed in bitter thoughts. It was unjust that a woman like Faithful, a goddess on Earth, should belong to a man like that Steve Mutele. The bastard he was! How he strutted about in the village, showing off his blue metallic-coloured sunglasses and the project outfit he had received because he was the driver of Memsabu Veronica. One day he had driven into the village in the project jeep, and you should have seen him! He had stopped in front of his hut, called to Faithful to come out and get into the Land Rover next to him, and then he made a tour through the village while everyone had come out to look at them. So important had he begun to think himself that he no longer even respected the elders.

Joseph Polepole was at a loss as to what to do. How could he approach Faithful? He felt that she was not indifferent to his admiration but there was a major obstacle: the husband was a strong, fiercely jealous man, and even when he had gone from the village Joseph had, so far, not managed to be alone with Faithful. There were always other people around: her mother or Steve's brothers, and he had to be careful not to arouse suspicion. Several times these last weeks when he knew that Faithful had gone to work at Elephant Camp a few miles away, he had sneaked out of his village and hidden in the low bush that surrounded the camp, trying not to be seen while waiting for an opportunity to be alone with her, but he hadn't been lucky. On one occasion Faithful had passed by and he had made a movement to beckon her, but she had run away in panic without recognizing him. He had not waited and that was fortunate. That evening he had heard the story in the village: she had gone to get Steve and the bastard had searched the surroundings for more than an hour with a big machete, trying to find the intruder. After that Joseph Polepole wisely didn't push his luck.

Today, finally, he was at Elephant Camp in an official position. The previous handyman had left and he had been able to secure the job. The memsabu had explained what she wanted him to do and then had told Steve to drive her to Naboru. And today of all days Faithful was not there! He couldn't stand this much longer. What was he to do? Go to the witchdoctor and ask him to make Steve ill and Faithful desire him? That was really risky business, and he was not convinced that he should go to such extremes.

He tried out the new plank again and was about to hammer it on when he noticed that Faithful had arrived. She was a beautiful buxom woman, and as she walked past his whole being was irresistibly drawn towards her. The swaying of her full hips in a rhythmic movement charged with sensuality made his blood boil, and now she looked back at him over her shoulder with an unmistakably inviting expression in her eyes. This was too much to resist! This was his day! Without further ado Joseph dropped plank, hammer and nails, and went in pursuit of Faithful. And at the top of the landing, where the new secure railing was supposed to have been fixed, there was nothing but a bucket full of white paint.

25

That same afternoon a great jamboree was taking place at Kundimayo, one of the new villages encroaching upon the elephant reserve. Hundreds of people, men and women, had come from miles around to pay homage to their leader, and they were sitting on the dry grass with outstretched legs. Most of the men wore ripped trousers and old shirts, but some of the elders were still wrapped in blankets; nearly all carried long wooden sticks which were lying next to them on the ground. A few women continued to wear traditional outfits but most, especially the younger, wore bright-coloured dresses and had decorated their hair with shiny plastic combs.

The village elders were seated on metal chairs facing the people, flanked on both sides by a few askaris, standing proudly in their uniforms, hands on the barrels of their rifles. The centre, the place of honour, had been reserved for Mamabeka, Minister of Home Affairs, whose responsibilities included anti-corruption, family planning and now also wildlife. Although slightly greying, he was still an impressive man who had fourteen children by his legal wife and, it was whispered, had fathered at least another fifty in the innumerable extramarital affairs he had had in the course of a long political career, as he worked himself up from tribal spokesman to Minister of State. He sat there very upright, looking at the packed mass of men and women in front of him: these were the people of his own tribe. He was like a father to them.

After a long introduction during which the elders came to pay their respects and the Minister received some goats and a number of other presents, he rose from his chair to address the crowd. He knew how to work a crowd and capture an audience. His speech, in which greetings intermingled with references to local affairs and witty comments, made the people laugh. A huge, vastly overweight cheerleader repeated his most important remarks, throwing a long carved wooden stick in the air to underline the words while jumping up and down to loud applause from the cheering crowd. Many women were carrying babies, some suckling milk. These rolled off their mother's breasts and broke out into loud wails every time their mothers clapped their hands.

At last the Minister came to the central point of his visit: 'I have heard that you are not happy with the elephant reserve,' he said in a ponderous voice. 'If you have complaints, speak out! I am your father. I have come here to listen to you.'

'We complain about the elephants!' the people shouted back. 'They trample our shambas and eat our food!'

One of the elders now rose to speak. 'Minister,' he said in a singsong voice, 'our people are suffering. We work hard but when the food is ripe the elephants come and eat it, and we go hungry. This is not right. You must deliver us from these animals.'

Someone amongst the crowd shouted: 'Let's go kill them and eat them.'

The fat cheerleader now began dancing around, inciting the multitude to repeat: 'We shall eat them!'

Another elder rose. 'They say that we cannot do anything because the elephants belong to the reserve and are protected. But are we not also God's creatures? They say that the elephants are important. But are we not important too? Do we not have an equal right to live? I ask you: Who is more important? The elephants? Or us?'

When he heard this, the bulky cheerleader jumped up, bellowing: 'We are more important!' and the crowd joined in: 'We are more important!'

They finally quietened down, and the Minister now spoke again. 'What can we do?' he asked. 'The reserve is no longer ours. It has been taken over by foreigners. The boss of the reserve is a white person, a woman.'

'A woman!' repeated the fat cheerleader, wildly jumping up and down. 'Hear, hear! The boss is a woman!'

The most venerable of the elders now rose. 'Minister,' he asked, 'how can a woman rule over men? How can that be? Have we African men become so weak that a white woman is our master? A woman should serve her man. Cook his food. Bear his children.'

'I have been told that this woman has no husband and no children,' the Minister informed him. And he added in a tone that insinuated many things: 'They say that she prefers elephants to children.'

The venerable elder spoke again: 'It is common knowledge that a woman needs a child on her back and one in her belly to keep her from mischief.'

'Yeah,' shouted a voice in the crowd. 'Let's go and put a child in her belly. Then she will be occupied!' The people laughed heartily at the comment and a few men made provocative gestures.

Another elder now rose to speak: 'In the old days, when we needed more land, we took it from the bush. But today we are no longer allowed to do this. How are we going to survive if the reserve is there with all the animals protected, and we are boxed in and our hands are tied?'

An angry young man rose from the crowd, shouting: 'This land has been taken away from us by the white man. He has stolen our land to give it to the animals and make us poor. A white man can never be one of us. We must throw him out and take back what rightfully belongs to us. Then we shall be master over everything, over the land and the animals, and be rich.'

The fat cheerleader now began to hop about wildly, repeating, 'We shall be rich,' to the approval of the onlookers who clapped and cheered for a considerable time.

At long last, the Minister held up both arms, signalling to the people to quieten down. Then he proclaimed: 'I have heard you and am with you. Freedom fighters shall rise again as they did in the past to get rid of these last vestiges of colonialism, until we are our own masters. We do not want more bwanas. We shall not cower before the white man. We shall walk erect, as befits a proud people. We shall not tolerate injustice. Let our own law rule over our own country!'

At these words there was a thunderous ovation, everyone got up and they all started to sing and dance with jerky movements.

Then the Minister spoke again: 'I shall take your case to the President. I shall speak to him and defend your interests until justice is done and we are free!'

Upon this the Minister turned and walked to his car, escorted by the military. People rushed forward to shake his hand, but he had already stepped into his Mercedes and was off, waving to the happy crowds, while the goats and other presents followed in a pickup truck with the askaris.

26

'This thing no good, man,' said Mboko as if moved by a strong internal urge.

'What you mean by that?' Njoma took a deep drag from his cigarette, and for a moment the red glow it made was visible below the white of his eyes in the car's dark cabin.

'She's a woman, man. A white woman! There sure will be trouble.'

'Stop it, man! You not asked for opinion. You do what Boss say. And Boss say: 'You go kill her."

'I know ... I know.'

'You know Boss very upset. He give me this here special car to drive for special mission because his other car destroyed. Boss say this all white woman's fault. He very upset. And French Boss, he even more upset. He say white woman break his leg. They want revenge. They want to kill that woman!'

Neither spoke for a while as the big four-wheel drive vehicle, which was Luonga's greatest pride, slowly wound its way over the dusty track, the dimmed lights every now and then lighting up the umbrella-like forms of thorn trees. All else around was pitch dark.

Mboko finally said: 'If that there white woman can destroy car and break leg of French Boss, she very powerful. She full of witchcraft.'

'You stupid or what? Witchcraft is African, man. Belongs to us. White fellers they don't have no witchcraft.'

'Yes, but what about ghosts?' ventured Mboko after another silence.

'What ghosts?'

'You know, ghosts ... they are white. We are black ... but our ghosts are white. Now, white people ... they are white. Think of their ghosts. They must be very, very white, man. Very terrible. Just think of that!'

'You stupid or what? You ever seen a ghost?'

242

'No. And I don't want to see no ghost. But wise men in my village, they tell me about them ghosts. They terrible. They strong. I don't want to face no white woman's ghost.'

'Look, man. You not live in your village. You live in Naboru. Big, big city. No ghosts in Naboru.'

'Yeah, but this here white woman, she live in bush. This here is bush.'

'You think there are ghosts here?'

'Eeee-eee!'

'I never seen ghosts, man. What they look like?'

'People cannot see ghosts. They dead if they see ghost. But ghosts, they do what they want. Turn into a leopard. Or go through wall.'

'But why they come here to bush?'

'Perhaps to dance?' Mboko looked at his companion. 'Maybe to hold circumcision ceremonies? Who knows? Bush full of ghosts. They should be left alone. Especially very white ghosts. They very, very bad. We better turn back.'

'You not suddenly chicken? You remember training?'

'I remember training.'

'Then what you do?'

'I do what Boss commands.'

'When Boss say: "Go kill that woman," what you do?'

'I go kill that woman.'

'And if you not kill that woman and return, what Boss do?'

'He cut off my ears and privy parts and fry them.'

'So you better go kill that woman.'

They had arrived now. Njoma stopped the car outside the enclosure of Elephant Camp, switched off the headlights and got out. 'You go,' he whispered. 'Be brave! Got your knife?'

'Got my knife,' replied Mboko.

'Then you go kill quick. I mount guard here with Kalashnikov.'

Slowly, almost unwillingly, Mboko began to move towards the house: he had to do it or else his life was finished. He kept his fingers clasped around the handle of the knife, drawing courage from it, but as he got close to the house he hesitated again. What about those ghosts?

He had now reached the bottom of the wooden stairs. The woman slept in the room above, they had explained. Creep up the stairs, they had said. There is a small landing and a door to the left. That's the room. It was simple. It would be over quickly and then he would run to the car, and soon he would be safely back in Naboru where he was out of reach of those terrible ghosts. But he didn't feel entirely reassured. It was well known that ghosts waited till the last moment and then struck suddenly and unexpectedly. He wished it were all over. Lucky no one had seen him.

But he had been seen. Dumbo had been standing at the edge of the enclosure and was surprised to catch the scent of someone he didn't know. Maybe this was a new playmate. He'd better go and explore. Elephants can be extremely noiseless in spite of their bulk, and by the time Mboko put his foot on the first step, Dumbo was just behind him. This, Dumbo felt, was an ideal occasion to play one of the little tricks he so enjoyed. He advanced his trunk to within an inch of Mboko's neck and suddenly blew with all his might. As the wet blast and deafening sound hit him, Mboko jumped two feet up in the air, dropped his knife and shot up the stairs in the dark, frightened to death.

When he came to the top where the new secure railing was supposed to have been fixed, there was nothing but the bucket full of white paint Joseph Polepole had left when he had gone in pursuit of the irresistible Faithful. Mboko stumbled over it and went straight over the end of the landing. The toppled bucket hung a moment half over the edge as if undecided, paint dripping on the unfortunate man who was lying below, stunned by his fall, and then tipped over, emptying its contents on his head. Mboko gave a scream and shot off like a bullet, blinded by fear and paint, having only one aim: to get away from those dreadful ghosts as quickly as possible.

Where he stood on guard Njoma had heard a shriek and then some commotion. *Must be the woman*, he thought. *Hope that stupid Mboko killed her all right.* He reached into his pocket for his lighter and, as he lit up another cigarette, all hell suddenly broke loose. He was hit in the chest by someone running at top speed and knocked off his feet, and as he grabbed wildly around while falling he got hold of something white and sticky. A white ghost! Mboko had been right. This was surely the ghost of that white woman! It must already have killed Mboko, and now had come to kill him too!

They were both lying on the ground, with the white ghost

on top of Njoma who was gasping for breath. Panic got hold of him and he punched and kicked blindly. As Njoma's hand went down he got hold of some softer parts and at once it flashed through his mind: this was not the female ghost of the white woman; it was a male ghost! This was a different matter altogether: he was used to fighting males, ghosts or not, and redoubling his efforts Njoma decided to sell his life as dearly as possible.

Mboko too was convinced that he was fighting a ghost. After the collision he lay there for a few seconds, paralysed by fear, but when the ghost grabbed his testicles he was pressed into action and began to fight for survival. Clinging together in a deadly embrace the two men rolled through the dust and straight into a low-hanging branch of a thorn tree. Njoma yelled as a long thorn pierced his thigh. Mboko now had his fingers around Njoma's throat, while Njoma got hold of one of the white ghost's ears and, as he bit it with all his might, a sticky half-liquid substance filled his mouth. This was surely the stuff ghosts were made of. It was disgusting!

Mboko screamed in anguish, let go of his opponent's throat and struggled to his feet, trying to free himself from this new ghost's grip, but Njoma, who had also got up, kept clinging on to him. Facing the white ghost, Njoma suddenly perceived his opportunity. This was where his superior training would prove him the better of any opponent, even a ghost. In a flash he saw himself in Luonga's training grounds in Naboru, part of a group of ten, all lined up in front of the instructor. And the instructor had shown them how to neutralize an imaginary opponent they faced. He had taught them to go straight for the soft spot between the legs without further ado.

The instructor had shouted: 'What you do?'

They had all shouted back: 'We kick him in the balls,' whereupon all ten, using the left leg as a spring, had quickly jerked the right knee upwards, hitting an imaginary opponent with all their might between his legs. They had repeated this exercise over and over again, until it had become an automatic part of their fighting routine.

As Njoma faced the white ghost, he heard the instructor shout in his ears: 'What you do?' But Mboko had also been part of the group of ten and, as he faced his adversary, he too suddenly

245

saw the opening his adversary had left in his defences and also heard the instructor's voice shouting: 'What you do?' And so both right knees went up simultaneously and dealt a mighty blow to their opponent's balls.

The result was mayhem. Njoma and Mboko screamed as they fell to the ground, gripping their respective family jewels. Mboko was the first to crawl up and stumble away, bent double with pain and clutching the inside of his legs. He moved away half hopping, half running, but the paint blinded him, and he banged straight into the side of the car, knocked himself out against the hard metal and fell on his back, his mouth wide open.

A long, needle-sharp thorn went straight into Njoma's calf and another into his arm as he writhed in pain holding his testicles which seemed to be swelling to incredible proportions. Suddenly he rolled onto something long and hard: his Kalashnikov! A blind rage now took hold of him and, as he grabbed his weapon, he saw something white lying in the darkness, ten yards away, and he began to shoot, shouting: 'I'll kill you, white ghost!' The first bullet hit the windshield of the car and shattered it to pieces. The second bullet hit a tyre, which exploded with a loud bang. The third went straight into the back wing, blowing a hole through the petrol tank.

As the petrol spouted out, it splashed over Mboko, cleaning the paint off his face and running into his open mouth. This stirred him into action. He began to crawl into the bush on all fours, trying to remove himself from the scene of violence as fast as possible, spitting petrol while bullets whizzed past him. Njoma was now more enraged than ever. 'I'll get you ghost,' he gnashed between his clenched teeth, one hand on the trigger, the other on his private parts which by now felt as if they were swelling out of his trousers, and kept shooting till there were no bullets left.

One of the last bullets hit the electrics of the car, the spark hit the petrol and suddenly the darkness was lit up by a blazing fire. Gradually Njoma came to his senses. This was his Boss's precious four-wheel drive car, his pride, which he had entrusted to Njoma only because of the exceptional mission, and because his other car had been destroyed. He had warned Njoma that he would have to be personally responsible for the smallest scratch on the car body. This was not a scratch. It was a total write-off! Njoma felt instinctively that the Boss was not going to be pleased. He would be very, very upset – probably be more than upset. This was the end of Njoma's Naboru days, for sure. He had better disappear. There was a man who sometimes came to his village to hire people to work in the mines in South Africa. Better to die in a mine than to be skinned by his Boss in Naboru. And they said you could have lots of women there … although it remained to be seen whether his condition would allow him any more activity in that field. And slowly, waddling like a duck, he set off on the long road to his village.

Mboko, in the meantime, did not feel well. The drink of 98 octane petrol had not energized him as one might have thought. He burped every minute and felt dizzy. The paint had begun to dry by now, making his clothes heavy and irritating his skin. What worried him most was the condition of his testicles. They too had swollen considerably, making progress painful and slow. *I should have listened to the elders*, he thought. *Don't go to the city, they had said, it will be your downfall.* But he had been unable to resist the attraction of the bright lights, the money and easy women some of his friends who had been there had boasted about. And now what? He was a condemned man. He would have to hide for a long time, hoping his Boss would finally forget about him. And keep well away from provoking any more ghosts. If they wanted him back in his village, he would try to lead an honest life, marry and have children. But that was not so sure now. Fingering his swollen family jewels which hurt at the slightest touch, he wondered whether he would ever be a normal man again.

27

Sam Goldstein had come down late for breakfast. Kibu had gone up twice in the morning, knocking on his door to inquire if he was all right, but he hadn't answered. He had locked himself up in his room: he didn't want to risk a new encounter with that Veronica girl. He just sat there on the corner of his bed, brooding and getting hungrier and more annoyed by the minute, while memories kept assailing him. That awful female! The cheek she'd had. To shout at him, the great Samuel B. Goldstein Junior! To pour soup over his head! And to come back later to tell him that he was a criminal and that she was going to report him to the police for premeditated murder. To chase him with a whip! And after that she had installed herself for the night here in his own house. It was unheard of!

After what seemed ages he could stand it no more. He crept down the stairs while his eyes scanned the ground floor: there was no one, not a sound anywhere. He opened the door of the dining room very slowly and looked around carefully to make sure the coast was clear before entering. The room seemed to be deserted. Thank God that ghastly girl had gone!

Yet he didn't feel completely at ease, and as he reached for one of the pancakes, which were lukewarm by now, he quickly stuffed it into his mouth. One never knew with that girl: she might return at any moment. His mouth twitched nervously and he kept looking at the door while he gobbled down his breakfast as fast as he could.

Suddenly the face of that dreadful lawyer popped up in his mind's eye. He saw the conceited smirk on the man's countenance as clearly as if he were sitting right in front of him, and it put him in a thoroughly foul mood. That vicious guy had really got under his skin. He hated people who were out to get your money and flung the legal code into your face to support their claims. He just couldn't stand them! They should legally allow you to take a gun to lawyers who walked into your very house

248

threatening you with court cases. Sam kept muttering to himself, feeling irritated and restless, and the twitch around his mouth became more pronounced.

Everything appeared all right after the horrible events of the previous day, yet Sam knew it was not. There was nothing tangible, but tapping into a prevailing mood was like a sixth sense to him, and that sixth sense kept sending warning signals like a flashing light, telling him that things had changed for the worse.

Kibu always put the morning copy of the *Daily Star* on the table, and Sam now picked it up to occupy his mind. His attention was immediately caught by one of those improbable sensationalist articles which tabloids the world over love to splash all over their front pages. It carried the arresting title 'New Threat to Africa' and read:

It has been rumoured that AIDS was developed by the American secret services to depopulate Africa. Though one can never be certain of this, there is no smoke without fire, as the saying goes. Now an even more insidious danger may be threatening Africa. From a well-informed source, which unfortunately we cannot disclose for security reasons, we have gained knowledge that an American laboratory is secretly developing a chemical that strikes directly at the heart of African society. Mixed with our water supply this chemical is intended to make all African men who drink the water infertile.

Nothing seems capable of shaming the powers of the so-called developed world, or of holding them back when it comes to imagining despicable plans intended to harm us. This latest disgraceful scheme in a long list of sufferings imposed on the innocent African people seems to be their idea of solving what they call 'the African problem'.

The amazing fact, and a measure of the arrogance of those people, is that the laboratory producing this diabolical brew is not situated in a far-away country, but right in our very midst in Malavu Avenue here in Naboru. It goes without saying that we cannot let such a calamity happen and that we should act before the criminal minds behind this reprehensible scheme eliminate us from the world scene...

249

When he had begun reading the article Sam had found it extremely funny, even hilarious. He was just pouring himself a second cup of coffee when he came to the passage where it mentioned the address: they were talking about his own laboratory! His heart missed a beat, and he kept pouring out coffee without noticing it until it ran from the full cup over the table and from there over his trousers. He yelled and dropped the coffeepot, which fell on his cup, breaking it. He now became so enraged that he hurled the newspaper over the table, thereby knocking off more china.

This was the limit! How anyone could write such trash was beyond him. The worst was that the African readership was likely to believe such false, ridiculous stuff and that their reactions were unpredictable. This could easily run out of hand and have dire consequences for the lab. Boiling over with anger he went to the phone and dialled the number of the American Embassy.

Was it the dense morning activity of the Naboru offices, or the inadequacy of the city's overloaded phone network? He couldn't get through for more than half an hour, and when finally a secretary answered his call he was told that it was coffee break and that he should phone back later. He screamed with frustration, picked up a chair and smashed it against the wall. When he called back later, the embassy number seemed to be constantly engaged. After an hour he was finally connected to the head of security and began to pour out the gist of the article and his fears, into what he hoped was a sympathetic ear.

He hadn't even finished sketching the main story when the voice on the other side interrupted him. 'You civilians can be very excitable,' it said.

'Eh! What?' stammered Sam, unable to stop a sustained twitching of his mouth.

'You shouldn't take what journalists write so literally,' replied the voice on the other side. 'They blow things up, you know. Just remain calm and everything will blow over. Is that all?'

'But this is serious, can't you see?!' Sam screeched, on the edge of a nervous collapse.

'Surely you're not expecting us to send in the marines as protection any time a civilian feels offended by the lies published in newspapers?' the voice asked sarcastically. 'That's a good one. Haha! Phone back when they burn down your house. A good day to you, Sir.' And Sam heard a click as the connection was cut off.

He sat there for a while holding the receiver, shaking with resentment and shocked that a government official could behave so callously. Finally he put down the phone and knew for certain that his luck had run out.

28

'Hey, just read this,' said Phil Harriman, shoving the morning edition of the *Daily Star* under Monta's nose as they were having breakfast in their hotel that same morning.

'Please, Phil. I haven't finished my breakfast yet and I'm not in the mood. Yesterday was a horrible day.'

'But just read this and tell me what you think of it. It's not very long.'

'OK,' sighed Monta and began to read. 'What you want me to read such a stupid story for?' she commented when she had finished it.

'Don't you see? The address? Of course you don't know about addresses over here. It's the lab to which we went yesterday.'

'But then ... that article is a pack of lies!' exclaimed Monta. 'There's just John in that lab, lying there on a table with wires coming out of his head. And a lot of beeping things. I didn't see any chemicals in there! Whoever informed the newspaper about these chemicals must be dumb.'

'I was the informant.'

Monta swallowed a couple of times and then she said: 'Oh.'

'But don't you see how clever that was?' asked Phil, looking mightily pleased with himself.

'Well, yes ... no.'

'African crowds are easily inflamed. I'm certain that they will attack the house and destroy the lab before the day is done. And whose brainless body is inside and cannot be moved?'

'Well I never ... You *are* clever, Phil!' exclaimed Monta in awe. 'No one else would ever have thought of that. You do have brains.' She now put her hand on his. 'It is so reassuring for a woman to know she's in good hands.'

Phil did not withdraw his hand but smiled, saying: 'Shall we go up to your bedroom? We've got the whole day and nothing else to do.'

She nodded, looking at him with a hint of complicity, finished her cup of coffee and left the breakfast room, her arm hooked into his.

29

'I've just been up north,' said the Minister of Home Affairs, 'and there's quite a revolt going on. People are getting fed up with the elephant reserve and its privileges. The elephants attack them almost daily and destroy their shambas. No wonder the villagers are out for revenge. They claim that the government doesn't do anything to protect them and are ready to take the law into their own hands. If solutions aren't forthcoming soon, this could have grave political implications.'

The President eyed Mamabeka with displeasure. Yet, however much he disliked and distrusted him, the Minister was an important man from the second largest tribe in the country, and he needed his support.

'It's all very well to complain about the elephants, Minister,' he replied, 'but what can we do about them? There is too much international pressure to protect elephants. And these non-governmental organizations have observers everywhere. If you can think of a solution, you're welcome to tell me,' he added with sarcasm in his voice.

'I believe that we should approach the problem in a more businesslike fashion, President. I notice that this particular reserve is costing money, and this at a time when the whole world is talking about getting the accounts into balance and letting market forces rule. Everywhere, worldwide, enterprises have to pay for themselves. And what have we got here: no income.'

'What about the tourists coming to visit our wildlife parks?' objected the President. 'Don't they bring in money? Aren't the parks our goldmines and the animals our gold?'

'Indeed, President, indeed. The Ministry of Wildlife had money, but you know what the previous Minister did: Kimbabe ran off with the lot, even with the funds set aside to pay for an American specialist who was to come and help out with the problems of this reserve.'

'But can't the reserve pay for itself?'

'President, this is a reserve, not a park, and it has a special status. Nothing is organized here as it is in our parks. It is just an animal sanctuary. There are no visitors and no money coming in. The government is just pouring money down the drain while problems are growing beyond control. And what do the villagers who live around get out of it? Nothing but trouble.'

'Couldn't all that be organized differently?'

'Maybe, but not by the World Elephant Fund which is now running the reserve. All they ever worry about are the elephants, and nothing else.'

'What do you propose then?' asked the President.

'That we remove the present management from the reserve. The Americans want privatization. So let's privatize and give the concession to a private company that integrates everything.'

'That's easier said than done. Where are you going to find a company willing to take over the reserve?'

'As a matter of fact, in preparation for this meeting, I have put out a few feelers and found a French company that might be interested.'

'But as you just pointed out: how can this reserve possibly be of interest to a private company; it will want to make money?'

'As you rightly observe, President, this is indeed the crux of the matter. I have therefore discussed this particular problem at length with the French company, and am pleased to tell you that there may be a solution satisfactory to all interested parties...'

'Really? Tell me.'

'The problem is that there are too many elephants and that in the present situation we're powerless to do anything about this. Now, if we changed the status of the reserve and called it a private wildlife park, we could leave the running to a private company, which could cull the elephants. Getting rid of the excess elephants would remove the pressure on the villages around the park and relieve the tense political situation.'

'That sounds interesting so far,' the President said, nodding.

'There's even better. The company could at the same time sell not only the ivory but also the meat and all the rest. The French company would then pass on a share of the proceeds to the government. So instead of costing us money, the park would bring in revenue. No more worries for us; only revenue that would come in regularly. Just think what a relief that would be.'

The President did not have a very high opinion of his Minister of Home Affairs, but he had to admit that he was impressed by his solid reasoning. 'Minister,' said the President, 'let me congratulate you for your good work. It all sounds wonderful. But I see an insurmountable obstacle.'

'Which one?'

'I seem to recall that there is an agreement between our government and the World Elephant Fund you just mentioned, giving the concession to them. How can we break this agreement without creating a serous international incident – a worldwide scandal? We'll become pariahs and Western donors will withdraw aid. And what will we have gained then?'

'President, I have had this elephant reserve Charter analysed and discovered that there is a rider attached to it, stipulating that the details of the agreement are open for review every ten years.'

'And when is the deadline due?'

'As it happens, in three weeks' time. So we could exploit this to ask the World Elephant Fund for ten million dollars, which is the amount at which the French company has valued the private park.'

'Do you call ten million dollars a detail?' exclaimed the President, whose eyes nearly popped out of his head.

'It is somewhat big to pass as a detail, but keep in mind that it was your predecessor who signed the agreement, not you.'

'But he signed it in name of the government! Think what would happen if every new president changed the rules. There would be anarchy. Nothing would be safe, not even for retired presidents!'

'President, we are not rescinding the Charter. This is a dispute mainly about costs, a new direction, and a more modern approach. I'm certain that we'll be able to present our new approach in terms that sound reasonable and make it acceptable in international circles. Also, remember the political problems this is stirring up. We don't want an uprising of the people around the elephant reserve, do we? We don't want them to march into the reserve to kill all the elephants and eat them, which is what they are threatening to do. Think of the bad international press that would give our country. And it would not put a shilling into the government's coffers.'

'Right. Right.' The President thought for a while. 'Well, if you have a solution, go ahead. The Ministry of Wildlife is one of your responsibilities at present, and I appreciate your concern. But I don't want any unpleasantness. Let there be no attacks upon foreigners running the reserve. And keep the foreign press out of this if possible.'

Mamabeka now got up with a broad smile on his face, saying: 'I am pleased that we have found a way out of this difficult situation. Rest assured that all will turn out for the best for everyone.' He shook hands with the President and left the office.

30

It was dry season again and the matriarch was leading her herd towards a permanent watercourse. The moment they got near enough to pick up the scent, all the elephants rushed forward, hot and weary after the long march, and plunged into the cool waters in an access of joy, drinking their fill and showering themselves, splashing and rolling about. Then they retired into the shade, ready to sleep, their large ears cooling the blood and shutting out the world.

John was occupied with his little elephant and it was not until the late afternoon that he realized that this was the place where he had come face to face with the hominids possibly several years earlier, before the birth of his baby. Would they still be there? He had not seen any other creatures like them during his wanderings of several years through East Africa and felt quite convinced now that these were the only hominids around. He left his little elephant with the other females and moved to where he remembered the campsite to be. He found it, and as he approached it he noticed the slender apelike figures who observed him with suspicion, ready to flee. They were still there!

The elephants had been in the riverbed no more than a day or two when John saw a pride of lions emerging from the undergrowth of the forest into the open stretch along the river. They looked lean and aggressive because there were few animals to hunt in the area: the rainy season had been long and the rains abundant, and most herbivores were still out in the open savannah. The hungry lions monitored every move of the young elephants in the herd and kept hanging around. It was dangerous for the calves, especially when one of them was unable to mount the steep bank or got stuck in the mud.

A few days later John happened to wander near the spot where the hominids lived when he noticed that the lions were slowly crawling through the grass, ringing the campsite and gradually closing in upon the hominids. In a flash John understood their intentions: as there were few herbivores and catching them was difficult, they intended to eat the little people. There was not a second to lose! He charged forward towards the nearest lions, making them flee, while the hominids, alarmed by his thunderous approach and now perceiving the lions, screamed in fear and bolted up the trees. One lioness was so intent on catching one of the small creatures that she paid no attention to the elephant and got crushed under the heavy feet. The piercing cries of the hominids continued until the lions had retreated, chased by John, but the commotion went on for several hours.

These lions are hungry and will certainly try again, thought John as he returned to the herd. *If I don't protect the hominids and chase the lions away, sooner or later they will kill them. I can't possibly let that happen! I can't let them destroy the ancestors of humanity – my own ancestors. If they did, there would never be any humans on Earth. I must keep an eye on these ruthless predators.*

The following morning the lions managed to kill an eland and spent several hours crouched around the carcass, greedily eating their fill. Afterwards they just lay about on low-hanging branches and rocks, sleeping and digesting, and for the next few days everyone was left in peace, until the lions got hungry again and started prowling around the riverside in search of new prey.

After the first attack the hominids were constantly on the alert, but John didn't want to take any risks. He knew the lions' intentions and didn't trust them, even when they pretended to be moving in a casual manner. Whenever he saw them approach the campsite, he rushed in and chased them away. The lions couldn't believe what was happening and kept trying again, but after two weeks they gave up and left the hominids alone.

More animals began to cluster around the watercourse as the dry season advanced, and soon the lions were busy chasing bigger game on the savannah. They were no longer interested in small fry like the hominids now, and John was finally able to relax, spending his days educating his baby elephant and enjoying life with his family in the herd.

31

'*Donnerwetter! Donnerwetter!*' swore Klaus, fiddling with the knobs.
Little lights flickered on and off, the machine buzzed every now
and then, but there was no signal.

I just can't understand what's happened, he thought. *Where is
his brain? It can't be lost.*

He faintly heard people shouting outside in the street. A
crowd was gathering in front of the house and with every
passing hour more Africans were arriving, pushing against the
gate, trying to break it down. How long would it hold?

'The greatest experiment ever, and now this,' he fumed. 'I'm
disgusted! I've got to save my experiment! But how can I move
the table with John's body lying on it, the time machine and
all the equipment? It's impossible with those *Dummköpfe* blocking
the front gate. And where are all the others?'

As he left the lab and went into the house, the noise coming
from the crowd outside sounded much louder. He began to
shout: 'Is anyone there?' but there was no answer. The house
seemed empty. *What have we now?* he thought. *No one here? They
have left me alone to face a mass of irresponsible people who might
break in at any moment. Das ist doch nicht möglich!'*

'Yes, Sahib.' Kibu suddenly seemed to have materialized out
of thin air. 'You wanted something?'

'*Ach*, Kibu! You're still here.'

'I'm always there when I'm needed, Sahib.'

'Where's everybody?'

'In view of the critical situation the members of the personnel
have abandoned the premises, Sahib.'

'And Sam? Where's Sam?'

'I am afraid that Sahib Goldstein has a pronounced aversion
for mixing with the crowds. He let me know that he preferred
to remove his physical presence to some quieter spot, but asked
me to convey to you that he will remain with you in spirit.'

'Now, that's going to be a great help,' grumbled Klaus. 'We

are besieged, and you mean to say that there are only the two of us to defend the house against a mob of hundreds of overexcited assailants?'

'There remain three of us, Sahib. Don't forget Sahib Garfinger.'

'And what an asset he is! Our secret weapon, eh? With someone like him amongst us, what have we got to fear, eh? I'd better go back to the lab to see if I can stir some life into that secret weapon!'

32

John's herd had stayed near the watercourse for several months now. Life was becoming increasingly cramped and John was longing for the onset of the rainy season. Then, one day, he perceived low rumbling sounds as from far-away thunder, yet the sky remained bright blue. The rumbling kept coming back at intervals throughout the night and when morning broke John noticed a small plume of smoke rising from the nearby volcano. By the late afternoon the rumblings became more intense and the animals were showing signs of extreme nervousness, moving about without sense or direction. Just before sunset John heard a deafening explosion and the Earth shook under his feet as the top of the volcano was literally blown into the air and a stream of red-hot lava erupted from the gaping hole.

All the elephants scattered in fear and John found himself isolated from the herd. Large and small animals were charging out of control, coming at him from all directions, bumping into him, rebounding and then racing off in another direction. The wild stampede lasted all night as streams of glowing lava spouted out of the crater in a fantastic dancing blaze, lighting up the dark sky, while the Earth kept trembling and the volcano emitted deep rumbling sounds that sent the elephants into spasms of terror.

When the morning dawned, the soil and trees were hidden under a layer of ash and the Earth seemed dead. Animals were standing around everywhere in a state of shock, exhausted now and covered in grey dust. But where were all the elephants? Suddenly panic took hold of John as he thought: *Where is my baby?* He began to send out loud calling sounds while running about frantically. Then, from the riverbed, he heard a plaintive call and recognized the voice of his little one. As he reached the steep bank a most horrible scene unfolded before his eyes: there was his baby elephant, stuck in the mud, surrounded by

262

hominids who were attacking him with long pointed sticks. For a moment John's heart stopped, and then he rushed forward emitting a blood curdling trumpeting sound.

33

I must do something, thought Klaus, sweat dripping off his face, *I must do something whatever the risk involved.* He pushed his spectacles back onto his nose with a resolute gesture. *All right! Exceptional circumstances call for daring acts. This is my last chance: I'll set up the emergency call-back. Either it works or else he'll be lost forever. And even if he comes back his brain may be critically damaged.*

'Gott stehe mir bei,' he prayed as he started punching in some settings, diluting the time-component and putting the range at maximum.

Suddenly a very faint wave pattern began to appear on the screen. 'At last!' exclaimed Klaus, trembling with excitement. He now began to twiddle knobs, gradually narrowing the space-and-time range, until the signal became stronger and the machine began to beep. 'I got him, I got him!' he yelled and began pushing the handle very slowly, millimetre by millimetre.

There was a slight stirring in John's limp body. *Now*, thought Klaus as he kept pushing back the handle. *Come on, old boy! Do it for science. Do it for me. And for yourself! Come back or we'll both be killed.*

All of a sudden, John's body contracted convulsively. With a jerk he moved his head and began to shout: 'I'll kill you! I'll kill you!' his face contorted with rage.

Klaus had expected anything, but not this. It almost scared the wits out of him, and as John's forearms began to mill around wildly he ran behind his desk, picked up his chair and held it defensively in front of his face. He felt somewhat safer now, but his voice was still shaky when he asked: 'Are you there, John? Are you all right?'

John's torso began to strain against the straps that held him to the table, and he continued to shout: 'I'll kill you! I'll kill you!'

I must calm him down, thought Klaus. *He is still under the influence of the shock.*

'Don't take it so badly, man,' he said soothingly. 'You'll be all right. There's no need to kill me.'

'I'll kill you all!' shouted John. His eyes bulged out of his head and he looked a frightening sight with the wires hanging down from his scalp.

Klaus had been so worried, had hoped, yes, prayed for John's brain content to return to his body, but this weird man who was now staring at him with wild eyes fixing a point somewhere beyond his shoulder, was a total surprise. Maybe only part of the brain's content had come back whilst the rest had been lost somewhere in space–time? It was unnerving. How could it have happened? He was certain that all the formulas were accurate, and the electronics right and correctly programmed. Klaus did not understand.

He looked at John again. *I have no experience with madness*, he thought, *but this fellow surely has a mad stare in his eyes. What does one do in the presence of mad people? How does one approach them?* He now remembered that someone had once told him that madmen could be highly intelligent but at the same time a bit simplistic. *Better talk to John as if he were a child and not contradict him*, he concluded.

'So you want to kill us all then?' he ventured soothingly.

'Yes, yes! All of you!'

'But why?' asked Klaus, taken aback. 'Why do you want to kill us all?'

'Do you ask?' shouted John in disbelief. 'As if you don't know! After all I did for you? How could you? You ungrateful monsters! You're just cruel and treacherous. The world would be better off without you! And we elephants would be so much happier.'

Klaus sat down, puzzled. 'I do not understand,' he mumbled, looking in despair at his instruments that kept buzzing plaintively. 'I just don't understand what could have gone wrong.'

Then, abruptly, the wild gaze went out of John's eyes. He quietened down and looked around bewildered, as if awakening from a deep dream.

'Where am I?' he mumbled, staring at the equipment. Suddenly he saw Klaus, who was watching every movement he made, almost holding his breath.

'Is that you, Klaus?' he said in a surprised voice. 'What am I doing here?'

A great weight dropped off Klaus' shoulders. He was so overcome with emotion that he rushed forward to congratulate John, forgetting about the dozens of cables hanging about everywhere. As he hooked his feet behind several of them and pulled them along, they popped out of the time machine and one rack fell to the floor in a great crash, whilst Klaus disappeared amongst the leads under the table.

Moments later, after he had felt around for his spectacles, found them and fixed them back onto his nose, Klaus' head popped up at the end of the table on which John was lying.

'You remember me then? And my time machine? Do you recall my time machine? I whizzed you away to the past and I've just called you back. Tell me where you've been? I'm longing to know.'

A look of understanding came into John's eyes. 'Yes,' he said. 'Yes. I remember now.' Suddenly he became very angry. 'Why did you call me back at this critical instant?' he shouted furiously. 'Couldn't you have waited a few moments longer? I was just about to kill...'

'Yes...' Klaus nodded, all eager.

John opened his mouth, shut it again, waited a few seconds and finally made up his mind, saying: 'I don't want to talk about it.'

Klaus sensed that John was hiding a lot of extremely interesting information. 'All right,' he said soothingly, speaking as if to an obstinate child. 'Then just tell me where you've been...'

'I told you that I don't want to talk about it,' repeated John stubbornly, pressing his lips together.

'But your story is of the greatest interest. You must talk for the sake of science!' insisted Klaus. 'Tell me at least whether you found out anything about the hominids.'

'I don't give a damn about science!' exclaimed John suddenly. 'And to hell with all hominids, those ungrateful cunning bastards! Don't ask me about them. I hate them!'

Klaus realized that it was no use insisting for the time being. John was still in too great a state of shock. His reactions made it clear, though, that he had been in the deep past. It was also obvious that he had seen hominids and had had some very bad experiences he didn't want to talk about for the moment. Later, maybe, when he had calmed down, he would speak.

Everything had ended well and Klaus felt immensely relieved. He had pulled it off! Then a feeling of elation bubbled up inside him, lightness enveloped his whole being and his feet seemed to lift off the ground. He, Klaus Roderick Kundewust, was the greatest scientist ever. He was the first to have built a functioning time machine, to have sent someone into the past and brought him back. He had made history. He would be remembered in a thousand years hence – nay, forever. He had become immortal!

He began to sing Beethoven's '*Ode an die Freude*' in a high-pitched falsetto voice, took a few quick limping steps forward, jumped up in the air flapping his arms as if he were going to fly, and landed unceremoniously amongst the racks of equipment at the end of the laboratory, which hadn't been built to cope with flying scientists.

John had followed this outburst with a wary look in his eyes. *A madman,* he thought. *That's what he is. How I ever put my life into the hands of such a nutcase is beyond me? Better get out of here quickly.*

As Klaus attempted to crawl out from amongst the debris of his equipment John turned his head towards him. 'Hey!' he shouted.

'*Was ist los?* What is it now?' asked Klaus, back on Earth after having soared to the heights of immortality, and trying to extricate the mortal part of his being from the wires in which he found himself entangled.

'Can't you take those pins out of my scalp? They hurt, you know, especially if you keep pulling the wires to which they are attached.'

'*Was?* What?' inquired Klaus giving a good yank to one of the wires which had got wound around his neck. 'Can't you see I'm occupied? Damned wires! They're all over the place! What this laboratory needs is order!'

'Klaus, you stupid ass! Stop fiddling and take these pins off my head! And undo these straps. I'm numb and getting a cramp.' Then he looked at the laboratory with undisguised disapproval. 'And it is stifling in here. How you humans can stand living cooped up in such cluttered boxes is beyond me. Get me out of here! And quickly!'

'Hey! Hey! *Du Finkelstein!* A bit of respect, please.' This John

267

fellow was definitely getting on his nerves. He should have felt beholden to him for the honour. It was like having been offered the opportunity of being the first man on the Moon, and having your name go down in history books. As a footnote to his own, of course, but still! And look how ungrateful he was. Not a word of thanks, not a look in his eyes showing how much he venerated his great benefactor. There was only one explanation: he must be mad. And to think that he had chosen this madman for his extraordinary, unique, historic experiment. Come to think of it, the fellow had a reputation for being frivolous, and from what had happened to him and that girl Veronica every time he had gone to see her, it was obvious that he must be off his rocker. But he seemed much more deranged since he had returned from the past. The trip could well have completely unbalanced him. *Maybe he has become violent*, thought Klaus. *I'd better be careful. Not upset him and get him out of here.*

He had disentangled himself by now, and went over to John, trying to be as accommodating as possible. 'All right, all right,' he said while taking the wires off John's head and undoing the little probes that had been fastened all over his scalp.

'Awooh!' shouted John. 'You're hurting me. Careful.'

'Sorry, *mein Freund*, sorry,' replied Klaus. 'Can't help it. Your skin has grown over the probes.'

'Not surprising, considering that my body must have been lying here for at least three or four years.'

'Three or four years? You must be joking. How do you think we kept you alive for a couple of years? You've been lying here just over a week,' said Klaus, pulling out the last probes and starting to unfasten the straps that kept John fixed to the table.

When the last strap had come off, John sat up stiffly and began to rub his arms and legs. Then he climbed down and took a few uncertain steps holding on to the table.

'Just over a week,' he mumbled, bending his knees and doing a few stretching exercises. 'I do not understand.'

There was a knock on the door and Kibu walked in. He was just about to say something to Klaus when he noticed John. A smile lit his face as he spoke: 'Welcome again amongst us, Sahib. We have been worried about your health, and it is very appropriate of you to have come back at this very moment.' Then he turned to Klaus: 'I would strongly advise you not to delay departure,

Sahib. The front gate will not hold out much longer. They have brought a sledgehammer and are hard at work trying to knock the hinges out. The gate may come down any moment now.' Then he looked at John with a smile. 'I will fetch your bag, Sahib, to save you the discomfort of having to find new gear.'

'*Donnerwetter!*' exclaimed Klaus. 'I had completely forgotten. Quick! My papers. The formulas.' He rushed to his desk and began rummaging inside the drawers.

Kibu reappeared within a minute or two, motioning them to follow. 'May I suggest that you both come this way,' he proposed, 'and that we leave via the small door at the back of the garden?' And without further ado he preceded them out of the laboratory. Just as he unlocked the small door at the back, they heard a great crashing noise behind them, followed by the excited shouts of the angry mob streaming into the front garden.

PART
THREE

1

As they moved away along the backstreet, the racket made by the shouting crowd became gradually less audible. They continued at a rapid pace for some ten minutes, turned into an unlit side street and finally stopped in front of a low bungalow. 'I do apologize,' said Kibu as he stepped through the doorway, 'but may I ask the Sahibs to wait a moment while I make some arrangements?'

They heard muffled voices and a commotion going on inside. After a while the head servant reappeared and, making a gesture of invitation with his hand, he said: 'May I welcome the Sahibs into this humble dwelling?' He led them into a small room, beckoned to them to sit down on some low wooden chairs, and then left to organize the evening meal.

The two men remained silent for a while in the half-dark room, lit only by a petrol lamp. Finally John mumbled, as if to himself: 'I do not understand.'

'*Was?*' replied Klaus who was busily arranging his papers and formulas, oblivious of the situation.

'What's happened? Why this rush? Why did we have to leave the house?'

'Don't you understand? Because of the mob, of course. We couldn't delay any longer. A mob can be very dangerous, you know,' explained Klaus, nodding vigorously as if to emphasize the soundness of his logic.

'Klaus! I know there was a mob out there. I heard those people! I'm asking *why* they were set on attacking the house.'

'Oh that! I see now what you mean. It was because of that article in the *Daily Star*, don't you understand?'

'No. I don't! You can't expect me to have been reading newspapers while you left me brainless on that table, can you?

'Hah! Now that is a really interesting idea for a new experiment,' remarked Klaus. 'Provide entertainment for the pig from Guinea. *Ja. Eine sehr gute Idee!*' And he stuck his finger up in the air while his eyes shone with excitement behind his spectacles. 'I must follow this up.'

'Oh God!' murmured John, covering his eyes and shaking his head in exasperation.

Suddenly he heard someone clearing his throat, and turning towards the sound he saw Kibu standing nearby. 'Allow me to explain this unfortunate incident, Sahib,' said the head servant. 'This morning an article appeared in the *Daily Star* alleging that Sahib Klaus' laboratory was producing a chemical intended to make African men infertile.'

'You must be joking!'

'No, no,' interrupted Klaus, 'it is true. I read it with my own eyes. A strange idea that! I have been thinking about it and I wonder whether it can be done … maybe if one tried…'

'Klaus! Don't interfere!' shouted John. Then he turned to Kibu: 'But this is total nonsense.'

Kibu continued: 'I don't claim that the newspaper *deliberately* attempted to incite the crowds. It is common policy of newspapers the world over to come up with sensationalist news in order to be of greater interest than their competitors and to excite their readers. But African mobs, when worked the right way, tend to be somewhat inflammable, in particular when touched in what's nearest and dearest to them.'

'What puzzles me,' interrupted Klaus again, 'is that the article asserts that they have got the information from a well-informed source. But how can that source have been well informed when the information was not correct?'

'I wonder who's really behind all this?' said John pensively.

Kibu, who had stood there with a face that showed indecision, at last decided to speak. 'I have a cousin working on the staff of that paper and, although I would not normally reveal any confidential information, I feel that, in this particular case, it is my duty to make an exception. It was Mrs Garfinger's lawyer who passed this fabricated story on to the paper. It goes without saying that it was totally made up, but it incited the crowds and goaded them into action, resulting in the savage attack on Sahib Goldstein's property as we had occasion to witness.'

'Mrs Garfinger's lawyer?' asked John utterly surprised.

'Yes. He arrived here with the intention of making you sign some documents…'

'Make me sign documents? While I was lying on Klaus' time machine without a brain?'

Klaus was unable to keep quiet. 'I told him so!' he chuckled. 'I told him that hominids couldn't read or write, but he didn't seem to understand a word of what I was saying. I think he's a bit daft. That would explain how he got the information about the lab so totally wrong...'

'Klaus, please, can't you let Kibu continue?'

Kibu now carried on: 'The lawyer was of course unaware of your condition and had come out here accompanied by Mrs Garfinger...'

'By Mrs Garfinger?'

'Yes. The Sahib's wife whom we had the pleasure of meeting.'

'You mean Monta? My ex. But that's impossible! She's never left America.'

'I can assure you that she was here, Sahib,' countered Kibu unperturbed.

'Yeah. I saw her too,' interjected Klaus. 'It was quite funny. She was lying there on the floor of the lab with...'

'Klaus, please! Stop talking nonsense!' John shook his head. 'My ex lying on the floor of the lab! Can't you let Kibu explain everything?'

Klaus looked offended. 'I was just about to tell you a very amusing story...'

'Well, tell me later. Look! You've made me forget where we were...'

Klaus fell silent and sat there pouting, staring out over his spectacles with an offended look on his face.

'...Oh yes. How could Monta have been here? Nothing could possibly induce her to leave America unless ... yes, unless she's after a lot of money. Really big money. But...'

Kibu now spoke: 'That's probably what this was all about, Sahib. I have the impression that there is a large amount of money involved.'

'But how can that be? I haven't got a cent to my name: all I possess is an overdrawn credit card, a passport and a return ticket to Chicago. They were in my coat...' John suddenly looked up in panic. 'My coat didn't remain in the house, did it?'

'No, no, Sahib. Rest assured. I retrieved it from your room when I went to pick up your bag. Everything is safe.'

'Thank God!' exclaimed John in relief. 'I just couldn't face having to go to the American Embassy asking for a new passport. Please, continue.'

'Well ... it so happened that the lawyer left the documents he wanted you to sign on the table as he went in search of Mrs Garfinger after she had disappeared from the room, and I took the liberty of reading them. The documents stated that you had a thousand shares in a company called Biotech One, and the lawyer wanted these to be part of the divorce settlement.'

'Yes, Biotech One ... shares ... wait ... it's coming back. It's all so long ago ... it seems like a previous life.'

He had wanted to forget those shares. It had been such a painful episode in his life that he had erased their existence from his memory, but now Kibu had opened the doors of remembrance.

'Yes, indeed, I've got some shares ... but they are worthless!'

'They may have been worth very little when you obtained them, Sahib, but how long ago was that?'

'Let me think ... that must have been five years ago ... no, more...'

'Shares can go up tremendously in five years, Sahib. They may be worth a lot of money now; it wouldn't surprise me.'

'They must be, otherwise Monta would never have been induced to come out here.' Suddenly John looked up. 'What date are we today?'

'It is now the evening of the 25th of August, Sahib.'

'And I'm going to be divorced on ... let me see ... on the 27th. I think I understand everything now. They wanted me to sign before the divorce, that's it! They must have been under great pressure. Imagine their frustration then when they discovered that I was in no condition to sign anything.' He grinned. 'I wish I could have seen her face.'

'Permit me to ask you, Sahib, if you had died before the 27th, who would have inherited?'

John reflected for a while. 'As Monta would still have been my wife, I believe she'd have got everything.'

'I think that this explains why the lawyer went to the newspaper. He intended to provoke the crowd into attacking the lab. You would have been killed in the process and been eliminated from the scene.'

276

'Lord almighty!' exclaimed John. 'Of all the low bastardly tricks lawyers have up their sleeves.'

'Am I allowed to speak now?' asked Klaus, unable to contain his impatience any longer. 'I too have an important contribution to make, but you don't let me.'

'All right, Klaus, go ahead.'

Klaus hesitated. Now that they were at last waiting for him to tell his story, he didn't know where to begin. 'You see,' he finally blurted out, 'that wife of yours, she looked innocent, but she's not. She is a killer!'

'Klaus, you must be off your nut. Monta is a devious, unscrupulous schemer; she's a bunch of egocentrism, concerned only about her own comforts. But a killer? No way!'

'Ask Veronica if you don't believe me!'

'Oh God!' exclaimed John, holding his head. 'You're driving me mad! Do you really have to bring Veronica into this story?'

'Do I have to?' Klaus shot an offended look at John. 'You would be dead but for her! You don't even know!' he sneered. 'That's how ignorant you are. And then you dare tell me to shut up when you should be sitting there with your ears pricked up, you *Finkelstein!* Let me tell you that that wife of yours was ready to pull the wires from your head, when our little elephant girl caught her arm and wrestled her to the floor.'

'Klaus, you're pulling my leg! Veronica here? I wonder what you're going to tell me next?'

'I'm not pulling legs!' retorted Klaus. 'It was a scene I shall never forget. What a woman! She chased everyone out of the lab with a set of cables. The lawyer and your wife just ran for their lives. And Sam, who was full of soup you see, had to run too. We were all trembling. I never thought she had it in her. Such a slender woman! But how she handled those cables. Very impressive!'

'Klaus! Stop telling fairy tales!'

'No, Sahib,' intervened Kibu. 'Sahib Klaus is telling the truth. I saw her with my own eyes. She spent the rest of the day and the following night with you in the lab to guard you from further dangers.'

'Didn't I tell you!' exclaimed Klaus. 'You should have seen her. She was like a ferocious lioness defending her cub!'

'A miracle!' exclaimed John. 'A miracle has happened! And

277

to think that I wasn't there to see her ... at least ... I mean that my mind wasn't there.'

Kibu now cleared his throat. 'May I suggest that the Sahibs presently have their supper and retire afterwards. We have all had an eventful day and have to get up early tomorrow. I wish you goodnight.' And he turned and quietly left the room.

2

Next morning Klaus and John were woken up by the smell of fresh coffee. They had only just washed and dressed when Kibu brought in the breakfast.

Klaus gulped down his coffee with great gusto after adding three heaped spoonfuls of sugar, but he looked rather doubtfully at the pile of steaming maize cakes on the table.

'I apologize for being unable to keep up the high standards to which the Sahibs are accustomed,' said Kibu as he was about to withdraw. 'Unfortunately we shall have to make do with what the house can provide until our present difficulties are resolved.'

'I'm quite happy with these cakes,' stated John. 'They're a nice change from grass and leaves.'

Kibu looked at him, a puzzled expression on his face. Then he said: 'I'm afraid that I'm unable to grasp the meaning of the Sahib's words.'

'Well ... you know ... what elephants eat,' commented John, his mouth full of maize cake thickly smeared with golden syrup.

Klaus turned towards Kibu, tapping his temple with his forefinger. 'It's the time machine,' he whispered. 'Don't pay any attention.'

'Hey, I heard you! Are you implying that I'm mad?'

'I'm not implying that you're mad! I'm just trying to tell Kibu, who doesn't know you see, how badly the time machine has affected your brain. Mind you, I'm not accusing you. It's not entirely your fault. This is the first time such an experiment has been performed...' Klaus stuck out his chest in pride, '... *ever*. It was impossible to foresee how it would run and, considering the uncertainties involved, it's surprising that most of your brain's content seems to have come back. Ah, that reminds me ... I must check ... Tell me, do you remember your childhood?' Klaus looked at him as a psychiatrist might have looked at an unbalanced patient.

'Klaus! I'm not mentally deranged, do you hear me? Not de ... rang ... ed!'

279

'Oh no? And who wanted to kill me when he returned to the present, eh? Who screamed like a wild madman?'

'It wasn't you I wanted to kill! I wanted to kill all the hominids.'

'Kill all the hominids?'

'Yes, wipe them out. I was just rushing forward to kill them off when you called me back to the present.' John suddenly flared up. 'You stopped me, you idiot! Why you had to interfere at that critical moment is beyond me. You might at least have waited till I'd finished the job. But no! You always have to meddle, you annoying busybody!'

'*Was!* You call me an idiot. And a busy body! My body is not busy. My mind is busy. The most brilliant mind you ever had the privilege of speaking to. *Dummkopf* yourself! You do not understand anything and you dare contradict me, you *Finkelstein!* You are too stupid to realize that you could never have killed all the hominids.'

'Not killed them? If you hadn't stopped me I wouldn't have hesitated a second!' John was very upset now, and his voice became high-pitched. 'I would have destroyed them all. The lot! And it would have done the planet a great service. I would have got rid of the human race once and for all. Think. Just think what we could have had: unspoilt landscapes as far as the eye can see; vast herds of animals roaming the Earth; no polluted rivers – the freshwater animals would have thanked me; no cut-down forests – the trees would have hugged me; no killing of whales – the whales would have shaken my hand. And the elephants! They would have erected a statue to the mother elephant of two and a half million years ago who rid the Earth of the vilest, most destructive predator ever alive!'

'*Aber du bist verrückt!* That's not possible.'

'I know what you're going to say: that elephants cannot erect statues. I was speaking in the figurative sense of course. And what future is there now left for us elephants … I mean, for the elephants? And for all the other wild animals? What is happening today is no less than a giant mass extinction, not unlike the one that happened sixty-five million years ago, ending the reign of the dinosaurs. Only, to exterminate all the wild animals, humans won't need a meteor like the one that wiped out the dinosaurs. They'll manage it all on their own.'

'But I tell you that it's not possible,' repeated Klaus, shaking his head in despair at such obtuseness.

'Hey, your record has got stuck! You keep repeating the same sentence. What's not possible?'

'That you would have been able to destroy the hominids. If only you left me time to explain...'

'If that's what you think, you'd better think something else. If you, the great manipulator, had not flashed me back at that crucial moment, I would have wiped them clean off the face of the Earth.'

'But don't you realize the contradiction in what you're saying? Had you killed the hominids, you would have killed our ancestors, and eliminated mankind. That means everyone, including you and me.'

'Good heavens!' exclaimed John. 'Of course! You mean to say that by killing the hominids I would also have killed myself...' He thought for a moment. 'Well, come to think about it, I wouldn't have minded. If it needed my disappearance to save the planet, so be it. I'd have found consolation in all the smiling elephants I would have left behind.'

'Yeah! Smiling elephants! Smiling whales! Smiling trees! Smiling everything, but no smiling humans! You still don't seem to grasp the problem. Had you killed the hominids, we wouldn't have existed. And I would not have been able to make a time machine and send you back two and a half million years in time to put an end to the hominid line. See! Had you been able to do so, we wouldn't have existed and you would not have been able to do so. Don't you understand? In a space–time transformation you cannot possibly return to the past and be in a position to influence the present. The theory of general relativity prohibits it; or at least, the philosophical implications of space–time transformations do not allow it!'

'Are you saying then that everything was inevitable? That you had to intervene at that critical moment and call me back?'

'I suppose so. I don't really know. But I'm sure that you couldn't have killed the hominids.'

John sat there, deeply affected by Klaus' words. 'I didn't want to be called back!' he protested angrily, thinking of his last moments as an elephant. *I so wanted to save my baby elephant,* he thought with despair.

'Well, Sahib,' intervened Kibu who had been listening to the conversation, 'I for one am delighted to have you back amongst us. Allow me to ask: do you have any particular plans for the immediate future?'

'I have not given my future a single thought yet,' replied John, who was still trying to come to terms with his past – the sadness of losing his life on the savannah and his baby elephant.

'As you still have your return ticket, passport and credit card, Sahib, I would suggest, if you permit me, that you return to America without further delay and find out about those shares. I have a feeling that what you will discover may be of the greatest interest.'

3

Veronica had slept badly and woken up in an anxious state of mind. She had returned to Elephant Camp the previous day as she urgently had to monitor her elephants, leaving Klaus in charge of John but when she and Steve had got home they had found the burned-out wreck of a car. Steve had gone to inspect it and had returned very agitated. He said that there had been a fight and that he had found an assault rifle. What was all this? And she had come across a knife lying at the bottom of the stairs, the work on the landing had not been finished, white paint had been splashed all over the veranda and the handyman had disappeared. What was going on?

But instead of investigating these mysterious events first thing in the morning she decided to return to Naboru to make sure that everything was all right over there. She was extremely worried and prayed that Klaus had managed to bring back John's brain by now. Somehow she felt that she shouldn't have left him alone in the lab, defenceless.

When they arrived in front of the house she had a shock: the gate had been broken down and the place looked as if it had been hit by a hurricane. She called out as she entered but no one answered. The personnel, Klaus, Sam ... they had all disappeared. She ran towards the lab and her heart stopped: it had burned down!

She rushed back to her car, shouting: 'Steve, quick! Drive into town! We must find out what's happened!'

As they passed by a kiosk selling newspapers, Steve stopped. 'Maybe buy paper, Memsabu?' he suggested. Seconds later he returned with a copy of the *Daily Star*, which carried an article on the front page under the title: 'American Laboratory Attacked!' It read:

> Last night a furious mob attacked the American laboratory in Malavu Avenue which was denounced for producing a

chemical intended to make African men infertile. We were fortunate to have had one of our correspondents on the spot. He had mixed with the crowd and so has been able to give an eyewitness report of what happened. He declared that the angry crowd had been swelling by the hour, pressing against the iron front gate, when around 8 p.m. some people brought a sledgehammer and knocked the hinges out. As the mob streamed inside and surrounded the laboratory, Molotov cocktails were thrown through the windows, setting it on fire. The people next turned against the house, searching for the occupants, but the director and personnel had fled. The furious mob then ransacked the property, carrying off most of the belongings. By the time the police arrived, the crowd had dispersed, and the laboratory had almost burned to the ground.

A last-minute report informs us that a John Garfinger, of American nationality, was lying unconscious in the laboratory at the time of the attack. It is too early to confirm his fate since the police investigation is still going on at the time of writing, but it is reasonable to assume that he has been reduced to ashes. Needless to say, we will keep our public informed about further developments in this most interesting affair.

'Oh my God, no!' cried Veronica. 'This can't be true. John! They've burned John!' She felt sick. A great emptiness enveloped her and she started crying inconsolably.

4

Steve Mutele felt very troubled. The camp seemed to be under the influence of a spell. Faithful had been shy and distant these last days, and Steve wondered whether he should go and consult a witchdoctor. The Memsabu, too, was not her normal self. For two days now she had refused to eat. Only this morning Faithful had cooked her some tasty stew of maize-flour, rice, bananas and baobab leaves. She had put it in front of the Memsabu hoping that the delicious aroma would tempt her, but when she returned an hour later she'd found the bowl cold and untouched. No, the Memsabu was not well. Ever since they had returned from Naboru she had sat there on the veranda, staring out with empty eyes, and when he had asked her what there was to be done she had just made evasive gestures. How could he continue like that? Today he had told her that there was no cooking oil left and that they needed a fresh supply: she hadn't seemed interested. All she had done was to give him some money and tell him to drive to Bulamonga.

It was lucky he had done so because the owner of the Indian duka where he did his shopping told him to buy the *Daily Star* which, he said, contained an article about the elephant reserve. Although Steve could not read English, he had followed the shop owner's advice and bought it. He hoped that it would brighten up the Memsabu who definitely needed a change of thoughts.

As Steve handed Veronica the paper, she was about to put it aside when her attention was drawn to a big title on the front page: 'Government requests ten million dollars for elephant reserve.'

Her eyes scanned rapidly through the article:

In the framework of the decennial review of the Charter covering the elephant reserve near Naboru ... government believes that the World Elephant Fund should bear its part

285

of the costs ... only just and proper that a poor country should be paid for its services to the world community ... ten million dollars needed to cover costs ... deadline on September 14th ... otherwise the government will have to rethink the organization ... be forced to withdraw the concession from those running the reserve at present...

The paper fell from her hands, and she sat there stunned. John dead ... and now the reserve taken away from her ... This was the end.

As her head drooped, she noticed a title in the paper which had opened on page three: Further developments in the case of the American laboratory that was burned down.

Veronica picked up the paper and began to read with beating heart:

The commotion surrounding the laboratory that burned to the ground two days ago has now quietened down. We want to remind our readers that the laboratory in question was attacked on the evening of August 25th following rumours that it was the centre of production of chemicals that would render African men infertile.

It now seems that these rumours were without foundation. It appears that an American lawyer spread them with the intention of eliminating another American called John Garfinger, who at the time was lying unconscious inside the laboratory. This lawyer was working for the American wife of the dead man, and they wanted to kill the husband, which is why the lawyer spread these rumours. In fact, it was nothing but a very clever plot designed to get rid of the husband, which shows that American wives can be just as devious as African ones when it comes to scheming against their husbands.

Still, it is deplorable that such a despicable method was employed, making innocent Africans the executors of a crime masterminded by an American. It is truly inexcusable that this lawyer spread such base lies, knowing quite well how sensitive Africans would be to an attack upon the very core of their manhood. Luckily their criminal intentions backfired. Anger has now turned against the lawyer but he

286

has already fled the country and is, unfortunately, out of reach of our judicial system.

We also received a last-minute press release informing us that the aforementioned Mr. Garfinger, who was reported to have burned to death in the fire that devastated the laboratory on August 25th, escaped unscathed and is in good health. He was interviewed as he entered Naboru International Airport, where he boarded a plane for America. He did not want to reveal his intentions, but we believe that he is hot on the track of his assailants and that he intends to bring them to justice in his own country. So all is well that ends well, and we are pleased to tell our readership that peace and quiet have once more descended upon our beautiful capital.

John was alive! A miracle had happened! Veronica began to jump and dance around the house, waving her arms in the air while yelling wildly.

Steve and Faithful came running across the yard in panic and when they saw Veronica, Steve whispered in fright: 'Memsabu possessed by evil spirit. This dangerous magic. Quick! Go hide inside.'

Faithful gave a low moan and began to retreat hastily towards the kitchen.

Suddenly Veronica thought: *If one miracle can happen, then maybe a second will happen too. I'm not giving up the reserve. I'm going to fight back!*

She now turned to Steve. 'I want Faithful,' she requested. 'Where is she?'

Steve looked at her, his eyes wide with terror, not knowing what to say. Finally he answered in a trembling voice: 'I not know, Memsabu.'

'Well, find her and tell her to cook something for me,' said Veronica. 'I'm hungry!'

5

'Hello. I'm Mr Garfinger ... John's father. Could I speak to Monta, please?'

'Mr Garfinger!' answered a female voice. 'I'm Monta's mother. What a surprise! We haven't heard from you for years. How are you?'

'Oh, fine, fine. You're both OK too?'

'Yeah. Doing well. What's up?'

'Oh, I just wanted to find out how things are. How's Monta? Is the poor girl OK? I just wanted to say hello to her.'

'Well ... phone back in a couple of hours then. She's gone to the county court.'

'Whatever has she got to go to court for?'

'It's not her who's got to go to court. It's ... well, you know ... it's about the divorce.'

'Wasn't all that arranged months ago?'

'Yeah, but something new has come up. It seems that John had a lot of shares in his possession and didn't mention them during the divorce proceedings.' She hesitated. 'Did you know about this?'

'Shares? Oh! Shares? You don't mean those shares he was given by his boss at Biotech One? What about them? They're worth nothing.'

'It seems they're worth a lot of money now.'

'You don't say! A lot?'

'Yeah. We could be talking about a million dollars!'

'Holy Moses! That's incredible.'

'Yeah. And that's why Monta has gone to the county court with her lawyer this morning.'

'I see. And all this is going on with John away in Africa. Well, I'll try to phone again later then. What time do you think she'll be back?'

'You know what county courts are like – slow. She's one of many cases this morning. Better not to phone back before early afternoon.'

'OK. I'll do that. A good day to you, Mrs Macauley.'

As he hung up he looked at John who had been listening in. 'There's not a minute to be lost, son,' he urged. 'Jump into the car and drive off to the county court!'

6

When John reached the county court he prayed that he would not be too late, and rushed up the steps with beating heart.

Inside, the court case had nearly reached its final stage. Phil Harriman, pleading for Monta Macauley, was saying: '...So Ms Macauley's husband withheld the information about their existence deliberately, when these shares should have been part of the divorce settlement.'

'But I see here that the divorce has been pronounced and took effect on the 27th,' objected the judge. 'That's two days ago! Although I sympathize with Ms Macauley, it's going to be difficult to act retroactively.'

'I realize that, your Honour, but there have been new developments of which I'm going to notify you if you will permit me. You see, the husband, Mr John Garfinger, died on the 25th. At the time of his death he was in Africa in the town of Naboru where, during local riots, the house in which he lived was burned down with him inside. I've got documents to prove these circumstances and his death.' And he held up an article from the *Daily Star*. He continued: 'At someone's death his possessions pass on to his next of kin, and as at the time of his death Mr John Garfinger was still legally married to my client Ms Macauley, here present, his possessions, including the shares mentioned before, are therefore now legally hers.'

Monta had listened to the speech with mounting satisfaction. How well he was defending her! She smiled. Luck had been with her lately. She had gone to bed with Phil a couple of times since that day in her hotel room in Naboru, and everything had been perfect. Yes, she saw a bright future stretching ahead of her: she was going to be the wife of a famous lawyer!

The judge seemed to be less impressed. He sat there, hesitating. He lifted up his gavel, then put it down again. 'I'll have to wait for the official reports to come in,' he finally said.

'But your Honour, you know what African countries are like.

They just hush up any unpleasantness and pretend all's fine. One simply cannot rely on official African sources. At best an official confirmation is going to take a very long time, and at worst it'll never come. I was extremely lucky to have got hold of this newspaper article; otherwise we should have been waiting till doomsday for the law to follow its proper course. Wouldn't it be fairer to give my client provisional possession over her late husband's belongings while waiting for official confirmation?'

'You have a point there,' said the judge, nodding. 'Yes, you most definitely have a point. I admit that it is unusual to act in this way, but this appears to be a very unusual case.'

He was about to lift up his gavel and pronounce the case concluded, when John rushed forward shouting: 'Objection your Honour!'

'And who are you to burst into my court like that?' bellowed the judge, visibly disturbed.

'I'm John Garfinger, your Honour, and I've my passport to confirm it. I'm alive and well, and I also have documents to prove that my ex-wife and her lawyer were behind those so-called riots that were supposed to have caused my death. They lured the mob into burning down the house in which they thought I was lying unconscious. They wanted to kill me to lay their hands on the shares, but I escaped alive.'

The lawyer had remained dumbstruck since John had so unexpectedly resurfaced, while Monta looked as if she was seeing an apparition. Suddenly she jumped up, darted towards John and started hitting him with her fists while screaming hysterically. Then she kicked him hard in the shins, ran to the door and vanished.

7

'Welcome back to your old firm, John,' said Angus M. McDoughal Jr. as he got up from behind his desk and walked towards John with outstretched arms. 'So glad you've been able to come. And how well you look.'

John couldn't say the same about his ex-boss. He wouldn't have recognized him had he met him in the street: his hair had thinned and greyed, his cheeks had sagged, his face looked puffy and unhealthy, he had put on a stone or two and was potbellied. This was the man who, eight years ago when most of his colleagues had been fired, had promised John that he could stay on and that his salary would be raised if he helped his firm through the difficult times. All he asked from John was to exchange the genetic identification techniques which he had developed for a thousand shares in the company. John lived and worked for his firm, sacrificing his time and weekends, and if that was what it took to save his firm he was ready to do it, even if the shares were worthless at the time.

Not a year later his boss had called him into this same office to tell him with a painful smile that the company was going bankrupt and that he was forced to downsize as much as he could. John could still hear him say: 'Believe me, it's with the deepest regret that I have to let you go. I've pleaded with the board to keep you of all people, but there was nothing I could do about it.' He had been dismissed! John had left with hanging head and had spent two of the worst months of his life afterwards.

He had felt particularly bitter yesterday when he had contacted some ex-colleagues and learned that the firm had thrived on the techniques he had developed ever since he had swapped them for those shares. He now looked at his ex-boss calmly, smiling, showing none of his thoughts or feelings. 'So you wanted to see me to discuss my shares,' he said.

'Yeah, that's right,' replied his ex-boss. 'I understand that you've kept those thousand shares I gave you without doing anything with them, is that right?'

'That about sums it up.'

'Well, then, I've got good news for you. Those shares were not worth much at the time, but I knew that we'd get out of the fix in which we found ourselves. And today we've made good: we're now in a position to reward you for the confidence you had in us. I'm ready to buy the shares back from you and to pay you a large sum of money for them!'

John feigned indifference. He stared out of the window, then turned slowly towards his ex-boss and said: 'How much?'

The man looked at John encouragingly. 'Two hundred thousand dollars...' As John did not seem to react, he added: 'Believe me, that's good value. A share in the firm is worth less than two hundred dollars, but I'm prepared to offer you two hundred for each of your thousand shares to thank you for the good services you rendered to our firm.' He now put a document in front of John, saying: 'Just sign here.'

'Where do I sign?' asked John.

'Here on the dotted line. You'll be paid today,' said his ex-boss handing him a pen. 'In cash.'

John took it while his ex-boss held his breath and almost licked his lips when, without warning, John put the pen down and shook his head. 'No,' he said, 'no, no and no. I don't think I'm going to sell unless you do a lot better than that.'

His ex-boss looked visibly shaken and began to stammer: 'But ... but...'

Suddenly a loud voice became audible in the corridor outside, the door was flung open, and a short, red-haired, thickset man wearing gold-rimmed glasses appeared.

'Don't sell!' exclaimed Merrill B. Camson II as he stormed in. 'I'll pay more!' He looked at John. 'Are you the one who holds the missing shares?'

'I have that privilege,' replied John, appearing totally unconcerned.

'What the hell are you doing in my office?' thundered John's ex-boss who was trying to recover from the shock of coming eye to eye with his rival.

'I think he means business,' replied John, pointing his thumb at the second man. *How lucky*, he thought, *that an ex-colleague had let the cat out of the bag and that this man had agreed to come promptly when I phoned him.* John felt that he was going to enjoy the next moments. They were sure to become one of the highlights of his career as a biologist.

The second businessman resolutely turned his back on John's ex-boss, walked over to where John was sitting, and stared him straight in the eyes, expressing all his importance in his stance. 'You must sell to me, young man,' he said in a commanding voice. 'I have great plans for the firm. I'm going to transform it into a world leader if I get control. Look here, if you sell to me I'll pay you well. And I will keep you on the board!'

'Don't listen to him, John!' screeched Angus M. McDoneghal Jr. 'Remember that I've always protected you and given you the best I could. If the word gratefulness means anything to you, you must stay with me. I implore you to be faithful to your old firm.'

'Don't you listen to that bastard!' exclaimed the second man, grabbing John's shirtfront to draw his attention.

'Gentlemen, gentlemen...' John now rose, lifting up both his hands. Please, remain calm. Don't get so worked up. I don't care about the plans anyone has for the firm or a position on the board...'

'See!' yelled John's ex-boss triumphantly, as the face of the second man fell.

'...Nor do I care about the past. I have no feeling of gratitude towards the old firm...'

'And rightly so!' intervened the second man, who visibly cheered up. 'They've cheated you!'

'...So I am prepared to sell to the highest bidder. Gentlemen, may I now invite you to make your offers.'

'I told you how much your shares were worth,' said John's ex-boss with a voice like honey, 'but because it is you, and as a special gesture, I offer a million.' He looked at John hopefully.

When he heard this the second businessman let out a guffaw while clutching his sides. 'That's what he calls an offer ... hahaha ... a million, hahaha ... Well, son, let me tell you that I offer five million!'

'You damned interloper!' exploded John's ex-boss. 'If you think your money can buy control, you're mistaken. 'Six million, John. I offer six!'

'Ten million!' roared the second man.

'Eleven!'

'Fifteen!'

'Sixteen!'

'Eighteen!'

'You swine, you ... you ... twenty million! Come on, John, say yes. Think. I'm offering you twenty million dollars.' John's ex-boss looked at him with begging eyes. 'Please,' he added.

John looked at the man, a sardonic smile on his lips. 'Did I hear twenty million just now, or is it an illusion. Didn't you tell me a few minutes ago that the shares were worth only two hundred thousand?'

John's ex-boss looked pained. 'That was before this bastard here came in!' he shouted.

'See what a swindler he is!' exclaimed the second man. 'Don't even listen to him. He wants to get things on the cheap.' He turned to John's ex-boss: 'You need to be taught a good lesson, crook that you are! I'll get control and then I'll have the pleasure of kicking your filthy ass. I'll kick it from here all the way to Lake Michigan where you can cool down. I offer twenty-five million!'

'Is that so! Ah is that so! We'll see who kicks who! Thirty million!'

The second businessman went red in the face and he looked as if he might explode any moment, like a frog that has blown itself up to bursting point. 'You stinking skunk!' he yelled. 'Forty million!'

John's ex-boss was crimson now. His breathing was heavy and irregular, and John feared that he was going to have a heart attack. 'Forty-five million,' he said hoarsely.

'Fifty! Fifty!' exclaimed the second businessman.

John's ex-boss turned purple. His arteries stood out on his temples and sweat trickled down his brow. 'Fifty-two,' he croaked. 'Come on, John.' He looked at him pleadingly. 'Say yes.'

'Seventy million!' exclaimed the second businessman, looking the other defiantly in the eyes. John's ex-boss suddenly sank into his chair, his face ash-grey.

'I think he's had it,' said John, looking at the sagging figure. 'Here are the documents. Please fill in seventy million dollars and sign. He then opened the door and called in two of his former colleagues. 'Here are the witnesses who will sign with you.'

When the signing was over, John faced the second businessman. 'How soon can you pay?' he wanted to know. 'Tomorrow? That's fine.' He folded up the signed documents, put them in his pocket, and was about to leave, his hand on the door, when he turned around.

'Congratulations,' he said with a hint of a smile on his lips. 'You know, I'm so pleased that you licked that bastard over there and are kicking him out, that I would have sold you the shares for much less. But seventy million will do fine, thank you.' At that he went out, leaving Merrill B. Camson II behind, swallowing hard. He had not even had time to shut the door when he heard the man yell:

'Out, you bastard! Out! This is *my* office now!'

8

As John left the offices of Biotech One and drove to his parents' house, he felt in a state of euphoria. He was rich now. Immensely rich! He would never have to work again and could do anything he liked: no more job interviews; no more jobs; no more worries. *This is freedom at last*, he reflected, while his car moved slowly along the highway together with thousands of others coming out of Chicago.

Rush hour had begun, and as traffic grew denser it abruptly slowed down and then came to a standstill. After having sat in the huge traffic jam for a quarter of an hour, moving in fits and starts, with thousands of engines ejecting toxic fumes around him, John began to feel annoyed. His life as an elephant had made him forget the realities of the modern environment. He had lived in total freedom in pure, natural surroundings for so long that his senses had sharpened, and he seemed to have become acutely sensitive to any aggression and tension.

He had never given it a thought before, but he now realized that he was no longer master over the quality of his life. It was determined by the activities of millions upon millions of other people around him. There was no escaping them. They all affected each other as they pursued their own interests, even if they just honestly tried to create a good life for themselves. John felt like a molecule constrained in a narrow box with zillions of others, all banging into each other as they attempted to move and do the same things at the same time. *There is no longer any autonomy or real individual freedom, however much we try to convince ourselves that we have created the best of all worlds,* he mused. *Is this, then, the wonder of urbanized Western society?*

The following day he went to one of the big shopping malls that cater for the needs of suburbia. Now that he had money, he could at last buy some decent outfits and whatever else he fancied. Everything seemed beautiful, well arranged. Brightly lit shops announced special sales; the best offer, the highest quality

297

for the cheapest price. Some eateries had arranged their gaily painted tables and chairs on artificial grass around little fountains set in a rockery out of which sprouted artificial branches on which a few mechanical birds sang endlessly repeated pre-recorded birdsongs. It was a perfect imitation of the open-air terraces you find in some Mediterranean countries, and was intended to entice customers to sit down for a hasty meal while they could watch the hundreds of people walking past, gazing at what the shops had to offer. Humans had at last created a completely self-sufficient world. Nothing else was needed.

He entered several shops looking for something special to buy, but his visits turned out to be rather dull and uneventful. Shop assistants smiled their welcoming commercial smiles, everyone was polite and intent on supplying service to satisfy the customer, but somehow he felt a great void behind it all. This was exactly as you expected it to be. It all went smoothly – too smoothly. There was no longer any warm personal involvement, just an exchange of money to buy a smile that went with the service. He somehow missed the spice, colour and disorderliness of Africa. As he left the air-conditioned, artificially illuminated, unreal environment where the outside world was shut off as if it were something hostile, and felt the warmth of the sun outside and saw the real sky, he breathed a sigh of relief.

The next day was a Saturday, and his parent's neighbours were out manicuring their lawns while sitting on motorized mowers. A well-kept lawn was what everyone expected of their neighbours in suburbia, and this was the appointed time for that kind of activity. As he surveyed the succession of lawns and neat houses which looked almost regimented, he felt disheartened and withdrew into his room for the rest of the weekend.

He just couldn't see himself living like that day after day for another thirty or forty years. Was this the great adventure of life? The endpoint of four billion years of evolution? Where were the wide-open spaces? The wind blowing freely as he walked with the herd towards the ever-receding horizon? Where was the wild, untamed savannah? And where were the elephants? Then he thought: *I shall never be an elephant again, but at least there are some elephants left in the world and I'm going to do what I can to save those that remain.*

298

9

'Hello! Hello!' Twice already John had dialled the phone number of the World Elephant Fund, to hear a pre-recorded voice saying: 'If you want general information about our activities, press one; if you want to contact our sales and souvenirs' department, press two; if you want technical assistance, press three; if you want to make a donation, press four;' etc. And when he pressed one of these numbers he got another pre-recorded voice saying: 'We are sorry not to be able to answer your call for the moment. Could you please leave your name, phone number and reason for calling, and we'll contact you as soon as possible.'

He was getting very frustrated after the second time, and the third time he almost yelled: 'I want to speak to a person, not to a tape!' He wondered whether there were still any real people on the other side of a phone line in big organizations. *If they think I'm going to give up, they're mistaken*, thought John and tried again.

This time he pressed four for donations and let the phone ring a long time. He was about to despair when he heard a female voice saying: 'Good afternoon. Can I help you?'

John felt relieved. Someone to speak to at last!

'I'm phoning concerning a park in Africa,' he said, 'the Naboru Reserve.'

'Sir, this is the donations' department. If you want information about our parks you'll have to log on to our website...'

'No! No!' shouted John, frightened that the woman might hang up. 'I want to make a donation!'

'That's very kind of you, Sir,' replied the voice. 'Have you got the account number of the World Elephant Fund?'

'No! Listen. I want to make a donation for a very specific park. I told you: the elephant reserve near Naboru.'

'I don't know whether that's possible, Sir. Donations are normally made to the Fund which then distributes them according to needs and priorities.'

'Look here!' John spoke firmly. 'I want to make an extremely important donation, and it's going to be that reserve or nothing. So you'd better pass me on to a person who knows about this elephant reserve.'

'Oh,' said the voice, somewhat taken aback. 'I'll see what I can do. Could you please wait a second?'

John sat there for a whole minute without hearing anything, and was thinking that he had lost the connection, when someone said: 'Hello! Tim Palmer speaking. Can I help you?'

John now repeated the object of his call.

'I'm sorry to have to disappoint you, Sir,' replied the voice. 'We no longer take donations for that particular reserve. I'm afraid that they are useless. But we support several parks in other countries...'

'Hey!' exclaimed John. 'What's the matter with the Naboru Reserve? Why is it useless to make a donation?'

'That particular reserve has been taken off our list, Sir.'

'But why?'

'I'm afraid I don't know your name, Sir,' replied the voice on the other side of the line, somewhat coldly.

'I'm Doctor Garfinger, biologist. I'm not interested in other parks. I'm only interested in the reserve run by Veronica de Ville.'

'I'm afraid that she won't run it for much longer, Sir.'

'What? I demand to know why!' barked John, suddenly losing his temper. Then he added: 'I'm not proposing to donate just a few miserable dollars. I'm ready to donate millions!'

There was a short silence on the other side, and then John heard the man say: 'Oh ... I do apologize, Sir. I'll see if I can connect you to the President of the Fund.'

After a few minutes which felt like an eternity, John heard a disgruntled voice saying: 'Arthur Llewellyn speaking.'

'Oh ... good afternoon. I'm Doctor Garfinger. I'm ready to donate a few million dollars to the Fund...'

'... Welcome, welcome!' The President's voice had audibly mellowed.

'... But I want this money to go to one particular park: the Naboru Elephant Reserve run by Veronica de Ville.'

'But, my dear man, that reserve is a real problem case. Are you certain that you don't want to...'

'It's that one or nothing!' interrupted John in a firm voice.

'Ah! I see that you don't know ... the Naboru Reserve is going to be taken away from us.'

'But why?'

'I'm not sure whether I ought to tell you this...'

'Please tell me,' pleaded John.

'The government will take it away unless we pay them a large sum of money.'

'Maybe I can help?'

'I don't think so ... we're talking about a very large amount of money ... The government wants us to pay ten million dollars.'

'What! But ... why?'

'The details of the Charter covering the reserve are coming up for review in about ten days, and the government has used this to propose drastic modifications. The main point is that they are asking for ten million dollars to cover the cost of protection and resettlement of people around the reserve. I don't think that they have the law on their side, but they would certainly become very uncooperative if we resisted their claim. We have therefore decided that it's useless to stir up an international scandal and waste time and money on a case we're unlikely to win. However much we feel about this, the reality is that we have to live off donations and that we are strongly limited by our lack of funds.'

'But I have ten million dollars!' John blurted out. 'I'll buy out the Naboru Elephant Reserve!'

For a couple of seconds the President remained speechless. Then he exclaimed: 'You don't say! This is unexpected. This is ... this is extremely generous of you.'

'When can I see you?' asked John. '... Tomorrow afternoon, you say ... at the Fund's office in New York? All right, I'll be there.'

As he put the phone down he suddenly remembered Sir Arthur. In his mind's eye he saw images of a man chased up a thorn tree by Dumbo and ripping his trousers. Veronica had told him that he was wearing pink-striped underpants! *It's lucky for him that there are no elephants and no thorn trees in New York*, thought John, smiling cheerfully.

10

The next few days were a period of frenetic activity for John. Twice he took the plane to New York, and when he had done everything he had set out to do he collapsed and slept for a whole day.

He then began to wonder what he should do with all the money he had in the bank. Even after deducting the ten million that would go to buying out Veronica's reserve, he still had sixty million left. Hoping to find some inspiration, he bought a financial newspaper and was immediately struck by the big title on the front page: 'Giant bankruptcy!' An important hedge fund seemed to have gone under. *One more or one less, who cares?* thought John. *It's all money in the air, anyway.*

He started to scan the paper, trying to pick up some suggestions on where to invest. As he did so, his attention was drawn to an article on one of the inside pages which carried the title: 'Arrest of Sam Goldstein Jr.'

'Hey!' exclaimed John. 'What's that?' And he began to read with mounting interest:

Sam Goldstein Jr. was apprehended yesterday evening at Kennedy International Airport as he tried to board a plane for Rio de Janeiro. Samuel B. Goldstein Jr. is the son of the late Samuel A. Goldstein Sr. who was famous in Wall Street for his unfailing flair in buying and selling shares. For a while the son followed in his father's footsteps, having inherited not only his father's fortune but apparently also his outstanding financial gifts, but then he abandoned share trading and left for East Africa to pursue his interests in palaeontology. Having rejoined the financial world very recently he made some extremely risky investments, borrowing heavily to do so. Unfortunately he seems to have lost his flair for picking winners: he speculated on the hedge fund that collapsed so unexpectedly and yesterday's bankruptcy hit him fully.

He appears to have been unable to reimburse the banks from which he borrowed and tried to leave the country carrying a suitcase stuffed with cash. After his arrest he collapsed on the floor of the airport, where he received emergency treatment before being rushed to hospital. He was diagnosed as having suffered a slight stroke, but is out of danger now.

We hear that the banks to which he is heavily indebted have put Phil Harriman, a lawyer of international repute, onto the case. It is rumoured that he has decided to press for the maximum sentence. On hearing the prosecution lawyer's name Mr. Goldstein suffered a nervous collapse. He recovered after some hours, but his face seems to have been distorted by a severe twitch which he is unable to control.

While awaiting trial Mr. Goldstein has been transferred to prison where he is obliged to share a cell with common criminals and drug offenders due to the crowded conditions. Needless to say, we deplore Mr. Goldstein's bad luck and find it scandalous that a respected member of the financial community has been treated with so little consideration for his position.

Well, well, thought John. Good old Sam! Who would have believed it? He who had a sixth sense for money. He did push his luck, though.

John sat there for a while, pondering. Then he threw down the financial paper. *I don't want to be a second Sam*, he decided. *I'm not going to speculate until my face is deformed by a nervous twitch. Decidedly not!* John chuckled imagining Sam's face. *I don't want to be like him, investing all those millions to make more money. I'm not going to hoard them. We've only got one life, so what's the good of having a lot of money in the bank if you can't even touch it? I want to use this manna from heaven to do something constructive. I know I can't do much; I'm no more than a small pawn on the chessboard of life, but there are a few things I'm able to achieve now, and I'm damn well going to accomplish them!*

If other people are happy with modern life, John continued, *fine. It's their own choice, and who am I to tell them how they should live? But I have the right to choose my own path. I no longer feel at home in the civilized world. It's all too insipid, too artificial. Where are the warm colours, the bright sunlight and the disorder? The unexpected situations? What is life worth when there are no longer any surprises lurking around the corner? There's nothing here that can beat what a shop such as Shillingi Mingi's has to offer. Nothing to make your pulse race, and your heart pound like the throbbing of a drum. There's definitely a dimension missing here – or maybe two. I'll be glad to be back in Africa.*

11

Things had decidedly not gone well for Monta ever since John had turned up alive in court. When Phil had found her sitting outside on the steps of the county court, sobbing, he had not even attempted to console her. On the contrary, he had been enraged and had told her that she had made him do things that didn't befit a lawyer, that she had even turned him into a criminal. She had protested, but he had accused her of being a totally negative, egocentric woman who had only her own interests in mind and was ready to ruin any man's career if it suited her. He had said that he never wanted to see her again and that he would send her a bill for his services. Then he had just turned on his heel and left her stranded on the steps of the county court. How ungrateful! When she'd had such high hopes after what had happened in the hotel room in Naboru.

She had fallen into a deep depression after that and for several days had refused to leave her room in her parents' house. What was to become of her? She could not continue to rely on her parents forever. And her art didn't bring in much money. Ungrateful public! Instead of recognizing her great talent and paying for the privilege of having such an exceptional artist amongst them, they simply ignored her!

She had just gone downstairs to make herself a strong cup of coffee when the phone rang. She tried to ignore it but it kept on ringing. Finally she picked it up grumbling: 'Oh bother!'

'Monta! It's Minnie. I was just about to hang up. What luck you're there. Have you heard the news?'

'What news?' Monta's voice sounded dispirited.

'About John's shares.'

'I don't want to be reminded of those shares!' shouted Monta furiously. She was about to slam the phone down when she heard her sister's voice calling: 'Wait, wait!'

'What is it, then?'

'It seems that John has sold them for a fortune.'

'What! How much?'

'I really can't believe it, but one of his ex-colleagues who was there assured me that the amount is correct.'

'How much?'

'Seventy million dollars ... Hello...' She heard a crash on the other side of the line and then nothing more. 'Hello ... hello ... Monta? Are you there?'

'Se ... seventy,' came Monta's croaking voice finally. 'Did you say seventy million?'

'Yes. Incredible, isn't it?'

Monta felt her head spin and sat down, this time on the chair. 'Where is he?'

'I don't know.'

'All right. Thank you, Minnie. Bye,' she replied, slamming down the phone.

Her depression had suddenly dissipated like mist before a brilliant sunshine. At last she knew what to do. Her future stretched brightly ahead of her once again. Seventy million dollars! She was willing to go to the end of the Earth for that. She would do what was needed. Yes, she would be able to handle the situation. John had always been a despicable weakling. If she was clever and stuck it out, he would eventually surrender, she was sure of that.

She now looked up the phone number of John's parents and rang them.

'Hello. It's Monta ... I've heard the good news about John and I want to congratulate him ... He isn't there? ... He'll pass by before returning to Africa, you say? ... OK. I'll phone back later then. Bye.'

She thought fast: *A bag, some clothes, credit cards, my passport ... Quick, quick!*

12

John had just left his parents' house and was about to get into his car when a taxi drew up and Monta stepped out. She rushed towards him, flung her arms around his neck, kissed him and whispered in his ear: 'Congratulations, darling.' She smelled strongly of perfume and he recoiled.

'Hey!' he exclaimed. 'What's this?'

'A surprise,' said Monta with a big smile. 'I'm back. I knew you'd like it.'

'I don't like surprises!' protested John, but before he had time to react she lifted her bag out of the taxi, ran to his car, opened the passenger's door and sat down.

'You get out of here at once,' he said firmly as he got behind the steering wheel. 'I'm off to Africa.'

'John! Can't we stay in America?'

'We? What do you mean by *we*?'

'You and me of course.'

'Are you mad! We're divorced.'

'That was a terrible mistake. I should never have agreed to that. Anyway, we can always marry again.'

'Marry you again! You must be off your rocker.'

'Why not? We're older and wiser now. You'll be surprised to find out how well we'll get along. This time everything will be perfect.'

'Look here, I don't have time to talk to you! I can't waste a second more or I'll miss my plane.'

'If you absolutely have to go, I'll come with you. I made a mistake that time when I let you go alone to Europe, because I was too young then. This time you'll no longer be lonely. I'll be with you when you need me.' And she resolutely fastened her seatbelt and clung on to her bag as John started up the engine and drove off.

13

John had hoped that this nightmare would be over at the airport, but Monta had somehow succeeded in buying a ticket and had got on to the plane, fortunately far away from him. It completely spoiled his return to Naboru, and he kept racking his brain to find a way of getting rid of her. Of all the damned unexpected situations! Every now and then his ex came walking by along the aisle, smiling at him, trying to say something nice, and showing how concerned she was about his comfort and well-being. He tried hard to shut her out of his mind and think of Veronica, but he didn't succeed. By the time they landed in Naboru the next morning he felt thoroughly fed up.

He got through customs quickly and rushed away into the crowds attempting to rid himself of her, but somehow she had managed to follow close upon his heels. By the time he had finished hiring a car he found her standing by his side again, and when the man from the car rental company inquired politely whether the missus wanted to drive too, John nearly exploded. And then the stupid ass led them to the car and opened the door for her to sit down first!

'Now listen,' he said to Monta when he got into the car, 'this comedy has lasted long enough. I'll drive you to a hotel in town, we say goodbye, you spend a pleasant holiday and then you return to America.'

'I don't want to spend a holiday here,' said Monta with a stubborn intonation in her voice. 'I'm going to stay with you.'

'You can't follow me where I'm going!'

'Why not? I'll follow you anywhere.'

'You?'

'Yes, me. I've been in Africa once...'

'We don't want to go back over that again, do we?'

'...And I can do it again,' Monta continued. 'I can handle anything now. You'll see.'

John cut her short: 'I don't want to see it!' But when she

didn't move and just kept sitting there holding on to her bag, a decided expression on her face, he started the car and drove off. *This is going to end in murder*, he thought. *I can already see the title in the* Daily Star: *'American murders ex-wife in bush.'*

For the next half-hour neither of them spoke while John wound his way through the Naboru traffic, his lips tightly pressed together, and then turned off along the northern exit towards Bulamonga. Soon they had left the town behind and were heading for the open savannah.

'Hey, you're leaving the town!' objected Monta. 'Where are we going?'

'Where I want to. It's none of your business.'

'But ... but there's no one around here. This is all desolate countryside.'

'You're welcome to get out,' suggested John. 'Any time.'

'No! Certainly not here. There may be wild animals.'

'There are wild animals. And they love juicy American flesh,' he added in a cheerful voice.

Monta shut her eyes tightly, trying not to think of the hostile world outside, and hoped that they would soon reach their destination: she saw herself lounging in an easy chair under a sun umbrella around a deep-blue swimming pool, sipping a refreshing long drink.

After half an hour or so Monta spoke again. Her voice sounded shy this time: 'John, I've got to go to the restroom.'

'There is no restroom here. This is bush country. Why didn't you go before?'

'I drank a lot on the plane, and then I was so worried that I would lose you that I forgot to go and now ... it's urgent...'

'OK, I'll stop. The savannah is one giant restroom. Go behind a bush or a clump of trees.'

'What, here?' She looked around hesitantly. 'Are there snakes?'

'There may well be.' And then he added with perverse glee: 'Yeah. And there are plenty of lions too. They are all lurking in the high grass just there, waiting for a tasty morsel to walk up to them.'

Monta shuddered. 'I'll wait,' she said in a subdued voice.

They finally entered the little town of Bulamonga, an uninspiring cluster of small, square brick bungalows and sheds whose tin roofs shone in the sun. There were crowds of Africans just hanging about or walking the streets.

John stopped in front of a bar. 'Here you are,' he said, 'your restroom.'

Monta opened her eyes wide and shook her head. 'You don't want me to go in there, do you? There's no hygiene in that place. You're liable to catch anything there. And look at all those men hanging about! No I can't go in there.'

John sighed deeply. 'As you wish,' he said, 'but don't complain.'

They had left Bulamonga behind by a couple of miles when John heard Monta utter in a pleading, hardly audible voice: 'Could you stop, please? I ... I'll go in the bush.'

It was obvious that the situation was becoming very painful to her and that she was unable to keep up the effort. She got out, barely able to walk, and crouched behind a clump of trees. Suddenly John realized that this was going to be his one and only chance. He started up the engine and got moving while Monta emerged from behind the clump of trees pulling up her trousers and holding on to them, running after the car as fast as she could. John stopped after a hundred yards, lifted her bag out of the car, and dumped it on the road.

She had got to within twenty yards, when she heard him shout: 'I hope you're ready to handle anything now!' Then he quickly jumped back into the car and drove off, leaving a big cloud of dust behind him.

14

That morning Steve had driven Veronica into the savannah until they came upon one of the herds of elephants she hadn't seen for some time. There seemed to be quite a commotion and then Veronica noticed that one of the cows was about to give birth. This was an event she'd been waiting for, and she was overjoyed. A new baby elephant! They stayed with the herd the whole morning, and by the time the sun was high overhead and blazing down on the savannah, the little baby was on his feet and greedily sucking milk from one of his mother's teats. Soon it would be able to walk with the herd, which was getting impatient to move on to a shady place where the elephants could drink.

While she had been watching the magic of the birth she had forgotten about her present problems, but they came back with a vengeance when she returned to the camp. What was going to happen to that new baby and to all her elephants when she lost the battle for the reserve, as surely she would very soon? She couldn't bear to think of the disaster. She sensed that dark powers were at work behind this, evil powers so strong that they would eliminate anything that opposed them. They would wipe away all her work of the last two years, and would murder and devastate until there was nothing left to destroy. Only a miracle could save her elephants now.

They passed the burned-out car-wreck near the entrance of the camp. It had sat there for two weeks now, a dumb witness to a scene of unexplained violence. Steve had tried to find out what had happened, but had drawn a blank. It worried him: since the wreck had been there, Faithful seemed to be under the influence of a spell. He had asked the Memsabu to have the car-wreck removed, but she hadn't paid any attention.

As they drove into the enclosure Veronica noticed an unknown car and then she beheld an extraordinary scene: a man was standing in front of Dumbo, one arm around his trunk and the other at the back of his ear which he was scratching. At the sound of the approaching Land Rover he turned. It was John!

Veronica got out of the jeep and slowly crossed the short distance that separated her from him, while waves of strong feeling surged through her body. John! He had come back! She stood before him for a second looking up at him with eyes expressing at the same time uncertainty and infinite longing. Then she blurted out in a voice strangled by emotion: 'Oh John! I never thought I would see you again.'

John did not reply but simply opened his arms, and without another thought she buried her head in his shoulder while he folded his arms around her, saying: 'I've missed you.'

'I've missed you too,' whispered Veronica.

They stood there close together, their bodies and minds as one, expressing all the yearnings of a lifetime in their long embrace while the outside world ceased to exist and the brilliant-blue sky seemed to be whirling slowly around them.

The one who was not entirely happy was Dumbo. He felt left out and now began to shove, wanting to participate in the outpouring of feelings. For once Veronica pushed him away, saying in a reprimanding voice: 'Dumbo! Don't bother John!'

'Don't push him away,' pleaded John. 'He doesn't bother me at all. Look, he's upset now.' He went over to Dumbo and whispered something to him. The little elephant flapped his ears, then turned around and trotted away.

'John! How did you manage that? What did you tell him?' asked Veronica who had been staring at the scene in disbelief.

'Oh! I just told him that it's all right, that you're not cross but that we have important things to say to each other, and that he has to wait a while.'

'But how does he know what you're saying?' Veronica stared at John as if she had witnessed something supernatural. 'And how do you suddenly get on so well with Dumbo? Something is happening here that is beyond my understanding.'

'Oh ... it's really quite simple. You see ... Well ... I don't think I've got time now. It's a very long story. I'll explain later.'

'But this is a miracle! Everything is a miracle! You back here ... and you and Dumbo being friends ... and just when...' She swallowed hard and seemed unable to carry on.

'When what Veronica?'

'It's so sad. So very sad. Just when I'm going to lose all this ... John, you don't know. They want to take the reserve away from me. Oh God! I dare not think what will happen to the elephants. And to Dumbo...'

'Don't worry,' said John soothingly. 'Everything will be all right.'

'John! This is no light-hearted matter. This is very serious. I have moved heaven and earth. I've pleaded with the World Elephant Fund, imploring them to help me; I've been to the Ministry of Wildlife ... There's nothing I can do. They want me to pay ten million dollars within less than a week. Don't you realize what that means? It's a death warrant!'

'Don't worry,' repeated John calmly. 'I know what's happened. I've come to arrange everything.'

Veronica shook her head with pity. 'But, John! You're not a magician. You can't suddenly pull ten million dollars out of a hat!'

John reflected for a second or two. Then he replied: 'That's a very original way of putting it, but it sums up exactly what I've done: I've pulled ten million dollars out of a hat to buy out the reserve.'

Veronica stared at him, speechless. Then her lips began to tremble, she put a hand in front of her mouth and her eyes filled with tears. Suddenly she jumped forward, threw her arms around John's neck and covered his face with kisses, crying: 'John! Oh John! Is it true? Are you really a magician?'

'Yes,' replied John, stroking her hair. 'I'm your magician now. I've come back to Naboru to save the reserve. But I had to see you first. I wanted to reassure you.'

'Oh John, you have no idea how much you mean to me!' she cried, pressing herself tightly against him, clinging on to him as if she would never let him go.

'And you are all I ever dreamed of,' murmured John, caressing her cheek.

After a long while he held her at arm's length and looked deep in her bright-blue eyes which shone with hope now. 'I have to leave,' he said with a sigh, 'but I'll be back as soon as everything is over.'

They walked towards his car, arm in arm, and as they kissed

goodbye, Dumbo rushed forward to join them, trumpeting loudly. Then John drove off while Veronica stood there waving, an expression of ecstasy on her face.

When the car had disappeared she suddenly screamed: 'Yahoo!' and before Dumbo's astounded eyes she turned a cartwheel on outspread arms and landed unceremoniously amidst some tall red flowers she had recently planted along the edge of the enclosure.

15

John was in an elated mood, singing to himself and smiling as he drove back to Naboru. He had got to within a couple of miles of Bulamonga when he suddenly remembered Monta. *This is more or less where I dropped her*, he thought. He slowed down and began looking around but there was no trace of her – just the dirt road stretching away towards the south through a landscape of high yellow grass and scattered umbrella trees. He presumed that she had walked back to the town and was about to accelerate when he noticed a human shape waving at him from one of the trees on the side of the road and calling out to him. There she was, sitting on a branch like a brightly coloured bird in the dull yellow-brown savannah.

As he stopped the car and got out he heard her voice, trembling with fear: 'John! Please ... save me.'

'Have you been sitting up there all this time?' he called out.

She nodded her head, looking a bundle of human misery.

'So you couldn't handle it, eh?'

'Take me back, please,' came her voice, hardly audible.

'It was your idea to follow me out here, not mine,' John replied firmly.

'I would never have believed that you could be so nasty and cruel,' she retorted and began to sob.

'And you! You were not nasty and cruel when you wanted to kill me?

'I'm sorry. I won't do it again. I promise.'

'And you let your lawyer incite the mobs to burn down the laboratory.'

She tried to look apologetic. 'I'm very sorry. I didn't realize how bad that was. I'll be good from now onwards. You'll see.'

John shrugged his shoulders. 'Why are you up there?'

'I saw things move in the grass. I don't dare come down. I'm sure it's full of lions out there!' She looked at him with pleading eyes. 'Please, help me out of here.'

'But lions can climb trees.'

'What!' Monta scrambled down the tree like lightning, picked up her bag, rushed into the car and slammed the door behind her.

'Oh don't worry about lions,' said John without the slightest sign of concern. 'They're no more than big cats. When you see one come towards you, you just stamp your foot and chase it away. That's how you do it.'

Monta stared at John with eyes like soup plates. 'How brave you are!' she exclaimed, looking impressed. Then she added in a sugary voice: 'I feel safe now that I've got you at my side.'

John didn't reply but started the car and drove off towards Naboru at a good speed.

After a while Monta began fiddling with the handle of her bag which she was carrying on her lap. She was about to speak a couple of times but seemed to decide against it. Finally she could contain herself no longer and asked in a beguiling voice: 'John, do you still love me?'

'What makes you say such a thing?' replied John sharply. 'Is there anything in my attitude that could possibly suggest that I love you?'

'Don't get upset. I was just asking. One never knows with you. You've always hidden your feelings very carefully.'

'Do I really have to tell you? I don't love you. I expected you at least to have noticed that I haven't loved you for years.'

'But I've changed. The hours I spent up there in that tree have opened up a whole new perspective. It made me look upon life from a different angle.'

'Good for you!'

'Yes. And I've understood many things I never realized before. I'm ready to start a new life.'

'Is that so?' asked John thinking hard. 'Now is that so? So you're ready to start a new life ... Do you really repent for all your misdeeds?'

'Yes I do.'

'In that case I may be able to help you.'

'Would you, John. Oh would you?' Monta looked at him with big loving eyes, while congratulating herself for having had the courage to go through all this, and the cunning to pull it off.

'Well, anyway, I've got an idea,' he replied.

316

They entered Naboru an hour later. As they approached civilization, Monta began to cheer up. Although this was only African civilization, it was so much better than the bush. And the thought of all those millions of dollars was working wonders.

John was quiet, needing his full attention to steer the car through the traffic. Finally he stopped in front of a large white building. He took Monta's bag, motioning her to follow, and rang the bell.

A woman in uniform opened. 'Hello, Sister Anna,' he said. 'Is the director in?'

A moment later they were ushered into the director's office.

'Hello!' said the thin, ascetic-looking man, getting up from his chair and holding out a hand. Then, as he recognized John, a flicker of a smile appeared on his lips. 'Remember those hymns?' he suddenly asked. 'Have you been practising?'

'What? Oh the hymns! Well ... yes ... I have been singing ... one could call them hymns, I suppose. Why not? Although you wouldn't probably call them that ... They were very low-frequency hymns, you see ... infrasound.'

The man stared at John not understanding a word of what he was saying. 'Ah...' he said. 'Yes. I understand. You are coming to tell me that you have repented?'

John leant over towards the director as if he had something confidential to say, and whispered almost in his ear: 'I fear that you do not understand and never will. I'm worse than ever. I have become a confirmed sinner.'

'What!' The director recoiled as if bitten by Satan.

'But to make up for it, I've brought you a new member for your Congregation,' said John, pushing Monta forward. 'Please meet Ms Macauley. She is a reformed sinner according to her own words.'

The director was still in a state of shock and stammered: 'Well, I ... I'm not sure...'

'Oh yes, I almost forgot,' continued John. 'She loves hymns and has a most beautiful voice.'

'Oh well! In that case ... well, that's really wonderful!' exclaimed the director, thrilled now. 'A reformed sinner who loves hymns...' He got up and walked over to Monta, taking both her hands in his and making her sit down. 'Welcome, dear sister,' he murmured, holding her hands tightly, 'welcome to our community. Would it be too much to ask you to sing something for me?'

Before Monta could free herself John was already at the door, calling out: 'I entrust her to you. Take good care of her.' And he quickly turned away and left the office, a very broad grin on his face.

16

Minutes later John stopped in front of Sam's house, parked the car and went in. One side of the big double gate was hanging limply from its hinges while the other half was lying flat on the driveway; the garden was beginning to be overgrown and the house had been thoroughly pillaged by now. *What a shame,* thought John as he strolled through the abandoned property. *It was such a nice house when I lived here.*

He left through the back door and soon came to the narrow side streets into which Kibu had led them on the night of the attack. It took him half an hour of searching and asking around before he finally stood in front of Kibu's small bungalow. He knocked on the door and, as it opened, he looked into the surprised faces of three teenage children who stared at him with undisguised interest.

'It's the Sahib,' he heard the eldest boy whisper, and then they all disappeared inside.

Moments later Kibu appeared, extending a welcoming hand.

'Thank God, you're still here,' said John. 'What's happened to Klaus?'

'I'm sorry to have to tell you that Sahib Klaus is no longer his usual cheerful self, Sahib. I have the impression that the burning of his laboratory has somewhat disturbed him. He likes living according to a fixed schedule and is lost when he has time on his hands and cannot concentrate fully on his experiments. He has now retired to the back of my house where he is less bothered by the children, and has kept his nose in his papers ever since, jotting down formulas and doing calculations that surpass my understanding. He has also been complaining that he is losing weight, and I feel that he is not entirely happy with the type and especially the quantity of food I am able to provide. As to Sahib Goldstein, I am afraid that I have no information as to his whereabouts. His failure to return is creating a certain amount of problems because he has not made any payments since he left. He is in arrears with the rent of his house and the owners have now put it up for sale, being unable to let it in its present condition...'

'But I know what's happened to Sam!' exclaimed John. 'He went back to America, made some risky investments, went bankrupt and is now in prison.'

For once Kibu was somewhat taken aback. Then he regained self-control and continued in his usual manner. 'I'm sorry to hear about the misfortune that has befallen Sahib Goldstein. I was under the impression that he had lost some of his usual self-assurance when he left precipitately the afternoon the crowd collected in front of the gate, but I'm surprised to hear how strongly luck has turned against him. I gather that he will no longer need my services then.'

'That is indeed very unlikely,' affirmed John, 'though I'm certain it would greatly cheer him up to have you around where he is now.' Then he added: 'But *I* may need you.'

'You, Sahib?'

'Yes, Kibu. Do you remember those shares? I sold them for a fortune!'

'I surmised that they had a certain value, Sahib. I am delighted to hear that my advice has been of use to you. So, does the Sahib have the intention of staying here?'

'Yes, indeed. And I would like to retain your services if you are willing, Kibu.'

'I was in fact negotiating the terms of my future employment with an Indian firm that wanted to take me on, Sahib.'

'Has anything been finalized with the Indian firm yet?'

'I am expecting a definite offer any day now, Sahib.'

'You're still free then. Good. How much did Sam pay you?'

'The equivalent of fifty dollars per week, Sahib.'

That's not a very high salary. Why didn't he pay you more?'

'I'm afraid that Sahib Goldstein did not look favourably upon such a policy. He paid wages that are usual around here.'

'Well, someone with your brainpower deserves much more. I'll triple your previous salary if you stay on and keep running the house and staff at the same level of excellence as before.'

'Very well, Sahib.' There was a hint of a smile on Kibu's face. 'I feel inclined to accept such a favourable offer. But another problem remains: we no longer have Sahib Goldstein's house as a base.'

'Didn't you say just now that it has been put up for sale? I need a house here and I'm going to buy it. Could you immediately contact the owners with a view to purchasing it, and supervise the refurbishing and alterations afterwards? The grounds are very large and it would be to everyone's advantage if we could build proper quarters to accommodate the staff, and have a separate house at the back of the garden for you and your family. I shall be away most of the time and would feel reassured if you lived there, rather than where you are at present.'

'Indeed, Sahib. I would be delighted. You may leave all the negotiations in my hands. I'm certain that the owners will be pleased to get any offer for the house in its present condition. I also know a good builder who could start refurbishing the house within a short time.'

'Very well then, Kibu,' said John, ready to leave. 'And don't forget to tell Klaus that I want to retain his services too. Life wouldn't be the same without him.'

17

John had never been to see the villages that encroached upon the southern edge of the reserve, and he felt that it was about time to find out what the problems were. The moment he left Naboru behind, the scenery began to change and soon he came to a landscape of rolling hills, resembling a coloured patchwork: these were the shambas, the small family plots. Having started off as sizeable pieces of land, properties had been divided up amongst many children dozens of years ago, and then split again into even more reduced plots amongst the numerous grandchildren.

Men and women were toiling under the hot sun in the plantations of drooping banana fronds, manioc, waist-high maize and vegetables that surrounded their huts, but the parcels of land were so small now that trying to make a living out of them was becoming a losing battle. Soil fertility was falling and the cleared hillsides were eroding ever more with each passing rainy season. It was obvious that they needed new fields, and but for the reserve they would have kept spreading year after year, destroying natural landscapes.

Yet there was no feeling of animosity or despair. Some women were pounding manioc for the evening meal, carrying their children on their backs as they had done since time immemorial. Others were trudging along the road, their bodies bent forward under the heavy loads on their backs that were suspended by leather straps from their foreheads. As he drove by, the smell of freshly turned earth hitting his nostrils, men stopped working, leaned on the long wooden handles of their hoes and called out 'Jambo!' waving an arm, their faces beaming. Even the women, pounding the manioc or carrying loads smiled as he approached.

From time to time he met a couple of young boys maybe no older than eight or nine, coming towards him driving a herd of scraggy goats along the dusty track. He had to stop to let them pass, the herd splitting up and engulfing the car in waves of horns that every now and then banged into the sides. 'Jambo Bwana!' called the boys, smiling shyly as they tried to peep inside the car and stare at the wonders of the modern world.

School must be over, thought John, as he saw small groups of children, boys and girls mixed, coming down a hill. They all moved together in a sort of sustained trot, faster than walking but slower than running, the girls wearing red blouses with white collars, black belts and dark-green skirts, the boys yellow shirts and dark-blue shorts. Their school uniforms made them look like brightly coloured flowers flowing towards him, and their laughter was like the light bubbling of a mountain stream. As they passed John they looked at him with uninhibited curiosity and waved; their little voices were high-pitched as they screamed a 'Jambo'.

He now noticed the school building up on a small hill a hundred yards away, an uninspiring breeze-bloc structure with a corrugated-iron roof. In the open space in front girls and boys were washing their clothes, splashing about in a joyful splatter and babble of voices. They were the boarders who lived too far away and only went home during half-term.

They all looked so cheerful, so trusting in the future that John felt a pang in his heart. *If we want to assure the survival of the animals in the reserve*, he reflected, *we must include the people who live here. This is their land too, and they work hard to create a better life for their children. I honestly wish I knew how to solve this problem, but I don't.*

18

After having breakfasted in the small hotel which he was using as his base, John drove to Kibu's house hoping that he would be able to supply some ideas for the meeting with the Minister of Wildlife which was scheduled for the next day. He found Kibu his usual good-natured self, ready to lend an ear to John's problems.

'Kibu,' said John, 'I have been thinking about the problem of the people who live around the edge of the reserve. I imagined that it would be easy to stop further encroachment, but since I've been to visit the villages I'm not so sure.'

'Indeed, Sahib. I'm afraid that the problem is less simple than it seems at first sight. Agriculture and herding are not very profitable but what other way of subsisting is there for those villagers, considering that the reserve has produced no benefits for them until now? On the contrary, the elephants come to eat their plantations and sometimes destroy a year's work in one night. These people understandably do not look favourably upon the animals. The Sahib should be aware of the fact that if the local people refuse the elephants, these will eventually disappear. In order to change the prevailing attitudes, the villagers must be persuaded that a living wild animal is worth more than a dead one.'

'So it's really a matter of economics?'

'Isn't the refusal to take economic arguments into consideration the cause of many tragedies? In this particular case the benefits drawn from having an elephant reserve will have to outweigh those of other activities. That's why it is imperative to include the local population in the process of protecting the reserve and make them work for it, rather than against. They would probably be very glad to do so. It is really a matter of reorganization, and it would not even be very costly. The problem is that so far there have never been any funds for such a worthy purpose because what little money came in from tourism never reached the local people … Let's say that, for a number of reasons, the process of redistribution of wealth has not functioned well in this case.'

'Because the funds were embezzled?'

'I wouldn't put it as strongly as that. Let us say that the money tends to bypass those who have no connections. Solving this problem is no simple matter since it has its roots deep in our past. Men have always been held responsible for their extended families. If a man occupies a high position and is rich, all those connected to him will gather around to eat at his table. The system is being diluted today, but has not disappeared. That is one reason why politicians at the top want so much money, Sahib. It is not just that they are like big chiefs, and that big chiefs have to show that they are rich to inspire respect. They also have to feed a lot of people and distribute presents among their extended family, even among their whole tribe.'

'But can't people see how damaging such practices are? A modern economy cannot thrive unless all people are equal before the law, and are remunerated according to their efforts, whichever tribe or subgroup they happen to belong to.'

'Indeed, Sahib. But until recently, people over here never acted for the general benefit. The Sahib should realize that in the past there was never any trust between different tribes, or even between strangers. There were many enemies and only the extended family and eventually the tribe to count on. People even used to hide their true intentions. They approached their goals in a very roundabout way so as not to arouse suspicion and give an enemy the opportunity to interfere. Traditionally there are no straight lines in Africa. Now people are expected to think and move along straight lines and discuss their intentions openly with everyone. It is not easy.'

'But, Kibu, people are no longer living in tribal entities, but in cities such as Naboru.'

'Unfortunately, Sahib, the transition towards urbanization has happened so rapidly that the mindset has not always had time to follow. Traditional fixed rules of behaviour have broken down without being fully replaced by respect for the official law, which is supposed to govern dealings between people, and their conduct in modern society. There is certainly a lot of goodwill and enthusiasm for new things, but as yet very little rational thinking and efficient behaviour that would allow a modern economy to thrive. That is why education is so important. There is a great eagerness to learn among the younger generation, but, alas, our means are very limited. The problem is that there are many immediate needs, and that the possible benefits of education lie so far in the future that parents prefer their children, especially the girls, to help in the household. Many bright children over here have no prospect of any education beyond the most elementary level. It's a terrible waste, Sahib. An uneducated mind is like the soil that has not been fertilized. The possibilities of the mind wither and a precious plant that could have blossomed will be condemned to remain stunted for a lifetime.'

John remembered the smiling children. 'You are right, Kibu!' he said enthusiastically. 'The reserve ought to provide these children with a more rewarding life than their parents have known. They deserve a better future. I will put my funds into building schools and paying for education.'

'That is very generous of you Sahib, but I must caution you not to give anything for free.'

'Why not?' asked John, taken aback.

'If you give something away, Sahib, people will believe that it can only mean one of two things: either it has no value, or you wouldn't have given it but sold it; or else you have hidden intentions and give presents to make people dependent and obtain something much more valuable from them later. They must contribute their part, Sahib.'

'But how can they, Kibu? They are poor and have no money to give.'

'They can give their work, Sahib. They must erect the school buildings themselves; otherwise they will never have the feeling that the school belongs to their community and take pride in it and in their children's education. Donors often have the best of intentions, but if they don't work within the framework of African thought, all their efforts will be wasted. Western people are so impatient, Sahib. They want to see immediate results, but one cannot change minds overnight. And honestly, I don't think that Africans will ever become Europeans or Americans.' He paused, smiling ever so slightly.

'Thank you, Kibu,' said John. 'I'll try to think of all this when I'm discussing the new Charter with the Minister of Wildlife tomorrow. Is there any particular advice you'd like to add?'

'May I suggest that in his dealings with the Minister the Sahib tries to take into account the customs of this country without referring to them, and that he refrains from taking offence. And also that he keeps in mind that one needs to sacrifice a small fish to catch a big one. Good luck, Sahib.'

19

Minister Mamabeka was in a thoroughly foul mood. The President had entrusted him with the task of meeting this unknown man with a view to preparing the terms for a new agreement with the World Elephant Fund. At first he had thought that the President had given in to international pressure, and was about to speak his mind, but then he had been told that the Fund was prepared to pay the government ten million dollars. He found it difficult to believe this. They had no money, so how could they have come up with ten million dollars in such a short time? But the President had confirmed that the money would be handed over during the signing ceremony.

This was extremely upsetting. It thwarted all his arrangements with the French company. He had already spent a sizable portion of the million dollars he, or rather his ministry, was going to receive, promising payment within a short time. Where did this leave him? It would make him look like a fool and land him in an inextricable situation. What good was it to him that the President was going to cash in a ten-million-dollar cheque?

John had not expected a warm reception, but he was taken aback by the icy attitude of the important man in front of him. He was barely civil. He seemed to bark more than speak, merely holding a diatribe against the World Elephant Fund and foreign interference in general. John had not been able to get in more than a few words, and he instinctively felt that he would have to come to the heart of the matter soon, or all would be lost.

When the Minister had ended a long monologue and was drawing breath, John saw the opportunity to slip in a question and quickly asked: 'I don't know how I should pay you, Minister. Could you please make suggestions?'

Mamabeka, who was about to carry on, suddenly looked up. 'What?' he barked. Then, as the meaning of John's words began to penetrate, his tone changed. 'Do I understand that you are going to pay me ... I mean ... my ministry?' he inquired, wanting confirmation.

'Well, yes...' replied John. 'It's my own money and I would be delighted to help the World Elephant Fund and your country if only we can reach an agreement satisfactory to all interested parties. I imagine that I've got to split up the ten million dollars between different ministries of which yours is one, but I have no idea how to set about it and was counting on you to enlighten me.'

'Ah, oh, well...' said the Minister whose attitude visibly mellowed and who now attempted to smile amiably. 'As I said ... your proposal is most interesting, Mr...' He looked for the page with John's name, found that in his fury he had shoved it away, retrieved it and continued: '... Garfinger. Most interesting! I think that, under the circumstances, as Minister of Wildlife, I am ... I mean, my ministry is entitled to ... a million dollars?' He stared at John as if he wanted to tell him: don't let me down.

'That speaks for itself,' replied John.

Mamabeka, who had been holding his breath, now exhaled loudly, visibly relieved.

'But aren't you also Minister of Home Affairs?' continued John. 'Doesn't that Ministry also have an important role to play? For instance in all matters concerning the people living around the reserve?'

'Most certainly, most certainly!' confirmed Mamabeka. 'I was just about to remind you of it. As Minister of Home Affairs I'm entitled to ... how much would you say...' he looked at John with hope and expectation, 'another...'

'... Million dollars?' completed John. 'Yes, that's obvious.'

'My dear young man,' said Mamabeka who now got up, took John by the elbow and led him to some easy club chairs which were disposed around a low table on which sheets of paper and pens were lying, 'let us sit down over here. We'll be much more comfortable while we discuss the details of the agreement. A cigar?'

'No thank you,' replied John. 'I don't smoke.'

'A pity,' said the Minister lighting a long cigar and puffing a ring of smoke into the air. 'They are very good ones. Cuban. So you were saying...?'

'I would like to have your opinion on the villages that have spread into the reserve. Do you think that it's possible to lease their land? What do you suggest, Minister? If anyone knows the problem, it's you.'

'Dear man,' replied the Minister in a mellifluous tone, 'that's easy. These people all belong to my own tribe. If you are prepared to pay them for the loss of their land we simply move them out and create work for them around the reserve's edge, related to tourism and other activities.'

'Minister,' said John with a show of admiration, 'you have an answer to all my queries! But what do you think about the poachers? They really are a great problem. Can anything be done there?'

'It's obvious that all illegal incursions into the reserve and all killing of animals must be stopped immediately!' The Minister spoke in a determined voice that tolerated no opposition. 'Poachers must be dealt with without pity! The disrespect of those people is intolerable. They are a scourge and ruin our reputation abroad. If you pay, I'm ready to create special intervention units to patrol the reserve. We must counter brutal force with even more brutal force.'

Having agreed on all the important points, the Minister and John now set about working out the new Charter in its smallest details. The Minister seemed in a conciliatory mood and was even willing to agree on the new long-term lease of the reserve and on leaving Veronica as director. When everything was put on paper and all the arrangements were made for the signing ceremony, they shook hands like two comrades in arms and John left.

The Minister was in a jubilant state of mind. *What a most charming young man,* he thought. *And how cleverly I manipulated him: two million instead of one!* He rubbed his hands in contentment. Then he thought of that Frenchman who knew about his previous schemes and had now become an embarrassment. He had to be put behind bars together with all his accomplices before he upset the apple cart. And without further delay Mamabeka called for the Chief of Internal Security.

20

When John returned to the house on Malavu Avenue the next day he found it bustling with activities. It was no longer a house but a building site. Sacks of cement, stacks of bricks and other building materials were piled up on the front lawn and at least twenty workmen were erecting scaffolding, digging trenches for the new buildings and wheeling out rubble from the burned-out laboratory under the supervision of a few Indian foremen.

As John went in, he saw Kibu standing in front of a table covered with plans for the new buildings, together with a bearded and turbaned Indian.

'Welcome to your new home, Sahib,' said Kibu. 'I hope that you like the progress.'

'I'm impressed,' replied John. 'I didn't think you would be able to find a builder for at least a month.'

'Well, Sahib, Mr Patel here...' Kibu pointed at the Indian builder who nodded politely, 'was so good as to forgo other obligations and start immediately. Everything should be finished within a month. But a wing of the main house is in the process of being repainted and, if the Sahib wishes, he can leave his hotel in town and move in here tomorrow.'

'You're simply wonderful!' exclaimed John. 'Hey, and Klaus? Is he anywhere around?'

'I'm pleased to be able to tell the Sahib that Sahib Klaus had his usual breakfast this morning and appears to be happy again. He is busily working in one of the rooms on the ground floor which he is temporarily occupying.'

'I'll go and say hello to him then. Good old Klaus! He'll be so delighted to see me.' And he went off down the long corridor.

He heard a falsetto voice singing one of Schubert's Lieder behind a door and, as he pushed it, the door banged into a table just behind. When he slipped through the half-open doorway he found Klaus sitting there, looking shocked and holding on to a metallic-blue elongated object out of which a lot of wires protruded. It seemed to have fallen into his arms. 'Careful, you clumsy *Dummkopf*!' he yelled. 'You knocked my latest invention off the table.'

'I see that you're still your cheery old self,' remarked John sarcastically.

'If only curious people did not bump in at any odd time, poking their noses into what I'm doing and deranging my flow of genial thoughts, life would be much easier,' retorted Klaus.

'And what genial inventions are you producing now,' asked John, pointing at the object Klaus was pressing to his chest as if it were his precious baby. 'It looks like a vacuum cleaner.'

'A vacuum cleaner!' Klaus snorted. *'Du Finkelstein!'*

'Well, I was just referring to its looks, not to its contents of course. I expect that there's more inside than a paper bag to hold the dust.'

'What! A retarded hominid like you dares to laugh at one of the greatest inventions ever! If you really want to know: it's my Brain Extractor. It sucks out the brain's contents.'

John was about to say 'A vacuum cleaner, then,' but he abstained in the last split second. Instead he exclaimed: 'Extraordinary, Klaus! You are truly a genius!'

'I am the greatest genius ever! The world should have been at my feet after I successfully completed my experiment with the time machine. They should have erected my statue – a huge statue – with the inscription: "To Klaus the Great. From a humble admiring world." And what happened? My time machine was destroyed by a mob of *Dummköpfe*. And you...' he pointed an accusing thin finger at John, 'the only one who knows what's happened and can testify to my extraordinary invention ... you refuse to speak up! Under the circumstances, how can the world ever know what a genius I am and honour me? I've never been so disappointed in my life!'

He tugged at his hair until it nearly stood on end, and his eyes flashed angrily behind his spectacles. Suddenly he flared up, trembling with rage: 'That's why I have invented the Brain Extractor. I'm building it with the particular aim of drawing all the information out of obstinate people like you who don't want to reveal what's happened to them. One night I will sneak up to you and put it on your head, and then I will transfer your thoughts onto a screen and divulge them to the world. You just wait!'

'Well, thanks for warning me,' remarked John as he turned and left. 'I'll make sure that my door is securely locked at night.'

21

John had been so busy organizing everything since he'd been back in Africa that he'd had time for little else. Now he felt relieved. All the main problems had been straightened out and the official signing ceremony was going to take place tomorrow. Suddenly he felt a strong need for peace and space. He set off in his car and soon left the sprawl of shantytowns around Naboru behind. As he drove on through some scattered villages, slowly, almost imperceptibly, the landscape changed. He turned onto a rough track carpeted with red dust; after a while it began to descend towards the open savannah and then climbed again to the crest of a ridge.

He stopped the car, got out and walked a few paces to where a big boulder was lying. Birds whirled overhead and silence enveloped him, punctuated by the shrill chirping of the cicadas in some nearby acacia trees. As he sat down on the boulder in the shade of a tree, his whole being began to expand: he felt his senses sharpen and started to pick up the rich scent of the savannah which a soft breeze carried to his nostrils, a scent of dried grass mixed with the dusty smell of the earth.

He looked around in awe. The world stretched at his feet, miles upon miles of rolling hills and bush. The plains seemed to go on forever, to the distant heat-blurred horizon and the high-piled cumulus clouds that filled the immense blue sky with majestic white shapes.

This is where I spent my life as an elephant, mused John. He had tried to suppress thinking of it since he had been caught up again in the whirlwind of modern human life. Now it all came back to him. Suddenly the last image of his life as an elephant flashed upon his mind: the hominids attacking his baby elephant, and the memory distressed him greatly. Had it survived the attack? Then he realized that only his mind had been called back from the elephant in which it had dwelled for some time, but the elephant mother must have continued to storm forward and John prayed that she had managed to rescue the baby. *It's a shame that I'll never know what happened,* he thought. *I'd have loved to see my baby elephant grow up. I would have been so proud to see him grow into a mighty elephant.*

He tried to push that painful last memory out of his mind and thought again of the many seasons he had spent with the elephants: the tranquil life and long wanderings with the herd in the savannah, the company of the others surrounding him with loving care. It had been paradise on earth and it saddened him that it was lost forever. *I am human again now,* he said to himself, *but something of the elephant will always remain in me.*

The shrill cry of a startled bird shattered the silence, and from the corner of his eye John perceived the faint movement of a frightened lizard vanishing into the undergrowth. As he looked out over the vast landscape below his feet, he felt as if he were the first man to sit on this particular boulder and set eyes on the magnificent panorama that stretched endlessly before him. Nothing seemed spoiled or sullied, grass bent before the wind, a buzzard soared and crickets trilled ceaselessly ... There was peace all around.

There was something in the sweeping views, the brightness of the colours and quality of the light that no other continent possessed. It conveyed a feeling of belonging that one did not experience anywhere else. This was the Africa he had come to love, with its wide-open spaces and ever-retreating horizon. This was the cradle of mankind. Once upon a time all the people of the world had been Africans, until the ancestors of Asians, Europeans and Americans had left the continent, maybe sixty thousand years ago. *We are all emigrants,* John reflected. *We all came out of Africa. This is our birthplace and we should care for it.*

The shadows were lengthening and as John got up facing the immense expanse of grass and trees, now stained red by the rays of the setting sun, suddenly the thought came to him: *I am an African emigrant who has returned after thousands of years of restless trekking. This is the land where I belong. I'm back home at last.*

22

The next day an article appeared in the evening edition of the *Daily Star* under the title: 'Official creation of the first World Heritage Park. It read:

We are pleased to announce that the dispute concerning the status of the Naboru Elephant Reserve has been satisfactorily resolved. After the World Elephant Fund paid a compensation amounting to ten million dollars to different government departments, it was agreed that the reserve will be leased out to the Fund for a period of ninety-nine years. During a meeting held today at the Presidential Palace, a document was signed by our President and Sir Arthur Llewellyn, President of the World Elephant Fund, in the presence of the UN representative for Africa and Minister Mamabeka.

We are also happy to inform our readers that the status of the reserve has been changed at the insistence of our President and Minister Mamabeka. Thanks to their visionary initiative our country has created the first World Heritage Park and our President has expressed the hope that other countries will not hesitate to follow this outstanding initiative.

The park will be a showcase for the whole world. Under the competent leadership of Miss de Ville, who has been confirmed in her position as director and was present at the ceremony, the park will become a role model for the new approach to projects of this kind. Part of the revenues it generates will go to the government; a large part will also be invested in educational and health programmes for the local population.

Minister Mamabeka, who played an essential role in brokering the deal with the international organizations, and who supplied many of the brightest ideas that characterize the new approach, declared afterwards that 'We are certain that the whole world will be watching us closely. We must all collaborate to make sure that this becomes a tremendous success.' He added that the reputation of our country depended on it and stressed that the government will clamp down on any illegal activity liable to damage the park, drawing particular attention to the problem of poaching. 'The wild animals are our heritage,' he said, 'and their future is also our own. We cannot tolerate their being killed for short-term gain by unscrupulous bandits.' He declared in words that left no doubt that '...we shall declare full-scale war on them and fight the poachers until we rid our country of this scourge!'

He also spoke long and convincingly of the need for an integrated free-market approach in running the park. 'Unless the economics are right,' he stated, 'our efforts are doomed to failure. Tourism and the protection of the park must be integrated into a web of activities that include the local population. Revenues must be sufficient to cover all expenses. These are the requirements of any healthy modern enterprise, and the management is committed to running the park upon these principles in collaboration with the appropriate government services and local councils.'

The Minister concluded: 'We are proud today to show the world that we are in the vanguard of modern park management, and we will give what it takes to turn this unique project into a worldwide success that will be the envy of other countries.'

23

There was one problem John had been unable to solve so far: how to deter elephants from straying out of the park and uprooting people's shambas. He had learned that several methods had been tried out in wildlife parks elsewhere, from electric fences to ropes smeared with a pungent mixture of grease and hot chilli peppers – a combination elephants seemed to abhor. Villagers living around parks also spent time on elephant watch, equipped with firecrackers and searchlights to scare hungry elephants away from their fields at night. It seemed all very laborious and costly. It was also impractical around a huge park such as Veronica's and John wondered how they could possibly stop the elephants from straying across the boundary.

After leaving his luggage in a room in his new house John went in search of Klaus, hoping that he might be able to help him. As he entered the large backroom where Klaus was setting up a temporary laboratory, he found it littered with piles of half unpacked crates. Racks of instruments were rising like miniature skyscrapers among the boxes and computers; bits and pieces of electronic equipment were lying on tables and chairs, and wires were trailing all over the floor.

That's Klaus in action, thought John as he surveyed the scene with an amused look in his eyes. *With the thoroughness and methodology Germans are so admired for. But where is he himself?*

'Klaus!' he called out. 'Are you there?'

He was about to leave when a bespectacled head rose from behind one of the higher crates.

'*Eh? Was?*' said the head that seemed to be floating by itself above the crate.

'Listen. I've had an idea...'

Klaus at once cut him short. 'You cannot bump in here like that with ideas!' he said in a firm voice. 'This is not the right time. Can't you see that I'm concentrating on my task? I have to proceed with order and method. I'm building up this laboratory according to a strict plan and my thoughts cannot be interrupted. Come back in a week or so.'

'I know that you're very busy but there's an urgent task that can't wait.'

'If it can't wait you'll have to ring a repair service or something like that. They must have services for emergencies. Look it up in the phone directory and call them. I'm sure they'll send a specialized technician.' And Klaus' head vanished again behind the crate.

John stood there at a loss for words. The events of the last weeks didn't seem to have improved Klaus' character. He insisted: 'It's nothing like that. It's a *real* problem.'

The head reappeared, the gold-rimmed spectacles on the point of the nose and the eyes spitting fire. '*Donnerwetter!* Are you still there? What is it?'

This needs a more diplomatic approach, thought John, *otherwise we'll get nowhere*. And he began to speak coaxingly: 'It needs a big brain to solve this kind of problem, you see. And only you have such a brain.'

'Aha! It's that kind of problem.' Klaus now sat upright, a contented look on his face, saying magnanimously: 'Tell me about it.'

'We need a system to scare the elephants away from the villages around the reserve. They're in the habit of moving in at night to eat the crops of maize and trample the fields, and the villagers don't like it a bit. So we are looking for a foolproof system that scares the elephants but doesn't annoy the villagers.'

'What have I got to do with that? I don't know anything about elephants. That's more in your elephant girl's line.' He was about to turn away again, but John stopped him.

'Just hear me out to the end. I have experienced that elephants are extremely sensitive to sound. They love gentle sounds such as those made for example by ... bubbling water, but are utterly frightened of deep rumbling noises such as ... well ... those produced by the eruption of a volcano or something like that. I believe that repetitive deep drumming sounds would scare them. Now, you are a great connoisseur of music...'

'That's true!' exclaimed Klaus without even a hint of modesty. 'You can call me an authority on German music. Any of the works of Beethoven, Schumann, Schubert's Lieder, ...'

'The problem is that elephants will probably like that kind of music and draw nearer to listen to it instead of running away. No! We don't want melodious music. We've got to find music they abhor, and furthermore play it in infrasound.'

'Why is that?'

'Well, elephants carry on most of their communication in infrasound. We humans cannot hear it, but they are attuned to extremely low frequencies.'

'Aha! I see now. You want a soundtrack elephants abhor, and play it the whole night in infrasound so that humans cannot hear it. That's easy. I've got an idea already.'

'So you can solve the problem?'

'Of course,' declared Klaus sticking out his narrow chest. 'Did you doubt it?

24

Her daily tasks over, Veronica was hanging out of the window of her room in Elephant Camp smiling, lost in thought. The last week had been the most exciting week of her life! First the miracle of John coming back, telling her that he loved her. And then yesterday: she had been to the Presidential Palace for the signing ceremony! Who would ever have believed it? Her name was on the new Charter. For ninety-nine years, imagine that! She had felt so proud afterwards, standing on the steps of the palace between the President and Sir Arthur. Then the President had made a speech and when he had finished he had pushed her forward, asking her to add a word. And before she had realized what she was doing she had opened her heart and made a passionate plea for the elephants, begging the world for donations. She had felt quite silly afterwards but the President had smiled and everyone had applauded while the photographers had zoomed in on her as if she were a celebrity.

She did not want to be a celebrity. She didn't care about it. She wanted John. He had been so occupied since he had returned from America that he hadn't even had time to come to the camp after that wonderful surprise a week ago. And yesterday she had seen him for no more than a few minutes just before the signing ceremony. He had not even taken part in it. He, who had arranged everything, didn't even have a function in the park!

She stood there, undecided, leaning on the windowsill, staring out towards the south, waiting for him to return. Surely, now that everything was arranged he would come back? Then she heard the sound of an approaching engine and her heart leapt. As she ran down and out of the house, a big safari bus turned into the enclosure, music blaring, and stopped with shrieking brakes.

'Oh God, not him!' exclaimed Veronica as Ron jumped out, a large smile on his face, showing two rows of sparkling teeth.

341

'Hi, Vee, old girl,' said Ron, coming towards her and giving her a peck on the cheek. 'Glad to see me after all this time, hey?'

Veronica stood there gaping at Ron, unable to speak for a few seconds. Then she stuttered: 'What ... what...?'

'I see that you are overcome,' remarked Ron with undisguised satisfaction. 'Naturally! The shock after having waited so long...'

'Oh, umph,' swallowed Veronica, unable to think of anything. Her brain seemed to have stopped functioning.

'Well, I just thought that it was about time I came to pay you a visit and talked about our arrangements for the park. I have set up an agency called Ron's Happy Safaris and, naturally, given our long and outstanding friendship, I'm sure that you have no objection to my running the tourist activities. I'll bring in the tourists and turn the organization into a thriving business. You know that with me everything is in experienced hands. You just leave that side of the problem to me and carry on concentrating on what you like best, namely caring for the elephants. I'm certain that we'll make a good team.'

Veronica couldn't believe her ears. Was this real?

Ron continued: 'I've read about your appearance at the Presidential Palace. You have become an important figure. Let me congratulate you!' Suddenly he added, as if he had almost forgotten: 'Oh yes, and I have a surprise for you.'

He carefully brushed the earth in front of Veronica's feet, bent down slowly on one knee, held up his hands in a theatrical way and bestowed his most flashy smile on her. Then, before her astounded eyes, he declared as if he were a comedian speaking on a stage: 'I'm doing you the honour of asking you to marry me.'

25

The sun was already leaning westwards as John drove towards Elephant Camp. Another hour and he would be with Veronica again. As he thought of her, pride welled up in him. How magnificent she had been yesterday! She had spoken so passionately on the steps of the Presidential Palace that her words had left a deep impression on the audience.

She would take over from here, and he felt relieved. He had played his role and now he just wanted to live and be happy. Little by little, as he moved along the dusty track through the savannah, the tension of the previous days started to drop off like a heavy cloak, and as he began to relax he felt utterly exhausted and had the feeling that he could sleep for a couple of days. *Heavens*, he suddenly thought, *I hope I'm not going to fall asleep the moment I get there. What a bad impression that would make on Veronica!*

He remembered the days long ago, before he had been an elephant. How insecure he had felt then every time he had gone to see her. How worried he had been when he approached the camp. And no wonder: she was such an extraordinary girl, whilst he could be such a clumsy fellow. The blunders he had made! Who could blame Veronica for having thought nothing of him?

The more he thought of Veronica, the more he began to doubt everything. Could it really be true that she loved him? She was infinitely more worthy than him. She was unique. And she was a star now!

His self-assurance had always had the bad habit of disappearing when he was going to be alone with Veronica, and it did so again. Suddenly the thought came to him that it was late afternoon already, and that he would have to spend the night at the camp. He remembered the last time he had proposed to spend the night there. Veronica had been very upset and had told him to go and sleep with Dumbo in his shed! Would it be the same this time?

Whenever he had approached Elephant Camp with high hopes, fate had intervened to do him a bad turn. All his attempts to make Veronica love him had turned into disaster. Something unexpected was sure to pop up again! He hoped that nothing untoward would happen tonight, and found himself once more preparing what he was going to say.

Do things repeat themselves in life? When he entered the enclosure he saw the big safari bus. *I was prepared for anything,* thought John with a shock, *but I had completely forgotten about him! The man with the flashy teeth has turned up again.*

As he stopped his car and emerged hesitantly, he witnessed a most astounding scene: there was Veronica, more beautiful than ever, standing as if in a trance, while that despicable fellow was kneeling in front of her, his arms stretched up towards her. Then she saw him and called out: 'John! Come and listen to this! Ron has just asked me to marry him!'

John felt his stomach turn and stood there stunned, unable to move or say anything, but Veronica didn't seem to notice and redirected her attention to Ron: 'Can you say it once again?' she demanded.

Ron looked displeased. 'Not with him standing there,' he mumbled. 'Where has he come from? I thought he'd gone forever?'

'Well, you can see that he's still here,' replied Veronica, smiling. 'Come on, say it again!'

At last Ron repeated in a flat artificial voice without the slightest hint of enthusiasm: 'I ask you to marry me.'

'No, that's not what you said!'

'I ask you to do me the honour of marrying me?'

'No, no! You actually said: "I'm doing you the honour of asking you to marry me." That's what you said. And I've never heard such a ludicrous thing in my life!' With a quick movement she put two fingers in her mouth and produced an ear-splitting whistle.

'What's that?' exclaimed Ron. 'That's not an answer!'

'Yes, yes, it is! You'll see. Wait!'

Suddenly Dumbo came charging into the yard trumpeting loudly and made straight for Ron.

'Hey!' he yelled, getting up in fright. 'That fellow's gone crazy! Hey, stop him!' he kept yelling as he began to run, surprisingly fast for someone so pompous. Within seconds he had vanished down the drive with a loud-trumpeting Dumbo hot on his heels.

Steve, alarmed by Dumbo's wild sounds, came running along shouting: 'Things OK, Memsabu?'

'Steve! You've come at the right moment. Could you drive that bus over there along the track until you catch up with the owner? But drive very slowly,' Veronica added with a smile. 'The man needs some exercise.'

John had been standing there all this time, dumbfounded. Now Veronica rushed up to him and flung her arms around his neck. 'Oh, John, you have come back,' she murmured. 'At last!'

'Hem ... I ... eh ... I can always sleep with Dumbo if you want,' stammered John, attempting to pre-empt all possible embarrassment.

'John! What are you talking about? Are you not well?'

'Well ... eh...' Suddenly words came out of John's mouth like a flood. 'Veronica! You're famous the world over! Do you realize that millions of dollars have been pledged to help you just in one day? You've become an icon overnight! The phone never stopped at our centre in Naboru. And I have to tell you that five offers of marriage have come in already.'

'Six,' corrected Veronica, pointing gleefully towards the southern horizon.

'He doesn't count. But some proposals are not to be looked down on. They are from very wealthy men. You certainly don't want a clumsy fellow like me now, do you?'

'But John! I don't care about wealthy millionaires. I'd rather be your number twenty-one than Mrs Millionaire.'

'My number twenty-one?'

'Well yes, considering that you've known twenty women already...'

'Wherever did you get such a ridiculous idea from?'

'Sam told me and he sounded as if he knew...'

'What a damned lie! How could he do such a thing?' He looked at Veronica. 'And why anyone ever listens to such obvious lies is more than I can understand. No wonder I've acquired such a bad reputation!' John seemed thoroughly vexed. 'If you absolutely need to know, I've had no more than four relationships. One was my ex, and I've had three other short, miserable affairs.'

'Does that include your Bulgarian conquests?'

'There was nothing to include there,' replied John grumpily.

'I'm sorry to have upset you,' said Veronica in a sweet voice. 'But there are things a girl wants to know when she's about to ... Oh John,' she pleaded, 'shall we forget about the past?'

'I wish we would,' replied John.

26

After he had got his safari bus back, Ron was assailed by dark thoughts as he sped towards Naboru. What had come over that girl? How anyone could be so ungrateful was beyond him. She had ordered that little monster of an elephant to chase him away. After he had proposed to marry her! Why they had kept her on as director of the park was beyond his understanding. How could Le Tellier have failed so miserably in his plans? A real shame it was. Everything would have been so much easier with him. *I would have worked with a reasonable man who understands business,* thought Ron. *But no, they force you to do business with a hysterical girl instead!*

It had seemed a good idea to ask her to marry him when he had learned that she'd been reconfirmed in her position. He would have been sitting on a bed of roses, directing all the tourist activities. But he realized now that it was altogether lucky that he'd got out of it. Imagine the price he would have had to pay: having to live with someone as unbalanced as that girl. It would have been hell on earth. He shuddered at the thought. Still, his prospects suddenly looked much less bright than they had a couple of hours ago. He had spent his last savings on this tourist agency and had even borrowed, counting on Le Tellier to arrange everything. *I'd better get out of this country,* reflected Ron, *and drive to South Africa. There are lots of well-functioning parks in that country. Maybe I'll be able to set up as an independent operator there?*

Dumbo on the contrary was very pleased with himself. He had chased that unpleasant man for well over a mile, but the fellow had run surprisingly fast and he had been unable to catch up with him. Still, it had been great fun! Dumbo had felt hungry afterwards and had spent an hour browsing in the bush until night was falling. When he returned to the enclosure, he was just in time to see his mother and his new great friend go up the stairs, their arms around each other, and disappear inside the bedroom. As he began to drink from the water barrel underneath he vaguely heard their voices, and then the lights went out. He felt immensely happy and stood there for a long time, gazing at the sliver of a moon hanging low over the horizon and at the stars which began to twinkle brightly. Then he walked towards his shed, made himself comfortable inside and fell asleep contentedly, in harmony with the whole world.

27

The next morning Veronica and John had breakfast on the veranda in almost complete silence. There was an unwillingness to break the spell and speak of ordinary things. There was also the shyness of two lovers who have to look into each other's eyes in broad daylight after the intimacy of their first night.

When breakfast was over Veronica went to Dumbo's shed. John's eyes followed her receding figure till she disappeared inside, and as images of last night whirled through his head, he got up and began to walk alongside the house in the full glory of the African morning while waves of strong feeling went through his body – there are moments when happiness is so great that it is nearly impossible to bear. He noticed Veronica leaving the shed, and when he saw the gracefulness of her movements, the sheer beauty of her silhouette against the immensity of the African sky as she came towards him, he was overcome with emotion. After all those wasted, lonely years he had found the one soul akin to his own! It seemed so incredible that he had been chosen. He was almost unable to believe it. Could it really be true?

Veronica looked at him as he was standing in front of a clump of tall elephant grass. Such a handsome, sweet man he was ... she couldn't believe her luck. But he seemed so quiet this morning, almost absent. Was he disappointed in her? She was such an ordinary girl, whilst he ... to think that everything would have been lost but for him. And he had not even given himself a role in the organization! Why had he done that? Maybe ... maybe he knew that he wasn't going to stay? Maybe he was going back to America?

Suddenly she was assailed by panic and before she was able to stop the words, she blurted out: 'John, you're not thinking of going away again, are you?' She just couldn't face having to live without him. 'It ... it would be so lonely without you.' She looked very despondent.

John stared at his feet. 'Oh no, but...'

'But what?'

'Do you really want me?'

'How can you ask such a question?'

'What I mean to say is...' John turned red and resumed gazing at his feet. 'I ... I ... would you marry me?'

For a second Veronica looked at him in utter surprise. Then she yelled: 'Yahoo! I will!' She leapt up at him, flinging her arms around his neck and throwing her legs around his hips with such force that John fell over backwards, and they both disappeared into the clump of tall elephant grass and tumbled into the nearby plumbago which grew in profusion along that side of the house.

Just then a car arrived and stopped in the yard, ten feet away. As Kibu got out he heard shrieks of laughter nearby in the grass and saw some wild movement. Then John's head popped up, a look of utter surprise on his face, followed by Veronica, her eyes glowing with excitement.

'I have not arrived at an inopportune moment, Sahib?' inquired Kibu hesitantly. 'I hope I'm not interrupting you while you are engaged in some important business? I can always come back...'

'No ... ahem ... it's quite all right,' replied John somewhat bewildered. 'We just happened to fall down...'

'What a pleasure to see you here!' exclaimed Veronica, her face flushed with happiness. She crawled out of the grass on all fours and stepped forward to shake hands with him.

'It's a great honour for me, Memsabu, to be so well received in your abode,' answered Kibu, modestly averting his eyes while she was busy pulling some of the sticky blue plumbago flowers out of her hair.

'And what brings you over here at such an ... opportune moment?' asked John, on his feet now.

'Well, Sahib, following your instructions I have been trying to find some extra personnel, not only for your house in Naboru, but also for the Memsabu's house here. And I believe I have found a perfect candidate. His name is Bongo. He is strong and I find him willing and good-natured. He says that he knows the area, is excellent at spotting animals, and can even drive a car if necessary. Here he is.'

Bongo had just managed to extract his bulk from the small

car and now came towards John, his face split by a huge smile. 'Good morning, Boss,' he said. Then he hesitated a second and added, as if he needed to be reassured: 'I hope that you won't mind me calling you boss, Boss?'

Veronica suddenly exploded in mirth. 'I know him!' she shrieked. 'He's an important government official. We'll take him.'

John didn't know what to make out of this. 'Do you really want a government official?' he asked surprised.

'Yes, yes! He's great fun.'

John looked puzzled, but called for Steve and told him to explain some of the tasks to the newcomer. As Bongo was about to follow Steve he turned once more to John and said with a look of conspiracy on his face: 'Thank you, Boss. And I'll put some spring in my step.' And he went off with a studied bounce in his gait, leaving John totally perplexed.

When he had gone, John turned again to Kibu. 'How's Klaus getting on?'

'Well, Sahib, only this morning I heard him say that, as the elephants were not going to come to his lab, he would have to go to the elephants. I must admit that I do not really understand the meaning of his words.'

'Is Klaus coming here to see elephants?' asked Veronica. 'I can let Steve drive him into the park if he needs to see elephants.'

'But, Memsabu, isn't that somewhat dangerous for Sahib Klaus, given how distracted he is at times?'

'It's probably more dangerous for the elephants to let Klaus loose on them,' laughed John. 'So how is he getting on with the music?'

'Music, Sahib? I have indeed noticed that Sahib Klaus has been singing a great deal in German lately. He has also been playing a lot of music, even the "God save the Queen", without showing the slightest respect, imagine! But I cannot really tell, Sahib. I can confirm though that he is eating properly and full of energy, and that he is his old self again. I trust that under the circumstances he will soon come to the successful conclusion of whatever he is doing.'

'Very good!' replied John. 'And how is the other part of our research into the elephant problem coming along?'

'What problem are you talking about?' Veronica asked sharply.

'The Sahib is referring to our attempts to prevent overpopulation, Memsabu.'

'I don't want any elephants killed!' shouted Veronica defensively.

'Don't worry, Veronica,' replied John calmly. 'I wouldn't dream of killing an elephant. Elephants are extremely sensitive to acts of violence. They remember those who die for a long time. They will stop if they find the bones of one of their dead companions in the savannah and touch them with great tenderness. Believe me, it's a traumatic experience for elephants to see one of their family killed. If they are shot at, they will also bear an ever-lasting grudge towards humans and steer away from them, which is no fun for tourists who want to see them. They may even become dangerous and attack humans. No, killing excess elephants is not an option. We must intervene beforehand and avert overpopulation by limiting births. I have asked Kibu to look into the state of the research to intervene in the reproduction cycle, which is at present carried out by several American laboratories. That's what we're talking about.'

Veronica looked at John with awe. 'But, John, how …

'Just trust me, Veronica,' John carried on. 'The elephants are safe with me. I love them as much as you do.'

He now turned to Kibu: 'Have you been able to gather the information?'

'Yes Sahib. It seems that the experiments to develop vaccines that would prevent the female's eggs from being fertilized are already well advanced. Several methods are being tried out and some vaccines are ready for use. They could be injected with dart guns which would allow park wardens to vaccinate the elephants from a safe distance.'

'Wonderful!' exclaimed John. 'Could you contact the companies concerned? We are going to try out all the different methods and select the safest one.'

Veronica still stood there, gaping at John. 'But I … but I didn't realize that you were doing these things. And how do you know all this? I don't understand…'

'There is a lot we shall never understand,' replied John mysteriously.

'John, you surprise me at every turn. You seem to know much more about elephants than I do. You should really have been the new director,' said Veronica, working herself up. 'The top job should have been rightfully yours anyway since it was you who saved the reserve. It's highly unfair that you have no role in the organization!'

'I don't want any more jobs,' replied John calmly, taking her hands in his. 'But if you are willing to accept my help I'd love to assist you.'

28

Two days later Klaus turned up at the camp and, assisted by Steve and Bongo, he transferred some bulky sound equipment he had brought to Veronica's jeep and mounted a loudspeaker on the roof. Then they went off in search of elephants. When they returned a few hours later Klaus looked jubilant. He told Veronica and John that all was ready, and invited them to accompany him into the park.

After some time they made contact with a herd of about twenty elephants which were browsing peacefully. They drew nearer very carefully, stopped with the loudspeaker turned towards the elephants, and Klaus put a tape into the equipment. As he played it, the elephants became agitated and showed signs of displeasure.

'Now, this is a normal reaction,' said Klaus, sticking up a finger as if he were lecturing. 'Good! Let me show you their reaction to another sound track.'

The elephants' reaction was the same: they were visibly disturbed, their ears were flapping, but they didn't move away.

'I can't hear anything!' protested Veronica. 'Can't you switch on the sound?'

'The sound is on,' replied Klaus as if speaking to a dumb child, 'but of course you can't hear anything.'

'It's infrasound,' clarified John. 'That's why you can't hear it. But elephants can.'

'*Genau*,' affirmed Klaus. 'You cannot hear anything because I have created an electronic device that transforms frequencies normally audible to humans into infrasound, which the human ear is unable to hear. But the elephants hear it well enough, as you can deduce from their reactions.' He carried on: 'So far I have shown you a few examples of soundtracks that elephants don't really like but are willing to put up with. Now listen to this,' he said, inserting a new tape. He looked at them for a moment like a conjurer, ready to pull a rabbit out of a hat,

354

and his eyes shone with an almost diabolical light as he switched on the sound. The effect was immediate. The elephants showed signs of extreme annoyance, turned and thundered away.

'Klaus, you've cracked the problem!' exclaimed John shaking his hand. 'You're a genius! Let me congratulate you.'

'I'm not a genius,' corrected Klaus. 'I'm *the* genius. All you now have to do is install transmitters functioning on solar-powered batteries in the villages around the park. They can emit this sound track the whole night. The villagers won't hear anything, but it'll keep the elephants at a safe distance.'

Veronica sat there gaping. 'This is incredible! The elephants looked thoroughly upset, almost disgusted. What is it you were playing?'

'Do you really want to know?' asked Klaus. 'Maybe it's better you don't.'

'That's highly unfair,' intervened John. 'I think that Veronica has a right to know. And I want to know it too. It's not a military secret, is it? What kind of music is this?'

'You really want to know? All right. If you get into trouble because of it, maybe it's better to know why. Anyway, it's not really my responsibility. Listen, I'm going to play the tape as you would hear it normally.'

Klaus fiddled with a few buttons, switched the tape on again, and suddenly they heard the ponderous tones of...'

'But this is...' stammered John, flabbergasted.

'Yes ... you recognize it?'

'...This is the Belgian national anthem!'

'You've got it!'

'How did you ever think of playing a national anthem?' asked Veronica, completely puzzled.

'Oh, it's all very logical, you see. John told me that elephants are peaceful animals and so I reasoned that music intended to whip up the human masses and make their chests swell with patriotic pride would probably have the opposite effect on elephants. I then started collecting several national anthems and this morning I tried them out on the elephants.' Klaus looked at Veronica as a professor would look at a somewhat backward student. 'As I thought, the elephants did not like any of the anthems but the effects weren't strong enough – that's what I wanted to show you by playing the first soundtracks. I was beginning to be discouraged until I played the Belgian national anthem. I've tried it out on several herds, on males and females, and the effect is always immediate: they just run away from it!'

'Who would ever have expected that?' commented John. 'The Belgian national anthem! It's absolutely astounding.'

'But, but...' stuttered Veronica, 'this is unbelievable. Why does this have such an effect on elephants?'

'I must admit that I don't know why,' replied Klaus somewhat reluctantly, 'but it works.' He now turned to John. 'I wonder how Belgians react. You who have lived over there, tell me: do they also run away like elephants when they hear their anthem?'

'Let's not go into such sensitive political matters,' said John, declining to make any comments.

But Klaus was not to be stopped. 'Can you imagine what great powers must be concealed in these solemn tones if they make elephants run?' he persevered. 'I'd like to understand.'

'This very simple,' intervened Steve who had been listening and thought it was about time to enlighten these ignorant people. 'This music is strong magic. Full of witchcraft! The elephants, they know. They scared.'

Everyone gaped at the driver who sat there while his face expressed the greatest respect for such powerful music.

'Well, who knows?' remarked John laughing. 'The Belgian national anthem has solved our problem and that looks very much like witchcraft to me.'

29

John had returned to Naboru for a few days to see how the work on the house was progressing. As Kibu was serving mid-morning tea with homemade scones, John was looking at him from the corner of his eye thinking: 'What an upstanding man he is in his bright flowing robes.'

'Kibu,' he said finally, 'there is something that has intrigued me for a long time. I would like to ask you a question, but if you think it too personal, don't feel obliged to answer.'

'Yes, Sahib...'

'How come you are so well educated and speak such good English?'

'That's quite simple, Sahib. I spent two years at Oxford University.'

'Amazing! I would never have thought of that. But why only two years?'

'My father, who occupied an elevated position in the previous government, had rented a house in Oxford where I lived with several other members of my extended family who were also studying. Unfortunately he fell out of favour with the previous President and the funds were cut off while I was in the middle of my second year. One cold, dark January day when I returned to the house, I found that the lights did not work. It turned out that the bills had not been paid and that the company had cut off the electricity and gas supply. We stuck it out for a few weeks, wrapped in blankets and reading by candlelight, but then a cold spell struck the country and it rained almost constantly – you know what it can be like over there in the winter. Then we found that the rent had not been paid either and we had to leave the house. I managed to move in with friends, passed the exams and finished the second year, though it was all very difficult and I often had to go hungry. I tried to do odd jobs but unfortunately it was impossible to raise the funds that would have allowed me to complete my studies. Upon my return here

I found employment with an Indian firm where my good command of English and knowledge of economic matters were greatly appreciated.'

'But that's awful!' exclaimed John.

'That's the way life goes, Sahib. One has to take the bad with the good.'

'How could you stand life over there?'

'As a matter of fact, I quite enjoyed my courses and the atmosphere, Sahib. The weather was not always pleasant and the cold somewhat difficult to bear, especially when we had no heating; the people were a trifle conceited and may have lacked the openness and ease of manner we are accustomed to here in Africa; but there was a richness of culture, a respect for the law, a readiness to discuss and exchange ideas and a political openness that were unlike anything I had experienced. By and large it was quite a unique experience.'

'But do you think that this makes up for the coldness of the people, the lack of concern for others and the egocentrism of the rich world?'

'It would be wonderful if we could combine the best of both worlds, Sahib. But alas, we humans are limited in our views and concerns.'

'You must feel bitter about the way fate has treated you?'

'I was very happy over there in spite of the many deprivations, Sahib. But I'm very happy here too.'

'But your career was cut short! I think that life has been extremely unjust to you.'

'Permit me to be the judge of that, Sahib. Those two years of education were a fantastic gift. I was very lucky to have been sent to Oxford.'

'Have you got any children, Kibu?'

'You have seen them, Sahib: two boys and a girl. Contrary to tradition over here I believe that it's better to have fewer children and care well for them. It's a shame though that I will not be able to give my children a good education.'

John reflected for a while. Then he said: 'It would be a pity indeed if your children in turn saw their education curtailed. If they have inherited only half your intelligence they deserve to be able to study.'

'You are too flattering, Sahib.'

'Would you mind if I paid for their education? And if they manage to pass and qualify for university, I would like to send them to any foreign institution of their choice that can provide them with top-level education.'

'It would be the joy of my life, Sahib, to see my children prosper,' answered Kibu. 'I would be infinitely grateful.' And this time there was a full smile on his face.

30

'Are you busy?' asked John as he entered Klaus' temporary laboratory.

'Can't you see that I'm working?' grumbled Klaus who was sitting in front of a large table littered with bits and pieces of electronic equipment. 'Why do people always have to bump in and bother me?'

'What are you working on now?' asked John, interested. 'Will you continue sending people's brain contents into the past?'

'Are you joking?' retorted Klaus. 'People are much too difficult. Just look at yourself. Can you think of a more ungrateful subject?'

'But I am very grateful for having been sent back to the past,' objected John. 'It has taught me so much...'

'Grateful! Pftt...' retorted Klaus who was not impressed. 'You should have felt honoured to have been chosen for that unique mission. And you were not even pleased. When you came back you were just shouting: "I'll kill you!"'

'But I wanted to kill the hominids, not you.'

Klaus held up a hand. 'You've explained that, but who knows? You're not trustworthy. Maybe it was really me you wanted to kill. Yes, that's what you wanted to do: kill me. Can you imagine what an irreplaceable loss that would have been for the world? No, no. I tell you, people are no good. Except I, myself, of course.'

He sat there for a while, his hand on his narrow chest, his eyes shining through his round, gold-rimmed spectacles. Then he carried on: 'No! No more space–time transformations for me. Enough is enough! From now on I'm going to work only with robots. You can program them. They are obedient, have no stupid inclinations of their own, don't dislike German music ... Hey, that's an idea! I'm going to make them like everything I sing. *Wunderbar!*'

'But it was wonderful that you sent me back in time,' protested John. 'Why don't you stick to people? Robots are so dull in comparison.'

'No, no!' objected Klaus. 'With robots at least you have no unpleasant surprises. You do not run the risk that their ex-wives will suddenly turn up with their lawyers and try to pull out the wires! Just think what this would have done to my experiment: it would have ruined it! And there will be no elephant girlfriends rushing in and using my precious cables as a whip! No, no, *mein Freund*. I don't want any more unpleasant humans. Only robots. Easygoing, docile, patient, intelligent, just perfect! The image of myself, *nicht wahr?*'

'Will they be able to walk?' asked John with a mischievous smile.

'Now that's an idea, yes! I could make them walk.'

'In that case, don't forget the slight limp,' remarked John as he was about to go out and return to Elephant Camp. 'And for completeness, add some gold-rimmed spectacles.'

31

Le Tellier was mumbling to himself: '... *Foie gras ... velouté d'asperges ... coq au vin ... fondue bourguignonne ... Reblochon ... Château Lafite...*'

'What are you grumbling about?' asked Luonga. 'I can't understand you.'

They were both dressed in dirty yellow-striped clothes and sitting uncomfortably on rough boulders somewhat apart from the other prisoners, while they were munching slightly burned corn that tasted of the charcoal on which they had cooked it.

'You wouldn't understand,' retorted Le Tellier. 'I'm not grumbling! I'm trying to keep myself going. A man needs something to look forward to. I'm thinking of what I'm going to eat and drink when I get out of *ce trou*. If the vultures don't get me first. Damned prison camp!'

He tried to kick a stone but didn't manage as his leg was still encased in plaster, and he shook his fist in frustration. How could all this have happened? He didn't understand. A few days ago he had been picked up by plain-clothes policemen. When he had asked why, they had just told him that he was accused of illegal activities, and had declined to elaborate. Illegal activities! But everyone was engaged in illegal activities. The whole of Africa was one huge illegal activity! He had requested to see Mamabeka but they had told him that this was impossible and had just driven him to this dump, where he had found his trading partner Luonga already well installed.

'Damned prison camp!' he repeated. 'They should at least provide comfortable chairs and sunshades when you eat. But no! They make you eat in the full sun wherever you happen to be, sitting on the ground like animals.'

'Talking of animals,' said Luonga, 'at least we are protected.' He pointed at the guards who stood at some distance, leaning on the barrels of their rifles, smoking cigarettes while chatting and laughing. 'No fear of being attacked by wild rhinos here,

362

see! And living in the bush is better than living in a big city … pure air and all that. It's supposed to be good for your health. Considering that we have to spend ten years here, it's better to look upon the bright side.'

His upbeat comments failed to cheer up Le Tellier. 'I hate it!' he yelled. 'All of it. But especially the food! Damned roasted corn. That's all they ever give you to chew on here.'

'Well, I want more of it. You need to eat all the calories you can get here. Look at me! I've already lost ten pounds in a week, breaking stones. If I don't get more food, I'll melt away till there's nothing left of me.'

'A lean diet will do you a lot of good, *mon ami*,' commented Le Tellier while giving his companion a disapproving look. 'You are grossly overweight.'

Luonga seemed stung. 'I'm not grossly overweight,' he retorted. 'I am a very good-looking upstanding man by our standards. But you! No woman would ever look at you. Your clothes are floating around your body. Or what you call a body.'

'*Quoi!* These aren't exactly designer clothes, *n'est-ce pas?* And if ever you went to La France you would see that all men of good upbringing take care not to have an ounce of fat on their bodies.'

Luonga shrugged his shoulders. 'Well, you'd better eat your corn because that's all you're going to get here.'

'Roasted corn!' Le Tellier seemed enraged. 'How they can torture people like this is beyond me! It's simply inhuman. I must get a message to the French Embassy.' And with a gesture of disgust he dumped the content of his dirty metal plate on the ground.

'Hey, don't do that!' exclaimed Luonga. 'Precious food!'

Le Tellier had got quite worked up by now. 'You expect me to live like an animal and subsist on coarse food? I cannot possibly do that! My stomach is very delicate. I need something more refined. *La cuisine* is an art, the essence of life, you see.' Suddenly he seemed to wax lyrical. 'Oh, to think of what I'm going to eat if ever I get out of here.'

'It's lucky you've got your leg in the plaster,' remarked Luonga cynically. 'Otherwise you would have to work with your muscles instead of your mouth and then you might realize what a real body is.' And he turned his back on Le Tellier and continued to eat with great gusto.

32

'Mike, come quickly! A letter from Monta.' Mrs Macauley opened the envelope with trembling hands as her husband rushed in, and began to read in a shaky voice:

Dear Parents,

Just a short word to reassure you and to let you know what has become of me after I left the house in such a hurry. I'm fine and in good health and spirits. As you see from the stamps I'm in Africa! You can imagine that I was very frightened at first, but I'm getting used to being here by now. I'm living in a sort of religious community and, although it was a bit strange in the beginning, I have to confess that I like it. I was accepted straight away and they are all doing their best to be friendly to me. We call each other brother and sister, and are really one big family. We share almost everything, but I do have my own room.

It feels so secure and peaceful here. I don't have to do any work, or cook or do things like that, but can just sit down for meals. Even more wonderful are the hymns we all sing. Within a day everyone had noticed my beautiful voice, and I have already worked myself up to the position of lead singer. Ernest, the director, seems to be very taken with me. He held both my hands in his while talking to me only yesterday. He is somewhat older than me, but he is a really charming and very trustworthy man. From what I have heard he has substantial means, and you know what? He is not married!

I'm going to stay here much longer than I initially planned. Do not worry. I feel very sheltered, very much at home. And my life has acquired a new meaning: I am aware that I have a mission to fulfil. Ernest has invited me for a stroll in the grounds and a long talk this afternoon, and I'm very much looking forward to sharing deep and intelligent thoughts with this outstanding man. We really have a lot in common, and I like being in close contact with him. I feel that I already occupy a very special place in his heart and have high hopes that I will be able to consolidate my position in the near future.

Pray for me.

Your loving daughter, Monta.

'Thank God she's all right,' murmured Mike Macauley.
'I'm going to pray straight away!' decided his wife Mary.

33

As John stood in front of the veranda of Elephant Camp and looked out over the savannah, memories of his life as an elephant came back to him. All of a sudden he thought of his baby elephant and felt a great emptiness. Then he saw that Veronica was looking at him with questioning eyes and began to feel uncomfortable. How could he explain all this to her?

'John,' said Veronica, looking him straight in the eyes, 'I don't want to be inquisitive but there are a number of things that have been puzzling me for some time. Take elephants for instance. I was certain that you didn't like them, but since your return from America you and Dumbo seem like two old pals who walk about with their arms around each other's shoulders. I've also noticed that you seem to know a lot about elephants now. Something must have happened in America that's beyond my understanding. And by the way, how did you get hold of those ten million dollars?'

'Oh that!' replied John, relieved to be able to answer the last question. 'That's really quite simple. I had some shares in the firm I used to work for before I came to Europe and I sold them.'

'But John! You don't sell a few shares for ten million dollars!'

'You're quite right,' agreed John, nodding vigorously. 'I sold them for much more than that...'

'All right, all right...' sighed Veronica, shaking her head. 'But what about the elephants? Where did you learn about them? At times I even have the impression that you communicate with them. It's uncanny.'

'Oh...' said John, getting confused, 'well, you see ... I have learned a lot about them since I've lived with them ... I mean ... since I have been on Klaus' time machine. I love them now and I would do anything for them. And let me add that no other female ... I mean person in the world ... is better qualified than I am to assist you with the elephants.'

Veronica looked at him with pity in her eyes. He appeared sincere enough, but he seemed to be talking sheer nonsense. *The time machine doesn't seem to have done him any good*, she reflected. *One never knows how such things affect the brain. But it has definitely transformed his attitude to elephants.*

'Veronica...' John's voice seemed shy. 'There's something I would like to ask you. I'm not certain that you will want to, but if you would, it would make me really very, very happy...' He stood there, looking down at his foot which was drawing nervous figures in the sand. 'You see...' he stammered, 'I would like to be a mother again ... oops,' he said, blushing, 'I mean a father.'

Veronica looked at him tenderly. 'I didn't know you had a child,' she said. 'Why didn't you tell me before?'

John went red in the face and was completely confused now. 'No, not a child. A little elephant like Dumbo!'

Veronica shook her head in bewilderment. 'I ... I really don't know what you mean.'

'Don't you understand?' John took Veronica in his arms and whispered: 'What I would like more than anything else is for us to have a little elephant of our own.' And to explain why he added: 'I feel motherless without one.'

Veronica's face was now a big question mark, but John didn't seem to notice.

'Oh John! I really don't know what you're talking about,' she blurted out. 'What is it you want? We already have a little elephant. Dumbo is ours.'

'No, no. I don't mean Dumbo. I mean a baby.'

'Would you want us to adopt another elephant? A small baby elephant?'

'No, I don't mean an elephant. I mean a baby. You know, you and me. Have a baby.'

'You'd like us to have a baby, is that it? I was getting all worried! Of course we'll have a baby if you want to. Why didn't you say so from the start?'

'I'm trying to but ... but you always overawe me so much that I get confused,' he stammered. 'And I keep mixing up things ... it's still so recent, you see. Of course, you have no idea. I swore to myself that I wouldn't tell anyone ... but if I don't you will probably think me mad. And if I do you might think me mad too and run away.'

He began pacing up and down, undecided. 'I ought to tell you,' he muttered, 'I really ought to. But I'm afraid that nobody will believe me. It's such a fantastic story.' He paused a moment in front of Veronica, saying as if to excuse himself: 'What happened to me was not really my fault. It was Klaus' time machine and it just happened like that.' Then he continued to move to and fro.

Finally he stopped in front of Veronica and put his hands on her shoulders. Veronica, who had been following the goings-on with mounting concern, now looked up at him with eyes expressing all her faith and love. 'Come on, John,' she pleaded, 'tell me!'

'All right,' he decided. 'I'm going to tell you. If anyone in this world will believe me, it is you. And you have a right to know. But it's going to be a very long story.'

'I love long stories!' exclaimed Veronica, all relieved and eager now. She took his hand, pulled him inside, pushed him onto the divan and sat down next to him, knees drawn up. 'Put your arm around me,' she said, nestling herself comfortably against his shoulder. 'I'm ready now. You can begin.'

'As I was lying on Klaus' time machine,' began John hesitantly, 'all sort of thoughts went through my head. Most terrible was the sense of having wasted my life, and, above all, of having lost you. Then my memory seemed to be drawn out of me and I lost consciousness. When I came to I could not believe my eyes. I was surrounded by...'